D0327266

PRAISE FOR
PRIVATE OFFERINGS

"...a timely fictional page-turner...she can tell a story..."
San Jose Mercury News

"'Private Offerings' flows at a breathless pace."
Mel Phelps
Former publisher Hambrecht & Quist Newsletter,
View; former writer, Upside

"Ann Bridges draws on her personal experience and insider's view of the world of Silicon Valley and IPOs to bring you intriguing, suspenseful fiction. Plus, she includes a ring of truth about the emerging influence of China on the high-tech, high-finance worlds."
Dinah Lin, MBA
Public speaker, author, former Fortune 500
international business executive

"...a high-tech tale of international intrigue, populated with promiscuous characters of dubious integrity...demystifies Silicon Valley with a story of love, greed and financial shenanigans."
George Koo
New America Media, former U.S.-China business consultant

"...Ms. Bridges dances [her multi-dimensional characters] through the perfectly captured intensity of the Silicon Valley business world...a compelling read: hard to put down..."
Pat Waite
Retired SV executive, San Jose political figure

PRIVATE OFFERINGS
A Silicon Valley Novel

Copyright © 2014 EndSource Management, Inc.

All rights reserved. No portion of this book may be reproduced, stored in a retrieval system or transmitted in any form or by any means, electronic or mechanical, including photocopy, recording, or any information storage and retrieval system now known or to be invented, without prior written permission from the publisher, with the exception of brief passages for inclusion in a written review for a magazine, newspaper, website or broadcast.

This is a work of fiction. Names, characters, places and incidents either are the product of the author's imagination or are used fictitiously, and any resemblance to actual persons, living or dead, events, or locales is entirely coincidental.

Hardcover ISBN 978-1-939454-48-5
Softcover ISBN 978-1-939454-49-2
Ebook ISBN 978-1-939454-50-8
Library of Congress Control Number: 2015935837
Cataloging in Publication data pending.

Published in the United States by
Balcony 7 Media and Publishing
530 South Lake Avenue #434
Pasadena, CA 91101
www.balcony7.com

Cover Art by Rex Perry
Cover & Interior Design by 3 Dog Design *www.3dogdesign.net*

Printed in the United States of America

Distributed to the trade by:
Ingram Publisher Services
Mackin
Overdrive
Baker & Taylor (through IPS)
MyiLibrary

PRIVATE OFFERINGS

A SILICON VALLEY NOVEL

Ann Bridges

NEW HANOVER COUNTY
PUBLIC LIBRARY
201 CHESTNUT STREET
WILMINGTON, NC 28401

BALCONY 7
media & publishing

For Dad,
whose words inspire so many.

Chapter 1

MAY 1, 1998

Northwestern University, Illinois

Gwendolyn Baker grabbed a white cardigan from the back of the desk chair and yanked it over her bare shoulders. Skirt ruffles swirling around her legs, she slammed the door on her bossy sister and stormed down the dormitory corridor. Her borrowed high-heels clicked against faded linoleum in time to her churning thoughts.

Pushing against the exit door handle, a warm breeze welcomed, reminding her of this afternoon's whipping winds over Lake Michigan. She hurried into the soft darkness, vividly recalling Eric's intense eyes, his lean body as he paced the cement jetty jutting toward the choppy waves.

Eric, she sighed. They'd never gotten around to trading last names. Eric what? With a wry twist of lips at her foolishness, she thought, Mrs. what?

Graceful arms of ancient maple and newer elm trees formed a continuous green arch above her head, their blended leaves sparkling in the gentle moonlight. Gwen followed a path cut between a traditional brick building and the bustling computer science labs. What technological promise awaited the June graduates! But tonight held a different kind of promise.

She shivered from more than the blood singing in her veins. She'd lied to Eric, and she needed to tell him the truth right away, before her little fib hurt both of them. Dreading the revelation, she shoved it from her mind, joining the throng of dancers at the elevated plaza. Soft strains of music wafted in the air. Warmed by her quick pace, she mounted the wide, flat steps and scanned the crowd.

"Gwen!" She turned her head, searching for Eric's familiar face.

"Over here! Gwen!" The voice called again off to her right. Trusting Eric would intercept her path, she lowered her head and pushed through the couples. She rammed into a very solid chest encased in a teal polo shirt and bounced back. She lifted her chin, scowling.

Eric stood in front of her, a smile flitting behind his scraggly beard. Stray strands of hair brushed his lean jaw. Hazel eyes glittered down at her. Words of greeting died in her throat.

"You look great tonight," he murmured. His glance swept the length of her body, pausing long moments at her exposed cleavage. He jerked his gaze up to hers. A slight flush stained his cheekbones. He abruptly stepped back a few inches, pivoting his khaki-clad hips at an angle, and grasped her hand.

Trembling in anticipation, Gwen stared up at him, fascinated by his intent look in the enveloping cocoon of silence. Frightened by the unfamiliar intimacy.

She gulped, courage failing her. She couldn't tell him the truth just yet.

"How...how did your presentation go?" After all, this was supposed to be a celebration of his success, wasn't it? She didn't want to ruin it for him.

"Not what I hoped," he replied, distress flashing in his deep-set eyes. "I'll tell you about it later."

Oh, no! Too bad. She squeezed his fingers and opened her mouth, but he shook his head, squelching her condolences.

His fingers grasped a curl escaping from the harsh clasp of the barrette and tucked it behind her ear. The gentle touch stilled Gwen's breath completely. His hooded eyes beckoned her to step even closer. She wanted him to breathe new life into her suddenly swollen lips.

Only she must tell him first. She'd delayed long enough.

"Eric, there's...there's something you need to know," Gwen began.

The musical chimes of a slow, popular tune interrupted her confession. Eric smiled and slid his arm around her waist, leading her toward the edge of the plaza.

"We can talk later. Dance with me first?" he cajoled in a quiet voice. His leg slipped between hers and his steps matched the subtle rhythms. "At least I think that's the point of this evening, isn't it?"

"But—"

"Let's just enjoy the dance, OK? I need to relax tonight, and what better way than with a beautiful girl?" His gaze was fiercely compelling.

Gwen melted into his embrace, swaying to the music and cataloging each new sensation: his arm firm and warm against her back, her left hand tucked snugly against his chest, the rapid thudding of his heart.

Eric danced her under a weeping willow tree. Its feathery arms draped close to the ground, providing a nest of privacy. Gentle breath caressed her hair. Her entire body throbbed with unaccustomed yearning.

Drawing her tightly against him, his fingers wandered around her neckline, toying with the soft skin of her throat. She couldn't help the sharp intake of her breath at the contact. He moved their clasped fingers to her jaw, gently nudging it upwards. His lips brushed hers, back and forth.

"You taste so sweet," he whispered. He nuzzled her mouth, his beard and mustache tickling. She eased away and scraped her lips with her teeth to stop the tingling. It didn't work.

"Gwen," he groaned under his breath, his arms tightening abruptly around her back, pulling her even closer. "Please…more!"

Gaining in confidence, Gwen opened her mouth and slid her arms around his neck. A soft explosion of moist warmth surprised her. His harsh breaths punctuated the quiet.

She rolled her hips against his thighs, and a soft jingle sounded. Glancing down, she glimpsed inches of glittering chain trailing out of his front pocket. He probably intended returning her father's silver charm to her tonight. But Gwen wanted Eric to keep it. Maybe it would improve his luck in the future, even though it hadn't worked today.

Her conscience twinged. She still hadn't told him!

"Umm, Eric?" Tugging on his ponytail, she slid her lips away and sighed.

Now or never. He deserved the truth

Chapter 2

SEVENTEEN YEARS LATER

Silicon Valley, California

Eric Coleman tore up Sand Hill Road, zooming past shining new Teslas and Ferraris, weaving in and out of the lanes toward the freeway. Raw buildings hosting brand new entrants to the decades-old venture capital community stuck out like sore thumbs, announcing their partners' lowly place in the financial pecking order for the hottest technology deals.

Pointing his vintage Mustang convertible south, he reveled in the wind rippling his short hair. The thundering noise battered his brain and calmed him, putting on hold his smoldering anger. Instead, he relaxed under hot waves of noontime sunshine. Rolling knolls dotted with grazing cows beckoned for his attention. These beautiful hills–sometimes green, now brown–always framed the valley below with their golden embrace.

Fortunately, he'd beaten the rush-hour traffic. He sped through the interchanges connecting eastern sprawl to western coast, northern cities and southern ranches. Usually they jammed up with workers pouring into the central hub running the western length of San Francisco Bay. Years ago, he'd studied Silicon Valley's commute patterns and bought his own little oasis in the eastern foothills of San Jose. Nestled within the steep canyon that originally provided respite and forgiveness to the Spanish missionaries, it had convenient access to both country roads and new expressways. His neighbors clung to their parents' homesteads in lieu of pocketing millions from an enterprising land developer, content to watch others scramble for newer housing.

He floored the accelerator on the last climb toward his rambling ranch house. Too bad Peter Baxter's head wasn't under his foot instead, so he could make him squirm and feel powerless, too. Grabbing his briefcase, he slammed the car door behind him and thundered up the front steps. He fumbled for his cell. Maybe his best friend would have an idea how to pull his butt out of this wringer.

"What's up, buddy?" Don Salazar's low voice rumbled in his ear.

"I can't believe it, Don," Eric barked, twisting the key in the lock. "Baxter put the proxy issue on the agenda and the board voted against me. I'm screwed. I've lost all control of my own damn company."

Pushing open the front door with his hip, he scratched Fred's ears, the mutt greeting him with head and body bumps. Sunlight poured through the skylight in the hall, lighting the way to his corner den, Fred pattering behind.

"You knew you risked this when you gave up your position as majority shareholder," Don reminded him. "As chairman of the board, Baxter's simply doing what's best for SDS as he sees it."

Eric winced. "Why not just come out and say I told you so?" His briefcase dropped onto the floor and he plopped into the scarred desk chair, its seat squeaking a protest. He'd screwed up big time, and this morning's vote just proved it. Fred's heavy sigh as he settled onto his ratty blanket matched his sentiments exactly.

"Because I'm not a jerk. You needed funding to get your technology developed, and the venture capitalists provided it–for a price. That's their job, including sitting on your board of directors."

Eric opened the bottom drawer and braced his feet on its edge. Yellowed papers and scribbled notes filled it almost to the brim, reminding him of his fruitless search culminating in this morning's catastrophe. "Yeah, but we always had the majority vote. They just took that away from me." He scratched his head with his knuckles. "Why the hell have I worked all these years if I have no say in how my ideas get used?"

Fatigue washed over him. Too many long hours. Too much agonizing. And for what? So he could be a pawn of his own company rather than its President? "I should just quit and let them handle the IPO and the Wall Street boys the traditional way."

"Stop whining. There's still time. What's the date you're up against?"

Eric pressed the button on his fluorescent desk lamp and squinted at his calendar. "According to Baxter, we have to be ready to sell shares of our stock to the public within two months, so we have to get all our existing shareholders in lockstep over the next few weeks." He grunted. "I guess Peter thinks they'll turn into goblins or something after Halloween."

"So we search some more. I can spend this afternoon re-checking my sources before I pick you up for the banquet."

Eric slapped his hand on the scratched oak surface. "Damn! I forgot all about that."

"If you're thinking about blowing it off–"

"Of course not. Those kids' dreams are too important. I wish there had been a program like that when I was struggling to figure out which direction to go."

He stared at the framed black-and-white photo adorning his desk. His dad stood so proud and tall in his white uniform at his Annapolis graduation ceremony. He had been in Eric's life for too short a time; just long enough to set him on a path, but not nearly long enough to guide him down it.

Don chuckled. "Yeah, I kinda think once Freeman introduced you to DuMont, your direction was set."

"Until today. Now I'm not sure where I'm heading." His foot slipped off the drawer, tilting it forward. A heavy necklace slithered onto the floor, its silver dollar coin winking up at him, reminding of the last time he'd relied on its luck. And the consequences.

"Keep the big picture in mind, kid. I haven't worked with you all these years just for a little obstacle to stop you. We need to wrap up this IPO with a pretty bow, and fast."

"I'm tired of the secrecy, Don." He picked up the necklace and swung it until it wrapped around his finger. His throat convulsed, guilt and lies tightening like a noose.

"Yeah, well, it's going to take even more of your Southern charm to sway the board this time. Frankly, I'm tired of bailing your ass out of muck you created with all this idealism and atonement crap."

"It should never have come to this. How can someone just disappear from the face of the earth?"

Silence filled his ear. "Death will do that to you, son."

Eric didn't dare consider all that Don's sympathetic tones implied. "Until we find proof, I won't believe that. The future of SDS is too important to make any assumptions. Not now. Not this close to the finish line."

"Whatever you say, kid. I'll get cracking on my search. Pick you up at six."

Eric tossed his phone onto the pile of old bills and buried his head in his hands. He'd followed Colonel DuMont's orders to the letter. Secrecy and scheming. Loyalty and lies.

Winning funding from the Defense Advanced Research Projects Agency had been the best and worst moment of his young life. Because he'd lived with that choice for way too long.

Chapter 3

BEIJING, CHINA

"Does the American Ambassador understand fully the consequences of this official position?" Zheng Yinglong strode down the wide corridor, shaking his coat dry. Pounding rain from the rising storm pummeled the red tile roof. Zheng pressed his phone tight against his ear. "The Premier is very disappointed there has been no movement on this issue."

Hearing the same excuses and affirmations of the negative message, Zheng terminated the call, pausing at the door, ajar and leading into the historic auditorium.

Enormous red flags with the symbolic five stars hung from the ceiling. Spotlights illuminated the raised podium, where a technician switched the microphone on and adjusted it to a precise height. Hundreds of the Communist Party faithful milled in the aisles, wearing their crisp gray suits with crimson ties, waiting for the signal that the Premier's speech would soon begin. The speech that promised to set a new direction for China.

Only the Americans weren't cooperating, as the Premier had hoped. As his speechwriter had written.

As Zheng had planned.

He searched the crowd for his three key strategists, masters of their particular spheres of influence. There, he spotted Tong Xiao, his silver cap of hair a beacon against the Western cuts of the youthful new generation, standing military erect. Across the room, Zhu Zhien lounged against a seat arm, an ever-present cigarette animating what was surely a lecture on investments. And Du Wenlin, huddled in the corner with his political lackeys, surveyed the chaotic crowd with cool disdain.

He sighed in relief. Good. The Premier could rely on his fail-safe option starting today.

Spinning away, he hurried down the hall into the anteroom. The Premier sat in front of an ornate mirror, the white cloth around his shoulders spattered with stray drips of black dye. His hairdresser fussed and combed his hair, applying gels and spray with abandon. His speechwriter hovered in the background, scowling at the papers in his hand.

"Premier, I apologize for my lateness." Zheng bowed low.

"You are forgiven—as long as you bring good news." The Premier flicked lint from his pants.

Zheng swallowed hard and faced his leader. "Actually, the Americans insist on the status quo until we meet their most recent demands to lift controls on the Internet."

A scowl crossed the Premier's face. "What do they hope to gain by holding politics over progress? What is it about their top-secret technology that is so special?" He whipped the towel from his shoulders and hurtled it across the room. "Heh? Don't we have engineers, too?"

"Of course. The best. But to catch up and surpass the Americans, we must have the same technological tools as they do—as soon as they do."

"So what's your solution, if they won't transfer the technology to us?"

"Long term, make our own and make it better. But in the short term—buy what we need. Whatever it costs. Whatever it takes."

Lifting one finger for silence, the Premier dismissed his hovering attendants with an impatient wave of his other hand. Zheng crossed to a low bench and sat down, keeping his eyes on the Premier's.

"What are you saying, Old Zheng?"

"We do not have to kowtow to them, Premier, like we did to the British centuries ago. We have a few ambitious leaders who have already taken the appropriate steps, positioning themselves, waiting for the right moment."

The Premier raised his eyebrows in silent query. Zheng knew he wouldn't officially sanction his now years-old plan, but that didn't mean he wasn't shrewd enough to recognize it—and leverage an opportunity.

"Think of it this way." Zheng pointed in the direction of the audience. "You are about to unleash the productive power of our population onto the world. We are ready to gather what we need for our people, our country, our future. This is what your speech will encourage, correct?"

The Premier nodded. His gaze remained focused, intent.

Zheng took a deep breath. "I harnessed three key scorpions over the years, powerful men who have been kept bottled up, unable to fight for their country, waiting for the time to escape their false confinement and follow their true nature—to fight and win at all costs. If I had let only one loose, the other two would have destroyed each other—and us—in their struggle for power. But all three...they kept each other in check."

"And now?"

"Now, we let them all loose immediately. The Party officials and their minions will follow your official guidance and policies to the letter, as they should. The three scorpions, however...they will make their own progress."

"And perhaps sting our American allies in ways to motivate them to change their policies?" A smug smile settled on the Premier's face.

Zheng bowed his head. "It is never good to be in the path of a scorpion."

Chapter 4

Lynn Baker sighed, letting the warmth melt her into a blissful puddle of oblivion on the stark, white hotel patio. California sun beat Colorado snow, hands down.

She shoved out of her mind the unread email from her mortgage company. They could handle another month without her payment. She'll call them in a few days and tell them she'd be starting a new contract. Surely they'll grant her an extension. The penalty fees might be high, but what choice did she have? At the rate her consultancy work was drying up, she'll be moving out of the foreclosed condominium before she could even finish unpacking her boxes.

She intended to lie here next to this gorgeous swimming pool and forget all about the business world until tomorrow morning. Then she would finally meet the President and Chief Executive Officer of her only client, the up-and-coming high-tech firm cryptically named SDS Technologies. Even with a hush-hush product, they'd gained a stellar reputation. Over breakfast, she would scan the last few pages of their web site to glean any tidbit of information she could use to wow him.

She'd better have a glowing recommendation at the end of this two-month stint or she might as well start looking for a regular job. All her prospects for new contracts had dried up in the last few weeks.

As jazzy music pumped into her earplugs, Lynn imagined names that would fit their mysterious acronym. "Silly Dumb Software"? "Sorta Does Stuff"? "Sends Data Somewhere"?

Her intended fifty laps in the pool faded away. She didn't mind at all when the music stopped and lazy murmurs of Sunday afternoon traffic drifted into her ears instead.

A shoe scuffed against the patio. She threw a languid glance to her right, her lowered lashes obscuring her vision. She glimpsed the back of a gray-suited man stepping into the riotously flowering oleander bushes lining the pool area.

Low voices directly behind caught her attention. Did she just hear "SDS" muttered? Tugging on the thin earplug cord, she tilted her head toward the conversation. If it concerned her new client, it was her business now.

"There is a woman close by who might overhear us," a man complained in a vehement whisper.

"Stop worrying." The scolding came from a heavily accented voice. Lynn couldn't quite place the modulation. Vietnamese? Chinese? Not Japanese. She heard the rustle of cellophane and the flick of a lighter. The acrid smell of smoke wafted through the bushes. "She cannot hear us. These Americans love their music players, and go into a world of their own."

"Is the press release prepared?" The first man's voice had sharpened. "We have to get it to the news agency by midnight Eastern time."

"Yes, it's complete and sent off already. My representative guarantees it will be the lead story of all IPO summaries for the week." The other man snorted. "It is so easy to control the American financial markets. They will carry any story sent to them, regardless of the source."

"And the release makes it clear there is a bug in the SDS software? We have to hold up their IPO if our most important customer is to have the negotiating advantage he needs. He may want to buy all the shares of SDS stock himself rather than let the American public get their hands on it."

"There will be no misunderstanding. The IPO will be delayed with news of this sort. Our customer will be pleased."

"He better be. He's paying top dollar for our inside information. We can't afford a mistake."

"I am delivering what I promised." Ire thickened the man's accent. "Do your part, and this will succeed."

"I control the American contacts, remember. I'll use them against you and cut you out of this and any future deal if you venture to insult me again."

An angry hiss was the only reply. The bushes parted near Lynn. She kept her eyes closed, tapping her foot in rhythm. She swore eyes raked her from the tip of her head to her aqua toenails. A muffled snort whispered above her head, and then the rapid tap-tap of hard-soled shoes on the patio deck faded away into soft echoes. Moments later the bushes rustled again, and the thrum of a second pair of footsteps diminished behind her.

Her eyes flew open. SDS was at a critical juncture. They had filed to go public three months ago, and hired Lynn as a public relations consultant to help with their marketing and advertising efforts during this sensitive time.

If these men had a negative press release ready to hit tomorrow morning, her job just got a lot harder–if not impossible!

Lynn scrambled to her feet, grabbed her flowered silk sarong and hastily wrapped it around her waist. She jammed her feet into flip-flops. Tote in hand and white plugs still stuffed into her ears, she hastened back to her room while keeping an eye out for anyone who didn't belong.

As if she would be able to tell. Who was she kidding? Playing spy games as a kid did not mean she was cut out for this cloak and dagger stuff.

How should she handle this crisis? Her business thrived on providing answers to her clients, but she drew a blank. How ironic was that?

Disgusted, she fought with the electronic card key to unlock her door before finally gaining access to the anonymous two-room suite. She dropped her tote onto the oak-laminate table and headed to the sink for a glass of water. Gulping too fast, she poured half over her chin. The cold shock of what spilled between her breasts and down to her tummy snapped her out of her stupor.

Pull it together, Lynn. Deep breaths. She sank onto the lumpy sofa, replaying the overheard conversation in her mind. Someone wants to damage SDS' reputation prior to going public, and is deliberately using the press to do it.

She gritted her teeth. No way. No one was going to screw her or the client she needed so badly. She had built a reputation that put her client's best interests first, and she saw no reason to behave differently this time. Despite possibly turning into a no-win contract.

Her gaze fell on the complimentary local newspaper delivered this morning. The initials "SDS" jumped out from a column of news briefs running down the left side, pointing to the full story in the business section.

She yanked those pages free from the clutter of advertisements. *Hmmm.* As Lynn scanned the news item, she pursed her lips. *Crazy, but...*She glanced at her watch and frowned at the time. *Maybe...* Jumping to her feet, she paced the small living area, muttering under her breath. Her plan might just work.

The cell phone's insistent ring wrenched her out of her thoughts. Grabbing it from her tote, she groaned. Her sister loved to chat insipidly for hours.

"Hi, Bernie," she sing-songed into the phone. The hated nickname would set off her temper and end the conversation that much sooner. Names were such a sore point in their family. Bernie had insisted she keep their father's last name, but Mom had changed Lynn's when Mitch had adopted them. "How's the snow?"

"Don't call me that," Bernadette sniffed. "If you do it again, I'll start calling you Gwendolyn. Would you like that?"

She shuddered. "No, thanks. The best decision I ever made was changing my name when I went to college. If only I could break Mom and the boys of the habit." She hated the name and all the bad memories associated with it. Especially the one of a soft voice whispering it in her ear.

"The snow is the least of your worries. There's a foreclosure notice tacked to your condo door! Where are you?"

Foreclosure notice? Her knees buckled, and she dropped back onto the sofa. Lynn could swear she had another month grace period. Unless that last email was her final notice. Ouch!

"Better go on home, Bernadette." Lynn fought to steady her voice. "I'm in San Jose sunbathing in eighty-degree heat. And don't worry about the notice. I've worked it all out with the bank. They're just making a point, and a rude one at that." She crossed her fingers, praying Bernadette would buy her story.

A lengthy pause met her announcement. "San Jose? Whatever for?"

"A client for Baker & Associates, of course. What else?"

"Well, I heard Kip was working in Silicon Valley again, and I thought maybe you two were getting back together." Bernadette's voice drifted off with a slight questioning lilt at the end.

"Nothing like that and you know it. Kip and I were over long before he checked into rehab." Did Bernadette really need to hear the facts yet again? What a protective mother hen. "The divorce is final, and we've both moved on." If having to still pay his bills and deal with her mental scars from his selfish disregard was moving on.

"Oh, well, that's good, I suppose." Lynn wondered at the relief in Bernadette's voice. "Have you talked to Mom recently? Mitch is worried about his lab test results. You'd think they'd hurry when every day counts."

Lynn winced. How could she have forgotten her stepfather's scheduled biopsy last week? When had she let her business problems trump her family? "I'm sure they'll get the results in a day or so. Let me know what they are, okay? I've got to run now."

"What? Don't you even take Sundays off?"

"One of the joys of running your own business, don't you know? There's no one to delegate to when you want free time. Besides, I just overheard a couple of guys talking about ruining SDS Technology's IPO and I've got to work tonight."

"SDS? Isn't that the company founded by that guy at Northwestern? The one who put the moves on you at the May Day dance when you visited me?"

Lynn blinked, clenching the phone tightly and swallowing hard. As if she could ever forget the night that started all her mistrust of men. "Are you sure?"

"I think so. I remember looking up his picture in the yearbook last year after some story came out about selling their software to the military." Bernie sounded confident. "What a nerd!"

Lynn remembered. He'd left her nothing but heartache. If this was the same Eric, boy, did she have a bone to pick with him!

"Gotta go, Bernadette. In my business, if you snooze, you lose. Bye."

Lynn punched the end button in the middle of Bernadette's protest. She'd live.

She picked up the newspaper again and re-read the details of the story. *"The CEO of SDS Technologies, Eric Coleman, will be presenting the annual 'Young Entrepreneur of the Year Award' to a deserving local high school student at the sold-out black-tie banquet held at the exclusive San Francisco Buena Vista Hotel tonight at 7 pm. The proceeds will provide a college scholarship for the winner."*

She gritted her teeth at the ambitiousness of her plan.

Not quite the relaxing evening she'd anticipated. But she had to talk to Eric Coleman, and fast. He'd never believe her unless they were face to face. And they needed to act tonight.

Lynn stepped into the bedroom, shedding her sarong and unclasping the halter neck of her swimsuit. She caught a glimpse of herself in the full-length mirror and hesitated.

The image staring back at her was a mass of contradictions.

Visible scars crisscrossed her torso and neck. The ones on her face were so slight they looked like premature old-age wrinkles. Body—good, but skin—ugly.

She still had a hard time recognizing herself with her new straight nose, high cheeks, and narrow chin. Miraculously her eyes had escaped unscathed, looking like crystal-blue, shattered marbles, scattered with hints of gray and green. She'd had laser surgery, so no more contact lenses. Her eyebrows were different, too—the reconstructive surgeon had given one of them a perpetual arch.

Lynn sighed at her tousled hair. White as snow, at age thirty-four.

Good thing having an indeterminate age helped her more often than not in her business. Some clients believed she had decades of experience that showed in her white hair and fine lines, while others thought of her as young and a bit eccentric.

To her, it was a daily reminder of her luck to survive and live each day to its fullest.

She could handle her life, even if she had to do it all on her own. She wouldn't risk getting hurt again—not her heart, her body, or her mind. Three times was more than enough for anyone to bear.

Entering the bathroom, she turned on the hot water in the shower, inspecting her sarong before hanging it on the nylon rope to steam out the wrinkles. She shook her head at the image she would make among San Francisco's society and business community.

"Nothing ventured, nothing gained," she quipped, ducking under the spray and grabbing the shampoo. "I never did learn to follow the rules, did I?"

Chapter 5

Eric squinted at the cryptic text message. "*1 of 3 Chinese scorpions loose.*" He hadn't heard from Paul Freeman since he'd recruited Eric from Northwestern University for DARPA. Did Paul discover his top-secret project became SDS?

Tugging at his strangling bow tie, he glanced around the noisy hotel ballroom. He wanted Don's take on this, since he'd known Paul longer. Not catching sight of him among the tuxedoed guests, he forwarded the message to Don's cell before pocketing his phone.

Usually Eric had too much work to attend the annual banquet in San Francisco, but this year the low-key publicity and goodwill it generated could only help the SDS IPO. Mingling with potential investors with gobs of money and established networks of high-level business and government contacts seemed the right thing to do. He approached a small circle of attendees to greet the organization's largest donor, C.J. Rogers, and stepped in close at the first lull in the conversation.

A warm hand inched along the front of his scarlet cummerbund. He flinched. His eyebrows shot up. His eyes flashed down. A huge diamond ring twinkled against his waist. He caught Crystal's too-friendly gaze. Wonderful, just wonderful. Roger's wife was making a pass at him. That's all he needed.

Tugging Eric toward the open bar, she smiled with a naughty suggestiveness. He rotated in the opposite direction, moving out of her reach. Her hand dropped, as he fully intended. Except Crystal dragged her palm over his crotch and winked, watching him out of the corner of her eye.

This was tiresome, as well as potentially embarrassing. His body, though, was paying attention all right. He struggled to keep it in check. Polite chitchat with Rogers be damned. He needed someone to rescue him discreetly–and soon.

A soft smack and dismayed cry caught Eric's ear. Turning his head, he saw perfectly shaped female hips and long legs, a lithe arm outstretched toward a fallen purse. Spinning deftly away from Crystal's advances, Eric assessed the rest of this vision–high heels, slender ankles, slim waist, bare and toned back. Without a conscious thought, he stepped forward.

"I was sure I put my ticket in here when I switched purses," a husky voice informed the doorman in an apologetic tone. "Eric will be so angry that I'm late, but I told him I just had to get my hair done today for such a special occasion. He'll kill me if I don't show!"

The doorman scowled. He squatted, helping her pick up the scattered cosmetics, muttering under his breath. "All right, ma'am, go on in. But next time..."

Her soft, low laugh drew Eric closer. "I know, I know. I'm such a scatterbrain. Thanks. You're a sweetie!" A slim hand patted the doorman gently on the cheek. The woman straightened to full height and a cascade of white hair tumbled over her naked shoulder. Eric stopped mid-step, stunned.

"Do you know where Mr. Coleman, er, Eric, might be? I have important news to tell him right away," the woman asked the doorman, stuffing a black scarf into her tiny handbag.

"Right behind you, ma'am. Have a good evening." The doorman nodded at Eric and returned to the top of the stairs.

The woman pivoted in slow motion. A stricken expression crossed her face. She took a deep breath, her breasts rising enticingly. Straightening her shoulders, she sought his eyes.

Eric crossed his arms over his chest, scrutinizing the mysterious interloper. Her snowy hair was loosely gathered in a pink scarf tied at the base of one shoulder. She wore a lacy top with a narrow, plunging neckline. The filmy swirls covered most of her skin, but the open pattern invited his slow perusal between the design whorls to gleaming flesh underneath.

Then there was her skirt. Angled low around her hips, contrasting green leaves and pink flowers shot through a background of the same teal blue as her top. A long slit ending at mid-thigh disclosed a silky leg.

Never before had he seen a woman's outfit so perfectly attuned to her body. It made the rest of the women's expensive gowns look dowdy by comparison. No jewels were necessary to make this woman glitter and glow.

"Mr. Coleman?" A deep, throaty voice reached his ears. He drew his gaze from her ankles up the length of her body, watching a flush rise from her slender neck to her high cheekbones.

He met turquoise eyes. "I thought I was just Eric." With a pointed glance at the doorman, Eric flashed a dimpled smile. "Remember? You did your hair special for me."

Annoyance flitting across her features, she arched one brow. "You like it? Most men prefer a younger look."

"I'd have to say it's very unusual, just like you. Did you really dye it for tonight?" He snagged one white strand curling against her exposed arm.

Her lips twisted in a rueful moue. "Nope, this is how it is all the time. Disappointed?"

"Actually, thrilled. I need an escort, and you fit the bill perfectly. No one will know if you're my mother or my date." He tugged her lock and released it.

Her chin jutted out and her eyes narrowed. "Your mother? I think not!"

Eric laughed, tucking her hand firmly into the crook of his arm. "At least you weren't horrified at the idea of being my date."

Grinning, he led her through the crowds spilling into the entrance of the ballroom. "Play along with me and don't let people know we just met," he whispered. "It will blow both our covers–and put you back on the street before you get a chance to tell me what's so important." He glanced down, wondering what had caused her to crash this event. "You were looking for me, right?"

His mystery lady nodded. "Just for tonight though," she cautioned. "And remember, whatever I say or do is because you asked me to pretend to be your date." Tension colored her husky voice

Although curious about her very clear boundaries, Eric shrugged. Since he needed her cooperation, he couldn't complain. But something about her caused the hair on the back of his neck to tickle with warning. And made the hound dog in him sit up and howl.

"Whatever you say or do this evening is fine by me. We'll talk later. Promise," he reassured.

Her breath came out in a relieved sigh. A broad smile crossed her lips as she twinkled blue eyes up at him. "Don't you even want to know my name…baby?"

Eric growled, pulling her close to his side and threading their way through the ballroom. "You're enjoying this, aren't you?"

She nodded with an unapologetic grin.

He tilted his head down. "What's your name, you shameless flirt?"

"Lynn Baker," she breathed into his ear, heating his blood. He shut his eyes, concentrating on controlling the surprising surge of lust, and felt a hard slap on his forearm.

Eric opened his eyes to Don's challenging gaze. "There you are," Eric exclaimed. "I've been looking for you everywhere. Did you get my text message?"

Don nodded, his brows arching and his shoulder lifting under his too-snug suit jacket. "We'll talk later." Don loosened the top button on his collar.

Eric studied Don's impassive face, but couldn't read a thing. Okay, apparently Paul's message about scorpions wasn't too urgent. "When does this banquet start?"

Don's gaze flickered over Lynn's hand. He scowled, further deepening the scar that furrowed his swarthy cheek. His silver mustache twitched as he scrutinized her with a speculative expression on his face. "Now. They want you up on the dais with the other honorees so this gaggle will get the idea and start eating the rubber chicken."

Eric nodded, pivoting toward the front. Don's firm hand stopped him before he had taken more than a step. "Who's this?" Don asked in a quiet voice.

Eric shook his head. "I forgot my manners," he chuckled, drawing Lynn closer. "Lynn, let me introduce you to my old friend, Don Salazar. Don, Lynn Baker."

Lynn smiled and held out slender fingers. "Don, I'm happy to meet you."

Don grasped her hand, shaking it briefly. He glanced at Eric. "I thought you didn't have a date."

Eric grasped for a plausible explanation. His work always came first–and Don knew why. So what was up with the third degree?

"Actually, we bumped into each other rather unexpectedly," Lynn answered. "Since I needed to talk to Eric about his business, he graciously asked me to join him." Her glance at Eric begged for corroboration.

Eric met Don's skeptical glare, guessing Don was more worried for his safety than offended that he didn't know Eric's plans. With the increasing dangers in the technology world, Don's FBI background came in handy. And given Paul's unexpected message, maybe Don was right to be on alert.

"Don't worry. I'm perfectly safe in Lynn's hands. I didn't notice a gun hidden anywhere, did you?"

Don relaxed his sturdy shoulders, glancing at the slinky material skimming Lynn's body. "I'll trust you've searched her thoroughly–or will eventually." He jerked his thumb to the front. "Lynn can take my seat. I'm happy to sit back here and talk to these young kids about their business ideas. They're amazing. Maybe I'll invest in them myself."

"Just check over their business plans before you part with any money," Eric called over his shoulder, pulling Lynn behind him.

Stepping into the glare of the footlights, Lynn glanced back at the other women heading toward the stage. Eric pulled out her chair, but she leaned into him instead.

"Let me sit down with Don," she hissed. "I'm not dressed for this!"

Quite happy to take advantage of the opportunity, Eric inspected her body again. It was the most luscious one he'd seen in years. "Why? I think you look beautiful. Everyone will be dying to know where to get an outfit like yours."

Lynn raised her chin and glowered at him. "Well, why don't you just go ahead and announce they can buy it online from Frederick's of Hollywood and Catalina Swimwear? That will make them all feel better."

Eric curved his lips into a lazy smile. "I will if you want, but maybe we should keep that our little secret. Though I admit it's rather titillating you're confident enough to wear lingerie in public to attract me."

Lynn snapped her mouth closed. A matronly woman and her distinguished husband paused to greet Eric. He quickly made introductions, overriding Lynn's objections.

The woman oohed and aahed over Lynn's stunning outfit. Eric bit the inside of his cheeks to keep a straight face. Lynn bowed her head in gracious acceptance and returned the compliment. The other dignitaries all stopped by as well, forcing Lynn to repeat her performance. Only the high color in her cheeks indicated her discomfort.

When everyone was finally seated on the dais, Eric felt her relax beside him. He picked up her hand and gave it a squeeze. "See, that wasn't so bad, was it?"

"No, it's actually funny when you think of it. Makes you wonder whether the fashion industry is as crucial to high society as it tells its customers."

He chuckled at her soft banter and dug into his salad. Lynn chatted with the gentleman on her other side, disclosing she was the owner of a small consulting firm, Baker & Associates.

As Eric overheard this exchange, it hit him. Of course. He had an appointment scheduled with her in the morning. With perfect references from another local firm, Eric hadn't bothered interviewing other candidates. Immersed in the IPO, he barely remembered their phone conversation last month.

But he should have remembered her voice. Sitting so close to Lynn now, in person, her low tones describing her education at Stanford rasped against his heightened nerve endings. They discussed trends in the technology world while her floral perfume tickled his nose. Asking polite questions about the organization sponsoring the event, she glowed with confidence.

She was a powerful package of a woman. He was looking forward to getting to know her much, much better.

Chapter 6

The waiters arrived with dessert and poured coffee. Excusing himself, Eric stepped to the podium, finally giving Lynn her chance to study him.

Wow! Was this really the long-haired, lanky nerd she flirted with and kissed eons ago? She never would have recognized him.

His sure command of the topic of entrepreneurship radiated confidence and leadership, probably from building SDS from scratch. Engineers considered it a real coup to work with him, now a Silicon Valley legend. But boy, she itched to give him a good dressing down for the way he treated her on that fateful night seventeen years ago.

Her mind wandered back to May Day at Northwestern, when they first met, by chance. He'd been nervous about his upcoming interview with the Defense Department, certain he'd blow his future because his software project wasn't good enough. She pumped up his ego, and then lent him her Dad's lucky necklace for his meeting. That night they danced and she let him believe she was his classmate, not the high-school senior she really was, visiting her sister for the weekend. Her heart was floating with teenage dreams–until he announced she was just someone to mess around with. As if that wasn't enough, he went on to say her advice and support before going into that crucial interview had been worse than worthless. Then he just walked off, without even a backward glance–and he kept her Dad's necklace to boot!

The audience laughed as he mentioned getting his initial funding from DARPA. Lynn crumpled the program in her fist, that old anger welling up again. He lied to her about winning his precious funding that afternoon. He'll pay for that, big time.

Because *this* time, her advice will come with a hefty price tag. She'll give him her professional best, of course. She could really have fun playing with his mind, though. He didn't recognize her! No surprise, given how much her appearance had changed since the accident. And besides that, he only knew her as Gwen.

Eric set his hands on the corner of the podium. She watched his fingers massaging the corners and remembered how those fingers felt as they ran down her spine. A warm, fluttering rush like heated brandy hit her. She always chalked up her impulsive actions that May Day to her youth. But maybe it was more. Maybe she had one of those pheromone reactions she'd read about.

Eric's well-fitted tuxedo showed off a magnificent physique. She took it all in as she sipped her coffee. Even his hair gleamed; Bernadette spent a fortune and couldn't get her highlights to look as good as his. He smiled, announcing the winner's name, and twin creases lined his lean cheeks, from his cheekbones to his square jaw. It wouldn't be too much of a hardship for her to lead him on and then dump him the way he had dumped her. Who could blame her for that? Fair's fair, after all–and she could finally put that teenage crush to rest.

Joining in the enthusiastic applause at the end of Eric's speech, she sighed. It's time to forget all that and concentrate on business. She ignored the pang of disappointment. Her work was worth more than any man, she reminded herself. But why did those words seem so empty this time? Because it's this man, or because her consultancy was failing?

She gathered her purse and put on her professional face. They'd put the threat to the IPO on hold long enough.

"Dance?" Eric whispered in her ear. His warm breath sent shivers along her nerve endings.

She grabbed hold of her ricocheting reactions. "Only if we can talk. It really is important," she added, noticing the disappointment crossing his face as he led her onto the dance floor. Good! Let him hang a bit.

"It can't wait until our appointment in the morning?" He whirled them into the first steps, his large hand brushing her bare back. Lynn hoped he missed how she arched into his touch, like that time long ago, when the moon shone over them and he'd kissed her–until Bernie suddenly found them and blurted out her real age.

Lynn squinted. "How long have you known who I am?" Who did he recognize–the roly-poly seventeen year-old with a crush on him, or the consultant he'd hired?

"Not until you started talking at dinner. I didn't expect you until tomorrow, so your name didn't ring a bell." His hooded eyes glimmered with heat. "I certainly wasn't expecting someone who looked like you to have such a dynamite professional reputation." His fingers drifted along her exposed shoulder.

A rush of warmth followed his caress, stimulating and hot, with just a tingle of warning. She frowned. "What's that supposed to mean?" She halted mid-step, waiting for his answer. He led her toward the edge of the thinning crowd. And, just like years ago, she followed him.

"Nothing insulting. Now, Ms. Baker, suppose you tell me what's so important that you crashed this party."

Lynn huffed, fighting to control her emotions, still prickling from his comments. She drew her professionalism around her like a familiar blanket.

"I overheard a conversation at my hotel about SDS." Somehow, she managed a calm voice. "There's a press release going out tonight announcing problems with your software, apparently to delay your IPO. Are you aware of that?"

The abrupt clenching of his arm around her waist supplied the answer. He jerked to a stop, holding her snug against his broad chest and bending his head down next to hers.

"Do you know who released it?" His deep voice was clipped and hushed, his gaze intent. He held her fingers so tightly his nails dug into her flesh.

She shook her head, dropping her voice even lower to match his. "I caught a glimpse of only one of the two men. He was in business dress, middle-aged, black hair. One of the voices had an Asian accent. That's all I can tell you." She bit her lip. "I figured it was better to let them think I didn't hear anything than confront them."

"You were right." He squeezed her briefly before dropping his arms. "Thanks for telling me. I'll see you tomorrow." He stepped away, scanning the crowd.

Lynn grabbed his wrist, twisting him back toward her. Surprise raked his features. "This is what I do for a living," she scolded in a whisper. "You need my help. After all, that's what you hired me for, right?"

"You know how to stop the press release?"

"No, but I know of a way to dissipate its effect. But we have to act tonight. Otherwise, you might as well give up. Those guys were serious about blocking your IPO."

He sighed. "All right. Can you give me a lift back to the office so we can work? Don can take my car home."

Lynn winced at the memory of her nerve-racking drive through the steep hills of San Francisco. "Couldn't I ride with you, and let Don drive my rental car instead?"

Eric's eyebrow lifted. "If that's what you want. Where's your car?"

"Valet parking." Lynn rummaged in her purse for the claim ticket.

"Excuse me, Mr. Coleman?" The bravado in the tenor-pitched voice barely covered its quaver. "Would it be all right if I asked your date to dance?"

Eric spun around so fast he almost knocked over the young man hovering behind him. A scowl crossed his features, and then a polite smile settled on his face. "Hello, Alex. Lynn, this is Alexander Tran, tonight's winner. Alex, Lynn Baker."

A teenager of Vietnamese descent, Alex's slight build reflected the hours he probably spent studying rather than building an athletic body. His thick black hair was close-cropped on the sides and stuck straight up on top. An eager smile flitted across his face.

Lynn extended her hand. "Congratulations, Alex. It's nice to meet you." She ignored his damp palm and gave it a firm squeeze.

Eric stepped aside, holding Lynn's gaze. "I'm sure Lynn would be happy to dance with you, since I have to find a friend before he leaves."

Lynn got the message, smiling at Alex while she handed Eric her claim ticket. "Why of course, I'd love to dance with the winner. You'll have to tell me more about your business plan."

Heading toward the dance floor, she caught Eric's eye over her shoulder. Would he return for her? He dropped his head in a brisk nod and disappeared into the crowd.

Chapter 7

Lynn gripped Eric's elbow as they left the hotel vestibule, pausing at the top of the steep street. A frigid fog floated over the hill in wispy waves, partially obscuring the million-dollar view of the surrounding mansions and the expanse of San Francisco Bay. The triangular top of the Transamerica pyramid loomed to the right above the fog belt, eerily detached from its foundation.

"Would you mind terribly getting the car and picking me up here?" Lynn drew her shoulders up and shifted behind him. "I'm freezing, and these hills are impossible to navigate in high heels."

A fierce windblast off the bay made her shiver. Eric nodded. "Of course. I'll just be a minute. Why don't you wait around the corner, out of this breeze?" He tugged the black scarf snugly around her neck and toyed with it a little longer than necessary. He surely didn't resent Alex Tran's audacity. On the contrary, it took guts to cut in. The kind of guts the kid would need if he wanted to make a name for himself in the tech world.

But Eric knew better than to lie to himself. He had felt envious. His time for fun was so limited, the brief respite of enjoyment with Lynn was refreshing–at least before she turned all cool and professional. Her shocking announcement refocused his attention like a laser onto business as usual. Never mind that she felt so right in his arms, cozy and stimulating at the same time.

Familiar is more like it. But he could swear he'd never seen her face before, or heard that husky voice that kept him aroused all evening

Wrestling with his unruly body as it responded to his vivid imagination, Eric jogged down the hill, pondering the threat to SDS. How did Paul's text message fit into all this? He would trust Don's assessment of its urgency, but his own gut warned him something big was happening, and SDS was right smack in the middle of it.

It only took three minutes to reach his vintage Mustang and roar back up to rescue Lynn from the harsh elements, heater on at full blast. Eric jumped out and helped her settle into the low-slung seat before climbing back in. Lynn nudged off her heels, tucking one foot under her and the other under the vent.

Wow, her knockout legs sure look hot against red leather.

Forcing his gaze away, he angled the long white hood into the intersection toward the sharp hill of California Street.

A jogger darted in front of them. Eric jammed the brakes.

Lynn gasped. Jerking upright, she gripped the seat with one hand and the dashboard with the other. The man slapped the hood, passing with a quick wave and a forced smile.

"These hills bother you?" He waited until she sank back into her seat before he pressed the accelerator again. "Join the rest of the tourists. I've seen cars roll backwards into traffic because the driver didn't know how to work the gears."

"It's just so easy to lose control." Her whispery voice seemed strained.

Eric reined in the powerful engine, keeping it from gathering speed on its free-fall toward the freeway.

"Nice car." Lynn let out a loud breath, finally releasing her death grip from the dash. "What year is it?"

"An original '64." Eric patted the steering wheel. "Three engineering friends from home fixed it up and gave it to me as a college graduation present. I've babied it ever since." Driving on the open road was the closest to freedom he got these days. When he turned onto Interstate 280, he accelerated well past the posted speed limit, the norm for the informal racetrack between San Francisco and San Jose.

Eric checked the rearview mirror. Yep, virtually no traffic. No cops either. He glanced at Lynn. "Okay, so what's your big idea for my company?"

She turned halfway in the seat, facing him. "How much do you know about the actual process of releasing press announcements?"

"Not much," he grunted. "We only started putting them out this past year. Whenever we had news, I asked Kay Chiang, our sales VP, to take care of it. I have no idea what happens once I approve the release itself."

"I do, so let me give you a quick overview," she said in a brisk tone. "You send PR News Alerts the final announcement with the date and time of release and they follow your instructions, including if you want it released overseas. The key to success is often the timing."

"It sounds like we're behind the eight ball on this one." Eric sighed. "Those guys beat us to the punch." Is this what Paul had meant? Had he somehow gotten wind of this damn press release?

"Not necessarily. Sometimes a release is buried because it's too early, just like one can be overlooked if it's too late. That's what I'm hoping we can do."

"Bury it? How?" He scrunched his eyebrows.

"Well, for one thing, we can put out a number of specific releases. Then theirs will be one of many, and the only one with a negative story to tell." Lynn drummed her fingers on her silk-covered thigh. Her slender legs peeked through that tempting slit, capturing his attention and notching up his body temperature.

Down boy, not now! Eric pulled his mind back to the discussion. "Aren't we under restrictions not to release any news prior to our IPO?" Joshua Stein and his investment firm's lawyers had pounded the narrowly circumscribed parameters of public disclosure into his head over the course of the last three months.

"I think if we can get this flurry of releases out ASAP, you'll still be able to meet your two-month deadline. But you'll be cutting it close." She gnawed on her bottom lip. "If the IPO is delayed a week, will it be harmful?"

Eric snorted. "Probably not. Even if we do everything right, we still have to wait until the stock market conditions are favorable. I don't pretend to know if the market will be strong two months from now."

"Then this should work. But I *do* need the truth on something first." She paused, as if searching for the right words.

He glanced at her, curious what would stop her now.

She cleared her throat. "I don't mean to insult you by my bluntness, but I really need to know. Um, is there any basis for the accusation that your software has problems?"

He glared at her through the darkness, and then turned his attention back to the striped highway speeding by. "What do you think?" he snarled.

Lynn twisted her fingers, sighing. "My job is to put your best foot forward now and set SDS up for the future. Believe me, I understand that no company is perfect. We can spin our press releases in such a way as to make even solving a problem like this into something positive. I just need to know the truth. Do we attack this as a pack of lies or an information leak?"

Okay, maybe he overreacted. He scratched the back of his head. "We've had an occasional problem, but Rajiv told me they were all fixed. Rajiv's my co-founder, right-hand man, and second largest shareholder—as well as the engineering expert. You'll meet him in the morning."

He hesitated. "I suppose it's possible there could be a problem that one of our customers reported, one we haven't resolved yet. They might have told someone else." He thrummed his fingers on the steering wheel. "It's still odd. We have a history of keeping our product in good shape. Even if there *is* a bug, people shouldn't react too negatively."

"We hope. It's possible to write a press release that hints at all kinds of greater problems without mentioning specifics. People read what they want into a release, you know."

"Yeah, I know." He couldn't help the defeat coloring his voice.

Lynn patted his arm with two short taps and shot him a mischievous grin. "Now comes the fun part. Have you introduced new features in the last product version?"

"Of course, we always do, but–"

"How about fixes of previous problems–were they included?"

"Yes, that's why we start with a new version. You see–"

"And you have specific plans for new features you'll be including in the future?"

He gave in with a wry smile. "Yes."

"New customers? New countries where your product has been introduced?"

"Let me see, there's that new one in–"

"Plans for participating in conferences? Key employees hired?"

Eric burst out laughing. "I surrender! Yes, yes, yes! Apparently we've missed all sorts of opportunities to toot our own horn."

"That's why you hired me, remember?"

"You've already proven your worth, and you haven't even set foot in our offices yet. Whatever your technique, I'm sure it will work for us."

A passing exit lamp illuminated Lynn's smug smile. "Mostly it's a matter of considering the information from a different angle and giving you back the confidence you need to take action."

"Great. You can focus on the PR while I try to figure out who is trying to tank my company and why."

"This IPO is very important to you, isn't it?" Lynn's quiet question filled the silence.

"More than you could ever understand." He punched the gas pedal when he reached the overpass, zooming above Stanford University's two-mile-long particle accelerator. The car's twin beams acted like spotlights on his scabbed-over memories.

Chapter 8

MAY 1, SEVENTEEN YEARS EARLIER

Northwestern University, Illinois

The limp strip of tissue paper hanging from the ventilation grate hadn't moved in an hour. No windows relieved the unadorned walls of the locked study room. Three nearly identical jackets hung over straight-backed metal chairs, and a single fluorescent light buzzed in the background. Eric felt as if he were facing a modern-day Spanish Inquisition in civilian garb.

"How can you make your software so flexible it will still be in use twenty-plus years from now?" Captain Kirk MacKenzie boomed at Eric, exposing his muscled forearms as he rolled up his shirtsleeves with precision.

"I don't know, sir," Eric admitted. "But I will make it my priority to figure that out." Darn, his presentation was weaker than he thought. He could just kiss the funding goodbye.

"You don't even have an advanced degree. How can you stay on top of new technologies?" MacKenzie threw his arms in the air.

Eric squirmed like a worm on a hook. "I don't think university professors are the best source for learning leading-edge programming, sir."

"Are you sure you understand what we're asking of you, son?" MacKenzie's ruddy cheeks had flushed a deep red, but the sage-green tie still nestled against the lean throat of the technical expert on the Department of Defense interview team.

Eric swallowed hard, the heavy weight of Gwen's lucky necklace under his sweat-dampened shirt a reassuring counterpoint to his rapid heartbeat. He focused on the memory of her encouraging eyes and compassionate voice, soothing his panicked nerves. She believed he could do this. It was just a matter of getting these hard-nosed military types to believe in his project, too.

Eric met MacKenzie's harsh gaze without flinching, just as his father taught him. "Captain MacKenzie, I understand you need innovative solutions to problems. My software will provide you with a methodology to approach problems in ways you've never considered before."

The three men exchanged looks. The oldest one leaned forward, his shrewd eyes boring into Eric's.

"That's not what we meant." Finally, Colonel George DuMont spoke, his deep voice harsh, sweat glistening bright against his black forehead. "Do you understand this will be tantamount to joining the military, and a top-secret part of it, at that?"

"Yes, sir."

DARPA was smack in the middle of the drive to find innovative new technologies and experts faster than terrorists could, now that high levels of computing and networking power reached every remote area of the globe. DuMont had final say in who joined his exclusive technology team. Eric bet part of his success as leader was due to his commanding physical presence. He towered several inches over six feet, as muscled and fit as his juniors despite gray curls crowning his head.

DuMont jerked his tie away from his throat and unbuttoned his collar, then slapped both hands on the metal tabletop. "You won't be able to tell anyone where you are or what you're working on for years... if ever. National security is at stake here."

Eric shrugged. "I don't have any family, so that doesn't matter, Colonel." The only so-called family he had left were his engineering mentors, last seen standing with him at his mother's grave at Christmas.

"Your girlfriend can't know, either," DuMont commanded. "We have zero tolerance for pillow talk leaks. Let me tell you, son, we've had to boot top men out on their butts because they couldn't keep their mouths shut in front of good-looking women." He shook his head, his gaze raking over Eric's chest. "You're no prize, that's for sure. In fact, you're downright scrawny. Maybe after our tough training, you'll bulk up some."

Eric looked him straight in the eye. "I don't have a girlfriend, so that's not an issue." How could he make these men understand he was dead serious? "Working on this project took any spare time I had."

"Believe me. We're impressed with your dedication." Paul Freeman's baritone rang with sympathy. "But let me warn you, Eric, for the next few years you can work on building a relationship with a sweetheart... or with us. Your choice, but it's final. If you want to bed some girl for the night, we'll look the other way. You want to get all lovey-dovey and serious, ask for weekends off–this just isn't going to work." Paul was the youngest of the three, with a wiry muscled strength that complemented the steel in his light green eyes, and belied the cherubic mop of blond curls and dimpled chin. "I know the relationship question is a tough one. So take your time answering," Freeman added, tilting back his chair to balance on the rear legs. He waved a hand, warding off his colleagues from interrupting the tense silence.

Eric had taken an instant liking to the young lieutenant during their previous two meetings. Evidently, Freeman had abandoned a plum post in covert operations to transfer into DuMont's handpicked unit as the team's front man. He had whet Eric's appetite with just enough background information to appeal to his ambition—or was it desperation? Freeman had emphasized they couldn't afford to make a mistake by investing in someone with poor judgment. It was critical to national security to get young talent who was as committed to this project and the country's needs as the career military men.

That's probably why they were probing his personal life so closely. To trust him with the highest level of secrecy, they needed to be sure of his loyalty…and his maturity.

Regret swept through him. He wouldn't even have the chance to get to know Gwen. What would be the point? They would only have six weeks until graduation. Then he would leave her for at least a few years. He'd have to risk that she would still be around when he finished his project. He certainly couldn't count on her waiting for him.

"I can handle anything, sir, if it means working with DARPA. I'll benefit more from working with you than from any other career path I could choose." Eric straightened his spine and pulled his shoulders erect. "If that means delaying pursuing personal interests for a time, I'm certainly willing to do so."

DuMont shot out of his chair and crossed to the rickety table at the end of the room, pouring the last bit of coffee from the pot. He grimaced after the first sip, heaping sugar and clumps of powdered creamer into his cup. Returning to the small group gathered around the conference table, he remained standing, glancing down at the neat stack of papers apparently comprising all the information they'd gathered on Eric.

Flipping through the pages, DuMont paused to scan one before pinning Eric with his probing eyes. "Your dad was a good man, son. I had the honor to serve with his SEAL team for a short stint in 'Nam. You anything like him?"

Eric opened his mouth to answer, but DuMont cut him off with a squinty-eyed glare, flipping a page in the file.

"Your friends from the Oak Ridge Labs tell me you helped your mother work through her depression after your dad was killed. They also say any success is yours and yours alone, that they only pointed you in the right direction when you were stuck. That true?"

One look at DuMont's fierce expression clued Eric to keep his mouth shut. The colonel jabbed at the next page.

"Plus, your profs here at Northwestern seem to think a lot of your skills and intelligence. They say you're the best student they've had in a long time. Are they right?"

Eric bounced his leg under cover of the tabletop, biting his tongue.

"Well? Answer me!" DuMont slammed the file closed.

"Yes, sir, to all your questions. Yes!" Eric blurted.

DuMont snorted. "Yes, you're the best? You have one hell of an ego, kid. We're talking about a lot of money if we fund your project. What makes your encryption software any fucking better than anyone else's?"

Eric gritted his teeth, refusing to give in to his nerves. Sweat gathered on his brow. He grazed the chain over his breastbone, wiped his forehead as he shoved the hair from his face, and met DuMont's gaze head-on.

"I used to help my father with his encoded messages when he was home. I incorporated a lot of unorthodox methods into my software most programmers wouldn't even know or consider worthwhile." *Damn!* His nervous twang was coloring his speech. Chagrined, he drew a deep breath. His hammering heart slowed. "But I know the military used them—maybe even still does—and because of that, my software will fit more cleanly into your needs than a program developed by someone else."

He saw the skeptical look still fixed on DuMont's face, and glanced at MacKenzie and Freeman. Their faces were impassive, gazes fixed on their senior officer, no hint they had anything to say. They'd done their jobs vetting Eric to this stage. Now it was DuMont's turn.

Seconds ticked by.

Eric notched his jaw upwards. "You need someone like me who is intimately familiar with the way the Internet is exploding for all sorts of uses," Eric continued. "I have classmates who respect my work and who will help me out, no questions asked. If you need discretion to stay on top of what is filtering through the technology community, especially at the universities, I'm your man. I have friends in both the business and government sectors who have helped me network with their own circle of contacts. They'll do it again if I ask."

DuMont raised his eyebrows at MacKenzie. "What do you think, Mac? Think this snot-nosed kid can just ask for information?"

MacKenzie aimed his index finger straight at Eric like a cocked pistol. "You understand everything is strictly classified? Whatever help you ask for will have to be under complete confidence. We can't risk betrayal of any kind, inadvertent or not. We're not gambling men, Eric."

Eric nodded, composing his face into a blank mask to match theirs, and wiped his damp palms on his dress slacks.

DuMont grunted, a sneer plastered on his face, and slapped his hands on the file. "Frankly, son, I don't trust a word you're saying. You don't have any other options if you don't get this funding. Tell me–what do you want to do with your life? What's your real dream, Eric? Fame? Riches?" His glare dared him to spill his guts, his large body looming over the table close enough that the stale odor of aftershave washed over Eric.

"I think that falls under strictly confidential, sir, meaning no disrespect." Yes! His voice hadn't quavered one bit. He relaxed his grip on his knees.

Freeman jerked, his chair dropping onto the floor with a loud thud. MacKenzie's brows shot way up. DuMont swore under his breath.

Eric gulped hard. "Captain MacKenzie is concerned I can't solicit help from my contacts without giving away the true reasons. I can't think of a better way to prove that than by keeping my motivations to myself. So, Colonel DuMont, you'll have to determine if I'm trustworthy enough even if I don't answer your question."

DuMont's lips twitched. He shot a grimace to MacKenzie, ignoring Freeman's stifled guffaw. "Well, now, that's as ballsy an answer as I've ever heard. Must have gotten some extra coaching from Freeman here," he added with a wink at the lieutenant.

DuMont thrust out his hand. "Welcome to the team, Eric. You'll be a good addition. Get your butt to San Diego a week after graduation. The assigned liaison for your project is Don Salazar. He'll get you the details on where to meet us. But you have your funding."

Eric jumped up and pumped DuMont's hand, grinning so widely he thought his face would split. "Yes, sir. Thank y'all. You won't regret your decision, I promise." He grabbed MacKenzie's and repeated the motion.

Freeman smiled as he shook his hand. "Remember the non-disclosure agreement you signed. All of this is top-secret," he reminded. "No one, not a soul, can know anything about what you will be working on or where you'll be until you complete the project. You'll virtually disappear from the face of the earth."

Eric wiped the grin from his face and nodded. "Yes, sir, I understand completely. I won't tell anyone."

The three men gathered up their coats and briefcases, stopping to shake his hand once more as they went through the doorway. Eric sank down in the nearest chair. Relief and the aftermath of adrenaline shuddered through him in strong waves.

He pulled the silver dollar out of his collar, squeezing it tight until he could force his body to obey him again. When he released it, his flesh carried the imprint of the dollar. Now Gwen's support was a part of him he would never lose. He could return the charm and still keep her luck wrapped around his life.

He was surprised at the strong thrust of anticipation shooting through him at the thought of seeing her again tonight, even if their first date had to be their last. If it hadn't been for her swift kick in his butt, he never would have won the DARPA contract. He literally owed her his future.

Chapter 9

CURRENT DAY

Swooping onto Highway 85, Eric passed the El Camino Real exit leading to his first office in Mountain View, a tiny one where he'd worked twenty hours a day programming breakthrough code to accomplish his goal of bringing the company public. He'd put his life on hold for years more, recruiting the best people to sell his ideas, to find the funds to be able to meet payroll each month.

He'd told himself at the time the incredible strain was worth it. But now, having to deal with a false press release? Or worse yet, a bug in his prized code within weeks of converting all that effort into tangible financial success through the IPO? As much as he hated to admit it, the IPO was a measure of his worth as an engineer, an entrepreneur—and a man. His life wrapped around SDS like ivy clinging to a tree. He couldn't separate the two. He'd purposely entwined his personal and professional personas to keep his sanity through the long, dark hours.

No one could get in his way now. He had an important debt to repay. A debt that gnawed at him every silent, lonely night.

"By the way, I asked Don to help us identify those guys you overheard," Eric informed Lynn. "He's a private investigator." His brain raced through the possibilities of who would have a motive to destroy his company. He hoped the press release itself could give him a clue. Or Rajiv. Or any of the other engineers who would know of the existence of a bug. Or Paul? Was that what that text message was all about?

He pulled off the highway at high speed onto Central Expressway's tunneled lanes, curving onto the empty road and into a large industrial park. He stopped in front of an innocuous building with SDS' name discreetly stenciled on the door. Turning off the ignition, Eric leaned over and unlocked the glove compartment, removing his handgun before slamming it shut.

Slipping the firearm into his coat pocket, he ignored Lynn's small gasp. "We've had a spate of executive kidnappings in Silicon Valley for years. This is only a precautionary measure that Don recommended, but one I'm glad I'm taking now. Who knows what these jokers may try to ruin SDS?"

Lynn nodded, fumbling for the door handle. Eric wondered if her trembling hands were from cold or fear of the weapon. Either way, she was in it with him now. After all, she had discovered the plot against SDS. He'd learned long ago that when reality bites, the niceties of life go by the wayside fast.

They walked to the entrance and Eric slid his magnetic security card through the reader, escorting her across the dim lobby. Only hallway lights gleamed through the connecting glass door. Passing the coffee area, Eric stopped to dump out old grounds, put a new pack in the coffeemaker, and flip the switch.

"I figure we'll need a caffeine boost before this night's over."

"Probably more than one," she agreed, following him past countless, cluttered cubicles.

He watched Lynn rub her hands up and down her bare arms. That skimpy outfit would provide her little warmth in the reduced temperature of the evening hours.

Digging out his keys, he unlocked his office door and motioned her inside. He'd managed to clear a space to work among the neatly stacked piles of paper covering the rest of his desk surface, but his in-box still overflowed with gaping file folders. The closed blinds over the huge corner window let in only glints from the parking lot lights.

He glanced at the whiteboard covering one entire wall. Rajiv's scribbled notes for the next release were written in different colors. The janitors had re-arranged the four large armchairs into a neat grouping around the glass coffee table, but had ignored the dust surrounding his laptop and the speakerphone sitting on top. Eric pointed to one of the armchairs.

"Can you work there?" He removed his tie with a swift jerk.

She nodded, dropping into the black chair and drawing her scarf tight around her neck. "Is there any way to turn up the heat?" She reached for the computer. Gooseflesh pebbled her arms, and he watched a deep shiver run the length of her body.

Eric laid the gun on his desk and whipped off his jacket. He draped it over her shoulders, tucking it around her back before crossing the empty sleeves in front.

"Nope, sorry. I can't raise the temperature. No one's yet designed an ice pack to wrap around computer servers, and they are our livelihood. But I'll see if I can scout out any floor heaters my employees snuck in, contrary to the fire code." He straightened. "The coffee should be done. How do you take yours?"

Lynn shot him a glance full of gratitude as she snuggled into the heat of his coat. "Cream, no sugar. Thanks." She started typing on the keyboard. "I'll get cracking, outlining my ideas while you're gone."

Minutes later, while sipping his mugful of caffeine and juggling hers, Eric stopped short in the doorway at the breathtaking vision before him.

Lynn had kicked off her pumps and lifted her feet onto the coffee table, her knees bent to support the laptop. Parted deeply at the slit, her skirt fell away to expose almost the entire length of her outer thigh, teasing him with glimpses of dark recesses even further up her slender legs. Astonishingly blue-topped toes gripped the edge of the table. Their color actually matched her lacy top, which peeked out from the edges of his coat.

Gathering his composure, Eric wondered about the contrast between her unvarnished fingernails and her provocative toes. What other secrets did she keep so well hidden? She intrigued him, more than any woman had in years. A feeling of great satisfaction settled within him at the sight of her lacy curves wrapped up in his garment. Almost as if he had claimed her already and it was just a matter of time before they acted on it.

"Sorry, no heater. Guess my employees actually do listen to me sometimes."

"Coffee works." Lynn glanced up from the computer screen and flashed him a thankful smile, accepting the steaming cup and blowing on it. "We need to write at least six press releases, with the most important ones going out last. I'll call my contact and confirm when the rogue announcement is set to be released, and then we'll just follow right behind." She sipped her coffee, squinting at the screen. "When people look for the news, ours will be the first stories they read, hopefully stopping before they get to the one about the bug."

Putting the cup down, she glanced up at him, her expression intent. She tapped her fingers on her thigh, gnawing on her lips. "Do you have a pen and some paper?"

He nodded, reaching into his top desk drawer and retrieving both.

She took them, tapped the blank pages into order, and met his gaze with arched brows. "I need the facts of any business that could remotely be construed newsworthy, and I'll prioritize and write," she ordered. "So start with the most trivial, okay?"

He settled behind his desk with ease, keeping the enticing view of her legs in his field of vision. It had been years since he'd allowed his body to respond so readily to a woman. He'd forgotten how enjoyable those latent impulses could be. "Why don't we make the first one that SDS hired Baker & Associates for PR? It would be logical to put it out first, and might encourage people to stop reading there."

"Good idea," Lynn murmured, jotting notes. She glanced at her watch. "It's almost two o'clock in New York, and that's when my friend gets to work. I'll find out everything I can about the other release so we know exactly what we're up against–where it came from, when it was submitted, and who the contact is."

"That would be a start," Eric agreed, knowing he'd be waking Don with the details later on. He hoped Inez would forgive him for disturbing her and the kids again. His late night phone calls to Don had tapered off after beginning the IPO process. He thought he was well on the way to reaching their goal. Apparently, someone had other plans for SDS.

Chapter 10

Joshua Stein yawned until his jaw cracked, scratching a belly that protruded over maroon pajama bottoms. He shuffled slippered feet into the so-called guest bedroom of his midtown Manhattan apartment, passing his father's legacy antique clock whose hands chided him, just as his father would, that he was ten minutes late to his usual start time of five in the morning.

The high-end PC glowed in the quiet dark, enticing him to get a jump on the rest of the Wall Street professionals by nosing through tidbits of news from the Asian and European markets floating through the ether. Joshua wanted, for once, the wealth to be his so he could finally stick it to his old man. In just a few more weeks, he would have it all.

He flipped the switch of the mini coffee maker he kept ready to brew, glancing at the fax machine standing like a sentinel set to spit out lucrative contracts at a moment's notice. Settling comfortably into the ergonomic chair, he typed in his standard search terms. While he embraced technology's innovations to keep close tabs on the firms his employer represented, Burns, Frankel, & Greenberg remained old-fashioned in their mindset and processes. But he refused to be destined as a minor player on the Street.

This morning he focused on his perfect opportunity–SDS Technologies. He'd spotted the company's potential last year, and had busted his ass to land BF&G as the lead underwriter for its IPO. The partners put him in charge, entrusting him to sell other investment banks on the deal so they could spread the risk of financing the company's debut as a publicly traded stock. And investment conditions were coming together for a successful technology launch.

He couldn't afford to screw it up. He had convinced the partners to bet big right before the last tech bubble burst. Bad timing. His advice left BF&G and its biggest clients with worthless investments. Not that anybody went broke. But they hollered, threatening to pull their money out of BF&G if there was another lapse in judgment.

Joshua watched over the years as smart-mouthed engineers still in their twenties walked away with hundreds of millions of dollars after selling their shares in the company they co-founded through an IPO. Joshua had done just as much work, or more, to bring them public. It wasn't fair, but it was predictable.

Already weary, he rubbed his hand over beard stubble, picking at an old acne scar before shoving his wire-rimmed glasses in place to read the news.

"SDS Wins Contract with Australian Stock Exchange" blared the top headline as Joshua's search results flashed across the screen.

"SDS Renews 3-Year Contract with Israel's Military" followed shortly thereafter.

Five more headlines hammered into Joshua's brain. Goddamn it, this was supposed to be the quiet period! The last blurb floated in front of his eyes.

"SDS Hires Marketing and Public Relations Firm Baker & Associates."

"What the hell's going on?" he yelled, smashing his fist on the desk so hard the PC shook. Coffee spilled from the tiny carafe. He pounded at the keyboard, searching for any other story mentioning SDS. One more showed up, released hours before the others. He gulped, his hands shaking so hard he could barely click the headline to pull up the entire story.

Joshua couldn't believe what he was reading. Some unknown outfit in China accused SDS of having a major bug in its software, making it vulnerable to hacker attacks. That would undermine SDS' worldwide reputation for secure data networks. How could he negotiate top dollar for the IPO with this crap hanging over his head? Someone was messing it up, trying to get the jump on him and setting him up to fail. That pissed him off royally.

Joshua grabbed his phone and accessed the stored number without hesitation. Only one person would have the answers he needed. Always have a backup plan, his old man had lectured. Now he understood why.

"Yes?"

Joshua wasted no time in formalities. "What do you know about the news releases on SDS?"

"Releases? I know of only one," an equally terse voice replied.

Joshua knew Sun Guibao considered the American style of informality insulting. However, Sun's covert behavior required losing the traditional niceties of Chinese society a long time ago. Joshua needed answers–now. While working at the Shanghai Stock Exchange, content to play a simple cog in a great wheel, Sun had developed a network of contacts outside his employer to protect his future–and pad his bank account.

"Must I remind you how perilous your situation is if anyone found out you're involved? Maybe you should do your homework before taking unilateral action," Joshua spit out. "There are at least eight additional stories released this morning. Who knows how many more will hit the wires today? What were you thinking about disclosing a bug?"

"I didn't say I released a story, simply that I was aware of one," Sun corrected in a raised voice. "My sources alerted me to the story about the bug earlier today."

"Well, apparently SDS has those same sources, because they came out firing all the PR guns they could find. Goddamnit, we'll have to delay the IPO until this all blows over," Joshua shouted. "And if there are questions about the quality of SDS software, it puts your plans on hold, too. Your butt is just as much in the wringer as mine is."

"What do you suggest we do?" Although his voice quieted, Joshua knew Sun was still irritated. Self-control was required to climb the ladder of success in China, and Sun usually excelled in that. No doubt his dealings with Americans gave him unlimited opportunities to practice.

"I suggest you find out who is behind the story in the first place, and what their agenda is," Joshua ordered. "If there is another bidder for SDS, the price just went up, and my fee along with it. I'll have to jump through hoops to keep my partners from walking away. Right now I can't come up with a good reason why they shouldn't."

Joshua slammed the phone down on the desk and ran his hands through his close-cropped curls, shoving at his glasses. He squinted at the screen, disbelief and denial rising in alternating waves.

Why now? He was so close to living his dream and retiring early on a private island in the Caribbean. Not like his father, who slaved for years at a desk, retired in Florida, and died of boredom. All those bribes sprinkled across influential people should let him pull the right levers when he chose, not when someone else forced his hand.

He'd garnered a promise from the senior partners at his firm that if the SDS IPO became a winner, he'd get a major bonus and promotion to senior partner. And if he managed to create an alliance with the Shanghai Stock Exchange, another huge bonus was likely.

But this time that wasn't enough.

He wasn't about to let anyone dictate his life ever again.

He tapped his lips. There was one other person who might have been behind the story. If so, what was her little scheme? Her unique contacts could hide the identity of the news source, and mask her own involvement behind a screen of innocence.

He grabbed the phone and punched in the number, glancing at the digital clock glowing red in the dim light. 5:30 a.m. here meant middle of the night on the West Coast.

Tough shit. This was important.

No one ever suspected a woman's hand in the rough-and-tumble game of financial power. But in his experience, they were always behind the scenes, egging men on to work harder. They wanted what power would control–unlimited wealth and influence–to stroke their own fragile self-worth.

And they had the nerve to laugh at male egos. What a joke!

Chapter 11

TAIPEI, TAIWAN

Du Wenlin stalked around the desk toward his assistant. "What do you mean, we have lost our negotiation strength? The U.S. military always sells Taiwan their most advanced weapons for the right price."

"I'm so sorry, Boss. But not this time." Chen Changgeng bowed his head and twiddled with his pen, avoiding his glare.

Du's gaze wandered to the window and the meandering Keelung River, finding its way to the Taiwan Strait. He could almost feel the presence of his hero, Mao Zedong, drifting in on the afternoon breeze, straight from the dominating portrait in Beijing's Tiananmen Square. How was he to launch a new revolution with whelps like these? What he wouldn't give for men with backbone and nerve, like the ones who had served by Chairman Mao's side. No matter the cost in money or lives, they had trekked hundreds of miles to accomplish their goal–a true people-run state.

"Why not?"

Young Chen shrugged. "Possibly there were rumors, unsubstantiated of course, of our true intent for the technology. You know the Americans don't have a similar weapons-sharing agreement with the Chinese Communist Party."

"And how are we to accomplish our mission of taking our rightful place in world politics if we are always beholden to the U.S. for the newest technology? Hm? Answer me that."

"There is always a way, Boss."

He paused, hearing the unspoken message in his assistant's confident voice. "You had better not suggest we cooperate with the Chinese military. Those lackeys only care about serving the current leaders and maintaining the status quo. We need to bring China back to its true peasant roots again—and on our own terms, not America's."

Chen Changgeng consulted his notes. "If you recall, a few years back you asked Weng Xilin to settle near Silicon Valley to keep an eye on all pertinent developments."

"Yes, yes. So what? How is he involved?"

"I am happy to report that Old Weng has made progress creating a network of people helpful in infiltrating key companies with leading-edge technology we can use in our mission."

"How? We are revolutionaries, not engineers!" Du slapped the top of his PC, scowling at the irritating blinking cursor. He'd learned to use it only because he had to. If he could, he'd destroy all computers and cell phones so the working class could return to its roots—cultivating fields for food, families for fortune, and culture for civilization.

"If I understand Old Weng's summary, Boss, we do this by using software to monitor our brothers in the homeland who are mostly against our efforts, and deal with them accordingly. The weak spot for capitalists is their money. Remember, the great warrior Sun Tzu wrote, *'Success in warfare is gained by carefully accommodating ourselves to the enemy's purpose.'* We will use their capitalistic desires against them."

"So this is not military weaponry?"

"No, it is categorized as advanced software. It will allow us to know who is behind all financial transactions worming their way into Chinese bank accounts. The Israeli military has used it to great advantage to fight their enemies in the Middle East."

"Hmm." Du paced to the middle of the room. "Zheng Yinglong told us some of these American companies are for sale. Has Old Weng explored that option?"

"Old Weng has studied many options. He believes the best price often comes after a company has made its splash on the world investment stage and then fades into oblivion. Six months after a company offers its stock for sale, many of its shareholders sell their stake, no longer caring about its future. That would be the time to wrest control of the company and bring it onto our shores. But we must be one of the initial investors to properly position ourselves beforehand."

"Bah! These Americans. Such a short attention span. How can they think to compete with our millennia of tradition, supporting our values? Our people?"

Young Chen hesitated, and then met his gaze. Finally, the whelp has courage. "They have done a very good job so far, Boss. I believe it would be a mistake to underestimate them."

"And I hope Old Weng has not. He has a fool-proof plan?"

"Old Weng's plan is his own, but I believe he has contacts throughout the technology and defense community in the U.S. And he has developed an understanding of financial markets as well."

Du twisted his lips, considering Weng Xilin's strengths–and weaknesses. "Make sure he delivers on his promises this time," he barked. "Old Weng has gotten too used to the soft American culture. His visa can expire on a moment's notice." He strode from the room, grateful for a six-month respite before pouncing on the unknowing company. He would have to develop new plans to take advantage of this special technology.

Chapter 12

A shrill ring pulled Kay out of her warm cocoon. Her body still ached from sexual gymnastics. Rolling to the edge of the bed, she fumbled for the phone. Her earrings tinkled hitting the floor. She swore under her breath, glancing at the glowing numbers of the clock. Who could be calling at this god-awful hour?

"Yes?" she whispered. Charlie's snores kept coming deep and even despite the racket.

"Kay, what the hell is going on?" The fierce shout jolted her awake. She winced, tilting the phone away from her ear. Joshua? This must be urgent.

"I don't know what you're talking about," she hissed, sliding out of the wide bed.

Her naked legs gleamed in the filtered moonlight, the beams caressing her as delicately as her lover. Her heavy hair cascaded to her hips, falling into its usual perfect smoothness.

She grabbed her satin robe with one hand and glided through the door. Leaving it ajar, she shrugged on the garment and sauntered down the short hall to the living room. Phone pressed to her ear, she listened to a torrent of anger and frustration.

"Joshua, listen to me. I don't know about any press release going out this morning." Kay crooned as though she was simply getting her young niece back to sleep after a nightmare. "It's just as important to me that the SDS IPO goes off as scheduled. What would I have to gain by leaking a story about a bug?"

Her back stiffened at his answer.

"You don't know me as well as you think." she retorted, raising her voice. "I told you the truth, but if you choose to believe otherwise, I can't stop you." She paused for two full counts. "However, if you're formally requesting to pull your firm out of its leadership position in the IPO syndicate, I'll be happy to pass that information on to Eric this morning. Is that really what you want?"

He mumbled a reply and she smiled in satisfaction. He was just a man, easily controlled by his need for dominance. Now he needed to learn to re-trust her.

"I'll look into it when I get to the office," she soothed. "If I find out anything, you'll be the first to know. I promise."

She listened to his reluctant apology, murmured her soft goodbye, and touched the end button on the phone. Walking to the window, she stared out the half-shuttered blinds overlooking the verdant courtyard below, catching glimpses of light coming from surrounding identical units. Engineers up early or working late, dealing with their far-flung customers. A 24-hour society, where she was never alone in the dark, even when she craved solitude.

Leaning against the cool wall as she stared into the darkness, she recalled setting her plan into action in college, when she'd first railed and rebelled against her family's rampant sexism. She'd truly surprised her parents and hovering brothers by going against the traditions of her namesake, her distant cousin and great Taiwanese rebel Chiang Kai Shek. Ignoring the hurt from their disdain and eventual disownment, she worked her butt off getting results on her assignments to break into the male-dominated ranks of power.

Thank God she met Charlie at last year's Emerging Markets Conference in San Jose. His recommendation got her the plum VP position at SDS. She landed contracts they never even considered possible. Only Eric kept dragging his feet to bring the company public.

Who was this new player threatening the IPO? She had to find out and bring him under her sphere of influence. She was so close to her goal she could taste it.

A door creaked, followed by a soft footfall behind her. She breathed a sigh of regret losing her brief moment of privacy. Another man to handle. She was so tired of it all—especially patriotic fervor. Maybe she would request vacation time after the IPO and before her next assignment. Stifling a sigh, she readied herself for Charlie's well-muscled chest, settling snugly behind her.

• • • • • •

Charlie slid his hands beneath the satiny smoothness of her robe and started stroking her firm stomach in slow, languid motions.

"Problems at the office, babe?" he breathed in her ear, swirling his tongue along the rim. Her breath hitched, and he nipped at her lobe, sliding the heavy black silk of her hair aside.

She was such a turn-on, from the tips of her small ears down to her delicate ankles, and her completely shaved ivory skin in between. She was exotic, erotic, and every man's wet dream, exploiting her sexual prowess each waking moment. That, too, enthralled him; a female with a fiery drive that was equal to his own, and demanded constant vigilance and feeding.

For brief moments, lying replete and satisfied after sex, he might catch her with her guard down, her eyes moist. Her softness and unfamiliar vulnerability would grab hold of him even tighter, in a place he hadn't realized existed except during a cocaine high.

She sighed, leaning back into his nakedness, clasping her arms around his head. Her silk-wrapped nails lightly stroked his nape, and her hips undulated against his thighs. "Nothing I can't handle. Just a rumor of a software bug."

He smiled against her ear as a warm wash of satisfaction ran through him. His plan was coming together. He could finally cash in on the bug he planted years ago. "A bug, huh? Won't that hurt the IPO?" He darted his tongue out and licked her neck, eliciting a soft groan of pleasure from her lips.

"Maybe. I'll take care of it. Nothing a few calls to customers won't tamp down. Unlike this." She dropped one hand and gently squeezed, her breathing quickening to match his.

"Good thing Lynn's there to handle all the press. Otherwise I wouldn't see you until after the IPO if you had to juggle this by yourself." He slid his fingers down and pushed deep into her slick, tight body. But she grabbed hold of his wrist and stilled his suggestive movements.

"Who's Lynn?" Her sharp tone set him on alert.

"My ex, honey. I told you about her." He squeezed her taut nipple. "I help her land jobs the same way I help you. I always do what's best for my women."

He exerted sheer strength against her clasping fingers, stroking her repeatedly while licking wide forays over slender shoulders, exposed by her slipping robe. He used the soft hair from his beard to tickle her damp flesh afterwards, his favorite trick. She'd forget all about work soon. They all did when he worked his magic.

"You landed her a job at SDS?" Kay's voice rose, but she squirmed and panted under his erotic ministrations.

"She's a marketing and PR consultant. I could see Eric and you were barely keeping pace now, with the IPO and all. So I put out the word that Eric ought to call her. She starts sometime this week." He yanked his wrist free and pulled her completely against his hard body, slipping between her thighs.

Kay clenched her legs together. "I can't believe you did that, Charlie. I've been working for months to get Eric to trust me, and you've gone behind my back and undermined any progress I've made. Lynn will control all the information coming out of SDS, and I'll be left out of the loop!"

He recognized the heated rage in her voice, but craved turning that fire into lust instead. He grabbed her thighs with both his hands and forcibly widened her stance, removing the cascades of satin between them by bunching her robe at her waist.

"Charlie, stop. I have to get to the office. This is a big deal."

She pulled away and stalked toward the bedroom, leaving him grasping only cloth. Angry, yet even more aroused, he pursued. He grabbed her shoulder and slammed her back against the wall. She gasped, eyes wide. He pressed the length of his hard body into hers, holding her tiny wrists high above her head, his fingers clenched tight.

"You have to get to Eric, you mean." Familiar jealousy shot through him. She was always running to Eric first, never to him. Even though Eric didn't give her the time of day. In fact, Eric seemed to go out of his way to avoid her overt advances. And he was tired of always coming in second behind a plodding nerd.

He grabbed her leg high, resting it on his thrusting hip. Plowing deep inside, he sought reaffirmation of his possession of her, wanting to brand her before sending her out to entice even more men. She moaned, meeting his eager thrusts with her own, her long nails spearing his back.

Lifting her into his arms, he headed back to bed. He had until dawn to remind Kay what screwing him was like–passion and pleasure, eroticism and exploration. Maybe it would be enough to keep her cooperative and make her forget her job.

Chapter 13

Inez slapped the platter of huevos rancheros in front of Don, the soft eggs quivering as if shaken with the force of a nearby earthquake. Stark sunshine bounced off the patio's terra-cotta planters and directly into their nook.

Don buried his head in the newspaper's financial section. As he shoved tortillas and chorizo into his mouth, he scanned the headlines, searching for even the smallest tidbit about emerging technology stocks. He scribbled any stock symbols worth exploring into his notepad in the hopes these possible investments could add a tiny portion to the kids' college funds. So far, he'd been lucky, using his gut and his experience. Sometimes he was wrong. Most of the time he wasn't.

He ran his fingers through his crew cut, the style that survived after his many years in the military. Reading with only half his usual attention, he stroked his mustache. Eric's news was unnerving. And Paul's alert only made sense in the context of the bigger picture. Add to that Lynn's chance eavesdropping on those two guys...well, he had to consider she made it all up just to get on Eric's good side. Or was she working with someone to tank the IPO? Hard to believe given the miracle she'd worked last night.

The major online news sources carried only the positive SDS headlines. Impressed that Lynn's non-confrontational offensive strategy had worked, Don mentally saluted her. He preferred the same style, working behind the scenes in a fight, gathering intelligence before he moved. Eric never could grasp the concept of controlled methodology. His passion and determination put him at greater risk than was necessary.

Maybe it was just the extra years he had on Eric–that and the time he spent as a kid outwitting roving street gangs in his neighborhood. The deep scar on his cheek served as a daily reminder to keep his emotions in check. Only with Inez and the kids did he drop his guard and let his good nature blossom.

"So is Eric paying you these days, or was he just feeling really friendly last night?" Inez settled her curvaceous hips into the seat next to him, turning to feed Isabella. Don Jr. had already left for kindergarten with the neighborhood carpool. Years of marriage had turned Inez from a carefree gang chica to a loving and devoted mother. She kept her black mane of hair short. Only the wild curls framing her face reflected her love of fun and excitement.

Wincing at her sarcasm, Don lowered the paper and set it aside. No point in antagonizing her further. "Someone is trying to tank the SDS IPO. Eric hired me to find out who."

Inez sniffed, carefully spooning away the food dribbling down the baby's chin. "All this effort simply to sell shares in the company from one set of investors to the other through an IPO seems like a lot of hooey to me."

"Actually, honey, the pros call it a 'liquidity event'–which is hooey with a lot more numbers after it." Don chuckled, hoping to thaw the frigid atmosphere. "The original venture capitalists want their money out profitably so they can invest it in the next tiny company with great promise. They figure they've babysat SDS long enough. It's time for the rest of us investing public to look like fools and chase a shot to make millions."

She paused, leaning her chin on her hand and studying him, her eyebrows lifted. "Feeling a little cynical about the fairness of the stock market this morning, hun?"

"Some idiot declares a company is 'hot' and everyone jumps on it." Don jabbed the paper with his middle finger. "No one thinks about the real losers; the innocent investors who give up their life savings to fund bad technology. Or the next start-up that gets spun around like it's just a pin-the-tail-on-the-donkey game. They lose direction, don't get funding, and perfectly good technology goes down the toilet."

"Well, I don't blame them. I'm amazed you can stay on top of all these changes." Inez turned back to the baby waving her messy fists.

"I can because I bother to. And it's just a hobby for me." He tamped down the familiar irritation. It got to him every morning.

He gulped down lukewarm coffee. "You know, I think the Wall Street boys make more money when entrepreneurs fail, because then their services are more in demand. Well-run companies don't need their money."

"Are you still worried about Eric?" Inez kept her compassionate brown eyes steady on his.

Don twisted his mouth. Inez always cut to the core of the issue. "Yeah, I am. His software is very good. He worked hard for his success and he deserves it. But I'd lay money down his independent streak will trip him up with the pros."

"I thought the whole point of the stock market was to make it an equal playing field." She wiped Isabella's face with the bib.

Don sighed, thinking of the bogus SDS press release. "I really wonder how fair it can ever be."

Inez lifted the baby out of her highchair and held Isabella to his face for a gooey kiss. Shifting her onto her hip, Inez pressed her full lips over Don's, brushing a crumb from his mustache into his mouth. "Don't take on the world, hon. Just handle our own little part of it, and we'll all be okay." She turned toward the door, but Don grabbed her fingers.

"Thanks for listening to me, babe." He smiled at the sweet picture she made. His own Madonna and Child, living with him every day. He thanked God his family kept him sane. "And I'm really sorry for last night's call. I'll speak to Eric about it."

"You're forgiven, and so is he. Just come home in time for supper tonight." She smiled over her shoulder and disappeared down the hall, her soft coos floating back to Don.

Walking over to the coffeepot, he poured a third cup of coffee, leaned against the counter, and took a hot sip.

He couldn't tell Inez about the special interest the government had in the financial markets these days. After the 9/11 terrorist attack rumors flew about someone behind the strike making a bundle of money by selling stock in the World Trade Center's insurance carrier the day before. If that was true, then terrorists could use the free market system to fund their activities. How ironic was that?

Balancing national security interests with the commitment to grow free enterprise worldwide was a tough job, and SDS was right smack in the middle of behind-the-scenes maneuvering. An unknown player showing up in this well-orchestrated dance would make the shit hit the fan all the way up the government chain. He hoped when it started falling back down Eric could avoid the splatter.

Of course, if Paul was on target, there were at least three outside players involved in the dance. Three scorpions in a bottle; each kept the other in check. If one got loose, the other two would sting each other to death. Could Eric avoid the rogue one, or would he get stung too?

He tossed the rest of his coffee into the sink. Eric had insisted on making foolish decisions when he incorporated his company. The impact of those decisions was already out of his control. Don prayed that Eric had learned enough to maneuver through this minefield with his butt in one piece. But he doubted it.

Chapter 14

SHANGHAI, CHINA

Cigarette smoke drifted from the jade ashtray sitting atop the intricately carved mahogany desk. Its lazy curl joined the haze, floating like a smog cloud in the ceiling of the high-rise office, a mirror image of the brown air concealing the skyline.

"What is the status of our effort to acquire SDS Technologies?"

The echoes of Zhu Zhien's sharp question reverberated off the windows. He stared in turn at the three men sitting across from him. His tailored coat draped over his desk chair, his extra pack of cigarettes bulging within easy reach from the breast pocket. He'd already smoked almost a pack this morning since he'd learned of the threat to his careful courtship of SDS by an unexpected press release. He stroked the close-cropped gray wings from his temples to his receding hairline and fingered new lines sprouting from his eyes.

His plum position administering the Shanghai Stock Exchange was contingent on keeping the political powers happy. That meant making certain excess money floated from the Exchange directly into their pockets. The official Communist Party propaganda railed about the excesses of capitalism, but they had no problems with excess profits that flowed reliably, free from government constraints. They trusted Zhu would deliver those profits. And he needed SDS to do so.

"It seems there are other compatriots interested in bringing SDS technology into our country. We'll have to deal with competition in our bid," Liu Tianwang answered, his voice gravelly from untold years of smoking.

Zhu frowned. The older man bowed his head, his heavy jowls swinging against a sunken chest. Zhu had worked with him since the beginning of his quest to marry the capitalistic institution of a stock market exchange with the current communist political structure. Zhu relied on his ability to be both truthful and non-judgmental as he tiptoed through the maze of new opportunities opening up after the Premier's economic call-to-arms speech.

"Who is it, Assistant Liu? We'll simply convince them to drop their efforts." Zhu made sure his tone was as bold as his words. He couldn't tolerate any doubt among his staff of the tremendous power he wielded.

Old Liu consulted his notepad. "Our sources tell us there is a small rebel group re-gathering on the island of Taiwan which wants to see the Chinese Communist Party return to its Maoist roots. They wish the central government to hold all economic power again, instead of following our current path toward blended capitalism."

Exhaling slowly, Zhu narrowed his eyes against the smoke. China couldn't go backwards. Not again. Mao Zedong had tried and utterly failed. His imitators still ruling North Korea hadn't learned that lesson, and their people were paying the price daily. A new political rebellion spreading into China would tear the world's carefully cultivated alliances to shreds. Just like in the old days under Chairman Mao.

Bad times were hard to forget.

"Anyone else?" Heavy silence met Zhu's question.

A polite cough came from the young man sitting in the junior seat near the door. Stuck in traffic, his boss had sent his assistant instead. Sweat stains darkened the armpits of his rumpled suit jacket. "Director Zhu, there may be at least one other player we should consider, although there is no evidence of their involvement–yet."

Zhu strained to hear the quiet voice above the construction noise outside. "Speak up, boy! That's why you're here." He took a quick drag on his cigarette. "What's your name?"

"Sun Guibao." The junior man cringed under the group's intense scrutiny, looking as though he wanted to run out the door. They weren't used to newcomers.

Zhu waved his cigarette. "Continue, Little Sun."

"As you know, SDS software is quite unique. It can securely encrypt a fast-moving and complex data stream from multiple sources." The youngster spoke with only a slight quiver in his raised voice. Well, good for him. He learned fast. "That is why so many military installations throughout the world are interested in it, as well as stock exchanges like ours."

"And why is that significant?" Zhu injected sarcasm into his provocative challenge, as a test. Would Sun Guibao pass? Zhu only trusted the opinions of those with the courage to continue in the face of deliberate rudeness. He prided himself on looking forward, steering away from political lapdogs who are only interested in protecting their own reputations and careers.

"I think we all know our government's desire for Chinese companies to dominate the worldwide economic chain without having to compete directly for that power."

Grunts of agreements met his blunt statement.

Little Sun's voice strengthened. "We've had a late start, true, but we can simply acquire better technology and then modify any promising product for our purposes while keeping the profit. Our engineers developed similar technology but it is inferior. Perhaps our military is interested in acquiring SDS to substitute for our own. It would allow them to secretly monitor foreign military communications and give our country a leg up on military dominance as well."

"Hmm." Zhu stroked his chin. "Can the SDS software be modified in such a fashion?"

"Yes, it is possible. The critical advantage of SDS software is the slight delay of the data from the point of transmission to the point of reception. It is those extra milliseconds that can give the owner an edge, no matter what the application–military or financial." A look of uncertainty swept over the young man's features. He took a deep breath. "Director Zhu, our sources indicate there is a flaw in the software, making it vulnerable without the customers even being aware of the process."

"Is this the flaw announced today?" Zhu turned, curious as to why his last advisor had remained so quiet. Wu Minggui wore an elegant suit and tie of the finest Chinese silk, a reflection of the executive status he had achieved through his hard work–and impeccable family bloodlines.

"I believe it is the same one, Boss," he answered with a smooth nod. "Our PR department traced its origin to a small marketing company near Beijing, but has not been able to determine who was behind it." Wu Minggui cleared his throat. "Of course, the news about the flaw is actually to our benefit. It was the flurry of other releases afterwards that don't help our effort to acquire SDS at a low price."

Zhu curled his lip. "Are you now trying to justify the release?"

"No, just pointing out the facts. And the fact is we desire to use the SDS software in exactly the way described–to allow the Shanghai Exchange a slight edge over the rest of the world markets so our own companies, investors, and brokerage firms can benefit. That is no secret to anyone."

Disgusted his plans were no longer confidential, Zhu made sure his look of displeasure was evident to every man in the room. He stubbed out his cigarette in the overflowing ashtray with fierce jabs and reached for his pack to light another one.

Fresh smoke joined the cloud pooling at the ceiling. Zhu pointed his cigarette at the participants in turn. "We will get SDS under our control," he ordered. "Find out who initiated that press release, and then we will make our offer. I don't care what you need to do. Just make it so."

Waving his hand in dismissal, Zhu swiveled in his chair and stared out the window. The men filed out in silence, and he shrugged aside any turmoil his unequivocal order may have caused. His own life would get a lot more complicated if he now had to battle compatriots in order to set China on the right path. Greater men than he had died trying.

Chapter 15

Lynn dropped into Eric's Mustang in the pearly morning light, hoping she didn't look too worse for wear. Worries about the quality of her work interrupted too few hours of sleep. Instead of caffeine, her morning jolt had come from reading her mortgage company's email, informing her in oh-so-polite terms that she had no more than thirty days to pay up or clear out. This was truly trial by fire.

Eric raked wide eyes over her severe blue suit, high-collared white blouse, horn-rimmed glasses, and French twist hairdo. "Wow! I have to admit if you'd showed up at the banquet looking like that, I would have introduced you as my mother instead of my date. I like last night's outfit much better."

"For your information, my company's image is as important as yours, only I don't have product announcements to help shape it. Only me." Lynn didn't mean her response to be so sharp, but his unstated criticism stung.

Eric's brows shot up.

She smoothed her skirt over her knees, surprised at her irritation. What did she expect? He'd proven he was a jerk years ago when he'd lied. Multiple times.

She sighed, reminding herself she was an adult now, and a successful businesswoman. "I dress this way to reassure my clients of my professional abilities." She prayed her technique worked in Eric's case.

"I'm impressed by your words and actions, not the way you dress." Eric put the car in gear and turned out of the hotel parking lot. "I didn't mean to ruffle your feathers." His lips quirked in a half-smile. "You look great, just...different."

Lynn leaned back, mollified. Bernadette gave her the same grief about her business clothes. Lynn knew her conservative image made her look at least ten years older. Usually it didn't bother her, but Eric's comment rankled.

Maybe she was just tired. Or maybe she wished this particular client would see her as a desirable woman so she could pay him back for rejecting her years ago. And after she helped build him up on that wind-swept pier overlooking Lake Michigan.

Glancing at him from the corner of her eyes, she mentally shook her head. He seemed to be no worse for wear for lack of sleep. Even in casual business clothes, Eric was heart-stoppingly gorgeous. His black slacks contrasted with the dress shirt he wore, ivory sleeves already folded back to his elbows, his forearms tantalizing her with a downy covering of thick hair.

"I can't spend as much time with you today as we planned." Eric merged into heavy freeway traffic. "I have to fly to New York this afternoon to meet with the bankers in the morning. They're understandably upset about the press releases, and want to know what we're up to."

"Join the club," she muttered, closing her eyes for a brief moment, quelling the nervous flutter in her stomach. With her condo foreclosing and Mitch's medical bills piling up, she had no choice but to learn on the job. Not good. She glanced at him under lowered lashes, praying he hadn't heard her uncensored comment.

His brow wrinkled, and his head cocked to one side. He peered at the rearview mirror and changed lanes with a flick of his wrist. "I'd like you to join me there day after tomorrow," Eric continued. "The bankers will be more confident if they meet you. They'll undoubtedly reiterate the limitations we are under, and grill you on your background, references, et cetera. Then we can spend uninterrupted time on your marketing plan."

She gulped. "Is that really necessary? I mean, I just got here, and I was planning on learning a bit more about SDS before jumping in with both feet." She crossed her fingers in her lap, hoping her near terror didn't show. This was much more complicated than her expertise could handle. Shouldn't she confess her lack of experience with IPOs and back out of the contract? Her business might be on its last legs, but his was about to rocket to the moon. Was it fair to jeopardize his future because of her–and Kip's–failings?

"A little late, isn't it? If that had been the case, you wouldn't have come charging up to San Francisco to find me, or worked your tail off last night to deflect the bad press."

"Yes, but–" Images of a foreclosure notice tacked to her condo's door flashed through her mind.

"Lynn, you're working for me now, and I need you in New York. Okay?" His voice was stern, but his challenging hazel eyes glinted with questions she didn't dare answer.

"Of course." Pressing her lips together, Lynn nodded. Time to show him she was on board with his plan. "How long do you think I'll be there? I need to deal with my hotel room and rental car."

"I'm not sure, so just give up your room for now. I'll have Don return your car. You can use mine tonight and leave it here until we come back."

She eyed the muscle car with trepidation. Its powerful engine rumbled through her pores as he accelerated through traffic. "You trust me with your baby?"

He burst out laughing, exiting the crowded freeway with a roar, hugging the tight curve lined with red-flowering bushes. “This is not my baby, believe me. And yes, I trust you. No one who works as hard as you did last night is inconsiderate.”

Slow warmth filled Lynn. Maybe he wasn’t a jerk anymore. “Thanks. So what’s our abbreviated agenda this morning?”

“I’ll introduce you to the key employees who can answer any questions you have, and load you up with IPO material for you to read on the plane.” His expression turned serious. “Just be careful. Keep all the information in your possession. We’re using confidential numbered paper copies so we can keep track of who has one. Believe it or not, old-fashioned security measures come in handy.”

He signaled and turned into the SDS driveway. Lynn checked her watch. Eight o’clock on the dot. What a difference six hours made. The parking lot was packed.

Eric led her toward his office and stopped in front of the desk of a woman judiciously jotting notes on a pad. She pursed her apricot-rouged lips, a perfect match to her cashmere sweater, and she peered over half-glasses.

“Good morning, Eric,” she said. “Lots of angry voice mail messages pouring in. Surprised?”

“Good morning, Steph. And no…not really surprised. I’d like you to meet out new PR consultant, Lynn Baker. Lynn, this is my assistant, Stephanie Medina. She really runs the place.”

Eric patted Stephanie on the shoulder and grabbed the pad from her desk. He glanced over the page, frowning.

Lynn extended her hand, catching Stephanie’s assessing glance. “Hello, Stephanie. Sorry if we gave you a rather hectic morning,” she added, tilting her head toward Eric’s messages. “We worked late last night on getting press releases out, and it looks as though they got a reaction.”

Stephanie returned Lynn’s handshake with a hearty squeeze. “It’s my job to handle the reaction. Though I have to admit I like having a little bit of advance notice." She waggled her eyebrows at Eric, a wry smile tilting her mouth.

"I figured you'd rather find out first thing this morning than in the middle of the night. Am I right?" Eric challenged.

"You bet, boss. The more beauty sleep, the better." She patted her hairspray-stiff coiffure. "Any travel arrangements you need?"

"Manhattan for me tonight, and Lynn joining me there tomorrow night. I don't know how long we'll stay to put these fires out. In the meantime, I'll introduce Lynn around. If you wouldn't mind helping her out if she needs a hand, I'd appreciate it."

"Sure thing." She turned toward Lynn exuding briskness and competence, pointing her thumb behind them. "The office at the end of the hall is all ready for you. Let me know if you need any admin help."

"Thanks," Lynn called over her shoulder. She hastened after Eric, who was heading in the opposite direction, scowling down at the messages.

"Problems?" she whispered, aware of the curious looks and hushed voices coming from the labyrinth of gray cubicles.

Eric shook his head. "We can talk about them later. Come meet Rajiv. He'll really be in charge while I'm gone, and we need to get him up to speed ASAP."

They turned a corner and knocked on an open door with a hand-carved wooden nameplate stating it belonged to Rajiv Ghosh. Similar to Eric's office, a white board hung on one wall, covered with colored scribbles and notations. Only this office looked like a cyclone had hit it. Scattered papers covered the desktop, reference books lay haphazardly open and marked with sticky notes, and pens and pencils littered the floor.

Standing in the middle of the office, scanning papers gripped in one hand with his briefcase still in his other, was a short, slender man with straight black hair worn almost to his shoulders, partially covering the mole on his dark cheek. Khaki pants and a golf shirt hanging untucked around his hips labeled him an engineer. High-priced athletic shoes completed the outfit.

His brown, heavy lidded eyes squinted at the papers as if he couldn't believe what they said. He glanced up as they approached, wide-eyed.

"Have you seen these press releases? What is Kay up to? And why would she release a story about a bug?" With each question his voice grew louder, until the last word rattled the ceiling tiles.

Chapter 16

Rajiv's breath came in shorts pants. Was it only last night he and Connie dreamed about how they would spend their IPO riches? So much for their goal of a great college education for the kids. Now he would be lucky if he still had a career! Word traveled fast in Silicon Valley.

Eric put a heavy hand on his shoulder and squeezed. "It's not quite as bad as it looks. But something's going on and I was hoping you would know why."

He lifted his other hand, palm out, stopping the flow of Rajiv's questions. "Rajiv, this is our new marketing and PR consultant, Lynn Baker. Lynn, meet my partner in crime here at SDS, Rajiv Ghosh."

Rajiv ignored her outstretched fingers. "You are the one responsible for all this? Are you insane?" Rajiv shook his fistful of papers in her face.

Lynn dropped her hand, shooting Eric a brief glance with one eyebrow arched. "Why don't we all sit down and discuss the problem? Eric and I need to brief you on what we worked on last night. Then hopefully you can update us on any engineering issues that may have started all this."

Rajiv opened his mouth, ready to defend the quality of his team's work. Eric's raised eyebrows and gleaming eyes challenged him. He snapped it shut. All right, maybe he did have an obsessive dedication to his software. Maybe that blinded him to problems. Over time, Rajiv had managed to handle himself and his team with much better aplomb when they received customer criticisms. Even so, this morning's unexpected bombshell shook his limited skills.

Pointing to the chairs in front of his desk, he slammed the door behind Eric and Lynn, and walked around. He dropped his heavy briefcase at his feet with a loud plop and sat.

Lynn leaned forward, her eyes reflecting concern. "We had a crisis on our hands, which started late yesterday afternoon. Fires needed to be put out before we could gather all the facts. It's not the way I generally start with a new client, but there it is. I hope you can accept that and work with me nonetheless."

"I am listening." He settled back in his chair, twisting his lips, perusing her conservative appearance and confident air. He still was not convinced an outsider should shape their public image, even though Chas had recommended this woman. Kay deserved the chance, especially given the high degree of confidential information involved. Eric seemed relaxed enough–was that a yawn he just stifled? At least Lynn looked like she had experience under her belt, not a young chippie cutting her professional eyeteeth on their IPO.

Lynn related facts, starting with the conversation she had overheard at the hotel pool and through their work in the dead of night. The more she shared, the more Rajiv accepted her critical role. This situation was indeed dire and required an expert.

Rajiv turned toward Eric, tugging on his ear. "But where would they get the idea there was a bug in the software? None has been reported to me." Pride warred with worry.

Eric shrugged, pointing to the press release. "I'd start with the customer they quoted and then go from there. I've already received phone calls from the CEOs of our two largest customers."

Rajiv pulled up his list of emails and scanned them. He puffed out a breath at the scope of the problem.

"I have many messages here, too. I will get back to them all personally this morning. In the meantime, I will have Scotty's team take apart the code line by line to see if they can find anything we missed. He warned me the engineers were gossiping like old ladies. I assume they have already learned the bad news."

Eric stood up and nodded toward Lynn. "I've got calls to make, and Lynn will be getting more information on the source of the release. Let's meet again in a couple of hours to see where we stand before I leave for New York."

Rajiv froze, swallowing hard. "It is so bad the money boys need to see you?"

Eric's lips twisted into a wry smile. "Once they got their hooks in to bring us public, they hanker to sniff out every tiny detail. Hopefully this will just be high-powered hand-holding, but I'd be foolish to deny this could have major repercussions on the IPO."

"I'll do my best to dissipate the negative impact of the press releases and keep you both posted," Lynn interjected quickly. "But please keep me fully apprised of any problem you may find, so we can get ahead of it instead of reacting to it." She pinned Rajiv with a hard look.

Rajiv met her eyes. "Yes, I understand what you need. As soon as there is anything to tell you, I will." It was a half-hearted promise, but she would have to take what she could get. He was nobody's fool, especially when his reputation was on the line. Some information should stay buried.

Lynn stood and extended her hand again. "I'm glad to be working with you, Rajiv," she said. "I've heard great things about you from my other clients."

Rajiv rose and shook her hand firmly, his cheeks heating in embarrassment. "Thank you. And I apologize for my reaction earlier," he conceded. "I do not like surprises, especially when it involves SDS."

Lynn squeezed his hand briefly before letting it go. "Loyalty like that is rare and precious. The company is lucky to have you."

Rajiv nodded his head, opening and closing the door behind them. He drew his first full breath since arriving at SDS this morning. Small tendrils of panic raced through his veins, panic he always kept tamped down in the presence of others. Someone was out to get SDS, and he intended to find out who it was. He sank back down in his chair and buried his head in his hands.

His parents' concerns about the risks inherent to a start-up had not tempered his ambition at all. Instead, he slaved for three years finalizing Eric's code and developing a quality engineering staff. He used consultants judiciously to maintain control. Each engineer learned only a part of the project–except Chas Wilkins. He knew the whole picture.

Rajiv squeezed his temples hard, pushing back the building pressure. Both Eric and Lynn assumed the problems were from new players in the marketplace making up rumors to tank SDS and the IPO. Only what if there really was a major bug? What if he had hired the wrong engineer in the early years?

Had he written bad software?

Had Eric?

What good did it do to place blame, anyway? Rajiv shoved the implications on his life's dreams aside. There would be plenty of time for regret and reassessment after the job was done. He reached for the phone and summoned Scotty.

Chapter 17

Eric leaned against the doorjamb of Lynn's tiny office, taking advantage of her deep absorption in work to study her. She sure had raised her professional barriers high this morning–as if her conservative clothes and schoolmarm hairstyle could cool his jets. Maybe it had worked with other men. Not him. Not in the least.

His garment bag swung from one finger while his other hand gripped his over-stuffed briefcase. He stepped into the room, making sure he still blocked the doorway. Lynn glanced up from the piles of pamphlets, business plans, sales presentations, and financial filings Eric had assigned her, and stretched her neck. A welcoming smile replaced the concentration marring her brow.

"Uh, Lynn, I need to ask you a big favor." Eric cocked his head, swinging his briefcase from side to side.

"Let me guess. You need me to go undercover as a secret agent and take out the bad guys one by one, punishing them for their dastardly actions." She threw him a broad wink, whipping off her glasses and pretending to look for hidden devices under the sole plant's wilting leaves as if her glasses were a gadget from a James Bond movie.

Eric chuckled, his mood lightening. She made him feel special, and he enjoyed every moment he spent in her company. Especially when he had the excuse of holding her close, like last night.

"Nothing quite that drastic, but I reserve the right to ask for that favor in the future." He grinned. "This is a little more prosaic."

Lynn pouted, drawing a hand across her brow in mock despair. "Rejected again for the role of a lifetime." She twinkled up at him. "Okay, let's have it. What can I do to help?"

Her blue eyes reflected a sunbeam trickling through the open window blinds. His breath caught at the sudden jolt of familiarity.

Shaking his head clear, he stepped aside. Young Alex Tran shuffled behind him, wide-eyed with curiosity and eagerness.

"Last night I agreed to let Alex spend the afternoon with me learning about SDS. Since I have to go to New York, I thought maybe the two of you could ramp up your knowledge together. You know, two heads are better than one, and all that…" He let his voice trail off. This was asking a personal favor from Lynn, not just a professional courtesy.

"Hello, Alex. Nice to see you again." She waggled her fingers at Alex and added a warm smile, one of her eyebrows quirking up. "Fine with me, Eric. I know you would rather deliver on your commitment personally since this is so important to you, but I consider it an honor to be your stand-in. Besides, Alex can probably help me translate this engineering gobbledygook before I really get lost."

Her gracious words put a proud smile on Alex's face, and he stood straight again, not slumping in disappointment as he had when Eric broke the news of his last-minute trip.

She was wonderful with people. Made them trust her and thank her all at once. It had been a long time since he'd met anyone like that. She reminded him of someone, but he couldn't quite put his finger on it.

Dropping his briefcase, he placed a reassuring hand on Alex's back and pushed him into the small office. "I'll make it up to you, Alex, as soon as I have a chance to breathe." He snapped his fingers. "Why don't you come to my annual Halloween bash with the rest of the employees? Steph will give you the details. In the meantime, at least you're getting an inkling of what it's like to bring a company public. It's no piece of cake, no matter what the legends running around Silicon Valley say."

"No problem, sir, and thank you for the invitation. I'll enjoy spending time with Ms. Baker. I'll be glad to help her in any way I can."

Alex's eyes glinted with teenage lust, yet he was smart enough to temper it with politeness. Good enough.

"I'll call you if I find out anything." Eric dropped his car keys on her desk, glancing from Alex's expression of eagerness to Lynn's look of chagrin. "Just leave the car parked here before you fly out tomorrow and I'll pick it up when I get back. Have fun," he added, flashing his dimple and waving goodbye.

• • • • • •

Lynn's insides heated at Eric's smile, but she tamped down her attraction. *Damn it, he didn't even remember their unorthodox past!* Why would she throw all her professional rules out the window? She didn't have time to deal with any more hurt in her life. That's all any relationship would lead to. With any man.

But he was so cute. He looked like a little boy asking forgiveness for breaking a window with a baseball. Wanting to help him tugged at her, even though she was knee-deep in alligators already.

"Good luck," Lynn called out to his retreating back, mentally juggling her priorities.

Turning her smile full blast onto Alex, she motioned for him to take a seat across the metal desk. "Care to see the nitty-gritty of the IPO?"

Alex nodded, perching on the edge of the seat. "I want to learn everything I can. They don't teach business in high school. I don't understand why not, since most of us will work for a business eventually."

"It doesn't make sense to me either, Alex." She grabbed the thick white booklet Eric had assigned her and tapped the cover. Red writing bordered the edges in stark contrast to the heavy, detailed black printing filling out the rest of the space. "This is a draft of the SDS Prospectus. For us ignoramuses, it should serve as good background material and answer our questions about the company. What's the first thing you want to know?"

"How about what the heck SDS means!" Alex exclaimed in exasperated tones. "I searched every newspaper article I could find, and even looked up their corporate filing on the Internet. All I could find were the initials."

Lynn regaled Alex with her theories of what the acronym stood for as she thumbed through the prospectus, looking for the paragraph on the company's history. She scanned it quickly, catching her breath when she read the details. She'd been wrong to assume Eric had turned into one of those skinny geeks frequenting coffee houses, so immersed in engineering problems they had no idea life existed outside of a computer. Look what he'd done with his life! So much more than she'd accomplished. She'd better buckle down if she wanted to earn that kind of respect in Silicon Valley.

"Well, I guess we'll have to ask Eric about the name. This only references initials, too." Lynn jotted a question mark next to the letters "SDS" on her note pad.

"Your turn, Ms. Baker."

"Lynn," she corrected. "I think we'll be working together close enough that we can stand a bit of informality, if that's all right with you."

Alex blushed. "Lynn, yeah, okay," he mumbled. "What's your first question about SDS?"

Lynn thought for a second. "I wonder who owns the company besides Eric. I know he brought in outside investors early on, but beyond that I'm clueless."

Alex grabbed the pamphlet and flipped pages. "Here, I think this is it. Eric Coleman owns 25% and Rajiv Ghosh owns 20%." He paused. "Who's he?"

"The Chief Technology Officer, or head engineer. I'll introduce you to him later."

"Silicon Valley Capital and Woodside Investors each own 15%, Vision Star Ventures owns 10%, the Coleman Trust owns 7%, and there are...one, two, three, four, no five more banking type names that each own 1%, And then there is an employee stock option plan that owns the last 3%." Alex studied the page. "Isn't it weird there's this Trust thing? Is that just another way for Eric, I mean Mr. Coleman, to control more of the company? Or is it for a member of his family?"

"I really have no idea," she confessed. "When a small company gets financing, especially from venture capitalists, the hardest part for the founders is keeping enough control over the company to run it the way they see fit, rather than let the bankers decide. This may be one way Eric could stay in charge. That extra 7% would put him and Rajiv as majority shareholders, and they could do what they want without worrying about outside investors."

Alex kept reading the dense type. A puzzled expression settled on his face. "This makes it sound as if SDS is a bad investment. I mean, they describe all the potential problems with the software, but most of what this says is true of any software company. Nowhere does it say how much better they are than their competitors, which I know is the case because I did my own research on their product and target markets." His voice reflected sincere aggravation.

Lynn steepled her fingers and tried to put in simple terms what in her opinion had become too complicated. "I think the purpose is to ensure anyone who buys their stock in the public market is aware of all the risks. Presumably, they are already aware of the rewards, or they wouldn't be considering investing. That's where public relations and marketing come into play—what I do for a living."

Alex gave her his full attention. "What are you doing for SDS?"

"Well, I'm preparing a plan to explain the company and its products to both its potential customers and investors in order to make SDS look good."

"How successful is it?"

Lynn flipped through the prospectus, opening the pamphlet to the back pages filled with numbers. "Can you read a financial statement?"

Alex scooted closer and hunched over the page. "I think so. I mean, I see they sell millions of dollars of their software all over the world." A glazed look filled his eyes. "Wow! Millions of dollars of revenue? They're all millionaires! Why doesn't Eric just buy the company back and control it himself again?"

Choking back a chuckle, Lynn pointed to the next line in the numbers outlining expenses. "Do you see all the money they need to spend to sell those millions of dollars?"

Chagrin darkened his eyes. "Oh, yeah, I forgot." He looked farther down the page, studying the numbers. "Well, at least for the last year they've made a profit, even if it is a tiny one."

"And they need the money from going public to invest even more into the company—to hire additional engineers and buy high-end computers, expand offices in other parts of the world, market themselves. All those things cost money, you know, and money doesn't—"

"Yeah, I know, grow on trees," Alex interrupted. "My mom keeps telling me that, too. She and Dad had to work really hard after they fled to America. She never lets me forget it."

"Well, it's a good fact for a budding entrepreneur to remember," she remarked. "If a business isn't profitable, it won't be long for this world. Profit is what allows a business to grow, to invest in more products, to hire more people. And, most importantly, to return to its investors a gain on their money. Otherwise, why would anyone invest in a company?"

"Got it. Hey, I've got another question. Why is a problem with software called a bug?"

Lynn burst out laughing. This one she had learned years ago. "Well, that term actually is based on a real-world experience, not a metaphor. Initially programming was much more basic and relied on large electrical circuits to run. Circuits filled entire rooms simply to draw a set of lines on a page. One day, a program stopped for no apparent reason. The engineers looked all through the software code they had written, and couldn't find any problem with it.

"So they got down on their hands and knees to examine the wires to see if there was a break, and voila! There was an actual bug fried in the circuit that kept the program from running. From then on, it was a joke to blame any software problem on a 'bug' instead of the code itself, even when the circuits became so tiny that no bug could ever affect the program."

Alex guffawed. "So now what do we do?"

"Now I think I should introduce you to Rajiv and let him give you an overview of the technology. When you're done with him, you can give me a layman's summary of what you've learned," Lynn said, rising. "Otherwise, I'll have to spend all afternoon learning programming mumbo-jumbo just to make heads or tails out of what's inside this prospectus. Would you do that for me?"

"You bet!" he exclaimed, jumping up and knocking over his chair in his haste.

"Let's go, then." She followed his slim body as he scooted out of the office and turned toward the engineering department. *He looks like a young puppy—so eager to please. Well, we certainly need all the help we can get today.*

Maybe a young brain can see what we missed. Like who might have the financial motivation to tank the company. She'd have to ask Eric to clear up the mysteries the next time she talked to him.

Chapter 18

BEIJING, CHINA

General Tong Xiao stood in front of a world map that covered his entire wall. He squinted against the blurriness and fumbled into his pocket for his reading glasses, shoving them onto his nose. His gaze naturally fell on the center–his homeland–so familiar, so precious. The Middle Kingdom's reputation had fallen greatly over the past few centuries, and only now could it reclaim a portion of its former glory.

He shrugged. The past decades crawling back with political and economic capability was a necessary first step. Soon, it would be time for a massive effort to extend China's power worldwide. By military force, if necessary.

Tracing his finger in ever-widening circles, he encompassed the broad continent of Asia, then the Pacific and Indian Oceans, then thrust his finger midway down the California coast.

"Bah!" he muttered, stalking to his desk and grabbing the file with this morning's briefing, dreading having to grapple with the complexities of all this new technology. Despite his protests, every day he was ignored or outvoted, his opinions labeled irrational and outmoded. Were youth no longer taught to honor the wisdom and experience of their elders? When would the current leaders, both military and political, punish such behavior? In the few years he had remaining?

He settled into his favorite chair facing the window. In the distance, he glimpsed the top of The Monument to The People's Heroes, a ten-story high obelisk set in Tiananmen Square. Its graceful lines and strong harmony provided a counterpoint to the crazy angles and reflecting glass the new generation of politicians preferred. Tong Xiao suspected they had been corrupted by Western values, instead of biding their time and waiting for the trust of their weaker enemy before decimating them. China could be strong again. But it would take commanding leadership, the likes of which hadn't been seen since the days of the great Emperor Qin.

Flipping open the file, he studied the short summary of his department's efforts to acquire military technology from the United States. Too much detail confused him. Yes or no, success or failure, how much and when—these were the only facts he wanted. Why did he need to understand the inner workings of finance?

With an approving nod, he pressed his embossed chop onto the bottom of a request to purchase a million chips needed to complement their own laser technology. With that order, China would become the company's largest, most influential customer. If the chips worked, they would either buy the company or control who they sold them to. Allies needed modern military gear too.

Setting that paper aside, he scowled at the words on the next page. His liaison in Washington, D.C. reported that a key experimental component required for their new weapons program remained classified under U.S. law, with a five-year waiting period. He tapped his fingers and considered his options. Many companies could serve as a phantom buyer and export the component directly to Beijing, undercover. He hated using them too frequently, however. One day he might have use of them to smuggle a large shipment before war was declared. The element of surprise was one he never wanted to compromise.

He learned many ways to gain cooperation; under Chairman Mao's tough fist. Humans were the same worldwide. Only the Chinese knew how Chairman Mao really gained control and validation. The refined techniques handed down through his military training, both on and off the fields of war, could be helpful–even in non-military campaigns.

Eventually, it all comes back to power. Who will gain the upper hand in the century to come?

General Xiao made no apologies for his true purpose–controlling China's budding capitalist marketplace to combine with their communist practices. Whether the economic experts labeled it blended or the critics shrilled that it was a mutant, he was content. Growing military prowess backed up the Communist Party's strategy. If capitalism delivered all it promised, the government would fill its coffers with the world's wealth, since Western investors overwhelmingly chased China's phenomenal growth. Then his dream of a powerful military could be realized. If capitalism imploded around them, they would already have stockpiled all the money they needed to set it right again through military might. Either way, China would dominate the world.

The General dropped the file to the floor and rested his head against the chair, his old bones aching. He didn't expect to see the day of victory. They were decades away from developing the kind of force necessary to take on the world.

But he could do his part now. His country still deserved his best. And his leaders expected it of him.

As General, he would accomplish his current mission before retiring. He had all the players in place, from Silicon Valley to Wall Street, ready to aid in acquiring the key SDS technology imperative to build China's burgeoning muscle.

Chapter 19

Lynn slammed down the phone, tired of leaving voice mail messages. She glanced at her watch. It was way past quitting time on the East Coast. What did it matter to her network of contacts that she couldn't uncover the mysterious source of the press release?

Today proved she lacked experience, lacked ideas, and would soon lack a client. She gulped, shoving aside growing panic. Time to take stock.

She had confirmed the press release originated in China. No surprise there–the accent of the men she'd overheard gave them that clue. While Rajiv confirmed they had a dozen Chinese customers, small and eager to use the software, it was unlikely they would bother with a purposely-misleading press release.

A soft slither of sound caught her attention. She glanced toward the door and her tired eyes snapped open. A slender, willowy Asian woman stood framed in the doorway, a short crimson skirt and hip-length, matching jacket clung faithfully to every curve. Her outfit emphasized an expanse of long legs ending with matching snakeskin heels, a vivid siren blast in business attire.

What would it be like to make such a memorable impression on every man or woman, instead of a stodgy one? Lynn tucked her white hair behind her ears and shoved aside a brief pang of envy.

"You must be Lynn Baker." The high-pitched voice had the same air of confidence as her appearance. "I'm Kay Chiang, VP of Sales. I've been meaning to speak to you all day, but it's been a little hectic, as I'm sure you're aware."

"Nice to meet you, Kay." Lynn winced at the contrast of her husky overtones modulating so much lower than Kay's. "I've got time to talk now. Come on in and have a seat."

With graceful steps, Kay covered the distance to the guest chair. She sat down and crossed her legs, exposing even more of a slender thigh and a hint of lace. Lynn couldn't help but admire Kay's guts to wear stockings, especially with such a short skirt. A whiff of exotic perfume drifted toward her, completing a total assault on her senses.

Kay pinned Lynn with narrowed eyes. "I've had to talk to almost every one of our customers and potential customers today to calm them down. What on earth were you thinking when you released the story about the software bug?"

"For the record, I had nothing to do with the story about the bug," Lynn corrected, on full alert from the animosity seeping into Kay's words. "I put out all the others to thwart its negative impact. Were your customers reassured?"

"Not enough to keep them from delaying their purchase orders," Kay replied, her voice rising in volume. "Why did you ever believe you had the authority to handle this on your own?" Kay tapped perfectly polished scarlet nails in an irritating, uneven rhythm on the desk. "I assume you're waiting to talk to me before you submit any new releases for approval."

Wow, this woman had nerve! A smirk flitted across her lips before Lynn had a chance to rearrange her expression to her usual, professional mask.

"Actually, Eric approved both the strategy and each press release before it went out last night. Apparently, he didn't think he needed your permission," she couldn't resist adding.

A flash of anger crossed Kay's face. "I've been taking care of all SDS marketing and PR needs, so from now on you'll have to work with me and through me." She flicked a long nail on the stack of paper nearest her. "You still have a lot to learn, I understand."

"Pardon me?" Lynn snapped.

Kay uncrossed her legs and tilted forward, her wiry body looking like a hardened Doberman ready to be unleashed.

"Don't pretend with me, Lynn. Charlie Wilkins told me all about the kinds of work you've done–and what you haven't. You've never taken on an IPO. You have no idea what SDS needs." She sneered at the last, leaning back and folding her arms across her chest.

Lynn swallowed hard, desperate to keep her expression impassive. How did Kip know about her contract with SDS? Did he hate her so much he wanted to ruin her reputation again–and permanently? She couldn't afford that. Time to fight fire with fire.

"Since I have no idea what relationship you may have with my ex-husband, nor do I care, I'll leave that alone. But perhaps you should consider why Eric decided to hire me."

She paused as she caught a flicker of uncertainty cross Kay's face. Triumphant from her tiny victory, she charged ahead. "Believe me, my clients are never ones with a functional and successful PR strategy and staff in place–only ones desperate for an alternative approach."

Twirling a pen in her fingers, Lynn gauged the effect of her verbal thrust. Too bad she had to be so nasty. Usually she avoided it at all costs. But this woman's attitude was downright antagonistic–almost as if she were purposely provoking her. Was it because Kay was used to being the queen bee in this man's world, or something else? Perhaps it was simply female jealousy over Kip. But why? She hadn't talked to him in ages.

Kay's lip curled. "Charlie and I have a very...satisfying...relationship, unlike the one he had with you, I understand. And as far as whether SDS needs help, if this is what you're offering you won't last long."

As if she wanted to hear about Kip's love life! "Is there more you wanted to talk to me about, Kay?" Lynn forced a politeness she didn't feel.

"Where did that first press release originate?"

Lynn tapped her pen twice on the desk, studying Kay's intent, watchful expression. The hairs on the back of Lynn's neck tickled.

"My contacts are tracing it down for me," she said slowly. "As soon as I know, I'll provide Eric with the details. You can ask him."

Kay's eyes blackened, her expression furious. "Eric is just a geeky nerd under all that sophisticated veneer, and really has very little experience in this. You can damn well give me the information directly." Her body coiled like a cobra readying to strike.

Relieved that Kay's emotional and very unprofessional reaction confirmed her suspicions, Lynn shook her head. "Sorry, no can do. Eric asked me to share that information only with him." Until she could speak with Eric, she wasn't comfortable revealing any details to this woman. After all, Kay was selling into Chinese companies. Maybe she had other contacts in that country as well. Contacts with no scruples about tanking SDS' IPO. "If you have a complaint, take it up with him."

Kay rose to her feet in a swirl of red, tossing her mane of black hair in disdain. "Be careful, Lynn. After I talk to Eric, you'll be working for me, not him. Frankly, I'm not impressed with what I've seen so far. I don't see how you can help SDS with your attitude and skills–or lack thereof." She left the office without a backwards look, the rat-a-tat of her heels echoing down the hall.

Lynn slumped in her chair, drained of energy. Whew! If only she could afford to renege on the SDS contract. Putting up with that woman definitely wasn't worth the effort, no matter what Kip might think.

Of course, Kip's opinion hardly mattered anymore. Kip's intellectual stimulation had been a safe, refreshing change of pace. No heart involved, only her mind. She'd been unprepared for the hurt Kip caused when she caught him compromising everything they had worked for. Drugs, women, and a careless disregard for both their reputations had destroyed any respect she had cultivated through their marriage. Saddled with the bills for his extravagant lifestyle while he dried out safely in a rehabilitation clinic only added to her bitterness. And made her business success her top–no, her only–priority.

Kip was involved with Kay now, hmm? And re-casting himself as Charlie to boot. Well, the two of them deserved each other. Beautiful to look at, flames to moths, but deadly in close quarters.

Given Kay's aggressiveness, she definitely saw SDS and its IPO as a stepping-stone in the business world. Lynn added her name to her list and put a row of question marks after it. What was Kay up to?

Chapter 20

"Rajiv, old friend, how's it going?" Charles Wilkins manufactured a cheery voice to boom over the speakerphone.

Charles heard the slam of the office door in the background, then Rajiv's voice speaking directly into the receiver. Apparently, he didn't want to risk anyone overhearing their conversation.

"I have had better days, Chas, I admit," Rajiv answered in quiet tones, using the nickname Charles had assured him he'd reserved for only his closest friend. "What is up with you?"

"My contract ended early, so I'm actually at loose ends." And he'd planned it that way. Rajiv should be running on ragged nerves by now, needing someone he could trust to hold his hand, as usual. The bug worked perfectly, setting a chain reaction in motion that nothing would stop. Excellent. "Need any help?"

"Actually, we could use your talents for a bit, but it might entail long days in the short term. Can you believe I have to report to Eric multiple times a day, even when he is in New York?" Petulance crept into Rajiv's voice, a sure sign of a bruised ego. It appeared they hadn't made any progress finding the bug either–since he was so anxious to hire Charles. Rajiv hated failure with a passion. And Charles was going to milk that for all it was worth.

"You know I'll always help out an old college buddy, no matter what it takes. Does it have to do with the press release I saw on the wires this morning?" Charles hid his inner glee. Any slip and it would destroy the trust and professional reputation he'd cultivated with Rajiv over the years. Just a little longer, and it would all play out exactly the way he'd envisioned.

"Yes, though it is not as bad as I originally thought. That PR lady you recommended seems to be handling it okay," Rajiv admitted with obvious reluctance. "I thought at first she was the one who released the story about the bug, but apparently it was someone else. We have worked non-stop all day because of it."

Charles stopped pacing between his living room and entranceway, staring at his captured reflection in the mirror and unfurling his brow before lines formed. He shoved his fingers through thick auburn hair, tousling it and re-smoothing the waves, only half paying attention. If he could get Rajiv to trust Lynn, his own job got a whole lot easier. The second-largest shareholder's opinion carried weight with the board of directors if push came to shove, especially when he was the one with the keys to the engineering kingdom.

"Lynn Baker is good at what she does. Just do what she says, even if it seems wrong. PR is a whole different ball of wax than programming, with more trapdoors and disguises than a mobile whorehouse." Charles walked into his living room and dropped into the recliner.

Rajiv guffawed. "Cannot argue with you there. Give me the black and white issues of code to read and write any day."

Smug, Charles settled back into the patched vinyl. Rajiv would run kicking and screaming from getting more involved in PR than he absolutely had to. "All right, spill what paths you've chased down to find this bug. Let's see if I can help you out of this maze."

A huge sigh rumbled out of Rajiv. He gave a blow-by-blow description of the steps he and his engineering team had taken thus far to find the elusive bug. Charles played the part of active listener, interjecting compliments when appropriate to keep Rajiv attentive.

"You are right, Chas, we should try dissecting that inner kernel of code. I had not thought a problem could be buried back that deep since that is one of our basic building blocks." Rajiv paused, his voice lighter than it had been at the start of the conversation. "Was that the code we wrote on my kitchen table over pizza that New Year's Eve?"

"And a six-pack of beer, too, if I remember correctly," Charles chuckled. "We should be more surprised that it hasn't caused a problem until now." And the trivial bug they found there would suck up all of Scotty's time and lead them away from the section of the code where he had buried the crucial one.

"Now Chas, you know that writing software is more art than science. Elegance and creativity is half the challenge. Otherwise how would we stay sane?"

"Many people would challenge your premise that we are sane."

"Speak for yourself. I will have you know I have wowed all the investment bankers and analysts we have met with." Rajiv adopted a snobbish tone, injecting the British-Indian accent of his parents. "They think I am just brilliant!"

Charles shook his head at Rajiv's ego, but made sure a full dose of sincerity carried over the phone. "That you are, my friend, that you are. You really are the best, and everyone in the Valley knows it."

"Uh, thanks, but–"

"No buts. You're the best, so hang up now and prove it by finding that bug. I have errands to run in the morning, but I'll be yours starting tomorrow afternoon. Usual terms for the contract?"

"Of course, but frankly if you help us pull this one out of the fire, I may have to come up with a special reward to thank you."

Charles laughed. Rajiv had no idea what kind of reward Charles had in mind from SDS this time–and it wasn't just a long-term consulting gig. "I may just hold you to that. Give Connie and the kids a hug from their

Uncle Chas for me, okay? And get home tonight at a decent hour! You know how Connie misses you when you work all night."

"So much she nags my ear off."

"That's what comes with marriage. Didn't anyone warn you?"

"No, but I already knew that after listening to my parents. Of course, I was not fully aware of the side benefits of having a beautiful woman in my bed every night. That is why old married men are willing to put up with a lot," he added with a lecherous laugh. "When are you going to try it?"

Charles hesitated. He juggled his contacts with precision. Like his various nicknames he reserved for special uses, he kept his private life away from his business contacts, preferring to exploit convenient truths or lies as the situation demanded. Rajiv knew him only as a bachelor, juggling different ladies with enough frequency to keep them distant. This was not the time to disclose Lynn was his ex.

"One of these days, but not now. You'll be keeping me so busy I won't even be able to keep my current lady happy, let alone a wife. See you tomorrow." He broke the connection during Rajiv's brief farewell.

Wasn't that the truth? Kay left the bed this morning thinking about SDS, not about him. If now he had to spend precious hours keeping Rajiv on a tight leash instead of pleasuring Kay to keep her as his ally, his sex life would suffer. It was like a giant chessboard–which piece would he sacrifice in order to win?

Charles pushed himself off the battered recliner, glancing down at the coffee table in the center of the tiny room. Instead of drug paraphernalia, these days technology magazines cluttered its surface. Every night he searched for nuggets of information to exploit, looking for the next big trend in Silicon Valley–and vulnerable companies willing to trust complete strangers in order to survive in this cutthroat, unforgiving culture.

Wandering into the small kitchen, he picked at the remains of his minimal dinner, shriveling on the dirty plate. He had gained two pounds in the last week because he'd skipped his usual gym workout. That's the kind of distraction that comes with having a regular girlfriend, especially one as hot as Kay. She had no idea how hard he cultivated his precise image of wealth and success, and he intended to keep it that way. No matter what it cost.

He rubbed a hand over his trimmed beard and mustache. Maybe he should call Lynn and get her perspective on SDS. She needed just enough time to ingratiate herself with Eric and Rajiv, but not so much that she would piss Kay off any more than she already had. It usually worked best when Lynn sorted out the critical information from the background noise.

Since he'd insisted she use her maiden name, no one ever suspected they were married. He and Lynn had tapped into the underground network that was the lifeblood of the Valley. Until he screwed up.

She had refused all his professional referrals, even after he kicked his addiction. This gig at SDS got her back in sync with his efforts. And removed all her other options. She had no choice now but to work with him.

He didn't intend to blow this opportunity. This time would be the last time he would need her.

Chapter 21

Lynn juggled an armful of files stuffed with brochures and white papers, and fished the hotel passkey from her purse. Running it through the electronic lock, she waited for the satisfying click announcing success.

Nothing.

Frowning, she settled her weight on one foot and glared at the door.

Great. No welcoming green light, and no blinking red one either. What did a girl have to do to get a working lock these days?

Making sure the card faced the correct orientation, she drew it through the slit again with a slow, deliberate stroke. She grabbed the door latch and pushed, praying the right timing would grant her access. Did technology really enhance her life when a metal key had worked perfectly for generations?

The door gave way and she bumped it open with her hip, concentrating on keeping one file from squeezing out from under her arm and spilling onto the floor. Her purse strap slid from her shoulder to her elbow, yanking at a stray lock of hair.

"Ouch!" She jerked her hand to her head. Papers cascaded to her feet in a colorful waterfall of slick colors. Muttering under her breath, she kicked the pile out of the path of the door and slammed it shut, groping for the light switch.

She blinked in the sudden glare and her back tightened in warning. She stepped sideways, stumbling over the loose files, and sagged against the door.

The battery chargers for her phone and PC lay in the middle of the room, their cords tangled together. Her personal organizer, usually neat and orderly, was in disarray, pages torn out and scattered on the coffee table. Through the bedroom door, she spotted underwear hanging over the edges of open drawers. Her suits created a jumbled heap on the closet floor.

Her blood pumping hard, she listened for any sound coming from the suite. There was nothing but the icemaker, humming down the hallway. Taking a deep breath, she extricated her feet from the scattered papers, kicked off her pumps, and tiptoed to the center of the room. The open doors were flush against the walls. No one could hide behind them.

She stretched to one side and peeked into the small bathroom. Fresh towels hung neatly on the bars. The tub glistened, white and empty.

She eyed the distance from the bedroom to the front door. Three long strides. She slipped inside the bedroom doorway, sliding her hand up the wall toward the light switch. Holding her breath, she flicked it on and crouched down to peer under the bed. Nothing but dust bunnies. She crawled to the windows, hoisted herself to a squatting position and flapped the drapes, hard.

Dust filled her nostrils, but no intruder leaped from a hiding place. She rose, coughing, and checked the windows. There was no way to open them. No broken glass. What had happened here? What were they looking for?

She shook her head at her stupidity. Of course. The words from the poolside conversation Sunday afternoon flashed through her brain. "*We can't afford a mistake.*" Was that was she was? A mistake that needed fixing? She'd bet her next mortgage payment it was one of those guys who ransacked her room. Especially after her interference with the press release offensive. If anyone had a bone to pick with her, it was surely those men.

She shuddered. What would have happened if she had surprised the intruder by being here at the time? Would they have only knocked her unconscious, or were the stakes with SDS high enough to kill her?

No client was worth her life.

She gnawed at her lip, staring at her fingers. Tiny tremors coursed through them. Her heart thudded against her chest. Should she renege on this contract and save her own butt? That seemed the most sensible course.

She planted her hands on her hips, allowing her heart rate to decelerate, and the exhaustion from two long days roared back. No time for rest now. She crossed over to the coffeepot, dumped in fresh grounds and water, and flipped the switch. While it brewed, she organized her clothes and her thoughts.

As soon as she could, she poured half a mugful of the hot liquid and plopped onto the sofa, her eyes resting on the SDS files scattered near the door. She grabbed her organizer and flipped through the pages, taking note of which sections seemed to have drawn the most interest from the intruder.

Anything related to SDS was gone. She took a long gulp of coffee. Her contact phone numbers, notes from her initial phone conversation with Eric, directions to the office. Plus, the pages with her bank account numbers and online passwords were missing, too. Only the jagged edges of the sheets remained.

Would the intruders return? She considered calling Eric, but it was already so late in New York. Don? Eric had said he was trustworthy, but she'd just met him, barely knew him. A hotel break-in didn't seem worth calling a virtual stranger at home. Besides, what could he do that she hadn't already done? Inventory the items missing, pat her on her head, and leave her alone?

A muffled ping from her cell phone reached her ear. Hopping up from the sofa, she extricated the phone from her purse, lying in a heap on the floor. She glanced down at a new text message.

She swore silently as she scanned the words with growing dread. Her mortgage company's final 30-day notice, apparently, since she hadn't replied to their email. Pay up or have her stuff tossed out, onto the street.

Unless...the intruders had hacked into her identity and altered her financial records. Would anyone be able to differentiate that?

As if it mattered. The bottom line was she'd missed too many payments. This text was for real. She had to come up with enough money to bring her mortgage up to date, and pay the penalty fees to boot, or she'll be homeless by November. Well, that made the SDS decision easy. She needed the contract now more than ever. Despite the danger. Despite the crazy intrigue. Despite her ancient grudge against Eric.

Memories floated through her head. Dancing with Eric in the moonlight, kissing under the willow tree. The gleam in his eye; his surprised expression–as if he too felt a special connection. But what did it matter now? When Bernadette arrived and told him she was a high school–not a college–senior, he mocked her, insulted her, and left without a backward glance.

Maybe it was past time to jettison the old hurt. After all, he hadn't done anything in their recent encounters to warrant any lingering anger. Maybe he had changed. She didn't dare risk losing the SDS contract now because of a bad attitude.

Unfortunately, her contract payment wouldn't be quite enough. She needed more, or she needed to wheedle a concession from her lender to accept a lick and a promise of a future contract, which she had better start hunting down now.

Going back to her organizer, she flipped to the pages with all her old contacts, took a deep breath, and started jotting down names. It didn't matter how sleazy the person–she needed a boatload of money. Fast.

Chapter 22

Eric clenched his jaw, struggling to maintain his patience. He stared across the massive oak conference table at the four men aligned against him, ignoring the Manhattan skyscrapers gleaming in the late morning sun. Angled rays bounced off shining steel and the mirrored glassiness of the nearby lake in Central Park.

"Gentlemen, I surely do understand your concerns about our reputation." Eric let his Tennessee drawl creep into his speech to slow the conversation's pace. "But SDS has a good name because of the way we handle problems, not because we never have them. Software companies have to anticipate bugs."

Sid Leavitt leaned over the table and pointed a bony finger at Eric. "I don't tell you how to do your job, son, so don't tell me how to do mine. I'm warning you–if you don't fix that problem soon, your IPO is a pipe dream for at least a year. Ideal market conditions like these don't last forever."

As the most experienced man in the syndicate, Sid's opinion counted heavily. Years of leadership had lined his face with deep creases and claimed most of his hair.

"I fully recognize we need to move fast. Believe me, we are." Eric strove to stay calm. "I spoke to Rajiv late last night and his team is furiously working on it. They are making progress, I assure you."

"Eric, you do understand that we'll need to delay the IPO for at least a few weeks, no earlier than forty days after the last press release goes out on this, right?" Mike McCarran's low rumble was uncharacteristically somber. He looked as if the strain of his financial dealings had finally caught up to him. Eric glimpsed the protruding paunch Mike normally tucked behind a snug vest, rumpling his pristine appearance. Somehow, it made him more human, willing to share the responsibility of the IPO instead of laying all the problems at Eric's feet.

"Your lawyers have tattooed the legal ramifications directly onto my brain. When I die, I expect my autopsy will make headlines." Eric hoped some comic relief might break the thick tension permeating the room.

Mike grinned, his gray eyes twinkling, but quickly became serious again. "I have to tell you, we're all uncomfortable about the PR firm you hired. Frankly, no one here has ever heard of Baker & Associates. Since this is a PR fiasco, we think you should find yourself someone new ASAP."

Eric took a deep breath and expelled it with deliberation. He tilted back in his chair and met the gaze of each banker. Except for Joshua, they were all gray-haired with hard, cynical expressions burned onto their faces. They had been around the block too many times to be conned.

Eric had to keep Lynn as his PR consultant. He couldn't afford to let these men know his true reason for using a no-name firm at this critical juncture. And he was flat out of time and options.

"Actually, the PR fiasco only came to light because of Ms. Baker's insight and initiative," he corrected. "Otherwise the situation would have been much worse. The only news out yesterday could have been about the bug. I would say she's done a phenomenal job so far, and I don't intend her to take the fall for something she didn't do. I don't do that to anyone I hire—employees, consultants, or even bankers." He paused, letting the silence carry his meaning. "This decision is mine, and mine alone."

"Grow up, son," advised Sid. "She's expendable–you're not. At least, not yet. If the board is dissatisfied with your decisions..."

Eric understood the implication. If he didn't take their advice now, not only was the IPO in jeopardy, so was Eric's role as CEO. The board members were anxious to get their money out. They had already put up with Eric's idealism longer than he expected.

"All right, gentlemen, I have an idea. Ms. Baker is arriving in New York tonight. We can meet with any or all of you tomorrow, if you would like to vet her personally." He rapped his knuckles on the table. "Of course, every minute we spend reassuring you is a minute we aren't working to make our potential investors and customers feel good. Which will it be?"

A full five seconds went by; the bankers glanced at each other.

Joshua cleared his throat and shoved his glasses up his nose. "Why don't I meet with you both in the morning? If I feel it's necessary to meet with anyone else, I'll set it up then. If you gentlemen would be willing to trust my judgment..."

Eric sensed the collective sigh of relief floating through the room. No one really wanted to waste time just to make the obvious point–they wanted Eric to manage the situation better.

Sid spoke up. "That'll work. You have the best understanding of all the technology issues, anyway. Just let us know." He reached for his copy of the prospectus and flipped it to a dog-eared page. "Now, let's get to the nitty-gritty. What price range do you think we can target for the IPO if it goes out in eight weeks instead of six? What other IPOs will we be up against then?"

Aaron Rayburn started speaking in his usual monotone cadence. He sounded as dull as he looked, the result of spending his whole life pouring over numbers. His somber tie was askew and thinning hair fell like wispy reeds, rooted in his pink scalp.

"Depending on what market sentiment is at that time, I think we'll still be able to command a price of $15-$20 per share," Aaron replied. "Assuming we stay with the initial projections of a 25-million new issue added to the existing 25 million–for a total of 50 million shares outstanding–that would give the company a market cap of up to $1 billion. Assuming the analysts cover SDS with any kind of positive recommendations, we should be able to keep that price range steady or better for the next six months."

Aaron peered at Eric over the half-glasses balanced precariously on the tip of his long nose. "And, of course, assuming that not only is the rest of the press good but also that the bug is fixed–and you are able to report sequential growth in your quarterly profits."

Eric bristled at the implied challenge. "If I didn't believe we could do that, I wouldn't be here today. Contrary to popular belief, my intent in going public is not to rape new investors just to put money in my pocket. It's to provide our company with the capital it needs to successfully expand and grow. And, of course, for the initial investors who took a risk on my idea to be able to make a profit so they can invest in the next start-up."

Sid snorted. "Pull my other leg, Eric. You'll make out like a banshee once you're legally able to sell your shares in six months. Until then, of course, you run the risk with the rest of us that the value will tank, and you'll be left with only a fraction of that. But owning over six million shares of a successful company gives you a hell of a financial cushion."

"Yeah, it'll be comparable to the amount of money your firms will make for the six months you worked to bring us public," Eric commented with a wry twist of his mouth. "I'd say that makes us about equal–except the IRS will be taking half of mine in taxes."

Aaron cleared his throat. "Let's stay focused, gentlemen. Last we talked, we had agreed to a pre-IPO price of $10 per share for the employee stock option plan. Of course, each set of initial investors has its own price valuation, ranging from ten cents for Eric and Rajiv, to one dollar for the VCs."

Joshua piped up. "And we still don't have the details on the Coleman Trust, do we Aaron?"

Sid turned to Eric, scowling. "I thought you were going to provide us that information last week."

"You'll get it prior to the IPO." Eric's cheek muscle twitched, his anger rising. He met Sid's gaze squarely. "It only really matters to the beneficiary of the Trust, doesn't it? Or do you get perverse pleasure out of comparing the size of yours to the size of everyone else's?"

Mike jumped in. "From what I understand from Sid's ladies, his pleasure doesn't come from comparison but from an entirely different activity."

"Gentlemen, gentlemen," Joshua chided. "Enough of the jabs, okay?"

Eric relaxed, grateful for Mike's quick wit and the opportunity to drop the subject. Eric and Sid butted heads often but he'd never lost his cool before or attacked Sid personally, no matter how stressed he was. This situation was testing his reserves. He was running out of time to deal with the Trust. And he still had no idea what to do.

"Why don't we break for lunch and continue later this afternoon?" Joshua suggested. "We still have a lot of details to cover and I for one need my nourishment." He pointed to his rounded belly. "I'm still a growing boy, after all."

The men stood almost as one, stretching cramped muscles and shrugging on finely tailored suit jackets while they argued over which restaurant was best. Their common pursuit of wealth always overrode any personal animosity, Eric observed with a cynical shrug.

Chapter 23

Slamming the hotel door shut behind him, Eric wrestled off his tie, barely feeling the silk against his fingers. The bankers debated each other until long after dinner had ended; no one was trusting the other to get the job done in an honest and fair way. And for good reason. They each had their own little secrets to protect. Including himself.

Eric hated this whole process. Years of dedication and hard work had now turned into a scuffle at the trough of instant wealth. This wasn't what he signed up for or pledged to accomplish. How had it suddenly become such a necessity? Thank God it would all be over soon. That is, assuming the IPO won't tank because of this damned bug!

Dropping onto the beige-and-white striped couch, he grabbed the phone and dialed Rajiv's office for the fifth time today. Rajiv usually progressed faster than this. Whatever problem they had was a big one.

"Hi, Eric," Rajiv greeted him. "It is late for you there, is it not?"

Eric glanced at his watch, shrugging. Already after eleven o'clock. He never could adjust his body rhythms to the constant time changes when he traveled. As a result, he was wide awake well into the night when in New York, and his mornings were hell.

"Any news?" He tried but failed to keep the impatience out of his voice.

"Only that we have gotten through the top three layers of code and still have not found anything wrong." Rajiv sighed. "I do not know if we will ever find it. But the customer certainly documented a problem. The bug is there somewhere. They did not make it up." His voice was strained and high-pitched. Eric could almost picture his partner tugging his ear in frustration.

"Let's get Don on the call with us. Can you conference him in?" Eric had already briefed Don on the status, asking him to wait for the call this evening. Within a few minutes, Don answered.

Eric didn't waste any time. "Rajiv, after talking with Don, I need you to consider the very real possibility that we are dealing with sabotage. Have you looked in that direction at all?"

Rajiv's surprised expletive answered his question.

Don jumped in. "I realize it's only a slim possibility, but it's logical given how well the bug is hidden and the coincidental timing of its so-called discovery. Have you had to discipline any engineer recently who has the skill to pull this off?"

"No, no one." Rajiv's disembodied voice bordered on the defensive. "Eric, you know how careful I have been hiring people over the years. Only the best, and only letting them have access to a small part of the program."

With an inward sigh at having to spend precious time and energy calming Rajiv's ruffled feathers, Eric opened his mouth. But Don cleared his throat first.

"It's impossible to anticipate every possibility," Don reassured in a respectful tone. Eric relaxed. "Even I was shocked when Lynn filled me in on the details of the conversation she overheard. It was a one-in-a-million chance you got the jump on that negative press. But we may not be so lucky finding the actual culprit."

"The other possibility is that it's a quality control problem with that customer's specific version of the software," Eric interjected. "Have you explored that avenue at all?"

"I asked Kay to talk to the customer directly and get as many details as she could about who worked with the software after we installed it on-site," Rajiv recounted. "I figured sweet-talking them might help."

"Great idea." Eric worked at keeping his tones flattering and supportive to keep Rajiv's spirits up.

"Well, it worked," Rajiv boasted. "They had hired their own team of consultants to write add-on programs, fully compatible with our software and within the terms of the license agreement. Those engineers had to access the core of the code to understand what to do. It is possible they messed up the program through their customization."

"But from our end, Rajiv, are we confident we shipped them the identical product that went to the rest of our customers?" For a moment, Eric dared to hope the worst had already been uncovered. "Maybe this is all just simple human error."

"Unfortunately, yes, it is identical. Which means that if they have a problem in our proprietary code, all of our customers potentially have a problem, too."

"Has anyone looked to see if your customer's competitors can gain by screwing with your product?" Don asked.

Trust Don to search every possible angle. "Yeah, Kay looked into that this afternoon, Don," Eric lamented. "No luck. This customer is so tiny, they're barely a blip on the radar screen. It's hard to imagine anyone setting up such a big sting on us just to bring them down. There are easier ways."

Don grunted. "Then we have to keep working under the assumption that SDS alone was targeted, and the purpose is to delay the IPO, exactly as Lynn described. I know you don't like to disclose details Eric but, based on your meeting this afternoon, did they succeed?"

Eric scratched his jaw, letting the silence drag on. He knew he could trust Don with his life and, yes, even the ins and outs of his financial wheeling and dealing. However, he never let too much detail from Wall Street meetings get back to Rajiv. His utter disinterest in the business side of the company had once led him to unwittingly disclose confidential information. This time, only Eric had the full briefing in detail. That was the only way to keep tight control on this final step of his plan.

"Let's just say the IPO is still on, but tenuous at best," Eric answered. "And I need both of you to forget I said that. Your jobs are to find out where the bug is and why someone put it there."

"Have you discovered how the story got out?" Rajiv asked. "Our customer swears they did not tell anyone. Unless it was the consultants they hired, and that is another angle to explore."

"Lynn's tracking that down through her contacts, but I've got to tell you, I don't have high hopes about ever knowing the truth." She had so little information to work with to uncover the actual culprit. Eric ran his fingers back and forth through his hair.

"It's obviously not very difficult to put out a story on a company with absolutely no one worrying about whether it's true," he continued. "Gone are the days when a reporter actually verified the facts before release. Internet time doesn't allow for accuracy. They stick something out there and let the subject of the account deal with any fallout." He snickered humorlessly. "Like nuclear winter. We just get buried in a bunch of radioactive crap, with little chance to clean it all up. Welcome to the 21st century."

• • • • • •

Don heard the frustration coloring Eric's voice. He had tried to warn him but, no, the kid had to make all his own mistakes. And neither of them had anticipated how effective a negative press campaign could be. They hadn't at all considered counter-tactics.

Rajiv spoke up. "Eric, I do not think I got a chance to tell you, but we lucked out. Chas Wilkins is available to help us. He started this afternoon on the base code."

"Who the hell is he?" Don jotted the new name down on his pad.

Surprise, surprise, Rajiv leapt to defend his friend. "He is a classmate of mine from Stanford. He worked for us almost since the beginning–right, Eric? He contributed to every product we have launched, and he is one of the best programmers in the Valley. I jumped at the chance to grab him."

"He's all right, Don," Eric concurred. "He does good work; we've never had any problem with confidentiality. I know he's had his hand in a number of government contracts, so he must have a high level of security clearance. He's the least of our worries."

"No problem with me double-checking, is there?" Don figured he was offending both of them. Tough. The FBI trained him to explore all possibilities, no matter how implausible. It wouldn't hurt to check. If it's a dead end, he'll know in short order. No way was he going to go tearing off in the wrong direction when Eric's entire company–and mission–was at stake.

Eric puffed out his breath. "No, Don, you do your job. Lynn is arriving later tonight, and we'll be meeting with Joshua Stein in the morning. After that, she and I will work at the hotel on our PR strategy. I want to hear from each of you no later than noon your time on any progress you've made, all right?"

Rajiv agreed, and Don grunted, staring at his notes and ignoring the brief goodbyes.

SDS had always relied on consultants to manage both their projects and finances. Don wondered if the Valley's informal work environment and trusting network had morphed over time into an unreliable and unsecure labor force, easily exploited by anyone with the motivation. This possibility glared at him because it was now obvious that someone was behind all this. Don knew it in his gut.

And Freeman's cryptic text message the other night confirmed it. He had called in some favors to DARPA and found out Freeman had transferred to a different branch of the Defense Department—one that no one was willing to disclose. Since the Cold War ended, enemies came in all shapes, sizes, and disguises. What were economic partners on one hand were potential threats on the other. Politicians the world over excelled at masking their true agendas, mouthing pabulum gobbled up by the television media for five-second sound bites, as if these complex issues could be discussed intelligibly between cereal commercials.

Freeman had mentioned three deadly scorpions existed, but only one was loose. What if the second had its stinger aimed at SDS? Or even the third? Either way, Don's job as mentor and protector just got harder. And he was the only one watching Eric's back.

He grabbed the phone again, and his old-fashioned Rolodex of business cards holding key contacts who could help him track down anyone in the world. Who wanted to interfere with the IPO? He'd better get answers and fast. Otherwise, DOD higher-ups would be calling him on the carpet to cough up how he could have let it happen.

Chapter 24

Joshua hit redial on his cell. His hand was shaking. He glared at the midtown traffic crawling by the taxicab's rain-streaked window. Horns blared around him, a cacophonous urban orchestra. His stomach roiled from the smell of vomit permeating through the rear of the cab, but the windows were jammed. He was in too much of a hurry to risk jumping out to compete for another cab in this downpour.

He had tried to reach Kay ever since he left the syndicate meeting, including through two high-priced scotches he downed at *Van's Cigar Bar* in an attempt to steady his frayed nerves.

Sid and the rest of the guys were cooling toward the SDS IPO. Bad press made their job more difficult, and there were always more firms to bring public. Why waste their time or reputation on a risk? That's what venture capitalists did, not investment bankers.

Joshua needed to keep the deal together, so respected professionals could create the highest market valuation for SDS. Then and only then would he have the options to play his cards the way he really intended.

That goddamn Coleman had been so close-mouthed about the software bug, checking in with his office regularly and reporting progress but not lifting a finger to sell the syndicate on his abilities to make them money. And he still kept the Trust beneficiary such a big secret! It was almost as if Coleman was testing them, instead of the other way around. As if Coleman was too good for them. Well, he would show Coleman who was in charge of the IPO.

"Yes?" A cool feminine voice answered.

"Kay, Joshua. What have you found out?" He didn't care that he was abrupt. He had run out of patience.

"Frankly, not a whole lot more." Kay's voice carried a hint of complaint. "Whoever planted that release wants to be hard to find, which makes me even more suspicious. How did your meeting go with Eric?"

"He's a total jerk. I don't think he cares one way or the other. It's past time he realized there are new players in this game who have power over him if he doesn't want to play ball."

Kay's purr rumbled in his ear. "I think you're right. I'll call my contacts and get them primed for the next move." She paused. "It will take exquisite timing to work this deal, especially since the bug issue fell into our lap. You sound a little stressed. Are you sure you're up for it?"

Joshua flared his nostrils at the insult. Raising his voice as much as he dared, he watched the cab driver for any reaction. These guys made good money turning over information they overheard.

"Honey, you don't need to ask me if I'm up for it." He injected a sexual tone into his voice, hoping the ruse worked. "I'm always up for you, aren't I? When will your pretty ass be out here?"

"Can you keep Eric busy so I can join both of you?" Kay countered. "I need to be part of the IPO road show, no matter what Eric says. These guys listen better to women in short skirts. If you're able to set up a meet with our Chinese investors, I'm sure I'll be an asset."

"He should be stuck out here for at least two days, so I'll try to set something up. No guarantees, though," Joshua warned. "Can Rajiv handle everything there without him?"

A soft chuckle filled his ear. "Probably not, but that's to our advantage, isn't it? The longer it takes him to fix the bug, the better negotiating power we'll have. If Eric comes back and jumps in, he'll probably get better results than Rajiv will on his own."

"We'll just have to keep him here, then, won't we, honey?" Joshua didn't care that his endearment was sarcastic. Kay always flirted with him but never delivered. One of these days he won't take no for an answer. After he'd made his millions. Then she would beg for him between her legs. Or in her mouth. Or...

"Set up the meet, and I'll let you know when I fly in. Talk to you then." Kay terminated the call, pulling Joshua out of his fantasy. That bitch was going to get what was coming to her all right.

The cab pulled up at Joshua's building and he hopped out, tossing a couple of twenties at the cabbie and stepping around the panhandlers crowding the sidewalk. He punched buttons on his cell but his signal dropped inside the elevator. He tapped his foot, counting the flashing numbers ascending on the panel. As soon as the doors slid wide, he tried the number again. Twisting his keys in multiple locks, he stepped through his door just as his call got through.

"Good morning, Mr. Zhu. This is Joshua Stein. How are you today?" He hated going through all these formalities, but the Chinese were particular about politeness with people they didn't know well–although Joshua had observed they progressed swiftly to a subtle rudeness to get results.

As head of the largest stock exchange in China, Zhu was a man of considerable influence in the financial networks. And that's why Joshua kept Tong Xiao on the hook too. His influence in the military circles was legendary.

Joshua waited for his grunted greeting before continuing. "I wanted to inform you that you should probably be preparing your private offer for SDS and be ready to act at a moment's notice. I don't know if you are aware of the press–"

"Why didn't you inform me of the problem in advance?" Zhu's sharp tones ripped into his ear.

He dropped his briefcase and shrugged off his wet raincoat. "I was as surprised as you, Sir, since the press release came from outside normal channels."

"So you don't know who was behind it, or their motivation. Why should I trust you with our money and reputation if you can't get a simple thing like this right?"

Joshua held onto his temper. "What's important to your bid to acquire SDS is that the bug is a threat to the IPO. I do know they haven't fixed the bug yet, so there is still time to act when the opportunity is exactly right."

"I do not go into battle until I know the strengths of my enemy," Zhu snapped. "You don't even know who might be bidding against us, correct? Why should I make any offer until you provide me with that information?"

Joshua crossed the room to stare at the rain-blurred skyline, listening to Zhu's tirade. All Joshua ever saw from his apartment were skyscrapers illuminated in pure blocks of amber and white, never the rat race driving the millions who called Manhattan home. He took a deep breath. "I'm working on that as we speak."

"And the Trust beneficiary? Do you know who it is?"

Joshua winced. "Not yet, but soon."

"Bah! You are worthless. I may have to take actions on my own to uncover the truth, actions you Americans might not appreciate."

Joshua had no problems believing Zhu would use any means at his disposal to obtain that information. But Joshua still had one trump card in his hand.

"Please remember that the final market valuation will be set by my partners as head of the banking syndicate established for the IPO—and no one else; therefore we still have some time. I will get all the information you require—and soon. When the price for SDS is set, you will be the first to know. Then we can refine the details of your approach and act accordingly."

"Your firm is not the only one on Wall Street. Do this right or we will take our business elsewhere."

Joshua nodded his head and tightened his grip. "I understand completely. I will not disappoint you. Thank you and goodbye, sir."

He ended the call and threw his cell onto the sleek damask sofa, sick to death of the games. How hard was it to buy a company? It's not as if these guys didn't have enough money to pay whatever price Coleman asked–and still have money left over to pay Joshua a hefty commission. They just wanted the thrill of forcing Coleman to crawl–and Joshua, too.

Joshua hated groveling. That's why he cultivated his contact with Kay. She gave him the inside scoop on the company's progress. He'd won the lead underwriter position for SDS and yet these Chinese guys treated him like a two-bit lackey.

He was good at what he did, despite that one mistake. The past was finished. Everyone could make money on SDS.

Unless they screwed it up with posturing and politics.

Chapter 25

Kay tossed her cell between her hands, pacing. The side street outside her office window was empty of traffic. Spinning on her toes, her gaze raked the wooden Chinese symbols draping the walls on either side of her closed door. Boy, did she need some of their good luck rubbing off on her tonight! The sweet pungency of freshly watered dirt infused her nostrils from the lush plants filling the far corners. Her teak desk gleamed in the fluorescent light, its surface clear except for her PC. Its cursor blinked at her, reminding her of the job still left to do.

Joshua's cowardice threw a wrench in her plans. She stepped around the guest chair upholstered in shades of gold and copper, and pivoted. What an idiot. If it was obvious to her he was losing his cool, it was obvious to the investors too. Now she couldn't trust him to deliver his part.

Good thing she no longer needed him for credibility. Her own network of contacts developed through selling SDS software to the big financial companies provided enough cover for her fishing expedition.

Shit. She wasn't any closer to identifying which clandestine players were the new force entering Chinese politics. Those on the winning side would be the biggest beneficiaries of that power shift. Money followed power. Right now, SDS was at the fulcrum of power. And she couldn't afford to let the Chinese military get the upper hand. Not that and keep her real job.

Her cell rang again. She glanced at the unfamiliar number, praying this was the call from Weng Xilin she'd been waiting for all day.

"This is Kay Chiang." Energy surged through her like a light switch flipping on.

Two seconds passed. Three. Kay held her breath. She understood caution, but did this guy want to move mountains or not?

"What do you wish to discuss?" A terse voice filled her ear. As the go-between for the Taiwanese-based Maoists and the Chinese mainland rebels, Weng Xilin was famous for his wealth of contacts. But he cloaked his efforts well since his boss, Du Wenlin, demanded total secrecy. Weng's complete discretion was probably what kept them both alive.

"I'm told you are the one responsible for our efforts in Silicon Valley," Kay said. Her parents could at least be proud of the respect she injected into her voice for an older man. "I was given your name from a mutual friend."

Weng grunted.

His rudeness irked her. Kay perched on her desk chair, staring at the cursor blinking like a watch hand, reminding her of her limited time. "We need to increase the pressure while our target is struggling. You know of the email strategy to get the attention of the CEO?"

"Of course." His sarcasm came through loud and clear. "I'm surprised you know of it, though."

She bit back an angry rejoinder, knowing her priority was to get the job done first. Insults come second. "Then implement it, starting in the morning. Understand?"

"Better than you. It will get done."

"It had better," Kay snapped, tiring of his cocky attitude. "Otherwise I will inform Du Wenlin that due to your misinformation about the recent press release, its effect is costing us precious time and money."

He knew as well as she that Du wouldn't tolerate failure from anyone working toward the greater goal. She raised her voice, letting all her frustration with the situation hit him full force. "How could you have been so stupid?"

"I suppose a mere woman could do better?" His voice dripped with mockery. "You're a fool, little girl! They just let you think you will have a place at the table so you'll work that pretty ass of yours off for our success. Then you'll be of no more use to us than the peasant women in the fields. Another pair of hands to do what is necessary, and that's all. Got it?"

"A mere woman has managed better many times, as you well know. You'd better change your view of women to match Chairman Mao's. When the power shifts in our favor, there will be many women superior to you." She paused, letting her words sink in. "Including me, you son of a bitch. Soon, you will be taking all your orders from me. Got that?" She terminated the call and slapped the phone onto her desktop.

She swore she would wield power over him, not the other way around. Her best chance to prove her worth would be in New York, at the analyst meeting. She intended to interpret more than Eric's glossy sell job. Her invited guests wanted the truth about the technology, and she would let them know exactly how the broad descriptions Eric used in his presentation could apply to their particular endeavor. They would learn the truth as she translated it. And after the successful IPO, she could join them at the power table.

Chapter 26

Lynn dropped her bags inside the door of the Manhattan hotel room, awed by its decor. The Hamilton Inn was very different from the chain hotels where she usually stayed.

Her room was downright cozy, with rose-patterned wallpaper, an antique headboard, and matching bed stand. Black and white photos of old New York street scenes hung between the windows. A polished pine armoire graced one corner, no doubt hiding the ubiquitous TV.

Two doors framed opposite walls. One she could see led into a spacious bathroom, the other probably a closet. But she was too tired to hang up her clothes right now.

She hadn't slept much the night before. She was on edge, thinking the intruder might return, despite switching rooms. The manager jabbered apologies and reassurances he had contacted a security firm to review their procedures. Procedures didn't do squat to stop a determined criminal. She didn't much relish being his intended victim.

It had taken most of her caffeine-induced energy to fight through the morass of automated phone systems and unsympathetic customer service reps to report the possibility of identity theft. Were they so mean because her credit score blinked red during their whole conversation?

Of course, compared to what Mitch and Mom were up against, her worries were downright petty. Bernadette's text message had come in just as the flight attendant announced the order to turn off all phones. Mitch's tests had come back inconclusive, which meant more expensive tests, more opinions–more money. Bernadette just assumed she would pitch in and help the family to pay the mounting medical bills.

Yeah, right. As soon as she dug herself out of her own hole.

Lynn winced at her selfish thoughts. Mitch's life was worth more than her condo–or credit rating. Maybe she should just let the bank foreclose on her, shack up with Bernadette when she was in Boulder, and make the best of her life. She was bound to land another client soon.

That is, if she worked her butt off on SDS and made their IPO a success. Only with the splash and fanfare that accompanied a successful IPO would she earn the accolades that could launch her into a brand new market of emerging technology companies ready to make a hit on Wall Street. If she succeeded with the current Silicon Valley darling, she couldn't fail.

This IPO had to come off without a hitch.

And she wasn't going to let any Chinese wannabe interfere.

Unfortunately, the last time she'd talked to Rajiv or Eric, neither had turned up any more pertinent leads. Her contacts had nothing new either. They were all hitting a giant brick wall, and Kay's caustic words about her inexperience still rang in her ears.

She puzzled over how Kip knew she was working at SDS. While they were married, Kip's good reputation around the Valley had managed to get her contracts based only on his referral. Had he somehow mentioned her name to Eric?

She would ask him tomorrow exactly why he'd chosen her for his PR push. Maybe that would help her figure out how to land her next client too.

A huge yawn cranked her jaws wide open. She stripped off her clothes, draped them over the chair, and dug into her bag for toiletries, a silk shortie nightgown, and a matching robe. She would steam out any wrinkles in her suit in the morning.

Heading for the bathroom, she paused to turn back the blankets, hastening her necessary night rituals before finally falling into bed and a welcome, blissful sleep.

Hours later, a quiet knock near her head yanked her from dreamless slumber. Lynn raised her head from the feather pillow's yielding depths and cleared her throat. "Who is it?"

"Your morning coffee," came the polite reply. She blinked, confused. Early morning light seeped through the curtains. She hadn't placed an order for room service when she'd checked in. Shrugging, she untangled her legs from the sheets and clicked on the bedside lamp. Bonus points for the Hamilton Inn. They read their guests' minds.

Pulling on her robe, she tugged on the door and opened it wide, backing up to let the waiter in.

Instead, a smiling Eric thrust a huge cup of coffee into her hands. His swift glance raked over her. His smile widened even further, eyes gleaming. Lynn gasped, struggling to keep from burning her bare legs with the steaming liquid.

"Cream, no sugar, right?" Eric asked in a cheery voice.

"What . . . what are you doing bringing me coffee?" All too late, Lynn remembered she was wearing her sheer nightclothes. She retreated into the room, yanking the edges of the robe together to cover her scars. Warmth filled her neck and cheeks.

"We share a suite." He squinted. "Didn't Steph tell you when she gave you the itinerary?"

Lynn shook her head hard, reaching for her tattered composure. "No. Steph gave me the address and told me to take a cab from the airport." She paused, glaring at him, remembering how she'd thought him a jerk for years. Didn't this qualify? "You have a hell of a lot of nerve, booking me into a suite with you!"

Eric raised his hands in surrender as his smile faded, backing away to stand in the doorway. "Hey, we all share a suite whenever we come to New York, regardless of gender. It's cheaper and easier, and the location is great. The only space we're sharing is a living room and kitchenette. There's nothing to be offended about."

"Sorry," she muttered, throttling back her temper. Setting the coffee on the bedside table, she dropped into the bed and pulled the covers over her exposed legs. "I was startled, that's all. And, umm, certainly not expecting to see you quite yet."

His warm chuckle soothed her frayed nerves. Surprised, she peeked through her eyelashes as he settled his wide shoulders against the doorframe. His eyes locked on hers.

"I just bet you weren't," he murmured. "Although I have to admit your choice of attire always leaves me guessing."

• • • • • •

And always wanting more, Eric admitted, trying to tamp down the rush of heated blood. His body's swift reaction to Lynn was embarrassing, its ferocity unnerving. Usually he had better control.

Maybe tousled white hair cascading over bare shoulders got him going. Was she even aware she gave him peek-a-boo glimpses through her thin nightgown? She was obviously uncomfortable in his presence. Either she was as attracted to him as he was to her, or she was not used to men in her bedroom—or both. He was happy with any of those possibilities.

Lynn's fingers plucked at the covers. "Would you give me thirty minutes to shower and dress before we start?"

"Actually, I was wondering if you were up for a brisk walk to chase those jet-lag cobwebs from your brain before you get cleaned up," Eric said. "We're right around the corner from Central Park. I try to squeeze in exercise whenever I travel, and early morning works best. Our meeting with Joshua isn't until ten. You game?"

Lynn brought the coffee cup to her lips, blowing its surface. "Sounds great. Give me five minutes to gulp this down and get dressed." She pointed to the doorway where he was standing. "Our living room is through there?"

He nodded, pulling the door behind him. "Just come on out when you're ready. I'll be waiting." He closed the door with an emphatic snap.

Pacing the adjoining room and swinging his sunglasses between his fingers, he stared at the stunning tenth floor view while battling his thoughts and his body. The morning sunshine bounced off the myriad buildings' shapes and sizes, creating long shadows and unexpected shafts of light.

Not since Gwen had he been so attracted to a woman in such a short amount of time. He had chalked that up to youthful lust and relief that he had landed the DARPA contract. He still carried guilt that he hadn't told her how much she had helped him.

Lynn intrigued him on all levels–intellectually, emotionally and, obviously, physically. Unfortunately, this was neither the time nor the place to indulge in play of any kind. They both had a job to do. He couldn't risk all his years of effort for a dalliance–or more.

He reiterated the familiar reasons to keep motivated, focused, and not distracted by women. Except images of Lynn's sleepy bedroom eyes kept interrupting these reminders–instead, enticing him to share the burden of his secrets with her. God, wouldn't that be great! With a frustrated sigh, he slammed his sunglasses on his face and whirled toward the sound of Lynn's footsteps across the hardwood floorboards.

"Ready?" he croaked, checking out the fit of her snug exercise clothes. She lifted her arms and tugged a red sweatshirt over her head. Thank God it ended well below her sweet butt cheeks; otherwise, he'd be a total basket case.

Her long slender legs in brief running shorts begged for perusal–along with her stunning blue eyes, of course. And her unexpectedly lush white hair, even though she had yanked it back into a ponytail. And her graceful neck. And…

Muffling a curse, Eric swept up his key card and opened the door, gesturing her to lead the way toward the elevator. He punched the down button with more force than necessary. They waited without speaking; the creaking and groaning of the approaching car filled the awkward silence.

Chapter 27

"Everything okay?" Lynn shot him a sideways glance, worried about the frown etched on Eric's face.

His lips twisted up at one side. He stepped through the elevator doors and punched the button for the lobby. "Sure. After all, what's there to worry about on this nice autumn day?" His sarcastic tone discouraged Lynn from probing further.

She couldn't read his eyes behind the dark glasses, but his body screamed tension–clenched fists, head down, foot tapping. Lycra shorts snugly encased his tight round buttocks and muscled thighs. A well-worn sweatshirt hugged his broad chest like a second skin. Warmth cascaded through her.

That boy had turned into one hell of a man. Ever since she had first laid eyes on him, her responses were uncontrollable. Years ago, she had blamed them on raging teenage hormones–what was her excuse now? Somehow, her ire about his prior dishonesty had melted into insignificance, now that she saw the very real man he appeared to be–one full of integrity, respected by his peers for his technological insights, and leading a grueling effort to make his company a resounding success.

Lynn pursed her lips. Maybe sharing a suite wasn't really such a great idea after all. She would have to behave on a strictly business level.

Sighing to herself, she counted off the remaining floors. She needed her energy for the ordeal of a walk in the city.

"The park is just around the corner?" Lynn confirmed as the elevator doors opened at the ground floor. Apprehension suddenly seized her back muscles.

"Mm-hmm. That's why we keep an account at this hotel. It's convenient to everything."

She nodded, pretending to stretch her arms as a warm-up to relieve her building tension. As they crossed the lobby, blaring horns broke the silence. Lynn blanched, twisting her neck to hide her nervousness.

Eric held the door for her and pointed right toward 74th Street. She rushed through and hugged the sidewalk next to the shops, pretending interest in the fresh fruit nestled among gaudy T-shirts.

Controlling her breathing with effort, Lynn made note of the obvious lack of speed with which the cars crept through heavy traffic, and tried to forget the impact of metal on her vulnerable body. She matched Eric's energetic pace and dared an upward glance.

An oasis of green trees and grass beckoned in the damp morning air—across the crowded street.

She gulped.

Eric didn't appear to notice her brief hesitation at the intersection. He weaved through the traffic and stopped cars with assurance. She, on the other hand, had no confidence that the drivers were aware of the two pedestrians' existence. She kept her eyes locked on his broad back, her toes almost scraping at his heels. As soon as her feet hit the sidewalk on the other side, she heaved a sigh of relief.

He stepped up his brisk pace to almost a jog, but Lynn didn't mind. She needed to work out the kinks from too many hours crammed in the middle seat of a crowded airplane. Amazed there was actually peace and quiet in the middle of this busy metropolis, Lynn forgot the crush and danger of automobiles lurking around its boundaries. The trail meandered among trees and along a lake. She drew her first full breath since stepping off the elevator. Her mind was finally clear.

"What would you like to accomplish in this meeting with Mr. Stein?" Lynn asked.

Eric glanced down at her. "I'd like you to blow him away."

Lynn eyes popped wide. She stopped dead at his bluntness, staring at his back. "You're kidding, right?"

He grasped her arm and pulled her out of the path of oncoming joggers. They breezed by, panting hard, and he tugged her forward again. "No, I'm not. The bankers are looking for someone to blame for the negative story, and you're a convenient scapegoat. I've already gone to bat for you, but they want to see for themselves that you're up to the assignment."

Lynn frowned at the challenge, but grabbed the opportunity he provided. "While I appreciate your support, I admit I'm a little surprised," she probed. "Most people would think a consultant is pretty expendable, and certainly not worth going up against the opinions of people who control the purse strings."

He scowled. "Do you really think I'm that spineless?"

"No, not at all," she protested. "But the IPO is important to you. If a public sacrifice is what it takes, it's obvious even to me I'm the right choice."

Eric stopped mid-stride, grabbing her arm again and spinning her around to face him. "You're right, the IPO is important to me. But if I have to compromise everything I swear by in order for it to succeed, it makes a mockery of all the years I've worked for it."

He paused for a long moment, his penetrating eyes staring into hers, oblivious to the strength of his grip. "I do what I believe in, no matter what. Nothing and no one gets in my way. I pay the price for what I want. That's my business, and no one else's. Got that?"

Lynn drowned in his essence. Quick, warm breath fanned her face. Sweaty musk filled her nostrils. His hazel eyes glittered, dark and intense. Lynn reeled from the impact of his touch, his voice. His passion. She couldn't help but wonder whether his voice would have the same intensity if it were whispering a different kind of passion into her ear. A passion for her, instead of his company. Was this what she had sensed years before? This basic magnetism that so attracted her, and then so bruised her tender heart?

What she wouldn't give to have the chance to do it all over again.

After she secured the job. After the IPO. And before she got any older.

• • • • • •

The morning breeze suddenly swirled, ruffling Eric's hair. Wisps of bright sun and hazy shadows filtered onto their frozen tableau. The coo of a pigeon floated in the air, its soft cry a soothing counterpoint to the distant roar of a jet streaking across the cloudless sky.

Lynn grasped his hand clutching her arm. "Got it," she whispered, her eyelids half-lowered over dilating pupils.

Eric caught his breath at her unmistakable reaction. She wasn't afraid of his strength. She admired it!

He stepped closer, reaching out to hold her other arm in a light grasp. "So you won't mind working with a hard-ass like me?" he asked, as alert to her response as a hawk hunting its prey.

She shook her head without looking away. "I would never mind working with you." She matched his hushed tones. "In fact, I've already enjoyed every second. You're my favorite client."

He couldn't stop the silly grin growing on his face. "I bet you say that to all your clients."

"No, you're the first," she confessed with a shy smile and even more huskiness in her voice.

Eric's grin faded. "If we didn't have more important things to do..." He stepped back, his fingers lingering in a soft, brief caress before he released her arms. "Let's get going," he muttered, clearing his throat of the unfamiliar rasp.

"Whatever you want," she murmured. Her simple words and throaty voice shot new bolts of desire through him.

He led her on a shady path toward their hotel, weaving in and out of the thickening crowds of joggers and bicyclists.

At the park entrance, cars swerved and accelerated in a manic pace of hurry-up-and-wait, running past the crosswalk at top speed. With a quick glance to the right, Eric hastened halfway through the intersection.

"Eric . . . wait . . . please!"

"Come on, Lynn," he urged, concentrating on getting them across safely. He waved an oncoming car to pass on their right while motioning another to swerve to their left.

A raucous horn pierced the air. A yellow taxicab barreled down at them. Drivers cursed. Tires squealed.

Eric stepped back to avoid one car. Plaintive moans reached his ears through a break in the blaring horns. He whirled around.

Lynn was down! She knelt right in the middle of the street, cowering. Her arms covered her head. Traffic parted like a broken stampede around her body, missing her by mere inches.

Panic shot through him. He rushed back to her side.

"Lynn! Get up! We have to get out of here!" Reaching under her armpits, he hauled her against his body. Her total lack of response startled him. He forced her chin up.

Stark terror filled her eyes. Her face was sheet-white. Her pupils had dilated so much that only the barest line of blue was visible. Fear gripped her features.

"Are you okay?" he demanded.

She nodded, closing her eyes. He lifted her legs, swinging her shaking body into his arms. Heading across the street with long strides, he fixed his glare at each oncoming car until it slowed. Reaching the safety of the sidewalk, he dropped her legs but kept his arm snug across her back, turning her face into his shoulder and hugging her tight.

"Shh, you're safe. Really," he soothed, rocking her back and forth like a baby. Lynn shuddered and went limp.

Dampness penetrated his thick sweatshirt. He lifted her chin again, swiping away tears coursing down her cheeks. Her heart hammered against his chest in syncopated rhythm to his own. His gut tightened at the terror lingering in her eyes. All his protective instincts ratcheted up to high gear.

"Can you walk to the hotel or do you need me to carry you?" He squeezed his arms to both comfort her and to remind her of his strength. If she needed–no, damn it–if she wanted him to carry her, he would do it. She looked like death.

Chapter 28

A passing bus coughed exhaust fumes into her face as it accelerated through a yellow light, leaving behind a trail of gray smoke into the cool air. For a brief moment, all traffic noise disappeared, until the silence was shattered again by the roaring race of engines, triggered by each flash of a green light.

Lynn stared up at Eric, blinking to clear her eyes of the welling tears. His offer to carry her barely penetrated her ears through the fog of cacophony around them. She would have to walk over a block with cars zooming by.

Deep breath. Turn off the noise. Concentrate on the here and now. Deep breath. Feel the strength in my hands. Feel the blood pulsing in my neck. Deep breath. Relax. Focus on my heartbeat gradually slowing. Deep breath.

She repeated the techniques drummed into her during therapy until she was calm again—at least outwardly.

Yes, she could do this. Again.

Lynn gripped Eric's shoulders, forcing herself to take a small step back, then another, until she could feel the cool glass of the grocer's display window behind her.

"I can make it," she said in a hoarse whisper, while avoiding his eyes. Shame swept through her and dispelled the freezing chill of the fast-moving traffic.

"At least your color is coming back," Eric informed her in a relieved voice. He slid an arm around her shoulders and turned them toward the corner, walking very slowly. "If you don't mind, I'll hang onto you." He gave her shoulders a light shake. "You scared me to death when I saw you curled up in the middle of the street. I thought you'd been hit by a car."

"Not this time." Appreciating his attempt to ease her tension, Lynn leaned into his hard warmth. Brakes squealed right next to them. She stumbled over her feet, seizing up in panic again. Eric's firm grip kept her upright and moving in the right direction, toward the safety of the hotel.

She watched their athletic shoes as they slapped the gray concrete in perfect rhythm, counting the steps, blocking out the relentless memories shimmering through her with every brake screech, every horn blast, and every breeze of exhaust expelled by the speeding cars. Only a little further. She kept her eyes on the pavement. He turned her again and pushed open the door to the lobby. She almost collapsed in sheer relief.

Eric kept his arm around her until the snug closing of the elevator doors sheared off the street noise. He punched the button for the tenth floor and eased his arm away, leaning against the elevator wall. She peeked up from under lowered lashes, noting his puzzled expression.

Lynn breathed deep but kept her face averted from him, crossing her arms under her breasts to protect herself. No doubt he'd ask painful questions. Everyone always did.

But without saying a word, Eric laid a hand on her lower back, guided her from the elevator, and opened the door to their suite. Nudging her inside, he closed the door and locked it.

"I'll get you a glass of water." He headed toward the kitchen. "Sit down on that couch before you topple over."

Lynn really wanted to curl up in bed and pull the covers over her face until her nightmares subsided. But she had to regain control. She couldn't regress. She had worked too hard to lose ground.

She sank onto the striped sofa and drew her legs into her chest. Laying her forehead on her knees and clamping her eyes shut, she listened to the comforting sounds of cupboard doors opening and closing, tap water running, footsteps returning.

Eric's weight sunk into the opposite end of the sofa. The smooth surface of a glass brushed against her fingers. Wrapping both hands around the tumbler, she raised it to her lips but couldn't control her tremors. Cool water splashed against her lips and chin. Tightening her grip, she poured it down her constricted throat.

A full minute passed in silence. "I guess I owe you an explanation," she muttered.

"You don't owe me anything," he corrected, staring at her with obvious concern. "Though I would like to understand what happened. Are you sick? Do you need to go home?"

She lowered her knees, tucking her feet under her hips. She turned to face him. "No, I'm not sick. I just had a panic attack, that's all."

"Panic? About what? The IPO?" Guilt colored his voice. "I never meant to put your life in danger."

She forced a smile to her lips. "I wish it were that simple. No, I panicked from the traffic. I was in a horrific accident years ago. I usually avoid heavy traffic whenever I can, especially as a pedestrian." It was why she preferred the wide-open spaces of the West, to both live and work, where people drove everywhere and sidewalks were more for decoration than for functionality.

Sympathy crossed his face as he inched closer, capturing one of her hands and giving it a gentle squeeze. "What happened?"

Lynn took a deep breath and expelled it to the count of five, concentrating on the warmth of his fingers instead of the deep chill inside of her. "I was crossing a busy street in Chicago, and a car ran into me. The bottom of the car caught on my clothes, and I was dragged face-down almost a block before I was torn loose."

Eric drew in a harsh breath and gripped her cold fingers, examining her face, curiosity clear on his. "How badly were you hurt?"

"I was in the hospital for almost a year. In and out for another year after that." Smells of antiseptic wafted over her as the buried memories tore free. "Let's see, I broke a couple ribs, my collarbone, jaw and nose. The pavement shredded the skin off most of my throat and face, and left me with severe friction burns on my stomach–not to mention bruises and contusions along my knees and hip, too."

"My God," he whispered, his fingers tightening around hers.

She swallowed hard. She rarely told anyone the rest of the story–but she trusted Eric with the full truth of her agonies. "After my bones set, they had to reconstruct my face and neck entirely. I don't look or even sound at all like I used to."

Isn't that the truth! It's no surprise he didn't recognize me.

She twisted her lips into a half smile, meeting his gaze for the first time. "I'm not sure when my hair went completely white. When I finally had the guts to look in the mirror again, there it was." She shrugged. "I guess it was from the trauma. I don't dye it to remind myself I've already come back from the dead once. Accomplishing anything else in life just isn't that hard."

Eric brought her hand to his lips in a silent salute. "I'm glad to know miracles can happen. You're one tough cookie."

"Obviously not tough enough." She frowned. Shame for her very unprofessional behavior warmed her cheeks. No way would she confess who she was now. It was bad enough he thought of her as a weakling. "Thanks for helping me. I haven't broken down like that in a while."

"Maybe that's because you've avoided places where you were exposed to danger again," Eric reminded her. "Understandable, even wise, but maybe those mental demons needed to be confronted one last time so that you could exorcise them."

"Maybe," she sighed. "But my reaction almost got me hit by a car again. It sure wasn't the great survival instinct that was supposed to kick in."

He shook his head. "Adrenaline works differently in people. You probably would have another reaction to a new danger. But this one you've already experienced before—and you know how painful it can be."

"It was terrible," Lynn whispered, drawn in by his compassionate tones. "I felt so alone. Except for Kip, no one could spend any time helping me get better."

"Kip?"

"My ex," she explained. "He visited me in the hospital more often than my own family did. He supported me through the all the physical therapy, complimented me even when my face was covered with bandages, and then helped me set up my company when I got out."

She tugged at the hem of her sweatshirt. "It's no wonder I thought I loved him. Unfortunately, I discovered too late that I only married him out of gratitude. We divorced a few years ago." She shrugged, gathered her tattered emotions and shoved them back inside. Time to act professional again. That's what he was paying her for, not a soap opera re-run. Regret tugged for a brief moment in her chest. Too bad they couldn't spend more time getting to know each other.

Eric squeezed her hand. "He probably was as impressed with your grit as I am. I'm sorry things didn't work out."

"Thanks, but I probably shouldn't have even tried marriage. My work always comes first." She squeezed his hand in return before breaking the contact. "Speaking of which, don't we have to get going?"

Eric rose from the sofa, stretching. "Yep. Are you up for the inquisition?" He reached down a hand and hauled her to her feet.

Lynn smiled like the Cheshire Cat. "I'll blow him away, Eric, exactly as you ordered." She sauntered into her room, her thoughts already turning to the impending warfare.

Chapter 29

"Ms. Baker, I appreciate the strategy you've outlined for SDS," Joshua droned. "Nevertheless, nothing you've told me thus far offsets your lack of credentials in terms of handling the PR of a firm during an IPO. The syndicate partners are concerned you simply don't have the experience."

Joshua glanced at Lynn's list of references and curriculum vitae before flipping the pages closed and tossing them aside. Eric suspected he was basking in his role of a powerful king, granting favors to pleading peons, ensconced in the power seat at the head of the conference table. A huge bouquet of mixed fresh flowers ornamenting the credenza framed his face like a living crown, their fragile loveliness a stark contrast to the harshness of his message.

Eric could tell by his flat, bored tones that Joshua hadn't yet been convinced.

All business, and seemingly unfazed, Lynn focused entirely on Joshua. Eric stared at the smooth line of her legs leading up to her hemline. Did she make time for pleasure? He hoped so. How ironic that he desired a woman more dedicated to her work than he was.

His term of service was almost over. Maybe hers would be too.

Eric unclenched his teeth and opened his mouth to set Joshua straight. Lynn's brief hand movement stopped him.

"Mr. Stein, I can understand your reluctance to accept a total stranger's expertise," Lynn remarked with equal courtesy. "But let me ask you, how much understanding do you and your syndicate have about the underlying SDS technology?"

Her perfect make-up matched an intricate hairdo, which created a sophisticated New York look. Her tailored black suit disguised most of her feminine curves, but she had given it her own unique style with a turquoise scarf somehow tied into an artful rose against her throat. Professional, through and through.

"I studied engineering at Cornell while getting my degree in business. I make it a point to stay on top of whatever comes out of Silicon Valley," Joshua boasted. "However, my partners' expertise is in the financial realm."

Lynn nodded her head and tapped her notepad with the end of her pen. "No marketing experts among you?"

At least Joshua had the grace to look abashed. "No."

"So you rely on experts in other fields to launch a public company, such as lawyers, just as Mr. Coleman has had to rely on your financial expertise. Is that correct?"

"Of course." Irritation seeped into Joshua's voice. "It's always a team effort."

Lynn shot a warning glance at Eric as he fought the smirk that lifted his lips ever so slightly. She leaned forward, wriggling her hips into her seat like a cougar readying for a stealth attack. "Do you recognize the names of the companies and marketing executives on my list of references?"

Joshua skimmed the page again. "Yes. I know many of them personally."

"And do you respect their judgment?"

"Well, yes, but what does that have to do—"

"Then you'll just have to take it on faith that I have the balls to use them as references because they believe in my talents and skills. If you won't trust me, then waste your own damn time calling them, and ask them directly." Lynn enunciated each word as precisely as a sharpshooter smacks the target. "Either way, you have all the information you need to support the choice Mr. Coleman made to hire me instead of one of them to market SDS. If you have a problem with Mr. Coleman's decision and not my abilities, you'll have to ask him about it, not me. I have better things to do than justify my existence to you."

Leaning back in the deep leather chair, Lynn crossed her long legs, looking completely unconcerned. Eric detected a slight tremor in her fingers but her expression remained confident and her eyes locked onto Joshua's face. Her slender foot, encased in a sexy black heel, swung back and forth.

Joshua's mouth dropped open. He stared between the two of them, blinking behind his thick lenses. He looks like a deer caught in the headlights, Eric thought with glee. He jumped into the opening Lynn had provided.

"As I told you and the boys yesterday, Ms. Baker is in New York to consult with me on handling the PR fallout and planning for the future. This is cutting into our time to work out our strategy. Did you get the information you need?" Eric made his tone firm and controlling, wanting nothing more than to end this interview.

Joshua blinked one last time, and then threw up his hands. "What the hell," he muttered, shrugging. "Ms. Baker, Eric, I will be happy to pass my opinion on to the syndicate that everything seems to be handled and there is no reason to find another firm."

Eric breathed a sigh of relief, and heard Lynn's matching exhalation.

Joshua wagged his finger at them, apparently not through with his petty power play quite yet. "However, there are confidential issues we still need to discuss. Since Ms. Baker will be representing SDS, I assume it will be all right to discuss them in front of her."

Tension shot through his back, but he nodded, crossing one ankle over his knee. "What is it, Joshua?"

Pivoting to face him, Joshua leaned on his elbows and pointed his fingers toward Eric. "You can't keep on ignoring the questions from the syndicate about this Trust you set up," he warned. "A 7% shareholder represents a large position in a company. The others are rightfully nervous about who the owner really is."

Eric uncoiled his body, readying for what felt like a down and dirty street fight. "And I've told you it is no concern of yours until the final filing for the IPO," he snarled.

Joshua fell back in his chair, wisely keeping a safe distance from his blistering anger. "It is our concern, and it is also the concern of your board of directors. In fact, one of them privately expressed deep reservations that you've kept such pertinent information hidden. It makes them all curious about what else you might be concealing," Joshua stressed. "Now this problem with the bug hits, and they're wondering if they can rely on your honest leadership. They have asked me to look at…other options."

Furious at Joshua for questioning his credibility, Eric clenched his jaw tight to keep from making a nasty remark. He rapped his knuckles rhythmically on the arm of the leather chair, narrowed his eyes and met Joshua's gaze, prepared to stare him down.

Silent seconds slid by. The Trust wouldn't be worth squat until they could set a value to SDS and find a willing buyer, either via an IPO or through a private deal. And he wouldn't disclose his true motivations until he found Gwen.

Vivid memories of her soft clear voice and softer lips were constant reminders of what he had tossed away for the DARPA contract, a contract he wouldn't have if it weren't for her. He owed Gwen for her unflagging support that afternoon, and the loan of her silver dollar necklace for luck. She had roused a yearning in his soul to share his lonely life, to live his dream sooner rather than later.

He'd meant to return her father's medallion with sincere thanks that night. The wave of betrayal over her true age had been tough to take.

He had almost been conned by a high school girl, his career potentially ruined before it even took off—just as DuMont had warned. But he saw her anguished tears after his harsh brush-off. When he finally got American soil under his feet again, he made it his top priority to find Gwen, but ran into dead-ends, despite Don's covert help. Even the letter sent to her sister Bernadette asking for her whereabouts got no response.

Overriding Don's harsh criticisms, he set aside SDS shares in a Trust with Gwendolyn Allen as beneficiary. It felt right, a sort of tithe or private offering, and a way to give back a little of what she so generously gave a total stranger. Besides Don, he'd only told Rajiv the barest facts about the Trust. He was under no illusion that Gwen would still be interested in him, and thought he had until after the IPO to find her by voting her shares by proxy.

Except now, his directors were refusing to honor the proxy, threatening to take away his and Rajiv's majority control. Those shares were what he and Don were counting on to make their strategy work. The board and the syndicate were merely interested in influencing the mysterious beneficiary's vote when they disagreed with Eric. And he couldn't afford her defection.

Time was running out. He didn't know where she was—or even if she was still alive. He would have to come up with a different plan.

Eric pulled himself back to the present and found Joshua eyeing him with a victorious gleam in his eyes.

"Well?" Joshua taunted. "Are you ready to do what's right and disclose what your Trust is all about?"

Eric suspected he was waiting to pounce on any sign of weakness. He rose from the chair and reached for his briefcase. "I'll disclose everything I'm required to legally, and not any more. You and the syndicate will just have to deal with that. As will my board." He turned toward Lynn. "Ready?"

Lynn nodded, slipping to her feet with not a trace of reaction to the strained undercurrents running between the men.

"If you'd like, I'll be happy to send you our completed publicity outline when we finish it, Mr. Stein," she offered. Eric hid a smile as he headed for the door, admiring her for poking Joshua one last time.

Joshua waved her off with a pudgy hand. "Don't bother. Your efforts are frankly immaterial to the real deals going on down here. If it's good, I'll hear about it. If it's bad, you'll hear about it. Either way, it's your reputation on the line, not mine."

Lynn followed Eric into the empty corridor. He leaned against the wood-paneled wall, pinching the bridge of his nose to relieve a brewing headache. She whisked the door closed behind her, and grasped his forearm through his pin-stripe jacket. She gave a gentle squeeze, almost as if she sensed he needed her unflagging support after his standoff with Joshua.

"How did we do? Was he blown away?" Releasing his arm, she whirled her cosmetic spectacles in a spinning motion and tucked them into her black handbag.

He didn't know about Joshua, but she'd already blown him away earlier this morning.

Her quiet courage had crashed through all his barriers. He couldn't forget how her eyes filled with tears, magnifying the shattered blue irises. Just hearing about her trauma tore him up inside. For the first time he noticed the tiny scars decorating her jaw, eyes and forehead. Her narrow escape on the street unsettled him in ways he couldn't name. Would she let him help erase the rest of those scars?

Eric guided her toward the elevator. His hand rested against the small of her back, not missing her small shiver at his touch. "I don't think he was quite expecting a dynamo packaged in such a demure wrapping," he chuckled. "I bet he doesn't lift one finger to check on your references. His ego wouldn't allow him to trust someone else's opinion over his own. Once you got him tongue-tied, he sealed his own fate."

She searched his face as the elevator plummeted down the skyscraper. "And did you blow him away over this secret Trust too?"

He narrowed his glance, assessing the sincerity of her question while fighting his uncontrolled reaction to the gravelly timbre of her voice. "I think I did, but he'll bring reinforcements when the time comes. What do you think?"

Suddenly it was imperative that Lynn was on his side and not just a neutral party. He wanted to challenge her, to test her dedication to SDS. Or was it her dedication to him? Maybe he didn't need to harbor secrets from her. Maybe he could trust her. Maybe...

Lynn flicked an invisible speck off her sleeve and answered over her shoulder as she stepped off the elevator. "I think you won this round, but you better have allies to help you next time."

She stopped short, fixing him with a distressed look. "Is there anyone who will step forward to help you when it's important?" Her fingers grasped his arm again.

"I have a couple of friends." He placed his hand over her warm one. "But I can always use more. Interested?" He held his breath, the seconds stretching into what seemed like eternity.

She squared to meet his intent gaze. "Yes, I am," she whispered. Blushing, she spun away, breaking the contact between them. She straightened her shoulders and moved toward the traffic moving outside the swinging doors. "Do you think we can have the taxi let us out before we get to the hotel? I'd like to re-do this morning's stroll."

Her willingness to confront her terrors so soon amazed Eric. He escorted her through the doors and onto the sidewalk. She hesitated, trembling. He wrapped his arm around her waist. "Sure we can. In fact, there's a little deli on Lexington a few blocks from the hotel. Why don't we pick up some lunch there? We can eat in the suite while we get to work."

A brave smile quivered on her lips. "Sounds like a plan." She kept one eye peeled on the cars zooming by.

Eric waved down a passing cab and opened the door for her, admiring her slender figure, all but hidden under her suit's boxy cut. If he didn't know what she looked like under these clothes, he would have mistaken her for a middle-aged, matronly woman.

Except his body remembered. In fact, it was almost constantly reminding him, despite his best efforts to keep his mind on their work. This afternoon was shaping up to be a bitch to get through.

Chapter 30

Lynn crumpled her napkin with a satisfied sigh. "Why is it that pastrami sandwiches taste so decadently wonderful?" She would need an extra hour of exercise to burn off the calories, but they were worth it.

"Because you don't indulge very often?" Eric wiped mustard from his lips and gathered the remains of their makeshift picnic from the coffee table. "I have a hard time believing you usually eat that much for lunch."

His gleaming eyes raked over her body. She tucked her bare feet under her, fighting a rising blush. They had both changed into casual clothes, and she wasn't sure where to stake that nebulous border between business and personal behavior.

"No, I'm set for the rest of the day," she admitted. "Lucky you—that leaves me more time to work."

"Slave-driver." He dumped the trash in the kitchen and returned with two bottles of water. "But you're right. Let's get started."

Grateful to resume her professional persona, Lynn grabbed the notepad from her briefcase and shuffled the pages, hesitating. "We can do this a couple of ways."

"I'm listening." He dropped into the overstuffed armchair angled next to the sofa and folded his hands across his stomach, like a contented Buddha.

"That's one possibility." Lynn shot him a wobbly smile. "The other is for me to listen. You can fill me in on some facts I need before I make a fool of myself and make silly recommendations based on only partial information."

"Nothing you recommend would be silly," he replied. "Actually, I'm rather curious about your powers of observation and ability to glean information from the prospectus and the other employees. Humor me. I'll listen and promise not to laugh."

Lynn quirked an eyebrow in his direction. "You'd better not," she joked, waggling her finger at him.

Turning serious, she flipped to the last page with her initial set of recommendations. She had worked hard on it during yesterday's flight as the Midwest unfolded beneath her. The flat, patchwork-quilt landscape reminded her of those crazy few hours when she'd had a crush on Eric.

Should she remind Eric they'd met? And danced? And kissed? After this contract was over, there would be no conflicting ethics, no worries about gossip in the tight-knit circles of Silicon Valley. Was she reading him right? Was he interested? Or had he already recognized her, and was avoiding acknowledging their past to keep her at a professional distance? Or worse. Toying with her emotions as a sort of power play?

Keep the conversation on business. She took a steadying breath.

"I think we succeeded when we were aggressive and out in front of the problem," she began. "People were upset about the actual bug, not the way we handled it. Most of them have been reassured that you have a solution and are working around the clock to fix the software. They trust you will eventually take care of it."

He grunted his agreement, slouching down and extending his khaki-clad legs onto the coffee table. The white golf shirt tightened across his broad chest. His buff physique chased the next comment right out of her head. Lynn took a sip of water and refocused her thoughts.

"I think we should continue to lead the situation, rather than respond to it," she continued. "I've booked you onto the *Business Best* show tomorrow morning. You'll have sixty seconds to answer any lingering questions and prove your confidence to the investment community."

Eric shook his head. "I can't do that. I need to keep as low a profile as possible. As CEO, any TV appearance could look as if I was purposely selling my company's future prospects instead of just answering questions."

Her shoulders slumped. She'd worked hard to get that television time slot.

"You're on the right track, only with the wrong person," he encouraged in a softer voice. "You should go on the show as our spokesperson."

She gasped. "No way! I couldn't handle ninety-percent of the questions they'll ask me. I don't know enough." She grimaced at the obvious panic in her voice.

Eric pinned her with his gaze. "Can't you get the questions in advance?"

"Yes, that's standard practice," Lynn snapped. "But there's a huge difference between booking the CEO and some lowly consultant to speak on behalf of the company."

"Of course there is. But if they don't know until the last minute I won't be there, and you very professionally show up in my stead so they aren't left in the lurch, won't they grab the chance to interview you instead?"

"Probably," she acknowledged, "but–"

"No buts. I can't go on TV, and the rest of your strategy is sound. For the record, you're not some lowly consultant," he scolded, sounding just like Bernie. He grabbed his bottle and unscrewed the top with a jerk, tipping it up and swallowing half the water in one gulp. "Regardless of Joshua's derogatory comments, I think you're doing a great job. You're exactly what I was looking for. I consider you the public face of SDS right now–especially since no one else can carry that ball for us."

Lynn gnawed at her lip and considered his logic, annoyed she'd forgotten that extra publicity was a no-no right before the IPO. But there was a significant problem staring them in the face.

"Eric, wouldn't you agree that people like to see a young and vibrant person representing a Silicon Valley company? That the mystique of the technology industry is the energy of youth?"

He tilted his head, his brows crinkled. "To an extent, maybe," he conceded. "There are others who like to know all that energy is harnessed by seasoned managers and executives. The '90s investment bubble proved youthful enthusiasm can go too far and evaporate investors' money. Gives the bankers a warm feeling in their tummies to see an adult handling the cash." He winked, returning the bottle to the table. "What's your point?"

"My point," Lynn enunciated, "is whether the best image for SDS is of an old lady with white hair talking about the hottest technology on the market. It would be much better coming from someone younger. And probably from a man since engineers, by and large, are still men."

He slapped his feet on the floor and propped his elbows on his knees. His eyes flickered with annoyance. "Why do you keep putting yourself and your appearance down?"

"I'm only speaking the truth." His fervent reaction unnerved her.

"You're not old. The fact that your hair is prematurely white is a reflection of trauma, not age. If you were a man, people would call it distinguished, wouldn't they?"

"Yes, but I'm not a man."

"No kidding. How old are you anyway?" Apparently, niceties went out the window when Eric wanted the truth.

"I'm thirty-four," she flared. "Not that it's any of your business."

"Well, Ms. Baker, my compliments that at such an early age, with the interruption of physical trauma and rehabilitation, you have managed to earn a well-deserved reputation for running a quality consultancy. It doesn't matter what you look like, only how you come across. And

I would be proud to have you represent my company on national television."

Lynn blinked back sudden tears. All her anger dissipated as quickly as it had come.

"All right, then," she capitulated. "Will you help me prepare for the questions?"

He scowled. "Of course I'll help. What else do you have to tell me?"

She ran through the highlights of her marketing strategy and how they could implement it after the IPO. Eric held to his promise, listening and nodding frequently, interrupting her flow of words only to clarify a point. When she was done, he looked pleased.

"You're the most insightful person I've ever had the pleasure to do business with. How did you figure us out so fast?" His voice was warm with admiration.

Lynn flushed, setting the papers aside and running her fingers through her hair, pulling the cascade over her shoulder.

"People tend to share information with me rather easily," she confessed. "I'm not sure why, but more than once when I've finished listening to clients they're surprised by how much they've disclosed–almost as if they couldn't help themselves." She shrugged. "I never use it to my advantage, only to theirs. But it helps to understand why people take actions, instead of believing only what's written in public documents."

"I know why they talk to you. It's your eyes. They're mesmerizing."

She met his steady contemplation. Her eyes widened as they stared into his and read the expression he wasn't bothering to hide.

Warmth, interest, and hints of hunger lurked below the surface. His hazel eyes had definitely turned a deeper green. She caught her breath as sexual heat warmed her blood, finally tearing her eyes away to grab the next stack of papers on the sofa.

"Your turn," she announced, unable to stop her voice from shaking. Her hands trembled as she shuffled the papers in her lap; the pages rustled and filled the expectant silence. She got them in order, smacked the layers against her pad, and straightened the edges. "I get to listen this time."

A ragged corner on one sheet reminded her about the intruder. She mentally shrugged. She'd tell him about it when she had her emotions back in check. After all, this had a deadline. The rest was just ancient history.

• • • • • •

Eric eased back in his chair and wriggled his shoulders into a comfortable position. He could tell Lynn was just as affected as he was. It was only a matter of time before they could act on it. Then he could enjoy instead of ignore the intense pleasure coursing through his body.

She certainly was as skittish as a kitten. The lingering silence was making her restless. She shifted her legs and her blue toenails blinked at him. They called to mind her much less demure attire the night of the banquet. She looked carefree and relaxed now in her tight black leggings and loose-fitting sweater. He was dying to slip his hands underneath the white cotton and feel her bare skin under his touch once again.

Reining in his thoughts, he clasped his itching palms behind his head and raised his brows.

"Shoot," he ordered.

"Why is your company called SDS?"

He shrugged. "Just a silly set of meaningless letters I threw together when I filed my incorporation papers. That style was popular at the time, so I grabbed three letters and they stuck." That was a blatant lie, but he would only share the true words with Gwen–if he ever found her.

"Names can be important."

"Sometimes. People often make up nicknames when it suits their purpose, or when they aren't particularly fond of their parents' choice. For example, do you like being called Lynn?"

"Yes, I do." She turned back to her papers. "Better than Gwendolyn," she muttered under her breath.

Eric flinched. He blinked several times. He stared at her long and hard, taking in her lean body, recalling her throaty voice, and remembering her accident's horror story.

Her eyes. Her eyes were the same.

No, it couldn't be. But he should pay more attention to her behavior rather than her looks. Maybe a familiar nuance would trigger a buried memory.

"Here's one Rajiv couldn't manage. In simple terms, what makes SDS software so special? I mean, how can one piece of software be suited both to military uses and financial markets?" She looked up with a broad grin. "When I asked Rajiv, he went on for ten minutes with such technical jargon he lost me."

Eric chuckled, stretching his stiff arms high above his head before draping them along the back of his chair, flexing to loosen the muscles. His movements captured Lynn's attentive stare. Biting back a satisfied smile, he waited until she tore her eyes upward again, her cheeks faintly flushed.

"Basically, we have a piece of software that is uniquely able to secure data across extremely complex networks, knowing exactly where it is at every point along the way. Who received it, where, and when, down to the millisecond," he explained. "The military needs that kind of accuracy for reliable, secure communications, especially in the battlefield. The financial institutions need precision to deliver market data simultaneously to millions of potential buyers and sellers around the world. Otherwise, the marketplace wouldn't be free, open, and fair—or profitable."

She twisted her lips, tapping her pen against the pad. "So what does the bug do to harm it?"

Eric sighed, frustration eating at him. He clasped his hands between his knees. "It looks as if it might be imbedded in our core program, the one the rest of the software is based on. If so, it could affect the actual tracking of the precision clock and packet movements as they break up and re-form over the network."

"The Internet?"

"That, and any secure private network. Our program incorporates any custom system protocol. However, if a bug has gotten into just one protocol, it could have an impact on all of them." And an impact on the future of not only SDS but also on the technologists who rely on that security, he reminded himself. And the innocent citizens who rely on SDS' customers–both publicly known and confidential.

Lynn glanced at her watch. "It's almost noon in California. You haven't gotten a recent update, have you?"

Eric rose and started toward his room. "I need to check my email, and then phone the office. Why don't we take a break and re-group in about a half hour?"

"Sounds good to me. I'll take a first cut at the answers to the interview questions, except the ones relating to the bug. I hope you get better answers than we've had so far." She turned on her laptop.

Eric closed the door behind him, grabbed his computer off the bed stand and flipped it on. Only one new email waited–from an unknown sender.

Fighting back disappointment Rajiv didn't have good news yet, he clicked open the email.

"Don't fix the bug. Otherwise people will get hurt, starting with you."

What the hell? Obviously, someone had planted the bug with a nefarious purpose in mind. And that purpose must be damned important to warrant threatening physical danger. Eric grabbed his phone and punched in Don's number, committing the terse words to memory.

"Don, listen to this."

Don absorbed the missive but kept silent for a long moment. Confident that he would decipher its implications and run any possibilities through his analytical mind, Eric patiently waited for his response.

"I tell you, kid, someone's really got it in for you. You've got to take this seriously."

"You think?"

"Well, what do you want to do?"

Eric raked his fingers through his hair. "I want to find that bug and shove it up his ass!" he yelled. "No one pushes me around and gets away with–"

"Didn't the military teach you self-control? Calm down and react with your brains, not your ego."

How many times before had Don used those same exact words to cool his temper? Eric stalked around the bed, commanding his muscles to relax.

"I've already started background checks on all the consultants Rajiv has used recently, but so far nothing suspicious has turned up," Don informed him. "Have you learned more on your end?"

Eric hesitated, for once preferring to keep his head buried in the sand if it meant letting his youthful dreams have one brief minute of existence. But pragmatism grabbed hold and shook him. He needed to find out the truth about everyone and everything relating to SDS. And that included Lynn.

"Yeah, I found out Lynn has an ex named Kip, and she was in a hospital in Chicago for over a year after a car accident." He paused, fighting his reluctance to disclose the rest. "And her real name might be Gwendolyn," he sighed.

"Gwendolyn? As in Gwen?"

"Possibly. If Lynn is Gwen, I'll find out for sure and let you know. If so, it's more than a coincidence that she's here now."

"What an understatement," Don muttered. "I'll make her a top priority and have the information ready in three hours. Will that give you the time you need?"

If Lynn was actually Gwen, Eric would never have all the time he needed. His fascination with Lynn would only intensify if she turned out to be the sweetheart of his dreams. "That'll be enough time," he answered in a clipped tone. "Talk to you later."

Eric gripped the phone until its edges bit into his bones. He had to get his anger under control, otherwise he wouldn't be able to ferret secrets from Lynn. He forced his fingers to relax, turned off the phone and slipped it into his pocket. Feigning some semblance of calm, he strode back into the living room, hoping she wouldn't notice anything was wrong.

"Nothing new yet, so we may as well take a little breather." He dropped into the armchair. "Why don't you like the name Gwendolyn?"

Lynn toyed with her pen, averting her eyes. "Would you?"

"No, but that's probably a guy thing," he chuckled. "Don't most people shorten it to Gwen?"

"That was my name when I was a kid, but I hated it." She raised her eyes to his, looking downright defiant. "I changed it when I went away to college. The only person who still calls me Gwen is my sister, Bernie."

"Now that's an unusual name, too. Were your parents name-challenged?"

Lynn gave a wry smile. "We've often thought so. They got better with the two younger ones. My stepfather's influence, undoubtedly." She shrugged. "Actually, my sister's name is Bernadette, and she hates the nickname Bernie. But she deserves to be tormented sometimes."

His mind spun at the news about her sister. But he had to keep her talking to make sure. "Why?"

"Because she was the epitome of the domineering older sister when I was a kid, always butting into my business. I couldn't wait to get away from her when I left for Stanford."

"Did she go to Stanford before you?" Eric held his breath.

"No, she went to Northwestern around the same time you were there." Her teeth gnawed at her bottom lip.

"Maybe I knew her. Was she an engineering major, too?"

"Nope, fuzzy studies all the way—performing arts, drama, you name it. If it was a lightweight subject, she took the class."

Eric's heart lightened and fell at the same time. She had to be the same Gwen. "Northwestern has a good drama department, you know. Many famous actors got their start there. It's a highly-respected school."

Lynn looked stricken. "Of course it is, and it's a lovely campus."

"So you visited your sister, even though you dislike her?" Tension shot from his toes to his neck.

Lynn turned somber for a brief moment, not meeting his eyes. "Once, for a weekend in May. It was…memorable, to say the least." She twisted her fingers in her lap. "And I don't really dislike Bernie. I've learned to appreciate her protective, sisterly attributes."

Eric's mind reeled. He didn't know what to say. He'd longed for this day for so many years. Now he couldn't trust why she was here. What if she was involved with the bug? The silence lengthened between them.

"Eric, I have a confession to make." Lynn lowered her head, staring at her hands. "I probably should have told you before, but I didn't think it was that important. Now I'm not so sure." She picked up a coaster from the coffee table and toyed with it.

He clenched his jaw, his teeth grating together. Was she reading his mind now? Or did she recognize him too? "What is it?"

"The day after our press releases hit–you know, after you came to New York–I think someone ransacked my hotel room for information on SDS." Troubled blue eyes searched his before dropping again.

"What?" He bolted upright. "Did you tell Don?"

She shook her head. "I thought you all had more important things to worry about, and hoped this was only a simple attempt at burglary. But the more I've thought about it, the more I don't think so."

"Was anything stolen?"

"Only a few pages from my organizer with SDS phone numbers and some bank account information. I already called my bank, and nothing else was missing." She cocked her head to one side, perplexity sweeping over her features. "But my papers were ransacked, as if they were searching for information. It's possible one of the men from the conversation I overheard remembered me. He could have found my room after the press releases went out and searched it."

She raised her eyes to meet his, worry clouding her features. "Did I harm the IPO by not telling you sooner?"

"I honestly don't know," he replied. "I need to inform Don right away though." He rose to his feet and paused. "Anything else you want to come clean about?"

Please, he agonized, clenching and unclenching his hands behind his back. Just tell me the truth now.

Her brows arched high. "Why? Is there something you think I'm hiding from you?" She placed the coaster back on the coffee table with precise deliberation, not dropping her gaze from his.

Eric searched her eyes for long moments. He couldn't tell if she was hiding anything more or not. "No," he gritted out. "Excuse me."

Swearing under his breath, he strode to his room and slammed the door.

"You're kidding," Don exclaimed in reaction to the news of the break-in. "After all this time, there's probably not a whole heck of a lot I can find out, but I'll talk to the hotel manager anyway. I wouldn't recommend she go back there."

"She'll be in New York for at least one more day, so that's not an issue." He hesitated, taking a long breath. "I'm convinced she's the Gwen Allen we've been looking for. She must have taken on her stepfather's name, and that's why I couldn't find her. Did you make any progress?"

"Just a sec. The information is coming in now." Don paused, and then whistled. "Hang on to your hat, son, this is a doozy."

Eric sank onto the bed. How could it get any worse? "What is it?"

"Lynn's ex, Kip, is Rajiv's Chas Wilkins. The same guy. And get this. If I remember correctly, that's the guy who referred her to Rajiv. Am I right?"

Eric dropped his head to his chest. Unbelievable. "Yeah, Rajiv was where I first heard her name. But she came highly recommended by others too. That's not proof of her involvement."

"Not completely, no," Don concurred. "But Eric, Rajiv told me there are only three people who ever worked on the guts of the program where the bug is–you, Rajiv, and this Wilkins guy. My money says he's involved somehow. And it's no coincidence his ex-wife is running around supposedly putting out the fires he set. She's probably playing you for a fool right now, assuming you don't recognize her. After all, she hasn't breathed a word about knowing you from before, right? So she must be involved."

"I have a hard time believing–"

"Believe it. Damn it, kid, your butt's in a wringer. You need to face the facts staring you in the face."

Eric wrestled with the implications of Lynn's connections to Wilkins, ignoring the wave of disappointment washing through him.

Don heaved a long breath. "Sorry I'm being such a hard-ass."

"No, you're right," Eric acknowledged. "Rajiv was always very particular about dividing up the work. Usually we coded separately and then he fit the pieces together later. But I remember he used Wilkins a lot back then, so it's certainly possible."

"Do you know much about him personally?"

"Not really, especially nothing to shed light on his motivation to screw us," Eric reflected. "If you're right, he purposefully planned this years ago. I wonder if he's also the one behind the nasty email."

"I'm still working on that angle," Don cautioned. "I'll see if I can get more out of Rajiv on Wilkins's personal life. In the meantime, I suggest you take a chapter out of my book and use whatever methods you need to get Lynn to trust you and spill the beans. We need to find out who's behind all this mess, especially if they're making threats now." He paused. "You're a good-looking guy. She fell for you once, right? Get her to confide in you, if you know what I mean."

"I get it." Eric let loose his anger. "Use her, just in case she's using me. After all, the end always justifies the means, doesn't it? Even if someone gets hurt. Just like before."

"Hey, you're a big boy, playing in the big leagues now. I warned you it might get nasty, but you didn't want to believe me."

"No regrets, huh? That's always the Defense Department's answer."

"Look at it this way. You've finally found your precious Gwen, so when the time is right, you can ask her for that favor," Don consoled. "At least that part of the plan has been solved in time. You were running out of options, kiddo."

"Great, only she might not be so happy to cooperate. Maybe she already knows about the Trust and she's planning to convince me to spill the beans to her so she can get the information to Wilkins. Jeez, he undoubtedly has connections to the VC community, which means someone on my board could be behind all this too." Eric groaned, guilt and betrayal battering him. "What a mess!"

"Tell me about it. Watching dreams die is never pleasant."

"Thanks a lot, old friend."

"Good luck—and I mean it," Don replied, his sincere tones feeling like a warm hand on Eric's shoulder.

"Talk to you later." Eric ended the call, wondering just how many of his dreams would die tonight.

Chapter 31

"Hey, Chas. Have you found our bug yet?"

Patting his hair back in place and shooting his cuffs, Charles smothered his irritation and flashed a winning grin at Rajiv, who was peering over the top of his cubicle, tugging on his ear lobe.

Rajiv looked even grumpier than earlier–and downright messy with loose strands of his ponytail escaping that garish rubber band.

"Almost." Charles kept his voice confident. He needed Rajiv's faith in him at the highest level. "There are a couple of places in the original code where a bug could have been lurking. It might not have caused a problem until one of the new programs finally needed to access it. I'm working that angle now."

Rajiv dropped into the obnoxious orange chair squeezed next to the desk and heaved a huge sigh. "That is the best news I have heard all day," he admitted. "Eric has been all over my ass–probably because his is getting chewed out by the bankers in New York."

"Because of the bug?" Hah! Eric was finally getting his comeuppance.

"That, and because he is still so close-mouthed about the beneficiary of his Trust. The money-boys really hate not knowing every little detail."

"So what's the big secret?"

Rajiv shrugged. "Eric has always been reticent about her. Some college sweetheart named Gwen who helped him get his DARPA funding."

Bells went off in Charles's mind. Gwen? As in, Gwendolyn? Was there more between them than he'd guessed? If Bernadette hadn't pointed out Eric Coleman in her yearbook as the guy she'd had to chase away from Lynn at Northwestern, he never would have come up with his latest scheme. Threads of old conversations swirled in his mind, bits and pieces of trivia that now carried significance.

"Listen, I will assign two engineers to review the code with you so we can get this nailed down." Rajiv tugged on his ear again.

Charles calculated the angles of having assistants with rapid precision. "Great. Just send them to me and I'll show them where in the code. Maybe we can get this knocked out by midnight." If they found the phony bug he had already written to fool Rajiv, and overlooked the real bug, Charles's work was over—with style. Smug satisfaction settled into his chest.

"How did we miss it all these years?" Rajiv dropped his head into his palms.

"It was all my fault," Charles protested. Rajiv had to stay guilt-free about his own technical prowess, otherwise he'd dig too deep. His reputation with his family and employees meant so much to him. "You know how religious you are about checking every bit of code and running the quality-control tests afterwards. One of those late nights, I probably took a shortcut I shouldn't have, and now it's coming back to bite you in the butt."

He scanned Rajiv's face and saw only a little bit of relief creeping into his eyes. More chest thumping was needed. "I feel terrible this is happening at such a critical juncture. I'll burn the midnight oil until it's fixed. As a matter of fact, I won't even bill you for my time."

"No, that is not right," Rajiv objected. "You have worked as hard as any employee. Besides, the responsibility is mine, especially to our investors."

"It's the least I can do," Charles countered. "Your engineering reputation shouldn't suffer because of my mistake. You know how small the Valley is–you need your work here at SDS for a reference. I have a long list of clients who can provide me that pad. You can't afford it."

"Thank you, Chas," he replied in a gruff voice. "I do not know what I would do without you." Rajiv rose and squeezed his shoulder, stepping out of the cubicle. "I will tell my engineers to do exactly as you say."

Charles turned back to the computer screen, smirking. Rajiv was always so easy to manipulate. Just flatter his ego about his engineering talents. He rolled over like a puppy eager to show off a new trick. Not like the other engineers he'd cultivated in the Valley. They had cynicism to go with their brains, and sniffed out the insincerity in Charles's words if he went overboard with compliments. The only one who had been as naïve as Rajiv had been Lynn–at least in the beginning.

Charles recalled the first time he'd seen Lynn in the dorm, innocent as a kitten, striving to fit in. Someone to exploit. He asked her to call him Kip and convinced her to pursue a specialization in public relations.

After her accident, besides spending every moment he could with her, he sacrificed his own contacts until she was on her feet. And then he encouraged her to share every detail about her clients–gossip, rumors, mergers, problems. When he said a company would succeed or fail, he was unerringly right.

Lynn hadn't questioned his judgment on any level, and never asked how he knew. She had no clue of the money he earned on the side. Then he messed it all up with the drugs. *Shit. What a stupid mistake.* Lynn had turned away and never looked back.

Well, the pieces were coming together now. He would bet Eric's big, bad secret Trust had to do with Lynn. That would give him an extra fillip of negotiating power if he needed it. The money he made off SDS would make up for his mistake, and put his life back on the fast track.

• • • • • •

Rajiv stuck his head back over the top of the cubicle again. His eyes were gritty from staring non-stop at a computer screen. "Chas, my best engineers are in the conference room waiting for you. There are a couple more issues to run down before I leave, so I will be here if you need any help."

"Go on home. I'll take care of things."

"I am ultimately responsible for all this mess, no matter what you say." Rajiv owed it to Eric to take charge while he smoothed ruffled feathers in New York. Chas's reassurances had calmed him. It was past time he returned to management mode. The code obviously needed a thorough quality check. "Just do what you can to get the answer quickly. Please."

Rajiv would not burden Chas's shoulders with more problems, but a junior engineer had uncovered another apparent bug in one of the later lines of code. Maybe this one he could fix without Chas's help.

"Doesn't your family need you? After all, no one worries about me coming home late."

Rajiv wrinkled his brow. Why was Chas being so persistent? He shook his head again. "I have a job to do and it is not done yet."

"While we're working on that part of the bad code, you know no one else can work on it, right? I mean, what else is there for you to do until the three of us get it fixed?"

Chas's expression was sincere, but a small doubt grew in Rajiv's mind at Chas's Lone Ranger strategy. Did Chas covet public credit for finding and fixing the bug? Would that enhance his reputation?

"I will be here a while longer." Rajiv rapped the top of the cubicle. "I will let you know when I am done so you can fill me in on your progress."

Chas shrugged. "You're the boss."

Back in his office, Rajiv scanned the questionable code, both the lines Chas had pointed to and the new area Scotty reported. Similar programs, they mostly ran in parallel as a double-check.

A warning message flashed on his screen. Chas was right. Only one computer at a time could access the guts of the code over the company network. He would have to work off his personal copy to dissect the second flaw himself, the one he kept at home as a cheap insurance policy in case of fire or vandalism.

He packed up his briefcase and stuck his head into the conference room on his way out. "I am through here, but you can call me anytime if you need me," he said to the three men already hard at work around the console. "Good luck."

Two hours later Rajiv shoved back from his home computer, his head reeling. He recognized the code as work Chas had written, in both cases. His computer had all the different versions of the code, and he had traced the changes over each version.

They had found the bug and fixed it already–multiple times in fact. But it kept showing up in later versions.

Rajiv yanked his hair free from its band and rubbed his scalp, searching his memory. Each time the bug appeared correlated to when Chas worked for SDS. He would have to verify Chas's consulting invoices for the exact dates to be sure, but it looked like Chas had planted the bug on purpose. Multiple times.

Why?

He unearthed his phone from a paper pile. Rajiv wanted to run his theories by Don before telling Eric. After all, they both respected Chas. If Rajiv was wrong, he would only look like a fool to a private investigator, not to a fellow engineer, which might sully his reputation.

Don listened in silence to the facts. Rajiv blew out his breath in relief when Don agreed with his recommendation.

"Eric has his hands full with pressure from the bankers, so this level of detail is unnecessary," Don assured him. "I need to get back to him with other information, anyway. I'll give him a general overview of your progress without accusing Wilkins directly. In the meantime, figure out a way to prove your guess one way or the other, and fast, since he has his hands on your code again. Any ideas?"

Rajiv pondered the question. "The only way I can think of is to introduce the bug into another part of the code, point Chas in that direction, and see if he fixes both. In college, we designed traps and false doors into our code as a way to keep other programmers out. Only this time the purpose will be to entice Chas in."

"Assuming it works, then what?"

Rajiv scanned the code laid out in front of him, tugging his ear. "I will trail behind him to see if, after he fixes the bug, he plants it again. Either way, we should have confirmation."

"Confirmation may be good enough for you, but we'll need proof to press criminal charges."

"Oh, no! That would bring so much negative publicity down on SDS. It would not be worth it–especially since it would ruin the IPO."

Don's harsh expletives came across loud and clear. "Let's keep our eye on the ball. You do what you need to prove he's the problem. We'll let Eric take it from there. Agreed?"

"Agreed." Rajiv sighed with relief. "I will let you know as soon as I find out."

Don and Eric would handle it. All he had to do was deal with code. People problems were too difficult to manage.

Besides, Rajiv did not know which possibility he wanted confirmed. On one hand, he had found the bug and the IPO could proceed as planned. On the other hand, his judgment would be in question because he hired the wrong engineer–and that could haunt him for the rest of his career.

Chapter 32

Eric loitered in the kitchenette, perusing the label on the wine bottle. As the sun set and darkened their private little cocoon, neither had switched on the shaded lamps at either end of the couch. Moonlight spilled through the open curtains, subtly illuminating the intimate setting.

"More wine?" He tipped the bottle in her direction. Lynn shook her head. Eric topped off his glass and took a healthy swallow.

He needed all the help he could get.

Re-corking the bottle, he placed it on the chrome counter and snuck a furtive glance at Lynn nestled deep in the couch cushions. His stricken conscience battled for dominance. He wanted to be intimate with Lynn, sure, but not this way. Not for ulterior motives.

Don's planted suspicions tainted what should have been a joyous and pleasurable reunion. Now, if he wanted his plan to succeed, he would have to discover if they were true or false. Instead of losing himself in Lynn, he would have to hold back that part he always held back from women–except for that time with Gwen so many years ago.

He yearned to feel that freedom again, to not have to watch every word. Except that was out of the question.

Duty called.

He tamped down his frustration and rearranged his features to reflect only warmth and sincere interest. He headed into the living room. Taking a deep breath, he started the farce by sinking in next to her and setting his wine glass carefully beside hers. He leaned back and draped his arm behind her shoulders, not quite touching it.

"I think we've worked enough for now, don't you think?" he murmured, extending one finger to slide a thick strand of white hair over her shoulder, grazing her neck on the way with a bare caress.

Her eyes half closed as she shifted to face him. "It's been a long day."

He stroked the length of her neck under her ear, and then trailed his fingers to her nape, eliciting shivers.

"Eric, I don't know about this. We need to keep things professional."

"Why? Don't we deserve time off, too?"

She bit her bottom lip, her gaze uncertain. "We don't know each other very well."

"No time like the present, then, is there?" He cupped her shoulder and drew her closer.

"What about the past? And the future?" She pressed her fingers against his chest, keeping him at arms-length.

He stared into turquoise eyes. So familiar. So wary. Her pupils bloomed under his scrutiny. The soft pants of her breath wafted like spring sunshine across his face. "Is there some big, bad secret in your past you're hiding from me?" He forced a carefree smile, fought against tightening his grip.

She blinked and ducked her head. "Why would you think that?"

Eric narrowed his eyes at her expert avoidance of his question. "Okay, then maybe you have some nefarious plans to make millions off my hide." He kept his tone light. "But I gotta warn you, my bank account is pretty empty."

Her head snapped up, beautiful eyes gleaming with hurt and protest. "You're way off base!"

Weighing her reaction, he relaxed his tight control just the tiniest bit. "It doesn't matter. Why not forget the past and let the future take care of itself?"

Her fingers curled into his shirt and she tilted forward, raising her mouth to his. He brushed his lips across hers, savoring the familiar perfume of her breath. Snaking her hands around his neck, she tilted her head in unmistakable invitation.

Blood roared through his veins. His pulse jumped in military double-time. Settling his mouth across hers, he nibbled at her lips. Her eager tongue darted out and raked his teeth. He followed in kind, exploring her mouth, reveling in her sweet taste, her soft moans.

"I want to kiss your neck." He caught her gaze, praying she'd grant him permission. "It's been tempting me for hours."

"How naughty of it," she teased in her deep, throaty voice. She tilted her head slightly, leaning her body into his. "Go ahead."

He licked down the sensitive cord under her ear. Tremors rippled along her skin. Eric sampled more of her enticing flesh while his fingers cupped her nape, stroking and tugging at the tiny hairs. She dug her hands into his shoulders and pressed into him further.

His body throbbed and came to full attention. He lifted her legs so she was almost sitting on his lap and played with her toes. They had fascinated him all evening, peeping blue and bright against her naked feet.

Despite his discomfort, he was surprised by how much he enjoyed this slow pace of seduction. His legs felt like steel beams compared to hers, soft and yielding. Tight with tension, he kept a firm grip on his control. This was for a greater purpose, he reminded himself.

Yeah, right. I'll take what I can get and worry about repercussions later.

He tilted her in his arms and kissed her again, blotting out his mission, obliterating the past, focusing on the here and now and this willing woman in his arms.

The phone's shrill tones broke through the silence, shocking them to stillness. They stared at each other, panting.

"Goddamnit!" Eric fumbled for the lamp switch. Worming into his pants pocket for his cell, he stared down at Lynn in the light's bright glare.

"Coleman," he snapped, dragging his attention away from her. Every rapid heartbeat reminded him just how much he'd rather be prone with her than answering this call.

"I need to talk to you. Without an audience." Don's urgency carried through even the intermittent connection.

Eric pointed his thumb to his room and jumped up. She nodded, flicked on the second lamp and reached for her wine with a shaking hand.

"What's up?" Eric slammed the door behind him. He sank onto the bed and rubbed his neck muscles, shoving aside the fantasy of Lynn lying beneath him, naked and eager.

Don chuckled. "Sounds like progress buddy. Am I interrupting good times?"

"Cut the crap. What have you found out?" Eric scrubbed his hair.

"Rajiv has good reason to believe Wilkins planted the bug." All humor vanished from Don's voice. "Apparently, whenever he worked for SDS he took the time to reintroduce it into current versions. Therefore, it's logical to assume he put it there in the first place."

"Shit!" Eric hammered his clenched fist against the mattress. "Did you find any recent link to Lynn?"

"No, but I don't think it's a far stretch of the imagination to see her in it up to her big blue eyes. Any more on your end yet?"

"No," Eric growled. "She hasn't asked anything out of the ordinary. If she's trying to pry details about the Trust out of me, she's taking her sweet ol' time." His mind sifted through possibilities. "Any information on that email?"

"I've got people tracking it through the network servers to its origination point, but nothing so far. Lynn and Wilkins are our best leads, and you know it. Rajiv is keeping an eye on him, and it's your job to keep an eye on her."

"Yeah, only she's leaving tomorrow morning and I'm stuck here for at least one more day to meet with analysts. Got any ideas?" Eric rose and paced around the small room.

Silence met his question for a prolonged moment. "Hmmm. Actually, I do. Do you think you can get her to trust you enough to stay at your place instead of a hotel when she gets here?"

"Whoa, I don't know." Eric halted in his tracks. "We're not moving that fast."

Yet.

Maybe they could.

Would.

Should.

Eric's body battled with his mind over possibilities and promises–and potential betrayals.

"Why don't you tell her about the email?" Don suggested. "Coupled with her hotel room break-in and the general threat of danger, it's obvious someone knows she's involved. You just want to keep her safe. I can set up simple surveillance gadgets in your place before she gets there, and watch to see how she acts when she's alone."

"Maybe..." Eric couldn't share his friend's enthusiasm about actually spying on Lynn.

"Look, tell her you need an emergency dog-sitter, for God's sake. Just get her there. It's not like you're asking her to move in or anything–you won't even be there!" Don's impatience came across the phone, loud and clear.

"That does a lot for my ego, pal." Eric twisted his mouth. "Make up your mind. Do I make her fall for me or my dog?" His jest barely covered the harsh intensity in his tone.

"Whatever works. Sorry, kid, but too much is at stake to go slow. Unless I hear otherwise by morning, I'll assume you got her agreement and I'll set things up. Good luck."

Dead silence filled Eric's ear. Obviously Don was certain this was the best way to flush Lynn out, even if it meant steamrolling her.

Cursing under his breath, Eric flung the phone onto his bed. He flopped down on his back, rubbing his face with his palms. He hated this constant deceit with a passion. He thought he'd become used to his parallel games when he had first conceived the idea of SDS, but apparently he had a soft spot for Gwen–or Lynn.

Shit!

He glanced at his watch and calculated how much time he had to convince Lynn to believe his deliberate lies. Again. He pushed up from the bed and opened the door, pausing in the doorway to gaze at her slender body framed in the cascading moonlight.

He noted her rosy lips and flickering smile as she stared into her wine glass. Inhaling through flared nostrils, he savored the slight tang of her sweetness wafting from his own lips. He had wanted to salute her courage in overcoming her physical trauma, to reassure her that he would protect her. Now he had to feed her fears instead of eliminating them. He risked her distrusting anything he would ever say to her again. God, he hated this.

Swallowing past his tight throat, he started toward her, grimly wondering how best to convince her of Don's plan.

Chapter 33

Lynn ran one dampened fingertip over the lip of her half-empty wine glass, creating a low hum from its smooth surface. Her fingers still tingled, her mouth felt loose. Eric's kisses had released a torrent of liquid fire in her core, and she fought for control over roiling emotions.

Why hadn't he recognized her yet? His kisses were achingly familiar. With his eyes closed, couldn't he sense their past?

Of course not. I'm not the same. I've grown up.

A lousy marriage, a traumatic accident, and financial woes can change a girl.

Tipping the glass to her lips, she swallowed a generous gulp and prayed for courage. Time to tell the truth. Before they go any further. What was that saying? There's never enough time to do it right, only to do it over. Well, this time she would do it right.

She should slow things down.

Her stomach clenched in rebellion. Apparently, her body recognized the absolute rightness of being in his arms. They clicked with a compatibility that was too rare to ignore.

A huge sigh escaped her tender lips as she recalled just how well suited they were.

"Sounds like you're having second thoughts." Eric strolled into the living room, stopping on the other side of the coffee table, his hands jamming his pockets outwards.

Lynn tore her gaze from his crotch, heat flooding her cheeks. The wine glass almost tilted over. She grabbed it and set it upright on the coaster.

"I've had thoughts, but not second ones." Locking her eyes with his, she scrutinized his expression, and then patted the cushion. "Bad news?"

Settling his large frame next to her, he took a long sip of wine and then replaced the glass carefully on the table.

"Bad enough," he grimaced. "That was Don. He's been tracking down the source of a threatening email I got earlier, and he's had no luck. So he's asked me to take extra precautions until we know who's behind it."

Lynn jerked upright. "What kind of threat?"

"Unfortunately, the vague kind. Nothing we can wrap our arms around, but strong enough not to take lightly." He watched her with the steady attentiveness of a cat watching a mouse.

"To you? To SDS?" She wanted specifics, damn it, not dancing around the issue. Her whole life was at stake. If SDS was threatened, she could kiss her contract payment goodbye–and her condo, and Mitch's health. And her future.

"Yes, to both. And to you, too, since they broke into your hotel room."

Chilling fear shot through her. "Oh, my God. You think I'm still in danger?"

"Looks that way. But Don made a suggestion I think will keep you safe."

"Of course he did. Everyone is so full of suggestions after you need them." She regretted her harsh sarcasm as soon as she spoke. But damn it, why hadn't Eric deigned to disclose the threatening email before now?

Men and their damned secrets! Did they ever share?

A twinge of guilt nagged at her own humdinger of a secret. Only hers didn't rise to the level of bodily harm. It was a personal quirk, no link to SDS at all. Well, unless she counted it as a severe breach of professional ethics. She wasn't there. Yet.

Eric's cheek muscle twitched and his jaw clenched tight. "Don is a friend of mine, as well as the most professional private investigator and law enforcement official I have ever worked with. I think his ideas deserve a full hearing."

She squeezed his arm. "Oh, I am so sorry. I...I really didn't mean any disrespect. I'm sure he's doing the best he can under the circumstances. We all are. I wish you had told me sooner, that's all."

He tugged her into his arms. Her head fit into his shoulder's hollow perfectly.

"Don believes someone might have tapped into your credit cards so they can track where you are. When you return to San Jose tomorrow, he wants you to avoid staying in a hotel so they won't know where to find you."

"I already figured that might be an issue. I'll just pay in cash."

"Not good enough. You may be followed from the airport."

"Well, where am I supposed to sleep? Your office?"

"How about my place?" Eric's arms tightened.

Lynn tensed. "I don't think that's such a good idea." She withdrew from his warm snugness. And she thought she was moving too fast! Whew, Eric had her beat. Of course, maybe he thought she was easy. After all, he didn't know they'd met before. And she hadn't stopped any of his advances tonight. On the contrary, she'd been just as eager, just as disappointed by the interruption. So why shouldn't she trust him?

• • • • • •

Eric halted her skittish retreat by stroking the length of her spine and dipping into the open gap at her waist. He toyed with her naked skin.

With his other hand, he gripped her fingers and rested his thumb on the inside of her wrist. Her thrumming pulse was impossible to ignore, especially when it leapt at his lightest touch.

Time for the ultimate sales pitch.

"Why not? I'm stuck here for a while, anyway, so you'll have the run of the place. Except for Fred, of course."

"Fred? You have a roommate?"

"Well, he does like to curl up in bed with me sometimes, but usually, I sleep alone." Eric kept an innocent smile plastered on his face as bewilderment, shock, and then dismay marred her pretty face.

Lynn yanked herself free and stood up. She crossed to the other side of the room, shaking her head in disbelief.

"I'll take my chances with whoever is out there."

"Aw, come on. Fred's a fantastic watchdog. I'd trust him with your life."

"Watchdog?" Lynn exploded. "Fred's a dog?" Her look of astonishment was priceless.

Eric burst out laughing. He rose and crossed to stand in front of her. "Yes, Fred's a dog, and in desperate need of TLC since the little girl next door who usually takes care of him got sick."

Her expression didn't change.

"Are you afraid of dogs? Fred won't bite you. He prefers the taste of bad guys. Honest!"

She launched herself at him, lightly pummeling his chest with her fists. "You and Fred…you…you…joker!" Her astonishing blue eyes glimmered up at him with humor and relief.

A wave of lust pulsed through his body. Eric ignored it, focusing instead on the priority of the moment. Even though his needs were getting bigger by the minute. He captured her hands and stilled them against his chest.

"Seriously, both Don and I are worried for your safety. Do this for me, won't you?" Her expression hadn't betrayed any advance knowledge of the email. This time he wanted her close enough to read her body language.

She still hesitated.

Time for the clincher. "Fred really does need someone to feed him, but I'll leave it up to you whether you invite him onto your bed. He takes up a lot of room."

He pressed his body the length of hers without wrapping his arms around her, giving her the freedom to make her choice. Maybe with the promise of more pleasure he could convince her to agree to the plan. Very lightly, he pressed into the junction of her thighs. The rapid acceleration of her heartbeat in her exposed neck told him all he needed to know.

"I don't think Fred's the one I want on–or in–my bed," she whispered, curving her arms around his shoulders. "But if it means that much to you, I'll stay at your place."

Profoundly relieved, Eric kissed her with increasing ardor as she wrapped herself around his body. A low groan broke free from his throat. He gathered her closer and dropped his hands onto her hips, both of them swaying in sensual rhythm. Powerful, youthful memories of Gwen came roaring back.

He lifted his head reluctantly and put a few inches between them. "I don't know when I'll be able to grab a flight, so you can use my car in the meantime." He dropped a light kiss on her nose. "Think I could get a lift home from the airport?"

"Depends...if you're a good tipper..." Lynn purred, pressing her breasts against him.

"I'm as good as you want me to be, sweetie." He wrapped his arms around her and rocked her. "But not tonight."

She lifted her head, searching his eyes. Whatever she saw must have reassured her, because she relaxed. "I confess I'm glad this wasn't all an elaborate scheme to seduce me."

Eric dropped kisses on her eyes, closing them before she could catch the flicker of betrayal in his. His rampaging guilt would give him away soon, and he wasn't convinced she wasn't up to her silky neck in this whole plot after all. Why else would she make that nasty comment about Don? He had to keep his head clear, not let his dick lead him around.

He grasped to keep his honesty intact. "You've been a complete surprise to me. I'm not sure what's between us, but I know I want more from, and with, you."

"Ditto." Lynn dropped a light kiss onto his chin. "Tell me about Fred."

"He's a big mongrel stray from the pound. Ugly as sin, friendly as can be, and ears that hear squirrel farts a mile away."

"Sounds perfect," she chuckled, her blue eyes twinkling. "I haven't had a dog since I was a kid. Why did you decide to get Fred?"

"Last year I got tired of coming home to an empty house," he admitted, not bothering to disguise the loneliness echoing in his voice, just like the eeriness of his rooms. "Fred looked as if he needed someone, too."

He didn't add that Don's nagging about finding someone to love had motivated him as well. It hadn't been time to commit to a woman.

Not then. Maybe soon.

Lynn's eyes glistened with a moist sheen. "I know what you mean," she whispered, squeezing his waist. "I live with stacks of unpacked boxes. My condo is so empty and cold when I come home–and deathly quiet. Even the air is stale." She heaved a deep sigh, dropping her head onto his shoulder. "And no welcoming arms to hold me."

Eric rocked gently, offering what comfort he could.

"Now I'm definitely looking forward to meeting Fred." She frowned. "But how will he trust me if I'm a perfect stranger?"

Eric stroked her hair from the top of her head to the tips dangling down her back. "Don will meet your flight, show you around my home, and introduce you to Fred. Fred's his best friend," he confessed in a dejected whisper. "They try to spare my feelings, but they both like each other better than me."

"Poor baby," Lynn crooned, a wide grin creasing her face. "I guess you're worried Fred will find me irresistible, too."

"I saw you first, sweetheart, just remember that." Eric punctuated his comment by running soft kisses over her face.

Years ago, and she had haunted him ever since.

Did she remember him? If so, was it with the same longing he felt, or was it just to use him for the money and power his software could bring to the winner of this little game?

Chapter 34

Eric picked over the remains of his cream-cheese bagel, intrigued by Lynn's performance on the morning business show. Despite her detectable nervousness, she answered the interview questions with confidence and aplomb, even one that hadn't been on the advanced list.

This morning she looked almost grandmotherly. The buttoned-up suit jacket hid her lacy camisole underneath. Her cosmetic granny glasses added just the right touch. She'd even pulled her hair back into a tight bun, adding years to her image.

Eric found her white hair sexy. Its lush fullness and pearly color were surprisingly soft and smooth, a mirror image of her flesh. Fortunately, the television's sharp lens didn't pick up a hint of the burgeoning passion they had found in each other's arms.

Too bad she'd left for San Jose. He still had to prepare for the afternoon's gauntlet of analysts. He missed her already, and it had only been two hours since their sweet kiss goodbye. Maybe he could get a late flight out rather than wait until the morning.

Click.

All senses alert, he crept through the living room and hid behind the ajar door from Lynn's room. Was this the danger the email warned him about?

Cloyingly sweet perfume assailed his nostrils. He caught a glimpse of silk-encased legs crossing the threshold. Kay's long hair brushed against him as she sauntered by.

"Eric?" She turned in a tight circle, glancing around the empty room.

He stepped out from behind the door. "Why are you here, Kay?"

"And good morning to you, too." Her brow arched steeply. "I came to help with the road show. There are special Chinese guests who wangled an invitation from Joshua to join the analyst meeting today. I thought my presence here might be an asset."

Eric rubbed his jaw, both weary and skeptical. "I've told you before—the IPO is not your responsibility. It's mine, and I'd appreciate it if you would remember that. You're doing more harm than good."

Kay slithered toward him until he could feel warmth emanating through the canary yellow suit hugging all her curves. "Not this time. You need these guys."

"Who are they?" Eric demanded, tilting to the side. Kay epitomized everything he hated about women who used their bodies and sweet lies to get what they wanted. What made a woman become such a conniving bitch? He prayed his deception to Lynn wouldn't turn her into someone like Kay. She had been so sweet and innocent as a teenager.

Kay leaned forward and brushed her arm against his. He stepped backward and sat down in the armchair. She winked and sank onto the couch, crossing her legs so high her skirt rode up her thigh.

Eric kept his eyes fixed on her face, ignoring the tempting peripheral view.

"They are very patriotic Chinese who wish only the best for their homeland," Kay said in a soft voice. "Including the acquisition of the best technology to help their beloved country succeed."

Eric stilled. His irritation fell away. "What exactly are their government ties?" He snorted as she raised her eyebrow. "I'm sure they have some. The government puts up the money for all of China's acquisitions, even though they would never admit it."

Kay shrugged, slouching until her stocking tops peeked below her skirt. "You know how confusing it is over there," she pouted. "To the best of my knowledge, they're a rebel political group unhappy with the pace of change the current party bosses are dictating."

"So their goal is to push the Communist Party out of power? Is that it?"

"I haven't had in-depth ideological discussions with them, you know. That's generally outside the scope of our business dealings. But I think they call themselves Maoists." She played with the gap of her jacket, running her nails back and forth between the lapels. "I listen to the whispers and rumors behind the scenes. These men are no fans of the current government. They want change–fast–and they think SDS will help them achieve their goals."

"How?" Eric puzzled over this new twist.

"Does it matter?" She snapped upright, flinging her black hair over one shoulder. "They've asked for a way to pursue information leading to an offer to acquire SDS privately. I should think you'd like to have a possible buyer who could raise the market price of SDS at this point. After this PR fiasco, what can it really hurt?"

Eric tapped his fingers, pondering the best course of action. Kay was right. SDS' negotiation power increased tremendously if interested buyers determined its market value as well as the IPO syndicate. As soon as the investment banks discovered there were alternative buyers, they would be salivating at the chance to buy SDS stock just so they could turn around and sell it overnight at a higher price to naïve Chinese investors.

What use did they have for his technology? That was still a mystery, but maybe one Eric could uncover in a face-to-face meeting. Kay probably knew already. She would use it to further her power over the process, and Eric bet she wouldn't disclose it to him. At least not yet. She always exacted a price for her favors.

"You're right. It won't hurt to have them there. And I appreciate your initiative in coming yourself to facilitate–and help translate–the meeting." He strove for a cordial tone. She could be an asset in his strategic plan. Maybe this was the best opportunity.

She rose as gracefully as a cat and perched on the arm of his chair. Her crossed legs effectively blocked his escape. "You know, Eric, you could show your gratitude better," she murmured in a husky whisper, ruffling the hair at the nape of his neck. "We have an hour before we have to leave for the meeting."

He jerked his head away and jumped up, not caring that he bumped her so hard she almost fell on her butt. "Cut it out. We've been through this before. Your behavior is inappropriate and unwanted. You're my employee and nothing more."

"But don't you think I deserve a little reward for all my hard work?" She sidled up to his side, ignoring his glare. "Aren't you the least bit tempted to know what I'm wearing under my suit?"

She released the top button of her jacket, and the thin fabric parted. "Only completely bare skin," she whispered in his ear, brushing her breasts over his arm.

"Damn it, Kay, stop the games!" he yelled, jerking away. "I'm not interested in you, and that's final!" He took a deep breath, willing his anger under control. She would be at the meeting later, and he needed her on his side. "I have work to do until we leave."

Eric slammed his bedroom door and locked it with a deliberate twist, the loud click audible in the angry silence. He hated her advances. He'd once threatened to fire her if she didn't stop, but she had smugly pointed out that if he did she would be the one to cry sexual harassment. Moreover, she would probably win.

So he put up with it and eked out small favors, like allowing her to participate in the meetings this afternoon. That kept her in line. But she steps out of bounds so often it's getting downright tiresome.

Ninety minutes later, they stepped out of a taxi in front of a nondescript skyscraper off Wall Street. Eric was chillingly calm and civil, Kay, all seductive professionalism. No one would have guessed the animosity sparking between them.

As they entered the packed meeting room filled with dozens of faceless, nameless financial analysts of all ages and only one gender, all conversation stopped. Male heads turned as one toward the stunning contrast of Kay's sunshine suit to their bland, gray and navy colors.

Joshua hurried forward to meet them.

"Eric, Kay, glad you're here. Now we can begin," he said louder than necessary, pumping Eric's hand and squeezing Kay's in a blatantly intimate gesture.

Kay gave Joshua a small peck on his cheek. "Have they arrived?"

"All the analysts are here, and we have special Chinese guests with a specific interest in the SDS technology," Joshua announced, his voice echoing off the walls. "Kay, perhaps you would help them with any translation needs they may have."

He pointed to a group of four men huddled in the far corner watching the proceedings with cautious eyes.

"I'll be glad to help." Kay sidled through the clusters of men with gracious ease, squeezing the arms of acquaintances, and saving her special brilliant smile for the guests.

Eric watched her seductive progress through the crowd, noting her unmistakable yet subtle power. As much as he loathed it, her behavior certainly kept her at the center of attention, including from another group of Asian men sitting military-erect on the opposite side of the room. When not ogling Kay, their gazes flickered over each analyst as if memorizing their faces. Were there more possible offers in the works than Joshua was sharing with him?

Joshua waved everyone into the seats. When the rustlings and quiet conversation died down, he introduced Eric and turned the meeting over to him.

Eric went through the PowerPoint presentation automatically. He had told the same story so many times he could do it in his sleep. At the end of his prepared speech, he tensed. The Q&A period always dissected the nitty-gritty issues.

"Mr. Coleman, that's a very pretty picture you've painted for us. But given the bad press you've received lately, don't you think your expectations are a little high?" grilled a young man, glasses perched on his nose, fingers poised expectantly over his fancy computer tablet. He looked like he had graduated from the best business school in the country in June and this was his first outing as an analyst.

"No, I don't think so." Eric held onto his temper. "We handled the press as well as could be expected. More importantly, we are diligently working not only to fix the problem but also to discover its source so we don't experience this again."

"Wrong, Mr. Coleman," another analyst interjected. This older man looked as if he didn't care if he was rude after so many years covering the exaggerations of CEOs. "That gal this morning really didn't help SDS' predicament at all."

Murmurs swept through the room, heads nodding. Eric read skepticism on the faces turned toward him.

"Thank you for your perspective, but frankly, I disagree." Eric swallowed, hard. By defending Lynn's performance in public, he was starting down a path from which there would be no turning back. "I asked Ms. Baker to explain the situation in terms that did not compromise the SEC restrictions on the IPO process. You gentlemen are all familiar with what can and can't be done around the quiet period."

The older man cleared his throat, tapping a pen against a dog-eared yellow notepad. "Seems to me your IPO is compromised due to the bad press, that's all I'm saying. Any possibility you'll yank the IPO and reschedule it?"

Joshua leapt to his feet and strode up to Eric's side. "Now, now, we are all here because our syndicate is staying on track with the SDS IPO. The press may delay it by a week or two, but you boys all know the market conditions might have done that anyway. I can assure you–my firm stands 100% behind SDS."

Out of the corner of his eye, Eric caught Joshua darting a quick glance at Kay. Was Joshua really behind the IPO, or just brokering a deal to sell SDS to the highest bidder? Either way, Joshua's firm was paid and Joshua would get a hefty commission.

Maybe it was time Don did more research on Joshua and Kay, and find out who they were working with behind the scenes. He couldn't afford being out-maneuvered.

Meanwhile he would meet the players, shake their hands, and get his own gut reaction to what their intentions were.

Chapter 35

Rajiv stared at the dates on the old invoices, sickened by the stark confirmation staring back at him. All the bugs correlated with times Chas worked for SDS.

Chas had betrayed him. To defend himself, Rajiv would need to destroy his best friend. Or the man he had considered his best friend.

Rajiv had arrived early in the morning to load a second new bug into the code and fix the one Chas planted. He also reassigned the other two engineers to a customer meeting for the rest of the day, just to make sure Chas would work alone.

If Chas found the new bug and declared it the problem bug, but re-activated his own bug again, Rajiv would have the confirmation he needed. For once, he was glad Eric had involved Don. At least Don was used to dealing with worms.

Chas stuck his head into Rajiv's office. A confident smile wreathed his face. "Good news! I found the bug–and fixed it too, so your problems are solved."

"Great!" Forcing enthusiasm, Rajiv came around the desk and slapped Chas on the back. "Show me your genius, old friend." He steered Chas out of his office and toward the cubicle.

"A new way to tackle the problem occurred to me last night, but it was so unorthodox, I didn't want to waste your engineers' time. So when I had a chance to explore my idea this morning, voila–it worked! No one was more surprised than me." Humility saturated Chas's smooth tones. Only this time, Rajiv recognized Chas belittling his own talents to stroke Rajiv's ego.

Rajiv studied the screen and scrolled through the software code. Oh, Chas was quite clever. Chas's bug was only in a single line, an unnamed variable buried deep in the bowels of the code. Rajiv could easily spot it now that he knew where to look.

Chas pointed to Rajiv's planted bug on the screen.

"See, there. I don't know how I missed it before, but that character sends the program in a parallel direction for the next set of commands, and that's when the program goes kerflooey–to use technical terms." Chas grinned. He seemed chillingly confident Rajiv would simply accept his word as final.

Rajiv patted Chas on the back, reigning in the wave of anger coursing through him. He needed to talk to Don. He could not reach Eric while he was knee-deep in meetings, but Don could handle this problem. All Rajiv needed to do was get Chas out of SDS, and fast.

"You did it again, Chas. Take the rest of the afternoon off while I look over your work. Tomorrow we will clean it up. I can at least tell Eric the problem has been completely identified and the solution on its way." His heart sank. He had never spoken truer words. What he really wanted to do was knock the teeth out of Chas's pretty face, but there was more at stake than his own career.

"Sounds great." Chas stretched and grabbed his trendy sports coat. "Call me if you run into a snag you can't handle. I'll be happy to walk you through it over the phone."

Rajiv dropped his hand on Chas's shoulder and steered him toward the lobby. "I am sure you are right, and you have found everything. You know your work has always been exemplary. That is why we hired you." Acid bubbled and burned in his throat at the lie.

"Thanks for the opportunity to correct my old programming. It's always an honor to work with you." His glib words belied the shrewd gleam in his eyes.

For the first time Rajiv recognized it for what it was–greed. With a quick wave to the receptionist, Chas disappeared out the doors heading toward his red BMW, looking as if he had not a care in the world.

Rajiv walked to his office and locked the door behind him before punching numbers into his phone.

"I have confirmation," he blurted the second Don answered. "Chas took the bait. He fixed his old bug again and blamed my planted one instead. He has been behind it the whole time." His shoulders sagged. "I cannot believe he duped me all these years."

Years, toiling away toward his dream. Unwilling to sever his Indian citizenship out of respect for his parents, as a non-citizen of the US he did not qualify for the highest level of security clearance that both Eric and Chas commanded. He had hoped his excellent work would someday give him an advantage to build his own company with the lucrative defense contracts percolating through Silicon Valley. With this fiasco, he would always work for someone else, never himself.

"I can't say I'm surprised." Don clicked his teeth. "Look, these things happen. You can't beat yourself up about it–Eric insists on sharing the blame, too. Besides, there may be other people involved."

"What are you talking about?"

"Eric got a physically threatening email, and Lynn's San Jose hotel room was broken into the day after she handled the first press release. That just doesn't strike me as Wilkins' style. He seems to work by finessing the technology, not by getting his hands dirty."

Rajiv hesitated. "In the past I would have agreed with you, but since it is clear I have no idea who Chas really is, I think I should keep my opinions to myself and let you draw your own conclusions."

"Did you ever meet Wilkins's wife?"

"Wife? Chas has never been married. He has paraded little foxes on his arms ever since I have known him. There is a different one every week." Rajiv harrumphed. "Connie and I have been hounding him to settle down, have a couple of kids, and give up such partying."

"Sorry to burst your bubble, but he was married until a couple of years ago. Apparently, his ex-wife agreed with you he needed to stop playing around, since the details of the divorce agreement included infidelity and his predilection for cocaine. In fact, you even know his wife."

Cocaine! Rajiv's eyes popped open. He had brought a huge risk into SDS with his bad judgment. And Chas had been married, too? He tugged on his ear, his guts spinning at his foolishness. "I only met a handful of Chas's women over the years."

"Actually, you met her recently. Lynn Baker."

Rajiv almost dropped the phone. "You are kidding me!" He groaned. "Of course. Chas is the one who recommended her to me, always praising the work she did for her clients. My Lord! Is she in on this too?"

A long silence met his question. "We don't know yet. So far everything she's done has been above board and in the best interest of SDS, but it may be just a matter of time before the other shoe drops."

Rajiv scowled. He had decided to apologize to Lynn for his earlier brusqueness. His customers were reassured and her efforts had given him the breathing room he needed in order to find the bug. Even her appearance on TV this morning had been full of positives about SDS.

"She divorced Chas? You are sure?"

"Seems she caught him with one of his girlfriends and lines of coke. She definitely wanted out, since she bargained for an uncontested divorce by agreeing to take on all his debt. What's odd is he referred her to you."

"Silicon Valley is such a tight-knit community," Rajiv reminded him. "Chas's recommendation would be enough to make or break her career.

Maybe she is playing smart by keeping on his good side. Professionally, at least."

"Yeah, or maybe she's been a partner in this scheme of his all along. We just don't know. Eric is keeping an eye on her, though."

Rajiv's tension eased. Eric never let a woman influence him. In all the years he had known him, he could only remember three times when Eric had dated anyone more than once.

"Well, since I did not even know Chas was married to Lynn, I certainly cannot be of any help with background information. But she strikes me as a straight arrow."

"Me, too," Don acknowledged in a grudging tone. "It would just be so much easier if this whole scheme was a plot by the two of them. But my gut tells me there's someone else involved."

"I sincerely hope not!"

"You'll be the first to know. Good work trapping Wilkins, by the way. If you ever need a job, give me a call. I'm light in the real guts of technology and could use someone with your expertise."

Rajiv basked for a moment in the flattery, but shrugged away the offer. He would never be satisfied chasing down criminals. He liked to create software and manage the whole process from start to finish.

"Thanks, but right now I have to nail down the fix and get it out to all our customers ASAP. I will probably work past midnight again."

"Understood. I'll let Eric know what's going on when he lands. And if you remember anything else Wilkins might have told you about Lynn–"

"You will be the first person I will inform, but do not hold your breath. Obviously, Chas was not as good a friend as I believed. Goodbye."

He ended the call, already worrying about how to confess to his wife and family his best friend's deception. Even if Eric hailed him a hero for finding the SDS bug, Connie would know the fiasco compromised his reputation. Somehow, he would have to make up for all his mistakes and make her proud of him again. Only he did not know how.

Chapter 36

Making his way through the echoing caverns of San Francisco International Airport, Eric swung his garment bag in a wide arc, dislodging Kay's clingy arm. He had arranged to catch the last flight out of New York partly to escape her cloying presence, but no such luck–she managed to nab a seat, too. Her blatant invitation to join the mile-high club in one of the cramped bathrooms sent him over the top. Only the hissed demands from their fellow travelers to keep their voices down prevented him from outright shouting at her.

He pulled up Don's number on his phone, anxious about what had transpired during his six-hour flight. Don's grunt of an answer made him wince. No doubt he just wakened Inez again. Better remember flowers the next time he drops by their house.

"Eric here. What's up?"

Eric felt the slightest tinge of relief hearing Don's summary of Rajiv's results. He had a solution to at least one piece of the puzzle.

"That's great. Did you catch anything on the TV show?" Glancing down at Kay hurrying to match his pace, he hoped she would guess he was talking about Lynn's TV broadcast and not the surveillance Don installed in his home. Kay seemed disinterested, flashing wide smiles at the attractive male travelers who invariably gave her the once-over as they passed.

"Nothing to go on. She seemed tired, and didn't make any phone calls except to thank a woman in the PR business," Don reported. "She worked on her computer, swam with Fred, and poked around your house a little, but no more than any woman would. All on the up and up, as far as I can tell."

Eric's tension lessened with every step. "Then we follow the plan, right?"

"I'll be at your house in an hour to chat with you and your lady friend, buddy. I hope you know what you're doing."

"Me, too. See you then."

Kay slipped her arm through his as they exited onto the wind-swept passenger pick-up sidewalk. "Can I give you a lift home? To yours or mine?"

"Kay, stop it!" Eric removed her hand, spotting Lynn behind the wheel of his Mustang just entering the area. He flagged Lynn to the curb. "The answer's no, to the ride and everything else. I'll see you at work tomorrow."

He jerked open the long door of his car and threw his bag and briefcase into the back, dropping into the passenger seat. He ignored Kay's pissed-off stance–hands on hips, one leg thrust forward.

Lynn's unique scent filled his car. His nostrils flared. Her baby-blue sweater clung to her breasts, and her snug leggings enticed his eyes to follow a path straight to the top of her thighs.

No time for this. At least, not yet.

Lynn stopped him from closing the door with a light touch to his knee.

"Does Kay need a ride home? I don't like leaving her standing alone this late at night."

"She's got her own damned car." Eric slammed the door. "Just drive, please. It's been a long day."

Barreling down the eerily empty freeway, Eric pretended to rest as his mind raced through the scenario he and Don had concocted late last night. If Lynn had done anything today to prove she was working with Wilkins, he would be escorting her to the police right now, along with her ex.

But her innocent actions left them no choice but to try entrapment. Unfortunately, if she wasn't involved in Wilkins' scheme, she'd be royally pissed they suspected her. He sighed deeply, hating all the choices.

Exiting in a wide circle, Lynn pointed to a small motel on the corner. "Why don't I stay there for the night? I'll grab my things and you can bring me back before turning in."

He shook his head. "Nope, that won't keep you safe. Besides, we still have a bunch of work to get through tonight."

"Work? Did something else happen?"

"You could say that," Eric answered. "Don is coming to the house to brief us. I only have a smattering of the facts, so it's better if you hear it from him first."

A short while later, she swung the car into Eric's driveway, catching a raccoon's bright eyes in the headlights before it scampered away. Peace and tranquility surrounded his house like a protective hedge. Welcoming lights brightened the windows.

"I hope that's not a bad guy we're interrupting," Lynn commented, turning off the engine. After a moment, nature's night instruments started up again–the rhythmic chirps of the crickets, the hoot of a hungry owl, even the crowing of roosters from a nearby farm.

"It better be Don with a pot of coffee." Eric unfolded his legs and stretched, working the kinks out of his back. He grabbed his luggage and slammed the car door, its loud clatter putting the familiar orchestra on hold.

The aromatic smell of coffee and Fred's wriggling body greeted them. Sniffing with satisfaction, Eric scratched behind Fred's ears and tickled his belly. He tossed his bags onto the floor with as much care as yesterday's garbage and headed toward the kitchen.

Ensconced in the oak nook, Don glanced up from a newspaper and sipped his coffee. The picture window created an eerily vacant backdrop, unlike dawn's stunning vista beckoning and rejuvenating Eric.

"Why don't we sit in the living room?" Eric grabbed two over-sized mugs from the cupboard and poured coffee and cream. "My butt can't handle any more torture."

Lynn led them into the sunken living area. Here plantation shutters shut out the darkness to reflect light from the Japanese lanterns hanging from the beamed ceiling. She nestled into the corner of the loveseat and tucked a loose thread from its gray and green plaid back into place.

Don dropped onto the matching couch and shoved the throw pillow and afghan to the opposite end, exposing a large rip. Fred settled onto the floor in front of him, grunting and draping his jowls on Don's shoe. Don stared at Lynn across the redwood burl table, stroking his mustache.

Eric settled into his old recliner with a sigh, happy to finally kick off his shoes and wriggle his shoulders deep into the padded leather. He picked up his coffee and took a long swallow. "Okay, Don, bring us both up to speed."

"Rajiv found the bug today, and also discovered who planted it." Don used his professional persona–abrupt, no-nonsense tones and narrowed, suspicious eyes.

"That's great!" Lynn threw an enthusiastic grin at Eric. He kept his expression neutral, and she frowned. "Isn't it?"

"It is for SDS," Don answered. "Rajiv discovered one of his contractors planted the bug years ago, and every time they fixed it, this guy would get another contract from SDS and replant it. He's very good–the best, according to Rajiv."

"Wow–Rajiv must feel terrible. He's the one who hires the engineers, right?" She turned toward Eric, concern etched onto her face.

"It's not entirely Rajiv's fault," Eric corrected. "I approved the hire every time, including in the beginning when I worked on the code alongside both of them. Any error in judgment is shared equally."

Don inched forward on the couch, ignoring its protesting squeak. "The contractor's name is Charles Wilkins." His stark statement boomed in the quiet room, his gaze locked onto Lynn's face.

She gasped. Her head spun toward Don. "Kip? Kip did all this? Are you sure?"

"We're sure. Rajiv set a trap that he fell for this morning."

Lynn wrung her hands, and pivoted to face Eric. "I, uh, I don't know how to say this, but Kip, uh, Charles and I were married once, and..." Her voice trailed off.

"We know about your marriage. Did you know about the bug?"

"God, no! Oh, you can't possibly believe I'd be involved!"

"Don has taught me to be suspicious of anyone and anything. And there's no getting around the fact that Wilkins referred you to us."

Lynn pulled her knees up in front of her body as if she was protecting herself. From what? More accusations? More questions?

More hurt?

She took a ragged breath. "I remember once he mentioned Rajiv's name as someone he had worked with in the past, but that's all. I always deal directly with the CEO. And you called me, Eric. You asked me to work for you. To be honest, I was never sure why."

She flung her hands palm upwards. At her anguished expression Eric's heart twisted. Only he couldn't reply to her silent supplication for help. Not yet.

"I alerted you to the press release, remember?" Her low tones carried a hint of desperation.

Don snorted. "Yeah, I remember. How convenient."

Lynn whirled on Don. "I worked my butt off to minimize the negative effects of that release. Why would I do that if I had planted it in the first place?"

"That's still a mystery to me," Don drawled. "Has Wilkins done this before?"

"Maybe. I've never been sure." Lynn chewed her lower lip. "He has an uncanny ability to be in the right place at the right time, you know? When his skills would be most in demand, when he could ask for top dollar because of the urgency of the situation. Somehow, he managed to support a high-flying cocaine habit without me noticing the incredible drain on our finances. For a while he had extra income coming in from somewhere." She dropped her gaze to her knees. "He conned his wife. It's not a stretch to assume he would con his clients, too."

"What did he do, bribe the companies to fix a problem he created?" Eric had to know his full exposure to Wilkins's meddling.

Lynn shrugged. "I honestly don't know." Her hands clasped together so tightly her knuckles turned white. "If I was involved in anything underhanded or illegal, I didn't realize it at the time."

"Like you may not realize it now?" Don sneered.

She flinched, but managed to lift her chin high and meet Don's eyes head on. "Kip hasn't talked to me about SDS at all. I don't know what he's up to, but I'm not his co-conspirator."

Eric spoke up. "Maybe he wanted to disclose the bug publicly just to get us to pay him again. Rajiv was desperate to use him once he was conveniently available. He could repeat this performance as many times as he could get away with it." A low growl of disgust slipped out of his throat. "But if SDS doesn't survive as a company, his ability to re-fix the bug would disappear. It would be in his best interest to get Lynn hired to put out the fire he started."

"Hmmm. I hadn't considered that angle." Don's brow knotted. "So you think he just treated Lynn as a pawn in his big chess game of life?"

Lynn harrumphed. "It wouldn't be the first time. Kip views himself as a master strategist who can control the outcome of any situation."

"He asked for a divorce?" Suddenly that little item became very important to Eric. Maybe she still had feelings for Wilkins. That would be motivation enough to plot SDS' demise with him.

"No, I left Kip. He even admitted he screwed up that little chess move. Since the only repercussion was to his personal life and ego, I don't think it affected his business game plan all that much." Lynn stifled a gasp. "Oh my God!"

"Wanna share?" Don's sarcasm was thick enough to coat the walls.

Lynn flushed. "Call me a naïve fool, but when we used to talk about business, I was fairly candid about my clients and what I was handling for them. Not confidential information, just the general thread of the contract. It's possible Kip used that information later on for his gain, and I never realized it. No one could ever tie problems back to me, so his little schemes were protected."

She turned toward Eric, tears dampening her eyes. "I'm so sorry."

Don's disclosures had clearly distressed her. Eric wanted to believe she wasn't involved, but whether she deserved his trust remained an open question.

The seconds ticked by. His mind whirled through the maze of possibilities.

"It doesn't sound as if you need to apologize," Eric said. "Both Rajiv and I were conned, too, as well as potentially scores of others. At least now we know who planted the bug, and what bug was up his ass to do so—pun intended."

"We're just guessing at his motivation," Don reminded him. "His style doesn't run to writing threatening emails, so there's probably someone else involved. Besides, there's a bigger issue here than just the bug." He pointed his finger at Eric. "Your turn."

Eric yanked the recliner into an upright position and leaned toward Lynn, resting his forearms on his knees. "Remember when you asked me about the Trust that owns 7% of SDS?"

Lynn nodded, her eyes wary. Eric could sense her misgivings all the way across the room.

"There's a battle going on at the board level for control of the voting rights of each and every shareholder." He took a deep breath. It's now or never. "The beneficiary of that Trust is turning out to be the key shareholder."

Steeling his nerves, he calculated this was the right time to shake her even more, despite her obvious fright at the previous disclosures. He hated using such ruthless tactics. But his feelings didn't matter. Proof did. He had to remove all doubt. "There are a lot of people wanting to know exactly who the beneficiary is, and which way the shares would be voted, in case of a private offer."

Lynn crinkled her forehead and twisted a long strand of hair between trembling fingers. "Private offer? I thought you were going public."

"We have to do what's best for the shareholders, and right now there is at least one company interested in buying us outright, possibly before the IPO," Eric explained. "I'm interested in exploring that offer and can convince Rajiv to stay open-minded, but the board members want to go public. The tie-breaking vote lies with the beneficiary."

"So what's the problem?" Lynn still looked perplexed.

Eric sighed. "The beneficiary doesn't know a damned thing about the existence of the Trust. I set it up years ago, and never dreamed I would run into a situation like this—even though Don warned me it could come back and bite me in the ass," he added, tossing a rueful smile at his friend.

Don shook his head, nudging Fred's jowls off his shoe and crossing his ankles.

"Let me ask you a theoretical question, Lynn." Eric kept his tone even. "What would you do if you were the beneficiary of such a Trust and had to vote the tie-breaking shares?"

Lynn frowned. "Well, hypothetically, I would follow the advice of whoever set up the Trust to begin with. After all, it's not like your beneficiary was an active investor like the rest of the shareholders, right?"

Eric nodded, not trusting his voice.

"Why did you set up a Trust in the first place? Isn't that unusual?" She had asked him the same question yesterday. Why was she so curious? He could only avoid her attempt to ferret out the truth for so long.

"It was meant to be a 'thank you' to someone who helped me early on, and one I wasn't sure would amount to much at all. Like a tithe," Eric said. "My mama always told me that success was never accomplished alone, only with the help of others. In this case, the help was so special I felt obliged to pay it back in a very special way."

"Then I would guess your beneficiary will do whatever you ask, Eric." Lynn relaxed into her chair. "Obviously you've gotten SDS this far, so your opinion should be the one that counts. Can't you just get a proxy from the beneficiary and vote the shares the way you see fit?"

Don lumbered to his feet, rolling his shoulders in circles. "You're a smart lady. That's what I keep telling Eric, but he's gun-shy about approaching the beneficiary directly. Maybe you can give him some pointers."

"Umm, sure. If I can help in any way, I'd be glad to."

"In the meantime, Inez will kill me if I don't get home soon. I'll leave you two to hash the rest of this out." Don stepped over a snoring Fred and walked out the front door, the automatic lock snapping in place behind him.

"The rest?" Lynn asked Eric, her eyebrow arched high.

Abrupt tension coiled his body. He'd anticipated this moment for seventeen years, but never imagined it colored by a tangled web of secrets and deceit. Would their relationship ever be simple?

Eric rose and held out his hand. "I have something to show you."

Chapter 37

Show me? As opposed to explain what the heck was going on? The conversation had gotten weirder by the minute, drifting into hypotheticals that had nothing to do with the real problems at hand. Like what was Kip really up to? Or what had she gotten herself into at SDS? She wanted clarity, not show-and-tell.

Especially as to whether Eric believed her innocence, despite Kip's treachery to destroy SDS. How else would they be able to recapture the sweetness of last night? Or move forward with a hazy possibility of a future together? She wanted to scream and cry about all the secrets and duplicities. Did anyone have an honest relationship anymore?

Yet she was just as much to blame for not bringing their past to light.

Gripping her fingers with surprising strength, Eric led her down the darkened corridor to his den and switched on the table lamp, flooding the ancient desk with a soft glow. The rest of the room faded into shadows.

Eric motioned Lynn to take a seat in the sagging gold armchair set in the corner. He plopped into the desk chair and spun around to face her.

"You wanted to know the name behind the company's initials, didn't you?"

Lynn managed a half-smile. "You should have heard the possibilities Alex and I came up with the other day. I hope the real meaning is better than those, otherwise my professional advice is to keep the name out of print."

Eric grinned. "You're right about that–there's no way I'd let it be known." He pinned her with an intent gaze. "In fact, no one but me knows the true name. But it's well past time to share it with you."

"I'm honored." The warm intimacy of his tone relaxed her. "But you don't have to tell me."

"No, I owe you this." He pulled out a leather-encased box from the lowest desk drawer and handed it to her. "This may help you understand why."

Curious, Lynn opened the box. Her breath stopped. Her father's lucky silver dollar necklace lay nestled in turquoise velvet. He knew! She shot her eyes back up to meet his.

"'Silver Dollar Sweetheart' is the actual name of the company, Gwendolyn. I named it for you, and hoped someday I could return your father's necklace to you too." His expression blazed with caring and pride, as if bestowing on her the ultimate honor.

Lynn dropped her eyes, a lump forming in her throat. For all those years, Eric had remembered her. And called her sweetheart. And named his company after her.

Oh, God. She thought she meant nothing to him. She certainly never expected to see him again.

How–better yet, when–did he discover who she was? Before he hired her? She stifled a gasp, the answer looming large. While they were making out in New York? A fuse of anger smoldered deep inside.

Taking a deep breath, Lynn met his eyes squarely, burning to know the answer. "How long have you known?"

Eric's smile faded. Her animosity must be clear as day. "New York," he admitted. "When you told me your name was Gwendolyn and had a sister named Bernadette you visited at Northwestern." He swallowed hard. "Before we kissed."

"Why didn't you tell me then?" Lynn could feel the familiar heartache returning, and tossed the box back onto the desk. His sweet caresses had fooled her. Again. He was keeping secrets from her. Again.

Nothing had changed. Just a repeat performance.

It didn't matter she knew. This responsibility was all his.

• • • • • •

Eric sighed and walked to the window. He stared at the moon-dappled swimming pool. Its shimmering surface reminded him of how they had first met, surrounded by churning water with unknown dangerous depths to explore.

But this time he could change the outcome.

"Look, you've got to understand. I was bursting to tell you, but Don had already linked Wilkins to this bug, and I didn't know whether I could trust you. That's why I insisted we talk as soon as I got home."

"And I suppose you have it all figured out now, huh? Like exactly how much you can trust me this time? And exactly which lies are okay to tell me? Or exactly which truths are okay to keep hidden forever?"

Her eyes glittered with repressed tears. Of anger, or of hurt? Either way, they dug a hole into his soul.

He marched back in front of her, grabbing her arms and yanking her up tight against him. "Here's the truth. I looked for you after the DARPA contract was over but I couldn't find you. Your sister ignored my letters. I didn't know your last name was different from hers, so I kept on hitting dead-ends."

He nudged her chin up with his thumb so she would meet his gaze. "I'm really sorry things ended the way they did at Northwestern. DARPA required me to hide from everyone that I'd won the contract. I hated it. I had already told you too much. And I sensed how much I hurt you when I lied to you."

He watched her doubtful eyes flicker, then harden again. "I really want to trust and believe you this time," he added.

Lynn squirmed against him until he finally let her go. "That doesn't justify hurting me." She stormed away. Retracing her steps, she went toe-to-toe, glaring up at him with a furious expression. "I was just a kid, and you purposely twisted a knife into my heart! Why? So you could go on your merry way and become a famous, successful entrepreneur, ready to make your millions with your IPO? Was your big secret really worth it?"

"I am so sorry." He grabbed her flailing hand, lifting it reverently to his lips. "I was a kid, too, only three years older than you." He forced her tense fingers open against his beard-roughened cheek, tilting his head to lay its weight against the softness of her palm. "And you lied to me as well. That hurt more than I would admit, even to myself."

Lynn quieted, staring at him with skepticism on her face, breathing hard. He sensed his ancient anguish matched hers.

"How did lying about my age hurt you?" she snapped, propping one hand on her hip.

Eric turned his mouth into her palm. "I hoped I had six weeks to see if what we felt was special enough to stand up to an extended absence. When you said you were only seventeen, you yanked my dream away from me. I lashed out." He met guilty blue eyes with his own. "I wanted to make it up to you by naming the company after you, so you would understand that I did care. I couldn't stop thinking about you, ever."

She swallowed. "I…I never should have misled you about my age. I was just so overwhelmed! I wanted you to think of me as a woman, not a girl."

"Believe me, I did, even after I learned the truth," he murmured, brushing her lips gently with his. He settled her into the armchair and sat back down. "If it hadn't been for your link to Wilkins, there never would have been any doubt in my mind to trust you. I was absolutely thrilled to have found you again." He expelled his breath in a sharp burst and his shoulders slumped. "I'd like to give us another chance. And, to tell you the truth, I was hoping you would feel the same way too."

"I've been carrying a damaged heart around for a long time," she whispered with lowered eyes. "This didn't help. It took me years to trust anyone again. I compared everyone I dated to you. Not many men made the cut."

"Wilkins did."

A chagrined look crossed Lynn's face. "Kip was a mistake. I was in such bad shape after the accident I let him take over my life. When I finally grew a backbone again, I realized I never should have married him."

"If only I had found you sooner..." He clenched his hands against the desktop.

"That's all in the past." She shook her head. "Kip's not important now."

"Unfortunately, he may be, remember? Besides, there's more I need to tell you." Could he trust her yet?

Lynn took a deep, shuddering breath and gripped her hands in her lap. "What else?"

He rose and squatted down on his haunches in front of her chair, taking both her hands in his. "That hypothetical question I asked wasn't just a brainteaser. You're the mysterious beneficiary of the Trust."

Lynn sat bolt upright, yanking her hands free. "You don't need to give me anything. I did so little to help you that day!"

Eric snatched her hands back and held them tight. "If you hadn't listened to me, supported me—damn, scolded me—I would have skipped the DARPA meeting altogether, and there wouldn't be any company at all. You inspired me to keep going. You believed in me when I didn't even believe in myself. You trusted me with your lucky necklace." He linked their fingers together. "You have no idea how precious that was."

Her eyes glistened with tears. "I'm glad I helped you. Obviously, you had everything you needed to succeed already. I don't want a part of your company. You earned it, you deserve it."

"Tough. It's my own private offering to you, so it's yours."

"Let me get this straight. I'm the critical shareholder whose vote matters so much, is that right?"

"Well, yes. Rajiv and I together own 45%. The board controls 48% as a block, since they vote the employee stock ownership plan now. You're the swing on any disputed issues between us and the board."

"And just how much is that vote worth?" Lynn whispered in an agonized voice. "All this seduction?"

"That's not fair." Eric gripped her fingers in protest and shook them. "When I presented you with the hypothetical scenario earlier, you said you would sign over the proxy to me since I set the Trust up in the first place, and made good decisions all along. Why would you think differently just because you're the beneficiary?"

"Don't you get it? Honesty and trust is a two-way street." Tears slid down her cheeks in slow but steady streams. "I learned that lesson very well from you. I divorced Kip when he couldn't handle that fact. Yet you expect me to simply accept everything you say at face value because... why? Because you have been so forthcoming up until now? How do I know you and Rajiv aren't behind the bug and press release, and you're not working behind the scenes to take control of SDS yourselves? How?"

"Shit!"

Eric leapt up and paced the perimeter of the small room, swearing under his breath. He had waited so many years for this moment. Now it was all blowing up in his face.

He took a deep breath. Lynn had a point. He had always avoided intimacy with other women under the guise of needing to keep these secrets. Lynn was different—he hoped—and he had kept too many secrets from her for too long. Even though he couldn't disclose everything, he could take the first step.

Eric dropped down on his knees in front of her and scraped the wetness from her cheeks. More tears streamed over her swollen lids. He kept at it, grateful he could offer a little bit of comfort when she was in such distress.

"Lynn...sweetheart...all I can offer you now is this simple fact. As beneficiary, you have every legal right to vote your shares based on whatever you believe. If you really think my game is to tank SDS or cut a private deal that's bad for the rest of the shareholders, then by all means vote against me for an IPO. I don't want your proxy. This is your privilege to vote what you think is right."

He met her startled glance calmly, ignoring the skepticism in her eyes. "No one can take that away from you, least of all me. You earned a share in the future of SDS, especially for your contributions these last four days."

He sank back on his haunches, hands resting on his thighs. "SDS started because of you. Now its fate rests with you."

Lynn hiccupped twice and wiped her nose with the back of her hand. She studied him with red-rimmed eyes, doubt and wariness shimmering across the turquoise irises like cloud shadows along a placid lake. She shook her head back and forth, hugging herself and rocking in the depths of the armchair.

Eric sensed desperation. He rose and extended his hand. "I think we've both had all we can take tonight. Maybe things will be clearer in the morning."

Her trembling fingers grasped his. "I just want to sleep. I can't handle more."

"Nothing more." He helped her up and wrapped one arm around her shoulders, pulling her in tight next to his body for reassurance. They left his office and walked down the hall toward the guest room. "I promise I won't let you get hurt again. Believe me?"

Lynn stared up at him in the dim light of the hall, guilt flashing across her expression. Why would she feel guilty? "Just give me a little space, okay?"

"Take whatever you need, sweetie. We have all the time in the world to do it right this time."

He brushed a light kiss over each of her swollen eyes, gave her a gentle push toward the open door, and flipped the light switch.

When she was completely inside, he shut the door behind her without another glance.

Fred padded up beside him, whimpering. His cold nose brushed his fingertips, almost as if the loyal mutt sensed his turmoil. Reaching down, he patted his back and headed for his bedroom.

Alone again, while the woman of his dreams slept only a few feet away. The woman who had set him on his life's path, and who now had the power to undo all his work with one simple vote.

Don's harsh lectures about this hare-brained plan echoed in his brain. How many times had Don warned him that his faith might be unfounded? That putting the security of the whole country in the hands of an unknown woman was crazy?

Eric couldn't explain it with logic. Gwen's belief in him when he hadn't believed in himself had given him strength. He'll rely on that strength to believe in her—even when the evidence pointed to the contrary.

He only prayed he had all the facts.

Chapter 38

Joshua shoved back his wrinkled shirtsleeve and glanced at his watch. Almost midnight. The flickering overhead lights in the outer office spread an eerie glow over the empty desks, emphasizing the feeling of isolation running coldly through his veins.

He was still waiting for the last call, this one from General Tong in Beijing. The military had first contacted Joshua only a month ago, fully briefed on SDS software and ready to act. Their only requirement: complete confidentiality. Joshua had decided to keep all of his phone calls with them off his cell, and through the company's phone system instead. Just in case. He wasn't comfortable with their brusque assumptions they were his number one priority.

Earlier, he had spoken with Zhu of the Shanghai Stock Exchange, but Zhu's reluctance to engage in a bidding war to acquire SDS made Joshua nervous.

Kay's Taiwanese contact had made their position clear hours ago. They stood by to act as soon as the IPO syndicate set SDS' final market value. Money certainly didn't seem to be an issue for them. But he suspected they would cut him out of any rewards, and break contracts with no compunction. Legal rights always came second to ideological fervor.

The phone's loud ring cut through the silence. Joshua jumped, his heart pounding, fingers quivering. Taking a deep breath, he reached for the receiver and lifted it to his ear. He pushed his sliding glasses back up his sweat-coated nose.

"Stein here."

"This is Tong Xiao. I trust you are able to talk freely," the heavily accented voice rose above what sounded like a vehement argument in the background.

"Yes, General Tong. What is your current situation?"

"We have discussed the matter at great length, and agree the pursuit of SDS should now escalate. We cannot wait until after they go public to make our offer."

The General might have less patience than the Taiwanese, but he also had a lot more power. Joshua hadn't a clue how they intended to use SDS software, nor did he care. But he suspected the Chinese military of pressuring the venture capital firms backing SDS, and they had to have the ear of at least one willing board member.

Joshua cleared his throat. "If you are in such agreement, what is the discussion behind you?"

A loud hiss filled the line, and the noise disappeared.

"I apologize for the disturbance, Mr. Stein. There was a debate of where we would be eating dinner, that is all."

Yeah, right. "No apologies necessary. You are aware you are not the only ones interested in SDS at this time, correct?"

Silence. "I would hope that you recognize the full benefits of guaranteeing we are the successful bidder in any contest to acquire SDS." Tong's tone brooked no argument.

Joshua squirmed, all too aware of the military resources Tong controlled. His decisions could affect the welfare and fate of over a billion Chinese. "Your influence is well understood. In fact, I would guess that you were involved in initiating the press release about the bug. Am I correct?"

Long silence.

Tong's lack of denial was confirmation enough. Maybe he also had a tie to SDS' customer in China who alerted him to the bug before even calling SDS. Joshua couldn't blame them–the Chinese military didn't forgive spies, even those on their own side.

"However, the other players are significant in their own areas as well," Joshua continued smoothly. "They are also highly motivated to acquire SDS and its unique technology."

"Mr. Stein, please be aware we will more than match the methods used by those entities, if need be. Money or tactics–or even political repercussions–do not limit us. A single person is certainly expendable in the scope of this opportunity. Do you understand me?"

Joshua gulped at the ruthless overtones. "Completely, General Tong. Nevertheless, I am only able to do so much to persuade Eric Coleman and his board without disclosing the true purpose. My role, after all, is to bring SDS public."

"I think not," Tong retorted. "I believe your role is to bring in as much money into your pockets and to that of your firm as you can. You promised to represent my interests. Do so, as pockets full of money on a dead man are not very satisfying."

"Look, don't threaten me." Joshua tamped down the bile rising in his throat at the calm way Tong discussed his death. "Coleman is the one with all the power. Between his and his partner's stake, and the stake of the Trust, he controls enough shares to make the board do whatever he wants." A flash of inspiration struck him. "Talk with the beneficiary of the Trust," he blurted out. "He will probably be easier to influence than Coleman, and could tip the board's vote in your direction if you wish it."

"Interesting. Who is that beneficiary?"

Joshua heaved a silent sigh of relief for diverting Tong's attention away from himself. "No one knows but Coleman. And he refuses to disclose it until he has to."

Tong snorted. "Well, Mr. Stein, make certain he has to. We will not wait any longer. If you can't fulfill your duties, we will find someone who can."

Joshua swallowed hard. "I'll take care of it, General Tong. It will probably take a couple of days. I'll call you when I have the information."

"Fast, Mr. Stein," Tong said with a menacing softness. "You've run out of time." The click of the call terminating resonated in Joshua's ear; it's finality reminding him this was his last chance.

"Shit!" He pulled his jacket on and slammed the door behind him. Guaranteed privacy would be necessary for his next call. Joshua stormed out of the deserted office suite and hailed a cab.

The identical quest for power in the three conversations tumbled around in his mind like socks in a dryer–haunting him. Although he wasn't their prey, he sure felt like their bait. Bait that these Chinese players would use, destroy, and discard as soon as his usefulness was over.

Joshua had spent too many years on Wall Street among American financial hunters not to recognize the telltale signs. He was just a minor player in an intense, international game. And unless he moved very carefully, he would be relegated to that role forever.

The echoing slam of his own front door book-ended his panicked thoughts. He hastened into the den and hit the programmed number on his desk phone.

"Hello?" Kay's silky voice answered.

"Are you alone?" Joshua yanked at his tie to relieve the tension locking up his throat.

"Unfortunately, yes. Too bad you're not here with me, Joshy. I feel like exploring an exciting new partner." Her wistful sigh carried straight to Joshua's groin, stirring him.

How often had she teased him and not delivered? He pushed aside her sultry promise.

"Listen to me," he snapped. "This is important. All our clients are anxious to make a deal happen quickly, but it keeps on coming down to who controls the votes of the shareholders. We need to make Eric tell us who this goddamned beneficiary is, and fast."

At this point, he didn't care how Kay would pull the information from Eric, just that she would do it. He closed his imagination to any methods Kay's contacts might use. One person, he reminded himself. It's only one person who might get hurt, like so much collateral damage, while so many others could benefit. Isn't that kind of sacrifice worth it? The kind they preach to recruit kids even into our military?

He shuddered as he realized if he were that one person, the same logic would apply, although he wouldn't be so willing to accept it. Because he would be dead. No doubt about it.

• • • • • •

"You have any new ideas?" The urgency of his tone wasn't lost on Kay. Something had broken Joshua's placid demeanor. She hoisted herself from a lounging position in front of her television.

"Can't you get hold of some Chinatown Triad gang members who might be happy to persuade Eric to fess up, for the right price?"

Kay blinked. "Are you suggesting violence to get information he'll have to disclose eventually anyway? You can't use legal pressure to get it?"

"You know Eric. He's a stubborn son of a bitch when he wants to be." Joshua's worry—or was it fear—carried across the miles. "We're out of time. What else can you do?"

Kay swore under her breath. Joshua was right. They had to take action and, as usual, it would take a woman to get the ball rolling. She had no time to get approval through normal channels. She'll have to go with her gut. "I'll call in a favor from someone I know. Nevertheless, I want everyone to understand I was the one who took care of it. You don't get to pretend you're the big macho hero in this."

Joshua's mirthless laugh sounded strained. "I don't think that image suits me at all. You're more than welcome to whatever glory comes from getting that beneficiary to vote our way. I only want results, no matter what it takes. Can you handle it?"

"Yes, I'll take care of all of it."

"Soon?"

"Tomorrow too quickly for you?"

"Nope, that's perfect. Call me when you have the answer." Click. Dead silence filled her ear.

Kay ignored his petty rudeness, already scanning her phone directory. This was her chance to prove herself an equal to the men. So many of them were wimps, unwilling to stand up when the going got rough.

Well, she would give her contacts the information first, which should earn her a place at the table when this whole episode was over. Joshua could just wait—she never wanted her bosses ever again to question her loyalty to the greater cause.

A smug smile crossed her lips. She'd let Weng know in advance what she intended to do, just so he'd realize how valuable she was to Du's team. Then, when she delivered, her credibility would be that much greater.

That phone call would come first. Then she would deal with Eric.

If he wouldn't play with her, he would soon find out just how formidable an adversary she could be.

Chapter 39

Squealing brakes. Hot metal, slamming into her. Knocking her flat. A fierce jerk, then smashing onto the hard road, bouncing. Skin ripping away, the slow burn becoming agony. Knees throbbing, toes and fingers scrabbling for purchase. Stabbing jabs of pain piercing her jaw. Squeezing her eyes shut, protecting at least one part of her body from torture.

Lynn bolted upright in bed, shaking. A scream started deep in her throat, threatening to burst free. Whimpering, she wrapped the blanket around her shivering shoulders and forced her consciousness out of the old nightmare, into the quiet stillness.

She fixed her gaze onto the lone pepper tree outlined on the hillside. Under a spotlight of silvery moon perched high above the hills, delicate limbs danced in a gentle breeze, caressing the contours of the land.

Deep breaths. Steady heartbeat. Come on, Lynn, you can do this. Think about today's problems, not the old terrors.

Expelling a huge breath, Lynn dropped her head into her hands, wrangling ricocheting emotions and buried memories.

Eric was still chock full of concern and respectfulness. And ambition. He may have kept secrets from her, but he hadn't forgotten her. Just as she hadn't forgotten him. Or gotten over him.

She had sworn never to give her affection that trustingly to anyone again. Now he was asking for her help. And to start over. How ironic was that?

Her hellish physical therapy sessions flashed through her mind. Sheer determination enabled her to push painful breaths in and out of her lungs. She lifted weights with weak, shaking arms. Every time the ever-present bandages were unwrapped from her face, she would grit her teeth and steel herself against the slow progress of multiple plastic surgery procedures.

She never thought she could do any of those things, but she proved herself wrong countless times. She was strong, not spineless.

So how could she have been so stupid not to tell Eric she recognized him before now? Or was it cowardice?

Did she want to wall herself off from the chance of love forever?

No!

Only now wasn't the time. She had to stay focused on saving her company from failing, didn't she? That was the most important priority in her life–wasn't it?

Maybe Eric had hired her with the best of intentions. Maybe he really thought she did good work. Except her suspicious link to Kip was indisputable, and could cause embarrassment or even harm to SDS in the future.

Now that she thought about it, why wasn't he terminating her ass?

Because she was a 7% shareholder, that's why!

No!

Sure, he had kept information from her, but she hadn't caught him in an outright lie. He even went to bat for her against his bankers. She could count on his professional promise.

Then why did she doubt his personal declarations?

Lynn groaned in frustration and leapt out of bed, pulling her robe over her nakedness and pacing the cold floor.

The present took precedence over the past. They would barely have a chance to talk tomorrow. Could she wait even another day to apologize for her behavior? Or to let him know she was interested in exploring where their feelings might lead? Seventeen years ago, they both thought they had all the time in the world. Look how that turned out.

Her hand twisted the doorknob and stopped, her cold fingers resting on the metal. Was he worth the risk?

Lynn considered the emptiness of her life in Boulder. She couldn't even call it home. It was a rest stop on the road to nowhere. If she didn't start taking charge of her future, she was in danger of it slipping away from her. Permanently. That was scarier than any possibility of failure with Eric.

Straightening her shoulders, she crept into the dark hall and felt her way toward Eric's room. His door was ajar, probably for Fred's convenience. She slipped through the opening and tiptoed through the semi-darkness. Soft thumps of the dog's tail greeted her.

Eric's hand dropped onto Fred's head. "What's wrong, boy?" Yawning, he lifted his head from his pillow.

Lynn curled up in the armchair next to the bed.

"Nothing's wrong," she whispered. "Is it okay if we talk?" Her breath came in short gasps and her hands trembled. A long shiver ran the length of her spine.

"Lynn?" Eric shot up in bed, his bare chest clearly outlined in the moonlight. "What…uh…why…are you sure nothing's wrong?"

"Yes, I'm sure. I just didn't think this should wait."

"What's up?" Eric stuffed a pillow behind his shoulders and settled back.

"I owe you an apology. I shouldn't have lost my temper…or my self-control."

"It was a lot to take in at once."

"I was afraid I'd get hurt again," she confessed, twisting her fingers together. "So I kept my distance."

"I really regret hurting you, sweetie. I had no idea you felt so strongly about me after only a couple of hours together."

"No idea? When you felt the same way about me after the same short amount of time?" She dug her toes under the cushion, seeking warmth.

He sighed, squirming beneath the blankets. "Actually, I denied I felt that deeply about you until I figured out who you were. Then everything made sense. The fact that I hadn't developed other serious relationships. My immediate attraction to you at the benefit. How right it felt to be with you. It all pointed to the fact that my old sweetheart Gwen had a stranglehold on me. But Don guessed."

Lynn tensed. "That's why he told you to stay away from me?"

"Actually, Don encouraged me to get real close to you. Only to keep my head this time."

"And you agreed?"

"Sweetie, I grabbed any excuse to spend time with you. But I also needed to find out if you were spying on me to help your ex."

"And now?"

"I feel like I'm trying to steer a tornado. I don't know what you want or need, babe. Can you help me out here?"

"Do you believe I had nothing to do with Kip's little scheme?"

"Since you told me you didn't, you didn't. Besides, I can't think of any plausible reason for you to plant a false press release." His tone was logical and businesslike, as if challenging her to contradict his belief in her veracity.

She gnawed on her lip. Dare she tell him about her dire financial straits now, or wait until later? She didn't want to be a hypocrite and accuse him of keeping secrets when she had one of her own.

"I'm not involved with Kip. In any way. But I am having other problems with my business," Lynn admitted. "And after all this is over, maybe we can spend time getting to know each other again."

He sat forward, anchoring the sheets low around his hips, drawing her gaze downward. He looked incredibly enticing.

Did it really matter that she'd recognized him? Or why she hadn't disclosed it? She wanted him again, as a woman, not as a teenager this time. She'd better end this now or she'd be in his bed too soon.

He opened his mouth, but she raised her hand. "We can talk more about it tomorrow. Goodnight." She uncurled her legs and rose, her balance unsteady on the cold floor.

"Uh, sweet dreams then. See you in the morning."

Turning toward the door, she caught a glimpse of his perplexed expression. She didn't blame him—she was confused about their future too.

Chapter 40

Charles slammed his cell down on the kitchen table with enough force to gouge another scratch in its battered surface. Where was Lynn? He had declined Kay's decidedly sexual invitation to spend the night at her place because he needed to talk to Lynn, and now she wasn't answering her phone. He hated leaving a voice mail if he could avoid it. They were so impersonal, so distant. The time lapse between his words and her ears would make it that much harder for him to exert his powerful charm.

He needed to find her. Something was going down at SDS.

Stalking the confining perimeter of his living room like a caged cougar, he stepped over piles of junk stacked against the walls. He had picked up rumors from an engineering chat forum there was a company interested in buying SDS after they went public. Charles needed to take the last step in his plan before it was too late.

The press release about the bug had worked exactly as he had hoped. But Coleman's unexpected trip to New York interrupted his plans. Now he had to rely solely on Lynn's influence over Coleman.

He stumbled over his old paper address book, retrieved it and absently thumbed through its pages, halting when he came across Bernadette's name.

Of course–Bernadette would know where her sister was. She couldn't help acting like a mother hen. He remembered how she nosed around in Lynn's business all the time.

Charles had used it to his advantage when he was married to Lynn, and there was no reason not to use it again now. After all, Bernadette offered him a standing invitation to her bed after he and Lynn divorced. She'll be glad to do him this favor.

He smiled, grabbed his phone and settled into the recliner, forcing himself to relax. Fortunately, Boulder was an hour ahead of San Jose. Bernadette would probably be in bed–and more open to sexual teasing.

He punched in her number and closed his eyes in anticipation.

Bernadette's gruff, sleepy mumble interrupted the ring.

"Bernadette, love. It's Kip. Sorry to wake you."

"Kip?" He heard the rustle of covers, imagined Bernadette tugging the blanket over her naked shoulders, her long limbs shifting in anticipation of their phone sex ritual. "Aren't you in San Jose? Is Lynn all right?"

"Everything's fine, love, as far as I know," he soothed. "I just didn't have the number of her hotel, and there's rather urgent business I need to give her tonight before the opportunity passes. Do you know where she is?"

"She usually stays at one of those national chains with the suites. Why don't you just call her cell?" Bernadette's petulant tone carried clearly over the phone.

"Her battery must be dead," he sighed. "It's too bad. This really is a great chance for her." Damn! He needed her to be cooperative and feel intimate with him, not pouty because she wasn't the center of his attention.

"Give me a minute to wake up." Bernadette cleared her throat and sniffed. "I think it's great that you help her out." Despite her polite words, Charles could tell she didn't really care one way or the other. "Any chance you're getting back together?"

Time for him to pour on the charm. "I don't think so, love. Besides, I married the wrong sister."

"Well, it's about time you realized it, sugar. When will I see you again?"

"As soon as I finish up my current project. By any chance, did Lynn tell you what she was up to?"

"She was running out the door to talk to her new client after she overheard some conversation about their IPO."

"Overheard? Where was she?"

"Soaking up rays near the pool. You know how it is these days. People shout their most confidential information over their phones without worrying about who's listening."

"When was this?"

"Sunday," she huffed. "That girl works seven days a week. No wonder she never had time for you."

Charles grunted in agreement, his mind racing. Who had been so careless? Had Lynn heard his name? That press release should have been a surprise. No wonder Lynn had put out so many counter releases that first day. "Well, I guess she'll have to miss this opportunity. Thanks for the help."

"Anytime, Kip. Anytime." There was no mistaking the sexual invitation in Bernadette's words. Charles smiled. His prowess was still strong, even over the phone.

"I'll see you soon, I promise. Dream sexy dreams of us," he crooned, dying to leave her thinking of him all night long.

She moaned. "I don't think I can help myself now. It'll be a wonder if I get any sleep at all."

Charles chuckled. "Good night, love. Take care."

"G'night."

He listened for the soft click of her phone before he ended the call. Women hated being hung up on, so he always made sure they hung up first. It was a simple action that helped them maintain the illusion of power.

This was getting too complicated for voice mail. He reached for his computer and mentally composed an email to Lynn while it booted. She needed to do exactly what he said, one last time.

Besides, she was as culpable as he was for the downfall of her clients, whether now or in the past. Threatening to destroy her reputation should convince her to go along with him. If that ruined her relationship with SDS, tough shit.

He wouldn't need her anymore after this.

Chapter 41

Lynn blinked open her eyes, discombobulated by the unfamiliar surroundings. A mockingbird sang its various calls in the early morning haze, seeking company to welcome the new day.

Her memories of the evening with Eric flooded back, and the stark morning light forced her to confront the possible truths.

Even though she and Eric had known each other for years, she could count on one hand the number of days they had actually been in each other's company. A relationship with Eric would definitely demand a higher degree of sacrifice than she had ever been willing to give a man before. His commitment and intensity would demand a matching response from her. Was she up to it?

She stared out the window, calmed by the pastoral setting of golden hills and valleys patterned in shadows of dark fir and oak trees. A small herd of deer foraged fallen fruit from an abandoned plum orchard below, occasionally waggling their big ears and lifting their heads to sniff the cool breeze. The moist air reminded her of those mornings with Kip, at their old house.

Kip. How was he involved in all this? Better yet, why?

This situation with SDS was huge—and Kip had deliberately involved her. This time, the law would be against her if he implicated her in fraud, or something even more heinous. Would she never get beyond her stupid choice of him as a partner?

Somehow, he must have found out about her tie to Eric from years ago. It was too coincidental that Eric called her out of nowhere to throw a contract her way. It had Kip's handiwork written all over it. But Lynn was positive she never told Kip about Eric. She kept that secret buried from the moment Eric turned her back on her…and on Bernadette.

Bernie. She was the only other person who knew.

Lynn slipped out of bed and tugged on her robe. She tiptoed to the living room and grabbed her phone, along with the afghan from the sofa.

Fred thumped his tail in sleepy welcome from the hearth rug, yawning and rising to pad after her. She winced at the front door's loud click in the early morning stillness. Opening it just enough for them to slip through, she settled on the porch steps facing the pulsing traffic noise drifting up from the valley below. What a startling contrast to the Eden-like setting at the rear of the house. It was enough to jar her back into the reality of the battle brewing in the business world she called home.

Lynn tapped her feet waiting for Bernadette to answer, the afghan around her shoulders tugged close to ward off the morning chill. Her sister couldn't have left for work yet, but she might be in the shower. She would give it ten rings.

"Hello?"

"Morning, Bernadette!" Lynn injected her voice with false cheerfulness. "Did I catch you lollygagging in bed?"

Bernadette sniffed. "For your information, I was starting a load of wash. So there!"

How quickly they reverted to their childhood styles, Lynn thought, amused.

"Hey, did Kip reach you last night? He called here to see if I knew where you were staying. It seemed really important."

Lynn clenched her fingers. "No, he didn't. Do you know what he wanted?"

"Gosh, I really hate acting as your go-between again. Can't you just talk to him and find out?"

"Bernie . . . "

"Okay, okay. Don't call me that! He mentioned some business opportunity. Then he asked a bunch of questions about when you called me from your hotel. You know, when you were crazy enough to see your new client on a Sunday night."

Fury ripped through her. "Why did he want to know about that?" Lynn worked to keep her voice casual. Bernadette had just confirmed everything Eric and Don suspected. Why else would Kip call Bernie looking for her?

"Beats me. He just said he needed to get in touch with you."

Lynn sighed. "Thanks. I need to go now, but I'll call you soon. Tell Mom and Mitch I'm working hard to help them out, no matter what happens." She ignored Bernadette's protests at her quick farewell, punching buttons to retrieve her voice mail, gritting her teeth when Kip's smooth tones ordered her to check her email.

With a muttered curse, she called Fred to her side and crept back into the house. She grabbed her computer and carried it into the kitchen. While it pulled up Kip's email, she started a pot of coffee. A fragrant cup of brew was halfway to her lips when she stared in disbelief at the screen.

"You better do exactly what I tell you or I'll announce your role at FutureTech, Interchip, and PST. A little more work of the same nature will save your precious little consultancy. I'll call to tell you what to do and when."

Her mind reeled in fury.

Those companies were originally Kip's clients. He had encouraged her to approach them after he completed his contracts, in each case to solve virtually insurmountable problems. They had paid her well for her efforts, but her recommendations were implemented too late to salvage any of the companies' reputations. They each went bankrupt, and swiftly.

Had Kip planned it that way?

Barely able to throttle back her anger, she reached for her phone and keyed Kip's number, ignoring her shaking hands.

Voice mail. Of course. "It's Lynn. Meet me at SDS at nine o'clock."

She ended the call abruptly, removing any temptation to blast him with her temper. Fuming, she slammed her computer lid shut and stuffed it into its carrying case.

Deep breaths. Take control. You can do it.

She concentrated on how wonderful Eric made her feel, not the panic demons threatening to surface. Although she hated to keep Kip's threat from him, this was her battle to fight, not Eric's. He had enough concerns. She was on her own.

Chapter 42

"Eric? You awake?"

Lynn waltzed in with two coffee mugs in her hands, Fred glued to her side, wriggling and licking her bare calf.

Lucky dog.

Eric blinked and rose onto one elbow, sniffing appreciatively.

"I wondered if you'd already left," he confessed, not bothering to hide the worry coloring his voice. He searched her eyes. "Any more thoughts?" He patted Fred on the head.

Lynn set his coffee cup on the bedside table. "Lots."

What did that mean? Eric grabbed her hand and kissed her palm. She curved her fingers around his jaw with a soft sigh. He tugged her down to the bed next to him and eased her into his arms, pressing tiny kisses all over her face. She smiled and grabbed his cheeks, holding him still for a resounding smack on the lips, reassuring him more than her words ever could. He set her away from him, eyeing the alarm clock.

"I have a conference call scheduled with New York in two minutes," he complained. Stroking stray strands of hair off her face, he noticed worry lines puckering her brows. "What's wrong, sweetie?"

"There's just a lot to plow through today." Her bright tones didn't fool him. Something was bothering her.

She jumped to her feet, and sipped her coffee. "I'll catch a cab to the office. We don't want to set off gossip." Her lips curved in a wry smile. "Though I suspect we won't be able to be so circumspect for long. I can't seem to keep my eyes off of you." She ran her eyes over his naked legs peeking through the tangled sheets, and sighed exaggeratedly.

"I won't be able to keep my hands off you if you keep looking at me like that," he mumbled, shifting to his side before she saw more than she probably wanted to see. "Are you sure you can't wait?"

Lynn grinned. "As much as I'm tempted, there's too much at stake to let ourselves get distracted." Her expression turned serious. "I'm not going anywhere–not this time. I trust you to not hurt me again." She blew him a kiss as his phone rang. "See you later."

Eric swore before he answered it. He was used to these early morning phone calls from East Coast bankers, but not with a throbbing boner distracting him.

A long hour later, he concluded his call with the analysts who were unable to make the in-person meeting the day before. He was tired of repeating the same information, giving the same answers to the same questions. There had to be a better way to get a return for him and his investors than to go public.

He rose from the bed and stretched, feeling the late night in his bones. Was Lynn tired and exhilarated too? She was hotter than any of his adult fantasies, better than any woman he had ever hoped to find.

And she wouldn't disappear this time. Maybe she was as serious about a long-term relationship as he was. He grinned like a fool.

His phone rang again. Was it Lynn? He couldn't believe he already missed her. It felt like a piece of him was missing and only her presence could make him complete.

"Don here," the gruff voice said, pulling him back to reality. "We need to talk."

"Sounds serious."

"It is if you and Lynn are an item." Don was a master of indirect conversation when he wanted to elicit information.

"I hope we will be soon. So what is it?"

"Did you know she called Wilkins this morning?"

Eric felt sucker-punched. A thunderbolt of doubt coursed through him. "No, she was up before me. What did she say?"

"Just to meet her at the office. She also called someone else, but I don't know who it was. We only have cameras on the outside of the house, and she called from the porch. Do you think she knew we were watching her?"

Eric sank onto the bed. He hated feeling these reservations, but he couldn't risk SDS because he was involved with her. He had to be sure.

"I don't know." He considered her reticence to talk in the den, her surprise visit to his bedroom, her hints at further discussion but unwillingness to talk more—even this morning. "I suppose it's possible."

"Look, we need to figure out what to do. Can you meet me at Walt's Waffles on Capitol Expressway in an hour? That will save time but still give us some privacy to hash this out."

"You buying?" His stomach rumbled at the thought of waffles and eggs.

"A fruit cup okay?"

Eric chuckled. "Point made. See you then." He tossed the phone on the bed.

What was Lynn really up to? Had he been a fool to trust her with so much information before they were sure of her loyalty to Kip?

Time to find out for sure.

He and Don had worked through worse crises in their lives. They would find the truth behind SDS' enemies—and Lynn wouldn't be one of them.

Chapter 43

Kip closed the door behind him with a sharp click. Dropping into the chair across from Lynn, he ran manicured fingers over his neat cap of hair and watched her with the eyes of a jackal considering its prey.

Lynn swallowed hard. She had to tamp down these lingering feelings of uncertainty. He won't dominate her again. She fisted her hands under the desk, a silent and private call for inner strength.

She took a deep breath and leaned back in the chair, uncrossing her arms as a gesture of confidence. "What is it you want?"

"Shares of stock. Those wonderful pieces of partial company ownership that create untold wealth in Silicon Valley. And you'll help me convince good ol' Eric to grant them to me for old time's sake." He caressed his trimmed beard, gaze unwavering.

"You've worked with him for years. Why can't you just ask Eric yourself?"

He eased forward over her desk with a threatening expression. "Because you've known him much longer, honey. He's been carrying a torch for you since college. You can wrap him around your little finger with no effort at all."

Bernie, what did you tell him, Lynn groaned to herself. She kept her face composed, only quirking one eyebrow. "Eric doesn't respond to anyone manipulating him, man or woman. I won't help you, Kip, no matter how many threats you make."

Kip smirked. "There are others who might respond, if you really feel your influence with Eric is at an all-time low, which I sincerely doubt. The board needs to know who the mysterious beneficiary of the Trust is. I think, in return for that advance knowledge, they would be happy to grant me stock."

He paused, gaze intent in the growing silence. Lynn prayed she hadn't revealed her dismay. This was Kip's little game to play. She mentally shrugged. So he made a good guess. She was just here to listen and learn. She tapped her jaw and waited for him to expose the rest of his plan.

"That is, if you want me to go behind Eric's back instead of asking him directly." Kip continued. "That's your business, of course, but he may not like it if you screw him over–in the figurative sense. I'm sure he'd like to screw your brains out, if you let him."

Oops. A red line. Better do more than just listen. "Look, Kip. For your own warped reasons, you're fixated on getting back at me, personally and professionally. Why do you need to involve others? Can't we just handle this between us, whatever it is?"

He snorted. "Do you have big bucks just lying around that I don't know about? That is, besides the money you'll make when SDS goes public?"

"Of course not. You know that, but–"

"Maybe I was too quick to divorce you." Bitterness crept into his voice. "If I waited until your boyfriend gave you the millions of dollars coming to you, I could have taken half."

Millions? Lynn swallowed hard and stared at her hands. How had she missed calculating the potential value of the Trust? She could use that money. Her mind cartwheeled through the possibilities–pay off her condo, help with Mitch's medical bills, re-capitalize her business. Her throat closed up as relief cascaded through her. Coughing, she fumbled in her purse for a tissue.

"I divorced you, and you deserved it." She pitched the tissue in the wastebasket with nonchalance. "And our past doesn't mean a tinker's damn to anyone but you."

"On the contrary, honey. A number of people would be very interested to know just how unqualified you are." His ferocious smile reminded her of a wolf–wily and dangerous. "Investment bankers don't take kindly to being conned, and the SEC has strict rules about misleading investors. It wouldn't take much to boot your little company out the door and blame your incompetence for this little fiasco with the bug."

She clenched the edge of the desk, resisting a temptation to slug him. "I had nothing to do with that!" For once, she loved the way her voice sounded–low and throaty, full of disgust.

"According to your sister, you found out in time to prevent it from actually hitting the wires. You sent out lots of other press releases instead, so you would seem indispensable," he mocked. "But you and I know better, don't we? Other companies relied on your advice, and look what happened to them."

She gritted her teeth. "I won't help you. Eric won't let anything hurt his company."

He rose, shaking his head. "You're a real fool, you know that? This won't hurt Eric or SDS one bit. The only people affected will be the new shareholders who buy into an overpriced IPO–like they always do. In the meantime, you'll make a bundle for your small effort and I, your humble servant, will finally make as much as the untalented clowns in this valley who've gotten filthy rich off my efforts." He notched up his chin. "I intend to get my cut this time."

"Don't count on me to help you." She slapped at her desk, dismayed that his egotistical power trip would bring him this far. "I can't, and I won't."

Kip reached across the desk and jabbed a hard finger into her chest. "You can, and you will. Because all those clients you're counting on to help you pay my debts won't hire you unless I say so. Why do you think you haven't been able to get any new clients? Because I still control your life. This time, you're following my orders exactly."

He straightened and buttoned his camelhair jacket. "I'll be in touch about our next steps. I'll expect more cooperation, or all hell will break loose–for both you and SDS." He stalked out of her office, slamming the door behind him.

Lynn groaned and dropped her head in her hands. Was he on drugs again? She hadn't noticed any physical signs, but he was definitely off the deep end this time.

If Don was right, Kip planted this bug years ago, waiting for the right moment to unleash his plan on her. It was eating him alive that they divorced too soon, that his cocaine habit had lost him half the Trust. But how did he find out? Did he have contacts in the government too, who could ferret out the confidential papers? Lynn wouldn't put it past him.

Lynn cursed under her breath. She had been such an idiot when it came to Kip.

She didn't dare think what that meant about her attraction to Eric.

Kip was right about one thing–he had all the information and contacts he needed to destroy her professionally. If not now, certainly later. He could threaten and blackmail her forever if she didn't figure out a way to stop him.

Otherwise, she could kiss Baker & Associates goodbye. Of course, she could change the name of her company and start all over. Surely, some loyal clients would serve as references after enough time had passed. Then, she could re-build her reputation. Couldn't she?

Only if she had a financial cushion to give her the time to re-build.

Lynn shook her head. If she didn't do her job now, there wouldn't be an IPO, and she could kiss any Trust money goodbye. Besides, that money belonged to Eric, not to her. Well, maybe a tiny portion of it would be nice. She would have to figure out later what would be the right thing to do.

In the meantime, she had a contract to deliver on. What could she do to help Eric keep the offering on track? It was her turn to step up to the plate.

And if her business failed, so what? She had resurrected herself before. One more time was no big deal. People did it in Silicon Valley every day.

And, maybe this time, Eric would be at her side to help her.

Chapter 44

Don scowled at the blaring headlines, ignoring the enticing aromas of waffles and bacon. His waitress refilled his coffee cup, splattering drops on his newspaper in the process.

Those so-called journalistic idiots didn't even pretend to be factual. They write an attention-grabbing headline, figuring no one would read the actual story, which mysteriously contradicts the headline. The poor fools who believe the big print dash off an order to their broker to buy or sell stock and get conned every day without even realizing it.

He blew on his coffee, considering the mystery of the SDS press release. A "nobody" started the rumor, and a good company expended an inordinate amount of resources to set things right. Sure, sometimes PR departments purposely distract the media from a negative fact, or Wall Street insiders start false rumors for the express purpose of sending the stock price skyrocketing. He just hadn't anticipated these shenanigans before the company actually went public. Shame on him.

Don glanced at his watch and frowned. Eric was fifteen minutes late. That wasn't like him.

Unless Lynn had stayed with him. Their mutual attraction shimmered unmistakably across the room last night. God knows, Eric had pined over her for years. Don only hoped she deserved Eric's loyalty.

He pulled up Eric's phone numbers. No answer on Eric's cell. Or at home.

Throwing bills down onto the laminated table, he dashed out. Eric must have forgotten about their meeting and driven straight to SDS. Or maybe a problem came up with the bankers and he had to deal with it right away. Don shrugged. He decided to drive to SDS. They could talk in Eric's office. He simply preferred the bustling, chrome anonymity of Walt's.

He strode through the SDS lobby, giving a familiar nod to the young receptionist. As he passed by the closed door of Lynn's office, on his way to Eric's, he could hear her muffled words. There was no question she was pissed. Her voice rose and fell in quick rhythm, punctuated with emphatic pauses and even a hand slamming on the desk. Don grimaced. He was still having doubts about her ongoing contact with Wilkins.

No matter what, Wilkins was a jerk. *Give him hell, Lynn.*

He stopped at Stephanie's desk. "Hey, Steph. Eric got a minute?"

Stephanie looked up from sorting the day's mail. Her perennially polite expression changed to a sincere smile. "Hello Don. I didn't expect to see you today. Eric isn't here yet, so I don't know his schedule."

"He hasn't been in at all today?"

"Not that I've seen, and I've been here since eight. Maybe someone who was here earlier might know where he is."

A warning bell clanged in Don's brain as he recalled the email threat. "Thanks. I'll check around. If I find out where he is, I'll let you know."

She nodded and returned her focus to the stack of mail. Don spun on his heel and stalked toward Lynn's office just as Wilkins turned the far corner. He knocked once and walked in, without waiting for a response. He caught Lynn with her head buried in her hands.

She glanced up and flushed, patting her disheveled hair back in place. "Good morning, Don. What can I do for you?"

"Have you seen Eric?"

She shook her head. "I haven't seen him here yet." Her eyes glanced toward the open door and pled for his discretion. "He indicated he would see me after a conference call with New York. I presumed that would be sometime this morning."

Don grunted his thanks and left just as abruptly as he'd entered. Coffee acid roiled his empty stomach. He strode through the maze of hallways and cubicles, stopped at Rajiv's office, and barged in after a brief knock.

Rajiv spun around. An annoyed look flashed on his face. Don waved his hand at the engineer standing at the whiteboard, asking for silence.

"Do you know where Eric is this morning?"

"No, Don, I am sorry. I have not talked to him since yesterday. As far as I know, he was coming into the office this morning. We have a number of things to discuss." He stared at Don. A quizzical expression replaced his earlier irritation.

"Sorry to interrupt, folks." Don backed out of the room and closed the door behind him.

Goddammit! What happened to Eric?

Exiting through a side door, he hurried back to the parking lot and jumped into his black sports utility vehicle. He quickly roared the engine to life and skidded out of the lot, praying for no traffic jams. As soon as he reached Central Expressway, he rammed his foot onto the pedal to keep the vehicle moving well beyond the speed limit, vying with jets gearing up for take off as he zoomed around the airport and onto the highway. Tracing Eric's usual route to SDS, he spun the wheel and tore through the Walt's Waffle's parking lot, searching for Eric's white car and praying his hunch was wrong.

No Eric.

Stifling his growing panic, he reentered Capitol Expressway and floored the gas pedal, eating up the miles.

Don turned at Eric's exit. He jerked his head from side to side, trying to simultaneously scan the traffic and the parked cars. Maybe Eric stopped to run an errand and had been delayed. Maybe he had a flat tire. Maybe...

Three miles from Eric's home, on a small twisting side street, Don braked hard.

Eric's Mustang lay tilted on the shoulder of the road. The driver's door was open. The rear right fender hung over a gully. No one was around.

Don executed a swift U-turn and parked behind the Mustang. He leapt out with the motor still running, shooting sharp glances at the surrounding vegetation and the sloping hillsides. This desolate road fed only local traffic into the more congested streets. There was no other way in or out.

A perfect trap.

Squatting, Don scrutinized a number of smeared footprints around the back of the car. It appeared like a simple accident scene; drivers gathering around the damaged area to accuse, blame, and swap insurance information.

But he suspected more. There were at least three different sets of footprints. Eric could easily have been overpowered if the guys had kidnapping on their minds.

He stepped gingerly around the prints. Not wanting to disturb the evidence, he approached the passenger side, crazily angled next to a juniper bush. Don opened the unlocked door and tried the glove compartment. Locked. He reached into his breast pocket and extracted a small tool. After a little fiddling with the lock, it popped open. Silvery gunmetal shimmered in the morning light.

Don swore under his breath. Why hadn't Eric taken the simple precaution of actually carrying his handgun? That would have made any kidnapper pause.

Don would have to alert the authorities—as soon as he confirmed his theory.

Hopefully it wouldn't be too late for Eric.

He returned the Mustang to the condition he had found it and retraced his steps to the SUV. Jumping in, he grabbed his phone, pulled up Rajiv's number, then slammed into gear and hit the gas.

He didn't wait for Rajiv's greeting.

"This is Don. We have an emergency. Get Lynn and meet me in your office in fifteen–no, make that ten minutes."

He hung up and concentrated on driving, whipping through the light traffic and running every signal he could, even hopping on Highway 101 just to shave a precious thirty seconds off his time.

His heart pounded in his chest as he considered possibilities. The worst ones he would keep to himself until he had other professionals involved. Rajiv and Lynn will freak out when they hear what might be happening at this very moment.

With a jerk, Don parked the SUV in the same space he'd vacated thirty minutes earlier and rushed into SDS, ignoring the receptionist. He made a beeline for Rajiv's office, quickly scanning the room for anyone who didn't belong. Don slammed the door, twisted the lock, and dropped into an empty chair. Lynn looked worried, Rajiv apprehensive.

Pity flashed through Don. These two had busted their tails putting out fires all week, and the mother of all infernos was roaring down on them. Don sure didn't relish breaking the news.

"Eric has probably been kidnapped," he announced, ignoring Lynn's suddenly white face and Rajiv's look of horror. "He was supposed to meet me for breakfast. When he didn't show up, I went looking for him. I found his car abandoned a couple of miles from his house, with signs of a scuffle among three men."

Lynn wagged her head. "Maybe he just walked back to his house to call a tow truck. Did you go there?"

Don raised his eyebrows. Years of experience told him not to bother testing her theory, but it wouldn't hurt. "Go ahead and try his house again. Rajiv, can you access Eric's email account so we can see if there are any new threats?"

Rajiv nodded, pulling his computer forward and typing furiously.

Don glanced at Lynn tapping her phone, gripping it as if she could will Eric to answer. Long moments passed. Lynn's hand dropped to her side with disappointment. She met Don's gaze, tears in her eyes.

"Kidnapped!" she whimpered. Wrapping her arms around her waist, she took deep breaths. Her eyes closed in a gesture of willed isolation from the clicks and clatter of the keyboard, and what more bad news they might bring. Don kept a close watch on her, praying she wasn't losing control.

Rajiv stood up and beckoned Don to sit in his chair at the desk to peruse Eric's incoming emails. As Rajiv leaned over his shoulder, Lynn jumped up to join them.

"Did you find anything?" she breathed, a ray of hope coloring her voice.

"Yeah, a ransom note," Don muttered, reading the email.

"We warned you. We will do whatever it takes to obtain the proxy rights of the Trust beneficiary, including killing your precious CEO. If you think your IPO can go forward without him, think again. We have very influential friends. We will be in touch shortly."

Lynn stumbled to the chair across the desk and stared at Don. "This is crazy. They kidnapped Eric because of me."

Rajiv scowled. "How do you reach that conclusion?"

Don nodded encouragement to Lynn. It was past time Rajiv knew her identity and Eric's years-ago promise.

The way he figured it, Rajiv and Lynn were the only two he was certain weren't behind Eric's disappearance. If she was involved, there was no reason to kidnap Eric. She could provide the proxy directly to the kidnappers. And Rajiv wouldn't risk harming the IPO. It was his dream come true. Eric's kidnapping was bound to delay, if not tank it, altogether.

"Last night, I found out Eric made me the Trust beneficiary." Lynn met Rajiv's glance squarely.

Don scrutinized Rajiv's expression, noting the hurt twisting his features. Eric hadn't trusted Rajiv with this last bit of significant information about his beloved company. Would it affect Rajiv's cooperation going forward?

Lynn wrung her hands and settled them into her lap, her fingers entwined. "I...helped him...with his initial proposal to get the DARPA funding years ago. As a thank you, he apparently decided years ago to repay me with a stake in SDS."

Rajiv glared at her, crossing his arms over his chest. "Was this before or after you married Chas? And helped him with his little bug?"

"Oh, no, Rajiv, I had nothing to do with Kip's–Chas's–schemes to plant the bug. Honestly," she protested. "This all happened years before I met Kip."

"And you do not think all this is related? I find that hard to believe," Rajiv pronounced, sounding like a high executioner handing down his sentence. Anger etched his face. Don couldn't blame him. His two best friends betrayed him, and Lynn was involved with both. But his eyes reflected intense worry, too.

Lynn raked her hand through her hair, pulling it free from the combs. It flowed in a white mass down her back. "I don't know," she admitted in a helpless voice. "There are too many parameters for me to sort through." She turned. "What can we do, Don?"

"Alert the authorities and wait for the next email. But you're right, Lynn. This is a lot more complex than a simple case of greed. Do you think Wilkins is behind this?"

"I doubt it," Lynn replied. "He came to talk to me this morning. He was full of demands."

Lynn recounted her conversation with Wilkins, and Don absorbed the nuances of Wilkins' behavior–taking the easy way out, avoiding confrontations. Probably not his style to arrange a kidnapping.

"He'd already guessed I was the beneficiary, and I think he'd be satisfied with a stock grant," Lynn concluded. "Besides, this just isn't like him."

"I tend to agree with you," Don said, catching the fury in Rajiv's face. "Look, Rajiv. I know Wilkins really pissed you off with that bug. But, think this through. He had his own plan in the works for years, and now he's able to pull it off. Why risk the IPO when those shares will finally be valuable?"

Rajiv muttered under his breath. He began pacing across his office, his face reddening. "After all these years I have dedicated to SDS and... still...Eric did not tell me the whole truth. To have it all fall around my head in pieces is too much!" He stared out of the window for long moments, his posture rigid, hands clenching and unclenching behind his back.

He whirled. "Our first priority must be to protect Eric. You are the expert, Don. What do you suggest?"

"As much as you'll hate it, we each need to work on what we're best at so there are no more weaknesses to exploit." Don scribbled notes on a piece of scratch paper. "That means you need to get the software code clean and bug free, Rajiv, so Lynn can crow to the heavens and squash whatever nefarious player is trying to ruin SDS' reputation. Let me take care of the rest."

Lynn jumped to her feet, smacking her hands on the desk and capturing Don's full attention with her challenging stare. "Not good enough. What exactly are you planning? I need to know. Otherwise, I'm starting on my own. I have contacts too."

God save me from amateurs. She looked like an Amazon warrior girding herself for battle.

Don sighed. He couldn't get away with brushing her off. "I'm calling in my old friends at the FBI. They'll go over the Mustang for clues. Then they'll need to see the emails and probably talk to us."

He paused, waiting for Rajiv's attention. "There are at least two different efforts trying to harm SDS that I can see, but there may be more. It will take pros to help us sort it all out. I need to work through the possibilities before I start talking to them. Otherwise, they'll spend too much time on the details and not enough on finding Eric. I find that unacceptable."

"So do I," echoed Rajiv.

"And I." Lynn nodded. "All right, I'll go with your plan. Why don't we leave Rajiv to get the code straightened out, Don. You and I can brainstorm in my office." She shot Rajiv a reassuring glance. "If we need you, we'll come get you, and tell you anything we discover. In the meantime, maybe you can also keep an eye on Eric's email so we know if a new one comes in."

Don admired her finesse smoothing Rajiv's obviously ruffled feathers while keeping them all at their most productive. He gathered up his notes and hastened out the door without waiting for Rajiv's reply. He had phone calls to make. He had to alert his friends at the Defense Department too. Their years-long strategy was now threatened, and they needed to know, ASAP.

Chapter 45

Eric squinted in the dim light. Where was he? His brain felt muzzy. The rat-tat-tat of little drummer boys pounded in his head, and his stomach rebelled with every breath. He fought back waves of fatigue.

One moment, he was squatting down to examine the damage to his Mustang's rear end and smelling a sickly sweet odor he attributed to the nearby vegetation. The next moment, he was here. Wherever *here* was.

He hoped chloroform had been their drug of choice. At least that wouldn't have lasting effects. He shook his head, blinking away the last vestiges of dizziness.

Eric tugged at the ropes binding his wrists and ankles, testing their strength. Too snug to budge. His arms and legs, threaded through slats of a straight-backed chair, kept him awkwardly upright. Numbness crept up his thighs, his own weight pressing against throbbing arteries. He was running out of time. A surge of adrenalin clanged his senses fully alert.

He closed his eyes and tried to focus on other clues. Smells of roasting fowl with heavy overtones of sesame oil seeped into his nostrils. Straining to listen, he caught the discordant, staccato rhythms of Asian dialect drifting through the window from the street below. A faint blast of a boat whistle reached his ears. His skin felt clammy in cool, damp air. He could almost taste the salty tang of the ocean.

San Francisco's Chinatown, in all its glory.

Why was he here? And who had taken him?

The screech of a heavy bolt sliding through its metal case broke the silence. Eric swung his head toward the door. A flash of light burned his eyes and he squinted, glancing up at a bare bulb hanging from a low ceiling.

Two muscular, young men with Chinese features entered the room. The tall one had the hulk of a football player. The other was short but lean, his relaxed arm ridged and hard, reminding Eric of the martial arts actor, Bruce Lee. He moved with a controlled grace, his weight perfectly balanced at all times. They closed the door behind them and stepped close to Eric.

"We can make this easy for you, or hard," the Hulk grunted. His very height was intimidating. "Tell us who the beneficiary of your Trust is, and we'll let you go, unharmed."

Lynn! Eric's brain screamed and scrambled. He'd put her in danger. All because he felt guilty and needed to make it up to her. He groaned to himself. If he had any idea this would happen, he never would have come up with the damned plan in the first place.

Eric didn't relish his choices. "Who are you? Or better yet, who's paying you?" He gambled with a sneer. "I doubt you're the brains behind whatever game is going on."

"Our boss has no interest in disclosing his identity to you." The Bruce Lee look-alike circled the chair with a menacing stride. "He only desires the name of the beneficiary. Tell us who it is, or you'll regret it."

"What does he want with the information?" Eric tensed.

"He just pays us to deliver it. So will you tell us, or not?"

"Not on your life."

Fists flew into his stomach. Numbing kicks to his legs and arms. Slaps against his temple, so powerful his ears rung. His head snapped from side to side with each blow.

"Do you wish to reconsider?" Even though Bruce Lee had thrown most of the punches, somehow he managed to keep his breathing measured and controlled.

"Nope." Eric took a deep breath, ignoring the pain shooting down his body.

They knocked him so hard, his chair toppled. He lay helpless on the floor, grunting, absorbing each blow on his exposed torso.

"We'll be back," the Hulk growled in his ear. "And we won't be as nice next time." They straightened their clothing and flicked off the light. The door lock's loud snap echoed in the empty room.

A tsunami of pain coursed through his nerve endings and into his brain. Eric let out a huge groan. He relaxed his body, trying to ease into the restraints, choking off his blood flow like an unwanted tourniquet.

One of the chair legs had cracked under his weight. He broke it off and pulled his leg forward, able to alleviate the worst of the pressure. Now lying horizontal on the dusty wooden floor, still attached to the back of his chair by his arms, he tried to rise. No go. Again. Nope.

He felt like a fish floundering in the bottom of a boat. Time to give up and think.

Whoever wanted control of SDS had ties to Chinese criminals here in San Francisco–obviously. But what would criminals want with SDS? Smuggled drugs or people forged the illegal black market between San Francisco and China. It didn't make sense.

Was the software bug related to his kidnapping? Violence wasn't Wilkins' style. But Eric would bet his last dollar whoever sent the threatening email hired these muscle guys, too.

Or was it someone linked to his board of directors? Possibly. But the board believed they'd already wrestled control of the proxy. Unless they wanted the certainty of having a signed agreement to do so, kidnapping him seemed a drastic step to take.

Then again, maybe whoever it was wanted to simply exploit the opportunity the bug provided.

A vision of Kay at the New York meeting flashed before his eyes. Maybe someone promised her a better future than she could get at SDS–if she delivered the mysterious shareholder. The Maoist political group? Possible.

Eric recalled the other small knot of Chinese men at Joshua's analyst meeting. That had been an invitation-only, ostensibly privileged briefing. Maybe they were behind his abduction somehow. That link, at least, made some sense. The bad press release came from China, and Kay hadn't been behind that–she'd jumped through hoops like the rest of them on Monday.

Joshua. Could he be involved? He could arrange the financial puzzle pieces; guaranteeing voting control of SDS in a certain person's hands as soon as they went public. If a client wanted to buy SDS, and was willing to pay a high enough price, he'd get it. Millions of dollars would motivate Joshua, who probably measured his self-worth by the cash in his bank account, without a qualm about how it got there.

A new thought sprang to mind. The secret he had buried as deep as a spring-water well. His covert plan had progressed suitably, and hadn't raised any hackles at Defense. But all his DARPA advisors, including Don, warned him what he was attempting could ultimately prove dangerous.

Years ago, Eric had brushed off their concerns with youthful disdain.

Now he wondered.

He tugged at his wrist restraints again, grunting with the effort. No matter who was behind his kidnapping, Lynn's life was in jeopardy. If his abductors had known she was the beneficiary, she would be here, beaten until she signed over her shares.

Eric broke out in a cold sweat.

Don would keep her safe. Don may be suspicious of her, but he trusted Eric's judgment. And he knew how deep Eric's feelings were for Lynn, despite the circumstances.

Neither he nor Don ever expected to need the insurance of the Trust. But it might come in handy, after all. Only Don understood enough to separate the issues and come up with a rescue plan without putting anything or anyone else at risk. They had to follow their original mission through to the bitter end.

Eric only hoped the bitter taste of blood in his mouth was the worst of it.

Chapter 46

Kay leaned her forehead against the cool glass of her apartment window, allowing herself sixty seconds of guilt and remorse. No more, no less. She was getting the job done, just as her superiors expected. If she were a man, they'd look the other way and slap her on the back with congratulations and hearty handshakes, despite her unorthodox tactics. Too bad if they were caught with their pants down in front of their bosses. Politics was always a messy business. Even more so, now that women were players too.

So why was she having second thoughts?

Shoving her conscience aside, she picked up her phone–and duties–again.

"Stein, here."

"Joshua, it's Kay," she lilted, sending out a long-distance caress. "Our dear friend has been, hmm, shall we say detained this morning. We'll have the information we need soon."

He gasped. "You had him kidnapped? A bit extreme, don't you think?" Joshua's voice carried a tiny tremor.

"Did you think asking him nicely would get us anywhere? You've been trying that for months."

"He can't be harmed," he hissed. "If it looks like coercion, the law enforcement guys will be all over this. Then the SEC will get in on the act, and everything will go straight to hell. This isn't China, you know. Here, we play by civilized rules."

That's a matter of opinion, Kay mused. She could write a book on how uncivilized America had become. Especially when it came to separating the good guys from the bad ones. "And that's why the good ol' USA is playing defense to China's ascendancy. You're playing in the big leagues, Joshua. If you can't handle it, get out before you get hurt."

"Be careful, Kay. I have contacts you need. If they hear you screwed this up, you can kiss your pretty ass goodbye. It won't be worth a penny, even as a washed-up whore in Thailand."

"Thank you so much for your concern." She didn't hide her disdain. "I'll fill you in on the necessary details when the time comes."

"You do that."

"I'll keep in touch. Bye-bye now."

Kay pushed the button to end the call without waiting for a reply. What little backbone Joshua ever had was disappearing by the minute. She would have to keep a close eye on him. In the meantime, she wanted to discover the name of the mysterious beneficiary before Eric's captors got the information first.

Her contacts in the Chinatown Benevolent Association had ties to the Triad gangs. Whatever information they pulled out of Eric they'd sell to the highest bidder–male, of course–and only then dole it out to a lowly woman. Even though she was the one who got them the job. They had the jump on her by a few hours already.

She dropped onto the small sofa and tucked her feet under her hips while she punched in Charlie's number. She suspected he was keeping information from her about SDS and had no idea how high the stakes had gone in this game. Time was running out to deliver on all her promises.

"Charlie," she cooed. "Did you miss me?"

His deep-throated rumble pulsed through the line. "I get hard just thinking about you, honey, and when you're not with me, I ache all night. Does that count?"

"Mm-hmm." She squirmed, her body responding against her will. Too bad their affair would end soon. He was a great lover, willing to explore even her most peculiar fantasies. "I may be tied up at work tonight, till late. Eric went missing."

"What?"

"Rumor has it he's been kidnapped. So hard to be a CEO these days..."

"Why on earth would anyone kidnap Eric? The SDS technology is good, but it's not as if they have a lot of money to pay a ransom yet. After the IPO maybe, but now? It doesn't make sense."

"Apparently, someone wants to get to the mysterious 7% owner of the Trust. And whoever that is will go to any lengths to find out." Kay feigned a sob. "I'm worried it won't stop with just Eric. What if I'm next?"

"Don't worry. Eric will tell them it's Lynn and they'll let him go. He has to reveal her identity soon for the IPO anyway. I doubt he'll trade his life for the information."

"Lynn?" Yes! Kay did a victorious hand pump. Her mind raced. "I didn't realize they had a history."

"They met at Northwestern. I'm guessing they cut a deal back then that gave her ownership." A long pause. "I could be wrong."

"Well, that would certainly explain their...um, how shall I put it? Coziness together?"

"Speaking of cozy, why don't you come over later? You can fill me in about these new goings-on at SDS, and then I'll take your mind off work all...night...long."

She had more urgent matters to handle than Charlie's libido. "No, thanks. I don't think you fill my needs anymore."

"What? Kay, what the—"

Kay cut off his protests with a touch of a finger and hummed, dialing the third number from memory. Weng's barked greeting filled her ear.

"Please communicate to Du Wenlin that I am happy to report the name of SDS' Trust beneficiary," she reported in a dutiful voice.

"And? Who is it?"

"I would like the honor of telling our boss personally. May I have his number, please?" Lord, she hated the expected groveling. Soon it would all be over, and she could tell these guys to shove it.

"He trusts me to guard his privacy–so, no. And he also reminded me that time is short if we need to take a different course of action."

Dammit, she'd just been out-maneuvered. She couldn't afford to start over with a new set of contacts. Quivering with frustration, she forced a steady voice. "Of course, I understand, but I trust you will tell Du Wenlin that I delivered what I promised."

"You haven't yet."

"Her name is Lynn Baker. Perhaps you saw her on TV, trying to undo the damage from the press release."

Silence. Kay shrugged. No getting out of spilling all her intelligence this time.

"She is a plain Caucasian woman, middle-aged with white hair. She wears very conservative clothes. You may want to confirm with Coleman that she's the one, but my source seemed fairly confident of his information."

Okay, that was a bit of a stretch. But her intuition told her Charlie was right. Eric was too tight with Lynn to have just met her. They definitely had a history, and Eric wanted it kept quiet.

"I'll keep you informed of her whereabouts this afternoon," she continued. "I'll be at work shortly, and will meet up with her there."

"Good." And that was that. Dismissed, even though her valuable nugget of information proved the worth of her uniquely female tactics. Let the men try to seduce the information from any of these tight-lipped executives. They only talked in bed.

Chapter 47

Lynn's office door crashed open, interrupting Don's low-toned musings. She stifled a shriek.

"There is another email!" Rajiv closed the door and crowded behind Don into the tight space. He shoved his phone out to them with a trembling hand.

"Lynn Baker must sign a proxy statement in San Francisco if you want him unharmed." An address followed at the end of the order. And that was it.

"Rather terse." Lynn ignored the gripping fear, wiping her damp palms on her skirt. "I'll leave now and get this over with…and get Eric back." Whatever they wanted, she would do it, to keep him safe. She'd never gotten over him, just as he'd never gotten over her. And look where it got them. Some dumb Trust putting both of their lives in danger.

"Not so fast," Don cautioned. "No one walks blindly into a trap. Let's try beating them at their own game."

Don drummed his fingers on the desk. A speculative expression settled on his face. He reached for the device. "How do I send a reply?"

"I will do it." Rajiv readied his fingers. "What is the message?"

Don's eyes raked over Lynn. "How adventurous are you feeling today?" Not an ounce of humor softened his hard, focused eyes.

Lynn met his glance with as much bravado as she could muster. "What do you have in mind?"

"A little public distraction so I can spring Eric before you sign anything. Are you game?"

"You bet." Eric trusted him implicitly. Lynn would do no less.

"I'll do everything to keep you both safe, but these kidnappers want their hands on you. If anything goes wrong, you'll be in danger, not Eric."

She grimaced. "I get it. I'll do whatever you think will work." She flashed him a weak grin. "I always had a secret yearning to be a spy. James Bond and I go way back."

Don chuckled, turning to Rajiv. "I need you to stay here and monitor emails and any other situation that might develop," he explained. "We still don't know if the bug is involved, and you're the only one who can keep an eye on that."

"I am happy to stay here." Rajiv's relief was obvious. "I have no hankering to be a spy. FYI, I have kept Chas out of our code today, so we have cleaned it up completely."

"Good. If you find anything else, let us know immediately. Now let's send that reply." Don gave up his chair to Rajiv and stared at the screen over his shoulder. "Send this: *Baker will be at the corner of Grant and California at 4 p.m. today. Have Coleman with you, and visible, or she won't sign.*"

Rajiv's fingers flew over the keys. "Okay to send?" His finger poised over the screen. At Don's nod, Rajiv sent the message.

"Come on. We only have two hours." Don beckoned to Lynn, hustling her out the door. "We'll call you as soon as we know more," he threw over his shoulder.

They rounded the corner and hurried into the lobby. The whoosh of the door opening blew Lynn's hair into her eyes.

"Hello, Lynn. What's the rush?"

Kay's calm question halted their frantic pace. Lynn matched Kay's composure, stopping directly in front of her and tucking her hair behind her ear.

"A bit of business regarding the press release," Lynn lied. "Don knows someone who might be able to shed light on the whole episode."

Lynn caught the flicker of surprise in Don's eyes at her ready fib, even as he kept his face blank. Little did he know how much she played spy games as a kid, practicing in the bathroom mirror until her face wouldn't give her away. She could handle his plan—whatever it was.

"Sorry, Ms. Chiang, but we are in a bit of a hurry. If you'll please excuse us." Don stepped between them to open the door, blocking her from Kay's view. Glancing back, Lynn caught Kay's speculative scowl as her eyes followed them out the door.

"Kay knows more than she lets on," Lynn murmured when they were a safe distance away.

"Yeah, I think you're right. She's moved way up on my list of potential bad guys." He boosted Lynn into the high seat of his SUV. Slamming the door, he scanned the parking lot before climbing in and turning the ignition.

He gave Lynn a hard look. "I expect you to honor your word and do what I tell you for Eric's sake. These guys are hard-core, and it will take a lot of fancy footwork for my plan to work. So listen up."

Breaking all speed laws, Don told her in graphic detail what part Lynn was to play in freeing Eric. She flushed clear to her ear tips, but nodded her agreement. If that's what it would take, she would do it.

Traffic slowed to a crawl as they approached San Francisco Airport. Lynn glanced at her watch to count off the minutes. The daily fog bank drifted across the narrow peninsula, snarling cars in both directions—thick enough today to delay flights. Don's muttered curses echoed in the car's interior as he wove through the slowdown, palm on the horn, taking chances that made her grip the edge of her seat.

Deep breaths. Nothing to fear. Relax. I'm safe.

Don dropped her off at the Embarcadero Center in downtown San Francisco with instructions to get her shopping and makeover completed within forty-five minutes. After that, she had fifteen minutes to take a cab to a street around the corner from their rendezvous, where he would call her to confirm he was in position. Then she was on her own to make her entrance.

In record time, Lynn combed through the racks of a trendy boutique, finding the exact style of clothes Don described. She plunked down enough bills to cover the purchase and rushed to a nearby store to buy the wig.

Next on the list: finding a thankfully empty restroom. She appropriated the handicapped stall, albeit with a twinge of guilt. She needed the extra width to maneuver the change of clothes–just for a few minutes.

Lynn had not even one pang of regret leaving her designer clothes behind. She studied herself in the mirror as she passed. Don was right. The kidnappers would never recognize her. They'll be looking for an apprehensive, white-haired business lady. Not someone like her.

Satisfied, she stuck out her tongue at her reflection, laughed, and dashed out to catch a cab. She couldn't wait to mess with the kidnapper's plans.

Chapter 48

Eric shuffled on the pavement, bulwarked between his two captors in the half-light of a foggy afternoon. He had guessed right. He was in the middle of Chinatown, on a street that definitely didn't cater to tourists. He stuck out like a sore thumb, towering over the milling population as they finished the day's shopping.

Old fish odors filled his nostrils. A background of burning incense added an intense layer to the stench of freshly butchered poultry. The discordant symphony of Chinese dialects was deafening, as people unflinchingly screamed their requests over the heads of those crowded in front.

Eric's guards kept him close. The jostling crowds buffeted their hard bodies against his bruised and battered one. He winced with each impact. They hadn't beaten him a second time. He couldn't decide if he should be grateful or not.

They apparently changed their minds after the first round in the ring. Returning with the name of the beneficiary, her signed proxy would now grant him his freedom. Eric's heart sank when they said "her." They must have discovered Lynn—anyone merely making a guess would have said "his." It was obvious they weren't bluffing.

How in hell could he keep Lynn safe with bruisers on either side? Don had always drilled him to be on the lookout for unexpected escape opportunities if his safety was ever compromised. Maybe, if he could break free—could he possibly outrun them?

Who was he kidding? The Hulk and Bruce Lee could track him through any back alley in Chinatown. There was nowhere to run, nowhere he could hide that they wouldn't know about.

What a picture they must make, two mismatched thugs escorting him down Grant Street's steep hill to a storefront doorway that just happened to be big enough for the three of them. It faced the fantastically carved gateway into Chinatown, arched in red and gold splendor. In stark contrast, plastic replicas of the Golden Gate Bridge, fake jade necklaces, and low-quality silk shirts filled the nearby window display, all priced absurdly high.

Eric pretended to be interested in the wares but used the glass reflection to study the street behind him. The ever-changing streetlight spit out waves of tourists. No one looked familiar. No cop he could flag down, either. His vision began to blur with worry. Was Lynn safe? Was Don protecting her?

The Hulk grinned and nudged Bruce Lee, spouting off a staccato of Chinese syllables. Bruce actually laughed out loud. Curious, Eric turned toward the street to follow their gaze.

A young woman—probably a tourist—was prancing around on the other side of the street. She wore a black micro-mini that set off her long legs to perfection. A hot-pink, cropped tee barely covered her ample breasts—and their very pointed nipples. Adding to this spectacle was the slightly darker, pink hair that cascaded down her back—so long it actually caught between her thighs as she walked. Swinging from her shoulder was a macramé, hemp purse.

Eric couldn't tell if it was the four-inch heels causing her to sway on the uneven pavement or the probability that she was stoned from a liberal sampling of San Francisco's other tourist crop–readily available pot from the medical marijuana clubs that anchored almost every block. Or maybe it was those outlandish, oversized sunglasses. They had to be more a hindrance than any help in the fog-drowned, hilly streets. Instead of blocking the sun, they probably hid her red-rimmed eyes.

Eric shook his head. What some women wouldn't do to get attention. But, boy did it work.

• • • • • •

Brakes squealed in Lynn's ears. She shuddered. Two cars were jockeying for position, pushing through the crowded intersection. Expectant spectators turned away with twisted disappointment when the cars roared away, undamaged.

Lynn filled her lungs with the damp air and held her breath for a measure of composure. She peered through the silly sunglasses, searching for any sign of Eric and his kidnappers. Don warned her they would remain hidden until they saw a woman who looked like Lynn. She had to keep her pace slow and deliberate.

Cold wind whipped through her clothes, making her shiver in spite of all the adrenaline coursing through her veins, and the embarrassment warming her face. Her nipples were so hard, they protruded through the thin cloth of the ridiculously tiny T-shirt, but there was no remedy for that. Don had insisted she look the part. Tourists wandered around San Francisco without coats all the time, unaware this California city rarely enjoyed beach weather–and froze in the fog instead.

She traced her exposed stomach scars with trembling fingers. A car gunned its engine to ascend the steep hill, and she pushed the nervous shudders aside. She didn't have time to deal with her old phobias. Not and still pull off this stunt for Eric's sake.

There! A block ahead, Lynn glimpsed a tall white man wedged between two Chinese men, guarding him like sentinels.

One of them looked right at her and grinned, motioning to his buddy and nodding in her direction. She froze, not daring even a breath. His partner in crime enjoyed a blatant once-over of her curves and laughed before turning back to stare into the crowd.

Lynn took a deep breath and climbed off the sidewalk, headed right toward them. After two steps, she stopped and swayed, as if she battled dizziness. Then, she placed her hand on her forehead, to drive the point home.

Without an obvious check of the traffic, she teetered across the street, teeth clenched, dodging oncoming cars and ignoring blaring horns. She sauntered up the hill, seemingly detached from her surroundings, stopping at every store window along the way and leaning against them in a perilous charade to keep her balance.

As she drew closer, she recognized Eric. His captors continued to scan the crowds in all directions. Looking for someone. Looking for her.

She flinched but kept on walking. No way fear would get the best of her now.

Don should be watching, ready to take advantage of any distraction she could cause. Thank God. Eric stood in an awkward position, as if he was favoring an injury. What had they done to him?

Lynn pushed the ugly picture from her mind. It wouldn't help her assignment. Only catching his captors' attention would.

With a vacant smile plastered on her face, Lynn paused at the window of the large souvenir shop, ignoring the men sheltered in its doorway. She leaned her forehead against the cold glass for a count of three, and then rolled her head toward the men without lifting it.

She widened her smile, praying all the while that her appearance was provocative and alluring. The larger of the two abductors seemed fixated on the enticing gap between her bare ribs and peek-a-boo shirt. It was the perfect invitation to sidle up to him and toy with the devil.

"Hi." She threw her voice as low and throaty as she could, extending her right hand.

Don was right—he didn't offer to shake it. She continued the forward motion, letting her body drift and melt into his chest. She brushed her bra-less breasts across a muscled arm, and giggled.

"Oops! Sorry." She grabbed onto his shoulder to keep her balance.

She turned her head to encompass both Eric and the other man with her smile, praying Eric would recognize her and know he had help on the way. "I'm looking for Chinatown. Can you give me directions?"

The wiry abductor snatched her hand from his partner's shoulder and gave him a glare, as if to remind him to keep his mind on business—no matter how alluring the distraction.

Unfazed, Lynn doubled down with an inviting smile and boldly reached for him instead. He swore and stepped back. Her body tilted toward Eric. Quick as a wick, the wiry one stepped in between them. He absorbed all her weight with a grunt, grabbed her elbows and stood her upright—a mere twelve inches from Eric. She kept her eyes riveted on Eric's face.

Come on. Come on. Look at me!

Eric drew a sharp breath and narrowed his eyes.

Yes! Eric recognized her!

Lynn gave them all a genuine smile and an awkward shrug of apology. Her purse slipped down her arm, pulling at her short sleeve to conveniently expose an enticing shoulder. "Sorry, cutie pies. This San Fran shit...is really...really good."

She wiggled her fingers in their faces and turned up the street, pausing to adjust her shirt strap. Bracing for the grand finale, she flung her hair back in a dramatic gesture, took four steps forward and stumbled, dropping her hemp bag in the process. It fell just out of reach. She bent at the waist, faking an inadequate grab and kept her legs straight. Her short skirt rose, as planned. She started counting seconds.

One. Anyone looking would see she was wearing absolutely nothing underneath.

Two. Lynn's cheeks burned from this compromising position, but she stayed in character, focused on fumbling for the silly bag.

Three. She was determined to follow Don's orders. He had assured her that no man would be able to resist the explicit shot she was giving—better than porn was how he described it.

Four. Peeking through her spread legs, she saw the larger of the two men finally step toward her. And Don, as he slipped through the door of the shop.

Five. Don grabbed the wiry one from behind and gave his throat a silent, lethal squeeze.

Six. Lynn miraculously maintained her unbalanced pose, swaying and now patting the sidewalk in front of her, with slow, stoned deliberation.

Seven. Her fingers finally found and grabbed her purse strap.

Eight. The large kidnapper stopped behind her, his gaze riveted by her bare flesh.

Nine. She sensed a hesitation in the constant movement of foot and car traffic, as if her erotic display mesmerized more than just Eric's captor.

Ten. The thug sagged unconscious into Don's arms.

She fell forward to her knees with a soft cry. Thrusting her hand behind her, she waggled it as if searching for help.

On cue, the kidnapper slipped his strong arm around her waist and slide his hand under her shirt, squeezing her chilled breast and hardened nipple as he drew her to her feet.

Lynn locked eyes with him over her shoulder. In her periphery, she could make out Don dragging his accomplice into the shop and pointing Eric toward the back exit. She needed to give Don just a little more time to spirit Eric to safety.

"It must be the altitude of these hills that got to me," she said, injecting breathiness into her husky voice. She didn't dare crack a real smile at the foolishness. Don had warned her: constant reassurance that she wasn't a threat would be the only way to protect herself.

Fighting all her common sense, she snuggled against him, and wiggled her butt into his crotch. He responded with an erection; it twitched and grew. Lynn shrugged her shoulder lightly, making the opposite shirt sleeve slip, revealing almost all of her ample bosom.

"You deserve a proper thanks." She twined her arms around his neck with a flowing twist, rubbing her breasts and crotch into his body until she felt his arousal thrust determinedly toward her soft flesh.

Harder than hell to run after Eric in that condition, Don had told her. Pun intended.

Bestowing a quick kiss on his cheek, along with a brilliant smile, she released his neck and sauntered up the hill. She ignored the hooting and catcalls from other men in the crowd, as well as the muttered curses and rapid footsteps behind her. The kidnapper must have discovered Eric and his partner were gone.

Lynn reached the first cross street and turned right at a leisurely pace. Quickly, she leaned down to remove her shoes and ran toward the garage where Don would be waiting.

The rumbling of an engine filled the cavernous darkness. She spotted the black SUV, and Don at the wheel. She frowned. Where was Eric? The back door inched open and a hand reached out to pull her forward, onto the floor. She landed with a grunt onto Eric's body. She threw her arms around him and gave a soft cry of victory.

"Nice floor show." Don threw the car into gear and peeled out of the garage, blasting his horn. "Ever consider a career in Vegas as an exhibitionist?"

Lynn blushed. "You promised you wouldn't look!"

Both Don and Eric burst out laughing.

"Sweetheart, the whole point was to make men look." Eric clasped her tightly. "Hell, I was so mesmerized I fought Don to let me stay there and watch." His fingers drifted along her bare back and under the short shirt, straying along the side of her breasts.

She shivered at the contrast of his hot wandering hand against her cool skin. Maybe she really was an exhibitionist at heart. For all she knew, Don could see Eric's exploring hands in the rearview mirror.

"You're safe, and that's all that matters," she said, injecting a bit of primness in her voice. "Oh, really, who cares who saw?" She chuckled. "If it freed you, it was worth it."

Eric tucked her head under his chin. "Thank you," he murmured. "I'm overwhelmed that you managed to walk into all that traffic without panicking."

"I'd do it again to keep you safe." Lynn cupped his cheek in her hand, pressing her body even closer, despite the awkward confines. "Are you all right?"

"Just bruises and bumps. You're the one in danger now." Eric's voice resonated with deep regret. "You'll only be safe when we find out exactly who's behind this, and what they intend to do with your proxy."

Lynn sensed the SUV finally hit freeway speed. Don was weaving in and out of lanes. She relaxed for the first time that day. Eric was safe. The SDS IPO was still on track. And he and Don would protect her. What else could she ask for?

"All clear," Don announced. Eric lifted Lynn up and onto the back seat. He untangled his limbs and followed her up with a soft groan.

"Head to the offices of Silicon Valley Capital," Eric instructed Don. "They're just off the Sand Hill Road exit. I'm calling an emergency board meeting, and that's as secure a location as any. Can I use your phone, Don, to let Rajiv know I'm safe? Apparently my kidnappers kept mine."

Don tossed his over the seat, meeting Eric's grim glance in the mirror. "When you're done, I'll call my buddies from the FBI."

"Agreed," said Eric. "Time to call in the cavalry."

Chapter 49

Joshua toyed with his microwave dinner as it cooled into a congealed mess in his lap. He stared distractedly at the muted talking heads on his favorite twenty-four-hour business show. Why hadn't he heard from Kay? Just thinking about the extreme measures she was using against Eric made gurgling pools of acid churn his stomach.

His preferred method was learned at the knees of Wall Street millionaires—in back-door discussions that would lead to handshake deals lining the pockets of all the players involved. Kay's method seemed so heavy-handed, utterly lacking finesse and subtlety. The exact opposite, in fact—mindless brute power.

The phone's loud ring made him jump. He grabbed it. "What?"

"We have the beneficiary's identity," Kay announced.

"That's just great." Joshua raised his voice. "Do you expect to hold onto Eric indefinitely? That no one will notice he's missing at the road show?"

"Actually, Eric is free. Our attention is focused solely on getting the signed proxy."

The antique clock filled the long silence. Tick-tock. Tick-tock.

"From who?" Joshua couldn't believe he had to drag this out of Kay. They were supposed to be on the same side.

"Believe it or not, Lynn Baker. Apparently Eric and she were friendly years ago."

Joshua tilted his head, considering his brief meeting with Lynn. "She's no pushover. She'll fight like a tiger if she believes she's making the right decision. Do you have anything to hold over her head?"

"Of course I do, Joshy. Have you ever known me to be helpless, babe?"

"I wouldn't be feeling so smug right now, Kay," he retorted. "We still don't have her proxy. You failed." He rubbed his forehead, reviewing his backup plan. It was the only lesson from his father that he followed religiously. If this fiasco spooked the private buyers, at least he would still have the legitimate IPO money in his pocket. Disappointing, but not the end of the world.

"I didn't fail! We got the name of the beneficiary." A defensive whine colored her usual dulcet tones. "The proxy is next, and I've got a contact who will help. We'll get it in a few hours."

"Yeah, right. And I've got a bridge for sale. Listen to me, 'babe,'" he laid the sarcasm on thick. "I've got phone calls to make. Any delay lies at your feet, not mine, and I'm going to make that crystal clear to all the parties. Get your act together on this, or your pretty little ass is grass."

"Joshua–"

. . . . . .

Her phone went dead. Not a good sign from your business partner.

Kay paced her office, putting off making the next, critical call. She had to nail down details of her plan to regain the confidence of the

Maoists. Joshua was right–she'd fallen short by losing both Eric and Lynn without gaining her signature.

But she wouldn't disappoint again. She needed to control Lynn's vote for her plan to work. Her assignment was clear–don't let the Chinese military get their hands on SDS technology. She had recognized the vultures hovering at the analyst meeting, not even bothering to take notes, only assessing Eric and the strength of opinions from the others. Joshua could finagle an end-around in a heartbeat with their support.

But Charlie could help her with Lynn. It was time for the tired, old groveling act.

She settled into her desk chair and took three deep, cleansing breaths. She tried to replay the last time they had sex, feel the sensual bonding and the thrill of exploration. The excitement of pushing someone's boundaries–and the feeling of victory the moment they yield.

Yes, that should work. Convince him her brush-off was a dominatrix act, the injection of a new element into their sex life. He would buy that. He may even enjoy the submissive role. After she'd exhaust him, he would do whatever she asked. He had zero love for Lynn, but an insatiable appetite for sex or money. Kay had plenty of currency to buy Charlie.

With a sigh of relief, she stretched her neck muscles and willed herself into the persona that could sizzle a phone line with erotic tension. It always worked before. It had to work this time.

"Charlie?" she purred when he answered. "I need you so badly tonight. I'm already soaking wet. Come over later."

"What game are you playing, Kay?"

"Oh, Charlie. You know I get all tense and jittery when things aren't going well at work. I just needed to be in control for a while, feel the rush of power again. But a great fuck just might take care of it. And you're the best there is, babe."

Only silence met her best seductive voice.

"I'll make it worth your while. I want to tap into your darker passions tonight." She dropped her voice to a whisper. "You can be my sex slave–or I can be yours."

"Oh, yeah? You'll do whatever I ask?"

"If that's what you want. It'll be as good as you want it to be. I promise. Please come over. I need it bad."

"Okay, babe. I've got a meeting first, so I can't be there until around nine. But you'd better be so hot and bothered by the time I get there that we don't even make it to the bed."

"Whatever you say, lover. Whatever you say..." For one last time, that is.

Chapter 50

Lynn dug in her four-inch heels. "I refuse to walk into the hallowed halls of the venture capital business community looking like a streetwalker."

Eric understood–her stomach scars blazed away for the whole world to see. "Don, help me out here. Don't you have something in the car Lynn can wear?"

During the drive, Eric updated Lynn with all the details. His board of directors had never been the most cooperative but, recently, they seemed to be blatantly following their own agenda. He had only turned to venture capitalists once in the past, and that was to buy out DARPA's position in SDS. He'd spent hours juggling their financial interests against his broader goals–not an easy task.

Perhaps the extra fillip of Baxter seeing the effects of his abduction might give Eric the edge he needed for their full cooperation, and maybe for the last time. Dried blood and bruises usually made quite a visual impact on the naive.

Burying his head deep into the SUV storage space, Eric swore under his breath. How could Lynn worry about her silly professional image at a time like this? He flipped over a stack of old newspapers. Don dug through a pile of rags. Damn it, didn't she realize the clock was ticking on her physical safety?

"How about this?" Don took a whiff of the sweatshirt and grimaced.

Wrinkling her nose and scowling at its oil stains and dirt streaks, Lynn tugged it over her head. It covered an inch more of her legs than her skirt, but it seemed to comfort her. She yanked the garish wig off her head to shake out her white mane and finger comb the worst of the tangles.

Eric grabbed her hand and pulled her through the glass doors of the soaring building nestled in a grove of eucalyptus trees. The money behind Silicon Valley's technology started here, in this little enclave of buildings that loom over Stanford University. Billions of dollars poured in and out of the hands of a speculative few, those who invested in tiny companies with the hope of spectacular returns when the rest of the public finally discovered them too–but by that time, for steep premiums.

The elderly receptionist took pause while putting a cover over her computer. "May I help you?" she asked, her eyes flicking to each of them.

"Is Peter Baxter still here?" Eric asked, glancing at his watch.

"I believe he is. Your name, please?"

"Eric Coleman. It's an emergency."

The receptionist's eyes grew wide behind her glasses. She turned away and punched buttons into the phone. Eric smiled to himself as he realized it was usually harried bankers in three-piece suits who tried to create an edge of urgency; not a start-up press favorite who looked rumpled, decidedly grumpy, and had a floozy as part of his entourage.

"Mr. Baxter says you can go right in," she invited, pointing to the corridor. "Do you know your way?"

"Sure do. Thanks." Eric headed toward the inner lobby door and into the hushed environment of rich wood paneling, vaulted ceilings, and early evening light filtering through skylights to the farthest office.

Rapping first, Eric pushed open the door and stepped back to let Lynn precede him. A startled expression crossed Baxter's face as he took in her appearance. At Eric's noticeable limp, his eyes opened even further. He re-settled his suit jacket onto the back of his chair.

"Eric, what's going on?" Baxter grouched. "My day started before dawn, and frankly I was looking forward to a stiff drink and dinner."

"I was kidnapped this morning because of an issue related to SDS. We need an emergency board meeting before more people are put in danger." Eric sank into one of the leather chairs at the small conference table with a sigh, motioning his companions to do the same.

Baxter rounded his desk and stopped in front of Eric, taking in his weary expression and torn clothes. "Oh, my God. Kidnapped! Are you all right? Do you need a doctor?"

"I'm not that badly hurt, just a little beat up. I'm serious, Peter, we need to get the other board members on the phone right now. I can't guarantee privacy at the SDS offices, so we came straight here after these two freed me."

Eric slapped his hand against his forehead. "I'm sorry, that was so rude. Peter, this is Lynn Baker, an old friend and currently the PR consultant for SDS. Lynn, Peter Baxter, the chairman of SDS' board of directors."

"How do you do." Lynn flushed, offering her hand. "I, um, I usually don't look like this. We took rather drastic measures to get Eric free."

"I'm pleased to meet you, Lynn. Don't worry about it." Baxter smiled at her, and then stole a glimpse of her bare legs tucked under the gleaming table. Averting his face, he winked at Eric.

"And you've heard of my old friend, Don Salazar, my DARPA advisor before SDS was even founded. He masterminded my escape." Eric clapped Don's shoulder, gratitude and pride filling him at his friend's daring.

"Mr. Baxter." Don rose and shook hands, seeming uncomfortable in this high-class business environment. Eric had felt like that his first visit, too. The sheer wealth created here every day overwhelmed even the most sophisticated players.

"I'm sure you'll only want to tell the story once," Baxter said. "Let me start my assistant on calling the other board members." He left the room at a fast clip.

"I need to text Rajiv and let him know he may be involved in the conference call, too. I hope he understands what I'm asking him to vote for." Eric paused. "Don, Rajiv may have questions. If he calls while I'm tied up, will you fill him in?"

Don's eyebrows shot to his hairline. "I'll give him the facts, but anything about a vote he'll want to run by you first."

"Just convince him to trust me one last time." Eric scrubbed his face, heavy weariness slowing his motions. "Then call your friends and have them meet us later."

Eric pinned Lynn with his gaze. "You, too. You may need to vote your shares. Are you ready?"

Lynn squeezed his hand. "As ready as I'll ever be."

Chapter 51

"Everyone is on the line except Simon, who is on his way to Beijing," Baxter announced.

Simon Hays, their newest board member, ran the international investments arm of Silicon Valley Ventures. He often missed meetings with his grueling travel schedule, but they had a quorum if only one board member was absent. It would have to do.

Eric spoke into the triangular contraption placed in the middle of the table. He introduced Don and Lynn to the disembodied board members before turning the meeting over to Don to explain what happened, trusting he'd omit Lynn's name as the beneficiary.

Allan Fleming, the founding partner of Vision Star Ventures, spoke first. "Are you sure you're all right, Eric? That was a traumatic experience to go through. Shouldn't we inform the press?" Eric suspected Fleming purposely created media hype about his high-profile technology companies before bringing them public. The more hype surrounding the IPO, the more press and future business his firm got. For once Eric was grateful for Fleming's flamboyant strategies.

"I'm fine, really," Eric reiterated. "You're correct–we need to take the offensive here. Private parties may be interested in buying SDS outright, but gaining control through a coerced proxy is illegal. We need to go public with all of this so whoever it is can't get away with stalking us in the shadows."

Murmurs of agreement floated over the speakerphone. Baxter's assistant crept in the room and whispered in Eric's ear Rajiv was on the phone. Eric motioned Don to follow the assistant out, turning back to Baxter.

"Ms. Baker will put out one press release announcing the complete fix of the bug, and another announcing there are private interests pursuing SDS at this time," he announced. "While the bug fix is good news, the possibility of an outside purchaser will delay the IPO indefinitely."

Chaotic shouts erupted from the little gray box.

"Out of the question! We need the IPO cash to promote our next fund."

"Peter! What's going on there? Private buyers? They'll negotiate us to death."

"What the hell are you thinking, Coleman? This is our money, not yours."

"Over my dead body. The IPO should be wildly successful on the first day."

Interesting. Not one person asked about the proxy. Maybe he was wrong one of them was behind the kidnapping. Keeping his cool, he took a deep breath and fired back.

Yes, he had met potential buyers when he was in New York. Joshua Stein was handling at least one of them personally.

No, he didn't know what their ultimate plans were with the SDS technology. After all, if they were a private company, it was their business what they did with it after they bought it, right?

Yes, the potential buyers were Chinese, but he wasn't sure whether they represented the government directly or a newly formed private enterprise.

No, he believed the bug's existence was unrelated to the kidnapping, since Rajiv had determined it had been there for many years, prior to SDS ever dreaming of going public. Nevertheless, Don would be following up with the authorities to uncover any possible ties.

Don snuck back into the room and gave Eric the thumbs-up. Eric sighed in relief. Somehow, Don had finagled Rajiv's support. However Don got it, Eric would take it.

Eric listened as a vociferous consensus developed to decline all private offers and proceed with the IPO as planned. Time to switch to Plan B.

"Gentlemen, let's take a vote," Eric interrupted. "I move to consider private offers. Will someone second that motion?"

No one spoke up. Baxter glared at Eric.

"Then let's ask the other shareholders to see if they agree." Eric suggested. He bet Baxter regretted pulling the board meeting together so quickly. Eric winced and rubbed his ribs in an exaggerated motion, catching Baxter's eye. "Peter, will you second my motion to hold a shareholder's meeting right now?"

Baxter caved. His worried eyes scanned Eric's awkward posture, shaking his head as if still in disbelief over the kidnapping. "Gentlemen, I think Eric has a far greater appreciation for the danger he may still be in. I second the motion to hold an emergency shareholder meeting. Does everyone agree?"

Angry mutters of assent floated over the speakerphone.

"Let's get Rajiv on the phone." Baxter motioned to his assistant.

Rajiv joined the call and greeted the others in a polite enough tone, but Eric detected the irritation in his partner's voice. No surprise there.

Eric rapped his knuckles on the table. "99% of all shareholders are now represented for a vote. Rajiv, to fill you in, I am waiting for someone to second my motion to allow consideration of an offer from a private firm to buy SDS, possibly prior to the IPO. Apparently, the board doesn't even wish to discuss any such offer. I chalk it up to their anger at the unusual events this past week."

Would any of them dispute his implications and admit that pushing the IPO forward would be against the best interest of all the shareholders? He smiled in satisfaction at the silence. He'd read their personalities correctly. They'd rather have a convenient excuse for pursuing the IPO than admit their egos were tied up with the prestige of Wall Street success.

Rajiv cleared his throat. "I second your motion, Eric."

"Thank you, Rajiv. I vote to consider all offers, up to and including an IPO," Eric announced. "Rajiv, how do you vote?"

One second. Two. Three. Sweat broke out on his brow. Finally, Rajiv's strained voice filled the silence. "I agree with you, Eric. We should at least consider all offers, even if it means not going public."

Eric nodded, tallying the rest of the board members. They voted in a block, racking up 47% of the shares versus 45% of those belonging to Eric and Rajiv.

Baxter rose and strode behind Eric, placing his hands on Eric's shoulders and giving them one hard squeeze. "Eric, I know these are extraordinary circumstances. Nevertheless, I'll remind you that the board revoked all proxy votes at the last meeting, since you were not forthcoming about the Trust beneficiary. You can't vote on its behalf until you disclose that information. Obviously, we're not the only ones who appreciate its importance."

Eric smiled in satisfaction. "Lynn Baker is the beneficiary of the Coleman Trust, and can vote her shares directly for the first time. Lynn, how do you vote?"

"Wait a minute!" Baxter pressed a restraining hand on Lynn's arm and leaned right into her face. "Ms. Baker, have you considered the consequences of not following through on the IPO? The chances of a private offer being anywhere near the amount of money you can make publicly is highly unlikely."

Eric shifted and watched Lynn's reaction.

Her glance flickered between him and Baxter. "Um…Mr. Baxter… gentlemen…I confess I only recently discovered Eric made me the beneficiary. If there's something you think I should know before voting—"

"I'll be happy to buy your shares immediately at a premium to today's valuation, Ms. Baker." Trust Fleming to jump in and make waves. "A verbal contract in front of witnesses is all I need to relieve you of the responsibility of this vote. And the money could be in your bank account tomorrow."

Lynn threw Eric a troubled glance, then shook off Baxter's hand. "Thank you, Sir, but I take my responsibility as a shareholder very seriously. Also, I'm not convinced a verbal agreement tonight would be legal." She dug into her hemp purse and unearthed a crumpled business card. She waved it under Baxter's nose. "I'll leave my contact information with Mr. Baxter, if anyone would like to discuss other options."

Unsettled, Eric tapped his foot furiously under the table and sat on his hands. He wanted to wring Baxter's neck for introducing an alternative for Lynn. Up until then, she would have voted with him, no matter what. Now, he wasn't certain at all. And he couldn't afford her defection. It involved more than just his emotions. His whole life was at stake.

Lynn leaned back in her chair and tapped a pen on the pad in front of her. She pressed her lips together, closed her eyes, and took three deep breaths. An anxious silence filled the conference room.

"I vote with you, Eric." Her husky voice carried too much uncertainty. Could she tell he'd maneuvered the board to go along with his plan? Did she really trust him, or was the reality of potential IPO riches finally turning her against him? "Let's bring all offers to the table and give them full consideration."

Resigned grumbles greeted her announcement. Baxter took his cue to conclude the impromptu meeting, signing off with a promise to keep the members informed. One by one, the callers disconnected, after some canned niceties. Reminding Eric to drop by the office, Rajiv hung up too. Baxter then escorted the three to the now-dark parking lot before making a beeline to his sporty Tesla. He rolled off silently, with a casual farewell wave.

The trio crawled into Don's SUV. Eric wasn't done with his plan. He twisted around in the front seat to peer at Lynn behind him. "I need another favor. A big one."

"What is it?"

He glanced at Don and back again at her. "I need you to put out a press release saying the bug hasn't been fixed, even though you just heard the opposite. When the shit hits the fan, you may have to take the fall. Can you do that?"

Lynn's jaw dropped.

He held her stricken gaze. She might sacrifice absolutely everything with that release. Her company's future. Her own security. Her professional reputation in Silicon Valley. She would never be able to make a living in this town again. The financial backers were even more ruthless toward non-performers than the engineering community. They would never forgive such deception or ineptness. Nor would they ever forget.

Was she ready for that?

Was he? While she may agree, as a paid consultant, she may never be able to forgive him for putting her in this situation.

"You're the client, Eric. Whatever you say goes." She reached around the seat and grabbed his right hand. She'll trust him. One last time.

The tight grasp of her fingers told him all he needed. Their safety was more important than any business. What was the worth of a good reputation if she were dead?

He prayed it would work out the way he had planned. There were other forces in motion that he knew she didn't understand. How could she? Hopefully, he could tell her the truth. Soon.

Chapter 52

Rajiv's face peeked through the blinds of the lobby as they roared into the parking lot, empty except for his gold Mercedes. Eric glanced at his watch–nearly eight o'clock and the evening was far from over. He crawled from the car, biting back a groan, and assisted Lynn down. They joined Don up the short walkway.

Rajiv opened the door and threw his arms around Eric in a brief hug. "Tell me everything." His expression anxious, Rajiv led them toward Eric's office. He paused by the coffee pot just as it finished its drip cycle.

Grateful that Rajiv remembered his caffeine addiction, Eric poured a mugful and turned to Don and Lynn. "I need to talk to Rajiv alone. You know what to do. How about you give us a half-hour, and then we can get out of here?" They both nodded and headed in opposite directions.

Rajiv followed Eric into his office and dropped into one of the armchairs, seemingly shell-shocked by Eric's battered appearance. As hard as he tried to be stoic, Eric winced in pain as he lowered himself gingerly into the leather chair, settling back with a forced stiffness.

"Let's bring each other up to speed." Eric chronicled his eventful day and, in turn, Rajiv detailed what he had done to entrap Wilkins and fix the bug. Eric breathed a sigh of relief that the damned bug would no longer be a threat to SDS.

"Good work," Eric complimented, running a hand over his face. "You make one hell of a chief technologist, you know that?"

"Thank you very much. Now would you mind telling me what was really behind that conference call?" Rajiv's voice shook with anger. "You have some nerve having Don do your dirty work, asking for my blind trust! I was tempted to ask an embarrassing question or two in front of the board. What the hell is behind all this secrecy?"

Astonished by his profanity, Eric met Rajiv's fiery stare. Part of Rajiv's uncharacteristic anger was understandable, given the long hours of worried waiting. "I never meant to keep you in the dark. Things started moving fast and I couldn't take the time to sit down and discuss them all with you." Regret filled him fast. He should have made the time. Rajiv had earned his trust. "There really are more ways for us to get a return on our investment in SDS other than an IPO. I need the flexibility to explore all options."

Rajiv's eyes narrowed. "Going public has always been our goal–and my dream," he said. His clipped tone spoke volumes. "In truth, it was very difficult for me to vote the way you asked. I deserve an explanation."

Eric set his empty mug on the table. "I can see you're upset. But let me ask you a question," Eric drawled. "Why is the IPO so important to you? Honestly?"

"Because it is a tangible result I can show to my family to validate the choices I have made with my life," Rajiv answered, tugging on his ear. "You would not understand. You are not an immigrant. To me, the respect of my family is very important. My parents expect me to support the whole family since I am the eldest. And they never condoned my career choice."

Rajiv's bitter laugh bounced off the office walls. "Their idea of success was for me to become a dentist–to enjoy stable hours in my own building, routine check-ups and teeth cleanings my entire life. To earn an honorary doctor's title without having to deal with the ugly emergencies. Technology and engineering is still a foreign, risky concept to them. The only way I can shut them up is to have proof of my success."

Eric propped his feet on the glass table. "I understand more than you think. I've seen how hard you work. So let me break it down for you a bit. Is it only wealth you're after?"

"Well, no. That is a big part of it, but not the only part."

"Does your family really understand the difference between a public and a private company?"

Rajiv shook his head, a chagrined expression twisting his features. "No, even though I have tried many, many times to explain."

"So it's a powerful position that's really important. And enough income and stature for them to understand you are a success. Correct?"

"Yes, that is essentially it." Rajiv jerked upright, his voice insistent. "And an IPO would provide all of that for me."

"So would the right job with a respected company who bought your ownership position outright," Eric pointed out. "You could get paid right away, instead of having to wait six months to sell your SDS shares on the open market. Who knows what the market conditions might be after we go public? There could be another terrorist attack, war, an economic slump, or just bad karma in New York. That's another form of risk, merely for the image of going through a grueling IPO process. Personally, I prefer a simple buyout, all things considered."

Rajiv sat silent, crossing and uncrossing his arms across his chest. "I see there are advantages to selling out without an IPO. As long as we get a good price. And I get a bump in pay and title," he added. "That is important to me."

Eric extended his hand toward Rajiv. "It's a deal. I won't consider any offer unless your needs are covered as part of the package. Agreed?"

Rajiv pumped Eric's hand. His face finally relaxed, making him look like he had years ago, when it was just the two of them, ready to take on the world with their engineering talents and vision. "Agreed.

I have always trusted you to make the right business decisions for the company. I will not start second-guessing you now. Only, please, keep me informed."

"No problem." Eric steeled his stiff legs under him and rose awkwardly to his feet. He draped his arm around Rajiv's shoulder, in a brotherly gesture. "Go home to your family. I bet they haven't seen much of you recently. I'll see you tomorrow–if I can make it to the office this time." He chuckled. "I think I'll get a ride in the morning. At least, that way, if I'm kidnapped again, I won't be alone."

Eric's black humor relieved only some of his tension. Thank God he'd been by himself this morning. He would have withstood any brutal beating from those thugs in order to protect Lynn, if they had tried to kidnap her too.

He hurried to Lynn's office as fast as his limp would allow. Papers were spitting out from her printer. She picked them up and handed them over with a wry smile. Leaning against the doorframe, he read the false press release, nodding with approval.

"You nailed it." He notched his thumb up. "Just enough information to keep them guessing about who the potential buyers are, yet apologetic enough that we still haven't fixed the bug. If this doesn't draw those cockroaches out of the woodwork to push us into negotiations while our back is supposedly against the wall, I don't know what will."

"Is that what this is all about? Flushing out the suitors?"

"In a way." He couldn't disclose too much to her yet. He needed Don's background information before he could proceed. "We need to find out who the buyers are, as well as what their motivation is to buy, before I know which offer is the best for all shareholders–if any."

Lynn opened her mouth as if to ask another question, and her desk phone rang. Glancing at the clock on the wall, her eyebrows rose.

"Who could be calling this late?" She reached for the phone. "This is Lynn Baker," she said in a cautious tone, tossing a wide-eyed glance at Eric. He didn't blame her for being nervous–it could be another threat.

A scowl crossed her face. "What do you want, Kip?" She pointed to the lobby. Eric walked through the hall and peered around the corner. Wilkins' shadow loomed against the locked outer entrance.

What the hell. Might as well deal with everything tonight.

He threw open the door. "Come on in, Wilkins."

Shoving his phone into his pocket, a charming smile graced Wilkins' expression.

"Coleman. Just the person I wanted to see. Has Lynn talked with you about our chat this morning?" His eyebrows lifted ever so slightly, as his controlled glance took in Eric's rumpled appearance.

Eric escorted him to his office, on high alert. He remembered Don's warning about Lynn's call to Wilkins. He had jettisoned his doubt about her links with the scumbag after she put her life on the line to save him from the kidnappers.

Now, a shadow of doubt was making a comeback.

As he passed Lynn's office, Eric motioned for her to follow them. Wilkins' eyes nearly popped out of his head when he took in Lynn's wild appearance. What would Wilkins think if he saw her without the sweatshirt, and with the pink wig, bending over for all of Chinatown to see? She had done all that to save his neck.

Or will Wilkins benefit from her actions too?

Eric settled into his desk chair and pointed to the two seats opposite. He needed distance until he understood what was going on between them.

"What can I do for you, Chas? Or is it Kip?" Eric challenged. "I seem to get it confused."

Even if Wilkins wasn't behind his kidnapping, his sabotage pissed him off, big time. He itched to pound that perfect profile under his fist. Instead, he clenched his hands and somehow managed a polite, professionally courteous expression. Better to find out everything he could from Wilkins before taking him apart.

"I know you're the man who really makes the decisions here, no matter what the board thinks," Wilkins said coolly. "So I'll lay my cards on the table. In order to keep me from tanking your IPO, you'll have to buy my silence about your software bug. I have no hesitation letting the world know you deliberately released your product with flaws, and compromised the world's financial markets, as well as military intelligence. That won't go over too well with your potential investors, will it?" Wilkins crossed his foot over his knee, appearing smug and confident he had the upper hand. Too confident.

Eric glanced at Lynn, cataloging her disgusted expression. "No, it wouldn't. What exactly do you want from me?"

Wilkins' eyes gleamed with greed. "I want you to write me a letter, right now, granting me half a million shares of SDS stock at the price of one dollar, with no conditions on when I can sell them. I know you have the authority to issue the grant, and the board will do whatever you say to protect the IPO. Even Rajiv jumps at your bidding."

Eric's mind raced. "At the price we're talking about going public, you'll pocket millions of dollars if you cash in right away. What makes you think you're worth that much?"

"If that's my take, you and Rajiv and your other investors will pocket ten times that, at least. My piece is just a tiny little expense to keep the IPO on track."

Eric studied him, keeping his expression blank despite his disgust. "And if I say no?"

Wilkins glanced at Lynn. "Lynn is quite an old friend of yours," he mocked. "I'll ruin her reputation if she can't convince you to play ball. She'll never work in PR again. Is that really what she deserves?"

Eric turned his stare to Lynn, his jaw clenched in an attempt to keep from responding to Wilkins' taunts. He didn't miss the blaze of anger turning her eyes into sparks of fire. There was no sadness or fear in her expression.

"Kip, I told you already I wouldn't help you in any way, and I meant it!" Lynn's voice shook. Her face flushed a deep red. "What is it about the word 'No' you don't understand?"

Eric forced himself to keep his butt firmly in the chair instead of sweeping her into his arms. Lynn was on his side, not Wilkins', despite being pulled in every direction since she came to SDS. Had it only been days ago? And he had just convinced her to destroy her reputation anyway, for his sake. How was he any different from Wilkins?

Regret swamped through him. She didn't know–yet–about the bigger picture. The sacrifices demanded from him all these years. Soon, she would understand that he never meant to harm her or her business–in any way. Somehow, he would have to make it up to her.

Right now, though, it was time to trap Wilkins in his own stupidity.

Eric grabbed a pad and pen. "I'm writing this here and now, and then you'll get out." He scrawled quickly, reading aloud as he wrote.

"Charles Wilkins is hereby granted 500,000 shares of SDS stock, for the price of $1.00, as payment for his work as a consultant. This grant will be effective on the date that SDS first begins trading in the public market. There will be no restrictions on his ownership or control of those shares as of that date, and he can dispose of them, when he sees fit, in the public marketplace. In return, these are the only shares that will be granted to Charles Wilkins as long as SDS exists."

A satisfied smirk settled on Wilkins' face. "Sign and date it, Coleman. I'll even make you a copy so you can jam it through at your next board meeting." He grabbed the paper after Eric swooped his signature on the bottom of the page, almost running to the photocopier humming outside of the office.

Lynn opened her mouth, but Eric raised a cautionary hand. Wilkins returned, throwing the duplicate on his desk. Eric grabbed his arm and yanked the jerk toward the lobby.

"Goodbye, Wilkins. You can be sure I'll tell Rajiv not to use your consulting services again. You've gotten your last dollar from us."

Wilkins' eyebrows lifted. "Oh, I wouldn't be so sure about that. You may be surprised when you might need me again in the future. Only then, I won't be so accommodating."

With a wave, he strode out the door, a victorious spring in his step.

Lynn joined Eric to watch him roar off. She slipped her arm gently around his waist. "I'm so sorry. That money has to come out of someone's pocket, and it will probably be yours."

Eric laughed, returning the hug and enjoying her warm body pressed snugly into his. "Your ex just walked out of here with a worthless piece of paper. It doesn't cover any contingency for us not going public, which at this point looks likely. I don't have to present it to my board unless that happens."

Lynn leaned back in his arms, blinking. "I didn't even catch that. How could he have been so careless? He must have been planning this for years."

"Most of his information came through Rajiv, and Rajiv believed an IPO was the only way for SDS to move forward. Wilkins assumed we were all as single-minded. He got caught up in Silicon Valley fever, that's all." He chuckled. "I'd like to see his face in the morning when he gets a look at your press releases. He'll be one unhappy camper."

Lynn shuddered. "That's putting it mildly. He has a terrible temper when he doesn't get his way. So look out–he may do all the things he's been threatening as soon as tomorrow."

"I can take care of Wilkins," he said. "Now let's get those releases out the door and go home. I don't know about you, but I'm bushed. And Don has more on the agenda this evening."

Chapter 53

Eric sprawled on the couch wearing his favorite sweatpants and an oversized T-shirt. Taking a long sniff, he sipped his favorite Kentucky bourbon, rolling it on his tongue before swallowing.

His body throbbed and ached in too many places to count. After he showered, the bathroom mirror confirmed his suspicions. Splotches of red turning to purple decorated his ribs, front and back, but he poked himself enough to verify there was no serious damage.

Still, he appreciated the slight dulling of his senses from the bourbon. When the FBI agents arrived, it promised to be a long night.

"While Lynn's cleaning up, tell me." Don leaned forward in the recliner, his voice low. "Did Rajiv agree to our plan?"

"Essentially, yes." Eric took another swallow, relishing the heated burn coursing down his throat and into his veins. "He finally realized his dream might not be as attractive in the light of day as it is at night. He's agreed to follow my lead as long as I take into consideration what he's been working for all these years. That seemed fair. We shook on it. Case closed."

Don's lips twitched. "I doubt it was that cut and dried, but I trust you have it handled." He paused, tapping his fingertips together. "I respect how you kept Rajiv focused on his role over the years. If you can manage his expectations, even in the midst of all this, you're a better leader than I realized." He raised his hand in a half-salute.

Surprised, Eric grunted his thanks. His friend didn't dish out compliments that readily. Eric had learned early to take his gruff feedback as a matter of course.

Now he craved a softer response to his intimate thoughts, to the baring of his soul. Lynn's compassionate eyes flashed into his mind. Was her loyalty to him great enough to warrant sharing his deepest secret?

Fred gave out a whine, and then he nudged Eric's hand before he gave it a loving lick. His soulful brown eyes flickered over Eric's prone body, as if sensing his distress. The mutt crowded close. Eric dropped his hand to stroke Fred's ears in an effort to comfort him. So great was the dog's instinct, he wasn't gamboling for Don's attention tonight. A man's best friend, when it counted.

The three of them sat in companionable silence, the men chomping on Don's thrown-together sandwiches. Eric listened to the quiet symphony of muffled sounds in a distant room, as Lynn took her turn getting back to normal. As soon as he heard her footsteps, he twisted his head and stared down the hall. She had changed into her own understated outfit—a dark pair of pants, white socks, a modest, yellow, cotton top, and hair piled carelessly into a top knot. The contrast from her previous outfit was too much.

He grinned at Don. "Hey, who's the stranger? Didn't we bring someone else home for tonight's fun and games?"

"Ha, ha, ha," Lynn said, tucking her head down with a brief smile. She lifted a sandwich onto a napkin. Was she embarrassed in front of Don? Eric prayed she would get over it. She would see a lot of Don in the future.

He hoped.

Eric eased his feet down, making room for her on the couch, and she plopped next to him, taking a huge bite of the sandwich.

"Look who's talking. You look like an old man, wincing every time you move," she mumbled, catching a crumb with her tongue. "If it hadn't been for me, you'd be in a lot worse shape. Just remember that."

Eric tucked her under his arm. "I do, every second." He dropped a kiss onto the top of her head and kept his face there for long seconds. An intense feeling of rightness washed through him.

The doorbell's melodic chimes broke the silence.

Don and Fred rose simultaneously and soon returned with two middle-aged men, dressed in somber suits, and each carrying a small briefcase. They paused in front of the couch with stern expressions on their faces.

With a chagrined look and tone, Eric waved his arm in a sweeping motion. "Gentlemen, welcome to my home. Please excuse me for not getting up, but my body went through hell today, and it doesn't want to move." He smiled down at Lynn. "Of course, it likes very much where it's sitting. Maybe that has more to do with it." He extended his hand. "Eric Coleman. This is Lynn Baker."

"How do you do Mr. Coleman, Ms. Baker," the first responded, his green eyes twinkling. His sparse frame bent into an L-shape to shake first Eric's and then Lynn's hand. "Special Agent Pete MacClaren here. This is Special Agent Emilio Chaboya."

Chaboya extended his hand. Shorter than MacClaren, with a mixture of muscle and slight flabbiness, he looked as if he spent most of his time parked behind a desk. His alert eyes glistened with intelligence and scrutinized them during the introductions. He momentarily relaxed his facial muscles to emulate a smile, and turned toward Don.

"We need to be briefed in detail, Don. Is there anyone else who should be here before we begin?"

Don hesitated. "There is another person who knows more about one of the issues, SDS' Chief Technology Officer Rajiv Ghosh. But he's not privy to the rest, and Eric wants it that way."

MacClaren gave a polite cough. "Frankly, we were expecting only to speak with you and Mr. Coleman. Meaning no disrespect, Ms. Baker, but could we continue this conversation in private?"

Lynn shifted to her feet. Eric pulled her back into his embrace, tossing a challenging glare at the agents. "Please, call us Eric and Lynn. Lynn's life was threatened. She has more right than most to hear your assessment. Besides, there's nothing to hide from her. Not anymore."

A soft blush flooded Lynn's cheeks. She snuggled into the couch, brushing her thigh with his. He pushed back just enough so she would know he accepted her silent gratitude.

Don motioned to the loveseat, settling into the recliner. "Please sit. Let's get started." Fred made three turns and settled at Don's feet.

Don detailed the chain of events in chronological order, starting with Wilkins' earliest involvement in planting the bug, through Lynn's overheard conversation at the hotel, and adding in the escalating dangers–the break-in of her hotel room, the threatening emails and, ultimately, Eric's kidnapping. The agents jotted frequent notes, only interrupting for a quick clarification.

Don had wrapped up his chronology when they arrived at SDS earlier. He turned to Eric. "Why don't you fill these guys in on what happened with Wilkins this evening?"

"Actually, Lynn knows more about that than I do," Eric replied, facing her. "You haven't told me exactly what happened between you two this morning."

Lynn twisted her fingers together in what Eric was starting to learn signaled her nervous tell. She took a deep breath and glanced at each of the four men in turn.

"He threatened to ruin my company if I didn't convince Eric to cooperate," she disclosed. "He claimed that whenever he referred business to me, he was actually using me either to cover his own mistakes or set me up to take the blame for his future actions. If he was ever caught, he planned on using me as a scapegoat." She shrugged. "Call me stupid, but I didn't realize what was happening at the time."

Eric jerked upright, ignoring the shooting pain up his back. "That asshole!"

Fred whined, padding over to plop down in front of the couch again, nudging Eric's hand with his cold nose.

"Calm down, Eric," Lynn soothed. "I know what kind of jerk he is now–that's why I divorced him. Besides, if he could ruin my reputation so easily, maybe it's not as strong as I believe."

Chaboya cleared his throat. "What kind of cooperation was he seeking from Eric?"

"He wanted to blackmail Eric into granting him low-priced shares of SDS, so when it went public he could cash in and make his millions."

MacClaren pivoted his piercing stare onto Eric. "Did he succeed?"

"In a manner of speaking." Eric waggled his thumb and pinkie back and forth. "I gave him exactly what he wanted in writing–SDS shares he could cash out, only in the public market."

A slow smile grew on MacClaren's face. "Pretty clever, aren't you?"

"You've lost me," Chaboya broke in, his heavy brow crinkled.

"There's no guarantee SDS will go public, not after this mess," Don explained, a broad grin slashing his face. "Even if there weren't buyers eager to make a private offer, the scandal of all these events would delay or eliminate any opportunity for SDS to go public. Wall Street boys don't like to have to sell a company whose reputation is somewhat questionable. Makes their job too hard."

Comprehension flashed over Chaboya's expression. "So he's pocketed a worthless piece of paper for all these years of plotting and scheming?" He chuckled. "Serves him right."

Don continued. "That makes Wilkins a less likely suspect in the kidnapping. He got his money through Lynn's involvement with Eric and the threat of future disclosure, not because of physical threats. He's a jerk, like Lynn said, and could be arrested, but at this point he's not the main player."

"Agreed," replied MacClaren, scanning his notes. "I know you want to keep this all under wraps, but kidnapping is a major offense that just can't be ignored. They might try again."

Eric cast a worried look toward Lynn, imagining exactly what kind of danger still lurked. "That's why it's important to find out who's behind it, and fast. How we resolve it will depend on who that is. This is a delicate situation you're coming into, gentlemen, one that Don and I have been working on for years."

"Who's your prime suspect, Don?" Chaboya quizzed. "I assume you have theories already fleshed out."

"We've looked at everyone except Eric and me," Don replied with only a quick glance at Lynn's stricken look. "I've narrowed it down to either someone at the investment bank–Joshua Stein, the likely contact there–and, or, someone inside SDS."

"Engineering staff?" MacClaren probed. "That Ghosh guy you didn't include here tonight?"

"I investigated him, of course, but couldn't find any link or motivation for him to disrupt the IPO," Don answered. "He did his best to find and fix the bug, and cooperated fully whenever Eric asked him to. He's not involved."

"Then who?" Lynn asked.

"Kay Chiang is up to her neck in this," Don answered. "She's the VP of Sales, and has had freedom to talk to potential buyers without anyone else knowing exactly what was said. Not only is she Wilkins' current lover but she's also had liaisons with the most radical element of a rebel Communist party based in Taiwan, the Maoists. She grew up in San Francisco and went to high school with known members of the Chinatown Triad gangs. Given that's where Eric was held this afternoon, I'd say there's more than enough evidence to pursue specific questions."

MacClaren looked up from his scribbling. "Before I look into her, did you also consider the other investors? Sometimes the venture capitalists have their own motivations for controlling the fate of a company. We've had a hell of a time breaking into their private dealings in the past, when we've had more information than this."

"I asked Don to look into everybody, Pete." Eric answered. "Fortunately, this time it looks as if our investors have been playing above board with us." He flashed a rueful smile. "Not to say they don't give me a run for my money–they're not very pleased with me right now. But since I'll make them a nice chunk of change one way or the other, they have no choice except to work with me, not against me."

"Wouldn't they financially gain from controlling Lynn's proxy?" Chaboya queried. "If they want to go public so badly to build their reputations, and her vote is what put your preference to pursue a private offer over the top, it seems like that's motivation enough for hardball tactics."

"It's possible, just not probable," Eric explained. "They would have to be colluding against me because I wouldn't give them Lynn's identity. All they had to do was wait." He shook his head in certainty. "Too much intrigue for a bunch of guys who barely have enough time to wolf down their meals before they hop on the next plane. I don't buy it. Not as a group. Possibly one of them individually, but Don couldn't uncover any obvious links of that sort."

Lynn shifted away a few inches and raised her chin. "Actually, I left my contact information with Peter Baxter to pass on to any board member who asks. I'm expecting a possible bidding war for my proxy in the next twenty-four hours."

"Lynn," Eric chided. "Those guys weren't serious." He crossed his fingers under his hip.

"Can you be absolutely sure? Are you willing to bet the future of SDS on it?" she challenged.

Eric captured her gaze, staring into her eyes. Was she interested in selling her proxy immediately to the highest bidder? Maybe someone had gotten to her already. He twisted his jaw to the side, letting disappointment slide through him like warm molasses. "I've been betting on the future of SDS my whole adult life."

Lynn kept her eyes on his, her expression intent. And her lips clamped shut.

"Okay," Chaboya said. "Let's get back to this...um...Kay Chiang. How well did you know her before you hired her?"

Eric tore his gaze away from Lynn, still unsettled. "She came highly referred by a number of local firms, but given Wilkins' involvement with her, I suspect his unscrupulous hand was behind those references. I have to admit she has done a fine job landing us business, especially in China. That's what we really hired her for."

"Has she acted suspicious?" MacClaren asked.

"She has an annoying habit of attempting to seduce me every moment of every day," he admitted. "She cleverly warned me she could scream sexual harassment, even though she's been the aggressor." He shrugged. "So far, it's just remained a threat."

"Because you agreed to her overtures?" Chaboya's eyebrows rose, his expression non-judgmental.

"No. Never. But not for lack of effort on her part."

"Having a high sex drive is not a crime, boys," Don interjected. "I think her ties to China may be significant, especially since the rogue press release originated there. We've reached a dead end identifying who's behind it. Maybe you'll have better luck."

"Any other ties that you know of?" MacClaren flipped through his notes.

Eric stiffened. "Now that you mention it, a pretty key one," he said, tapping his cheek with one finger. "Kay introduced me to Joshua Stein, singing praises about his firm months before we started the IPO process. He became the obvious choice to lead our effort since he got to know SDS in the interim."

"Interesting," muttered MacClaren. "Did he spend a lot of time with Ghosh and the technology behind it, or with you and the finances?"

"Both." Eric rubbed his forehead, recalling blurry details. "He's a frustrated engineer tied into the banking industry due to Daddy's influence. He loved talking shop with Rajiv as much as talking numbers with me."

"He pushed hard to know the name of the Trust beneficiary when we met him in New York, remember?" Lynn prodded. "You thought at the time it was extreme, didn't you?"

"Yeah, he was a little over the top. I think all my bankers suspect there is more going on with SDS than I've let on."

Chaboya cocked his head. "Is it true?"

Don and Eric exchanged looks across the room.

"Maybe," Don answered.

Chapter 54

"Now's the time to act," Joshua insisted, pulling the bathrobe over his chilled legs. He stared at an unauthorized copy of Lynn's press release. It hadn't hit the news wires yet. He only had a few hours to pull the deal together. "Offer as high as you can before anyone else bids against you. If we can get Coleman to give his word, he won't break it." He clenched the phone, holding his breath.

A string of curses filled his ear. "That is not the way we do business, offering a high price. We must bargain, make him come down off his price if we are to strike a good deal."

"Your bargain comes from controlling this software and not letting anyone else control it–or you," Joshua snapped, losing his patience. "If that's not worth it to you, I can guarantee it is to two other Chinese parties. I'll just make a phone call and let them know. They'll pay whatever Coleman asks."

A grunt was his only reply. Agitated voices in the background filled the line.

Joshua continued. “My cut is 1% of the price for SDS, plus 1% of the increase in the market value of your company after the SDS purchase, plus 1% of SDS’ total revenues as your subsidiary for the first year. All ones–you should have no problem remembering that. And I’ll expect the first payment in my account at Shanghai City Commercial Bank in six hours, or the deal’s off.” He typed the account number into the shared screen, watched it blink for a few seconds and then disappear.

Any other broker would ask for all his money upfront. Joshua prized the security of continued cash flow and the possibilities that a move to a tax-sheltered country might afford him, especially since he’d had the foresight to establish an account in China years ago. It would be stupid to lose half to taxes just because he was impatient. “I’ll send the terms of the offer to you in writing, and you can sign off on it before I contact Coleman. Agreed?”

“Yes. Agreed.” Joshua heard the sound of a match striking, then a deep drag on a cigarette.

Joshua smiled in triumph. Zhu may be irritated without his usual negotiation dance, but Joshua was dead right on one point–this was Zhu’s one and only chance to get his hands on the SDS technology before it landed in the hands of others with a political agenda.

Zhu’s network of spies undoubtedly informed him of the Chinese military’s interest to control SDS software. Once there, Zhu would never see it again. Frequent power grabs by the old guard defending existing turf were the norm. By purchasing SDS, Zhu’s financial success was a given, for both him and the Shanghai Exchange.

That was worth any price in the short-term. And Joshua intended to make him pay it.

“Here it comes.” Joshua hit the send button, transmitting the email before Zhu had second thoughts. “I’ll call you in fifteen minutes to finalize the deal.”

He punched the button to end the call and threw his hands up in victory.

Woo hoo! He'd done it! This deal would put more money in his pocket than any commission he would have gotten on the IPO. SDS still hadn't managed to fix the bug. The syndicate would yank the scheduled IPO today, and then reassign him to babysit the CEO of some second-rank company. He wanted out.

Twenty minutes later, with Zhu's return fax confirming the deal in hand, he called Kay. As he listened to the rings in the background, he couldn't stop grinning. He'd won!

"Joshua here," he announced, as soon as he heard her pick up. "I've just closed the deal with one of my contacts, so call off your dogs. They lost to someone willing to put dollars instead of threats into the deal."

"We'll counter-offer!" Kay's voice carried an uncharacteristic hint of panic. "I can get my–"

"No way, Kay, it's final."

Even if Zhu backed out, Joshua could use Zhu's offer to get General Tong to cough up an equivalent amount of money. Or not. Joshua quailed at the thought of negotiating to the wall when his life was at stake. He didn't doubt the military leader's threats of force. But Tong would keep searching for technology deals, and Joshua could make the money up in the future. His firm might even reward him with a great, big bonus for a direct link with the Chinese government. The military had a lot of influence with the right people in China.

Kay's rebels just weren't at the same level. Hers were last on his list, an extra measure of insurance. In any case, he'd only agreed to help them in order to tie Kay more closely to him. If she felt she could flaunt her sexuality to get favors, he would accommodate her. But since she didn't deliver, neither would he.

"Joshy, dear, does your buyer know a felony was committed on his behalf?"

"Keep your trap shut. If anyone suspects we knew about Eric's kidnapping, we could go to jail. That's not in my plans."

"I'll inform the FBI you were behind it. Let's see how far your friends will go to buy SDS on the word of a criminal."

"Don't even try blackmail." Joshua swallowed hard. "It won't work, and you know it. I have as much dirt on you. Squealing won't help either of us."

"Are you sure?" she purred. "My friends have very long arms."

Joshua ignored the frisson of fear racing down his spine. "Look, we both knew only one buyer would succeed. Your contacts wanted to wait until we priced the IPO. They lost. They'll have to come up with a new plan."

"Great. Where does that leave me?"

Was Kay actually whining? He felt magnanimous all of a sudden. "Listen, I won't leave you hanging out to dry. I'll help you find a better employer."

Any one of the men who met her at the analyst meeting would snap her up in a heartbeat. Whether she delivered on her alluring promises was her business.

He removed his glasses and rubbed his burning eyes. Right now, a quiet island in the Caymans with no corporate dealings sounded like paradise. Kay or no Kay. But no threats, either.

He closed his mind to the repercussions she faced by not delivering to her buyer. These guys thought kidnapping Eric was everyday business. Joshua would never cross that line again. "I'll call you if I hear of any new opportunities. Otherwise, I think we should end all discussions of SDS," Joshua reiterated, anxious to end this call. "Agreed?"

"But, Joshua–"

• • • • • •

Kay gripped the phone hard to fight back a wave of dismay. Taking her frustration out on Joshua wouldn't leverage her in a new direction. Her carefully cultivated network of contacts–and boss–would demand an explanation for her failure before she could tap into them again. She needed a new plan. Fast.

Joshua could get her in front of heavy players in the global financial industry, especially those willing to bend the rules. She had to suck up to him again. Even though he was such a weasel.

"Congratulations then, Joshua." She injected friendliness into her voice. "I'd appreciate any help you can give me to land a new job. I'll relocate anywhere, if that helps. And do anything, too."

She waited for his usual smarmy retort. Silence. He'd definitely moved on.

"Thanks for thinking of me," she murmured. "You've been a gem to work with."

"You too. Bye." The connection went dead.

Kay dropped her hand to her side, the phone sliding to the sofa cushion. Her head drooped to her chest like a deflating carnival balloon. She had bet her fast-track career on the SDS IPO. Eric had seemed so dedicated to bringing SDS public. Rajiv had talked about nothing but. Even Charlie had confirmed everything was on track. She had been positive her buyers would get their hands on SDS technology. Hadn't she gotten Lynn's name for them—and for Joshua? She'd even steeled herself to the idea of sleeping with Joshua, if necessary. How did she get out-maneuvered?

She fought back useless tears. Her buyers would find out the truth soon. And they'll be madder than her parents ever were at her antics. She needed to hide out until their anger dissipated.

Of course, they'll blame themselves for using a woman as the main contact. Any inroads she had made to join their precious club had not only disappeared but the chance of any woman breaking into their inner circle in her lifetime was also gone.

Not quite what she had hoped to accomplish with her idealistic fervor. How had she screwed this up so badly?

She closed her eyes, tried to shove aside the sense of responsibility rising up inside her. Yes, her boss deserved a call. But she needed to marshal her arguments first, or his sharp tongue would flay her to pieces. That would hurt too much.

After all, her conniving had netted partial results. They had gathered inside information about their enemy's tactics. They now knew who the key players were. It was simply a matter of using that intelligence in a different manner than originally anticipated. Yeah, she could sell that–if he stopped yelling long enough to listen.

Her doorbell rang, interrupting her thoughts. She glanced at her watch. *Who…?* Oh, right–Charlie.

He was of no use to her now. She checked her appearance in the mirror and sighed. Swinging the door open, she plastered a woebegone expression on her face. "Hi, Charlie. I hope you don't mind but I'm not feeling well, all of a sudden. This isn't a good time."

Charlie brushed by her with an exultant look. "Honey, this is a great time! I have a letter in my pocket worth millions of dollars. We need to celebrate. Got any champagne in the fridge?" He headed toward the kitchen.

"What happened?" She trailed behind him, her curiosity piqued.

Tearing the foil from the expensive bottle, he pointed to the cupboard where she kept her fluted glasses. "I hit the jackpot, honey. All my work finally paid off."

He worked the cork free, laughing as a whoosh of cold liquid splattered his hands. "Oops!" He upended the bottle and poured the icy bubbles into his mouth.

Kay grabbed two flutes from the cupboard. He over-filled them with a flourish, the liquid trickling in a sparkling golden waterfall onto her floor.

Charlie raised his glass. "To the two of us!" He gulped half the frothy wine in a grandiose gesture.

Skeptical, Kay took a small sip. "Us, darling?" Where had he gotten millions of dollars?

Charlie finished his champagne in one large gulp, setting his flute down on the counter with a clink. Grabbing her waist, he snuggled her against him. He took her flute from her chilled fingers and gave her a bruising kiss. "Us. Will you marry me?"

"Oh, Charlie," she fluttered, kissing him back with as much enthusiasm as she could muster while running through options in her mind. She needed a cover for her rapid flight out of town—wasn't passion and romance understandable in any culture?

Not that she'd tie herself down with Charlie, or any other man. Not now, when her beauty gave her so much power over men. She only had a few more years to use it to her advantage. Then again, maybe Charlie had his hands in more underhanded schemes than she had known. He might serve her purpose after all.

Kay stroked Charlie's neck with her tapered fingernails. "This is so sudden. Why don't we take a long vacation together and figure out what our future will be?"

She opened her eyes wide and forced a tiny gasp. "I'll quit SDS tonight! Then we can catch the first flight out to anywhere in the world. We don't even have to pack—we'll buy whatever we need when we get there. How does that sound?"

"It sounds wonderful." Charlie nipped her earlobe. "Only we don't leave for at least an hour. I have more pressing ways to celebrate with you." His hands pulled her blouse from her skirt, running up her ribs and cupping her exposed breasts. "After tonight, I'll do whatever you ask, Kay. You know I love you."

Yes, I know he does. Kay made herself respond, stroking and petting him back. She'd keep him until she figured out her next step. In the meantime, she'll enjoy spending every cent of his ill-gotten money.

Maybe he could add to his fortune at the gaming tables in Monaco. That would probably be far enough away to keep her safe.

She pulled back from her distracted thoughts and moaned at intervals. Charlie pulled her to the floor, yanking at their clothes, too impatient to wait until they got to the bed.

He'll be so easy to control. Not like the ones who had just beaten her.

Chapter 55

The phone in Eric's den rang in the background, soft and insistent.

Stifling a groan, Eric maneuvered off the couch, muttering excuses. He limped down the hall, his stiff back and pounding head stark reminders of his hellish day. Which apparently was not over yet.

He flicked the light switch by the door and glanced at his watch. This had better be good. It's too late to deal with anything except emergencies.

"Eric, this is Joshua Stein." His happy voice chirped into Eric's ear. "I just got a very attractive offer for SDS, and I need to fax it over to you right now. It expires in twenty-four hours, so you'll have to move fast."

Eric dropped into his desk chair, tugging out the bottom drawer to rest his aching leg on its edge. The box with Lynn's good luck pendant caught his eye. With a nostalgic smile, he opened the box and dangled the necklace from his fingers.

"Who's it from?" His fax machine hummed and sputtered, spitting out the first page.

"The Shanghai Stock Exchange."

Eric grinned, but he disguised any triumph from his voice. "The Exchange, huh? Did I meet any of these guys?"

"No. They've entrusted me to represent them confidentially."

"Why are they in such a hurry?" Maybe he and Don could put all their questions to rest if he could uncover their motivation.

"Um, they're aware of this morning's press release about the bug and the likely delay of the IPO. Don't ask me how they know," he added quickly. Too quickly. "They want SDS and they're smart businessmen using this window of opportunity to keep two other buyers at bay while you consider their offer."

Two other buyers, Eric pondered, listening to the slow whir of the fax. They must be Kay's political contacts and the military types lurking at the back of the analyst conference. Was it worth it to milk a higher price for SDS through a bidding war? Paul had warned him about three scorpions. Once one was out, the other two fought to their mutual death. Or stung an unwary spectator.

Glancing at his watch, he shook his head. He'd plain run out of time. He couldn't afford to take the risk. And the Shanghai Exchange filled his requirements nicely.

Eric plucked the three sheets out of the fax machine and scanned to the bottom line. Joshua was right, it was a very attractive offer, probably more than the investors would net from an IPO.

"I'll need to discuss this with my board, but that shouldn't be a problem," Eric responded. "We'll have terms and conditions of our own to negotiate, so prepare your party that this isn't a slam dunk."

He paused to ensure Joshua understood his next message. "But I have to tell you, this couldn't have come at a better time. We probably have a deal."

Joshua's sigh of relief was as clear as an early California summer morning. "Great. I'll pass on the information and be in touch with you this afternoon at three o'clock, Pacific time. Will you be able to call your board together by then?"

"If not, I'll let you know," Eric replied. "Thanks for all your work on this. Your firm probably would have preferred the IPO, but I confess I wasn't looking forward to constant travel for a month, spouting the same presentation over and over to analysts and bankers."

Joshua's chuckle seemed sincere. "Most CEOs feel the same. They hate the road show, but love the resulting money. If you can get the money without the work, I'd take it."

Eric tossed the necklace high, snatching it mid-air and tucking it into his pants pocket. "Thanks for the advice. I'll talk to you tomorrow."

He replaced the phone in the cradle and leaned back in the chair, relaxing his shoulders and rolling his neck. His mission was almost over.

He had to tell Don.

Eric walked into the living room. Curled up on the couch where he had left her, Lynn had her eyes closed and her hand resting on top of Fred's head. Don reclined in his chair glancing over his notes, and the two FBI agents huddled in the kitchen conferring in heated whispers.

He nudged Don with the faxed sheets. Don skimmed them, giving Eric a broad smile and congratulatory thumbs up. Eric beckoned the agents back into the room, remaining at Don's side.

MacClaren dropped onto the loveseat and studied his notepad. "Emilio and I agree we should initiate a full-scale investigation into Kay Chiang and Charles Wilkins for conspiracy to kidnap and blackmail Eric. There's enough evidence for a phone tap and a search warrant. The sooner we begin, the better."

Eric paced around the furniture. "No formal investigation. Those were Don's conditions when he invited you here. We only asked your help to determine the foreign interests willing to use such drastic measures."

Chaboya swore under his breath. "Mr. Coleman–Eric–you asked us here for our professional opinion. Pete here doesn't know you at all, but Don and I go way back to our days at the FBI academy. I know Don prizes complete consideration of all the possibilities. Are you of the same mind?"

Eric stilled next to Don's chair. "Yes, Don and I see eye to eye on that."

"And you'd still like Ms. Baker in the room?"

Eric walked to the couch and dropped next to Lynn. If Chaboya reverted to Ms. Baker instead of Lynn, whatever he was planning to say wouldn't be friendly. He clasped her hand. "Nowhere else."

Chaboya shot MacClaren a challenging glance. "Pete thinks I should keep my mouth shut given the circumstances, but I can't. My professional opinion is that in addition to Chiang and Wilkins, Ms. Baker is a prime suspect in these underhanded activities at SDS. There are too many coincidences to believe she wasn't involved in the early planning stages of one of these schemes. She stands to make a lot of money no matter what the outcome, and her knowledge of the Trust from years ago gives her plenty of motive."

Her grip tightened around his fingers at the agent's blunt pronouncement. Eric threw his head back and laughed. Only Don would understand the depth of the irony in Chaboya's statement. Even Lynn looked at him with puzzlement.

"Emilio, Pete, you'll have to trust me. Making money outside her contract was never Lynn's motivation for getting involved in SDS. She is simply a fantastic businesswoman working at her job, and handling all the personal ghosts of her past." Shooting her a tender smile, he squeezed her hand. "In fact, she compromised her own business on SDS' behalf. There is no way I would ever let you press charges against her." Lynn cast him a relieved peek under her lashes.

Sneaking a quick glance at Don, curious about his reaction to his strong defense of Lynn, he caught Don's reassuring nod, his expression light-hearted for once.

"Eric is right, Emilio, but thanks for your candid opinion," Don interjected. "You haven't been working with Lynn this week. She's been driving hard to uncover the source of the problems. I can vouch for the fact that until recently she had no idea she was beneficiary to the Trust."

Chaboya scowled. "Okay, if that's the way you want it. I still have my doubts. It's my job to keep looking for answers."

MacClaren stuffed his papers into his briefcase and rose, extending his hand to Eric and then Lynn. "I guess we're done here. I'll let you know if we find out more, but Don has done a thorough job already. Are you sure you don't want us to at least question Chiang and Wilkins?"

"SDS couldn't handle more bad publicity," Eric answered, twisting his lips. "There are only so many miracles Lynn can accomplish. But, with a little whisper from Rajiv, the Silicon Valley network will keep them out of the job market for a long, long time." He rose with aching legs and shook their hands. "Thanks for coming over and listening. You helped focus our thoughts, if nothing else."

Don and Eric escorted the agents out the door and closed it behind them with a firm thud. Eric eyed the comfortable couch, but Don grabbed his shoulder.

"Lynn, I need to talk with Eric in private. Mind a few minutes alone?"

"Of course not." She yawned. "I'll catnap while you boys chat. Talk away." She fluffed the throw pillow and lifted her feet onto the couch.

Eric draped the afghan over Lynn, wishing he could join her. Instead, he limped after Don into the den, closed the door and dropped his weight gingerly into the chair.

Don tossed the faxes onto the desk. "Did I read that right? The Shanghai Stock Exchange wants to buy SDS outright?"

Eric grinned in satisfaction. "Yeah. We couldn't have planned it better, could we?"

"Whew, you can say that again. How did they come into the picture?"

"Joshua set it up somehow. I suspected he had one or two potential buyers in the wings in case the IPO blew up. My guess is that he gets a cut of the deal, maybe even behind his employer's back."

Don paced the floor, his hands clasped behind him, head down. "Do you think Stein's behind the kidnapping? And the bogus press release?"

"He's definitely tied into very good sources," Eric mused. "He'd already read this morning's press releases, and he's smart enough to know how to leverage the bad news against us. But no, I don't think he's the mastermind behind it all. He's just opportunistic, looking to make money."

Don swore. "I don't think we'll ever find out who started the ball rolling with that press release about the bug. Wilkins clearly planted the bug but I haven't been able to tie him directly to any Chinese contacts. He needed you safe in order to take his money and run, and he was satisfied with the letter you gave him."

"The fool. If we accept this offer, he won't see a dime." Eric gritted his teeth. Anger swept through him again at Wilkins' attempted blackmail. "It serves him right. He deserves the inside of a jail cell." He clenched and unclenched his jaw.

"He's old news," Don reminded Eric. "Will the Exchange really be the right venue, given what the DOD asked of us?"

Eric stared through the moonlit window at the shadows weaving in the light breeze. Gnarled, old oak trees creaked and swayed, their twisted limbs looking freakishly dangerous, as if they were hunting for invisible prey floating in the night air. It reminded Eric of the political miasma in today's world. His country couldn't fight lethal enemies head on, and political enemies became economic competitors who cooperated at some levels, but definitely not on others.

When the DOD had first approached him about setting up a company with the express purpose of planting his cutting-edge software in the heart of enemy territory without anyone's knowledge, he had his doubts he could ever pull it off. DARPA had recouped their investment in his software early on by selling their interest quietly to Silicon Valley Capital, trusting Eric to carry out the mission without any more of their direct influence or guidance.

With Don's help and a lot of luck along the way, the perfect scenario just landed in their lap. And with perfect timing too. His software could only stay on top for so long before another competitor developed stronger, more attractive features. He couldn't ask for better payment for all his years of work. His efforts could help his country keep a close watch on terrorist activities.

"Ultimately, the Chinese government backs the Shanghai Exchange, so we accomplished our mission," Eric finally answered. "The Communist Party still believes in this blended economy concept. They can't afford to let capitalism take an independent foothold–they stand to lose too much political control."

"They've been willing to work with us to fight terrorism so far."

Eric chuckled. "It will make our military intelligence look that much more impressive when we can accurately pinpoint how the terrorists are getting their funding and laundering their money. There's nothing wrong in keeping our reputation sterling. And their military egos in check."

"Will you be able to get the board to accept the offer?"

"With Rajiv's and Lynn's votes as major shareholders, they can't stop us."

Don cleared his throat. "About that, Eric." He cracked his knuckles, avoiding Eric's eyes.

"Now what?"

"Well, I meant it when I agreed Lynn had no advance knowledge of her shares of SDS, and there was no justification for believing she was involved in any conspiracy. But..." His voice trailed off again.

Eric planted his feet firmly on the floor in front of him and leaned his elbows on his knees, forming half-fists. "Spit it out, Don."

"You remember I told you Lynn took on Wilkins' debts for the divorce?"

Eric nodded, his chest tightening.

"I did a little more digging," Don admitted. "Her company is on its last leg financially, which means she is personally, too. Her only asset is her condo in Boulder, and she's way behind on her payments. Her stepfather just developed cancer, and they've contracted with an experimental facility that his insurance doesn't cover. Also, they have two kids in college. If Lynn tries to help them out at all, she'll need a boatload of money. Now, not six weeks from now. You know she'll be blamed for the erroneous press release, no matter what you say, so she has no future income to count on."

"So what?"

"It may be faster and easier for her to sell her shares directly to one of the board members at a discount rather than wait for this deal to conclude. They clearly aren't happy with a private offer—and Lynn made sure Baxter had her email address."

Yeah, Eric hadn't been very pleased about that, either. At the time he'd chalked it up to just professional networking. But Don's spin forced him to look at it from a different perspective—one of suspicion.

"It's a piece of cake for him to offer her immediate cash for her shares right now—before the vote. Then you and Rajiv will no longer control the majority of shares. And the board will push for an IPO, with no guess as to what the future of SDS will be." Don shrugged. "Basically, there's no guarantee she'll vote your way tomorrow."

Eric swallowed hard. Don only envisioned the worst-case scenario, not what he really believed about Lynn.

Or did he?

His thoughts flashed back to last night, when she had admitted her doubts and fears in the dark. Had that all been a ploy to earn his trust so she could stab him in the back for money?

No! Why would she have confronted all her demons on the streets of Chinatown to save his ass if she was only interested in the money? Or be willing to sacrifice her company for his?

Didn't she know he'd be willing to help her out financially?

Idiot! How could she know? You've been so busy keeping secrets from her you forgot that a relationship requires honesty.

Eric's heart twinged. Guilt flooded his veins. Eric had hero-worshipped his father so much he forgot how his father's secrets had undermined his marriage. Yet he was risking destroying his growing relationship with Lynn for the same reason. Again.

Would he ever learn?

He paced to the window, staring at the moon high up in the sky. His mission had finally sucked him dry. "I have to trust her to vote with me," he sighed. "If I don't, I don't have a prayer of a relationship with her."

Eric pivoted. "I'm tired of all the secrets. Tired of not sharing my worries with anyone but you. Tired of not having a woman to share my dreams. Just flat out tired of always being alone."

Don opened his mouth, but Eric cut him off. "I'm taking a chance here, but I understand and accept the risks. Do you understand the rewards?"

"Listen, kid, I know this is really difficult for you." Sympathy gleamed from Don's eyes. "I'm not blind to what's going on between you two–in fact, I'm happy for you both. I hope it lasts. You haven't had a lot of joy in your life, so if Lynn is able to give it to you, she's all right in my book. But–"

"But what?"

"Do you really think you can compromise national security because of your feelings?"

"She won't betray me." Eric punched a fist into his palm.

"It's your call. It always has been."

Don rose and walked to his side, clapping a hand on his tense shoulder. "What else needs to be done so our mission succeeds?"

He welcomed changing the topic back to the sane and prosaic. "I'll need to modify the terms so Rajiv is taken care of, but those are pretty minor in the scheme of things."

Eric resumed his seat, pulling out the necklace from his pocket and fingering it as he talked. "Go ahead and alert your contacts at DOD to tap into the back door I built into the SDS software once the network's installed in Shanghai. They should be able to monitor financial transactions for at least five years before our technology becomes obsolete. We've done our job."

Unless Lynn betrays me. He pushed back the unwanted warning flashing through his brain.

"Any regrets selling to these guys?" Don leaned his back against the dark window.

"No, not really." Eric scrubbed his hands over his face, but when he finally met Don's gaze his spirits lifted. "I was hoping the IPO process would attract the right kind of buyer for this stage of the game. It obviously did, even if we had unexpected help along the way." He shrugged. "I really didn't want to go public. It's too onerous to have to jump through the hoops the SEC set up. They couldn't pay me enough to stay with the company in the current environment."

Don studied Eric, his expression affectionate. "You've done it, kid, and I'm proud of you. You were one of the best projects that DARPA ever funded, and I don't just mean your software. You were the right man for the whole job. Whether anyone else thanks you for all the sacrifices you made to make this happen, you have mine."

"I couldn't have done it without you or Rajiv." Eric hesitated, doubts crossing his mind. "I hope he likes the new situation. He really had his heart set on an IPO."

Don sniffed. "Once he'd spent one week on the road with you he'd have realized it was overrated. This way he can pocket the money and get on with his life. There's nothing preventing him from starting his own company one day. He's just been too comfortable to get out there and try."

Eric stared at his hands.

After a full minute, Don broke the tense silence. "Now you're brooding. What's up?"

"I'm not sure how much of the past to tell Lynn," Eric confessed. "I wouldn't even be here if it weren't for her. It seems wrong not to tell her our ultimate goal. She has a right to know what her namesake was all about."

"Her namesake? What are you talking about?"

Eric tossed the silver dollar necklace at Don. "SDS stands for Silver Dollar Sweetheart. I named the company after her when the good-luck charm she gave me to wear to the DARPA presentation worked. I won't hide part of my life from her again. Last time, I lost her for years when I lied to her about this."

Don studied the necklace, and then pressed it back into Eric's hand. "All of us with security clearance grapple with the same issue. Inez accepted it, and Lynn will too. Just tell her the truth–it has to do with national security and you're not at liberty to disclose all the country's secrets, no matter how much she means to you." He paused, capturing and holding Eric's gaze. "You love her, don't you?"

Tension flowed out of Eric. Yes, he loved her. Had for years. He had been so busy keeping secrets, he'd kept the biggest one from himself.

"Absolutely," Eric answered with conviction.

"Then don't worry about it. From what I've seen, she feels the same way. In fact, I'm feeling like a third wheel here, so I'm going home to crawl into bed and remind my wife how much I love her." He winked. "It's not only you young studs who get all the action, you know."

Eric chuckled, slapping Don on the back and leading him down the hall. "After the beating I took today, I don't feel very studly, but thanks for the thought. Good night, Don, and thanks again for everything."

"'Night." Don hurried out the door.

Chapter 56

Eric perched on the edge of the couch and nestled his hip against Lynn's curled back. He leaned over, kissing her exposed neck until she responded with a soft murmur and a subtle wiggle. "Wake up, sweetie."

"Mmm. Is Don gone?" She stretched full length, her hands twisting above her head. The afghan fell away, leaving her bare midriff exposed.

"He just left." Intrigued, he traced the irregular patterns of scars scattered across her pale flesh. "I know it's late but would you like to soak in the hot tub with me?" He winked. "Our own kind of home entertainment."

Lynn's eyes fluttered open. "Sounds fair. If I'm throwing myself to the dogs tomorrow, at least I should get eye-candy as motivation tonight."

He drew her into his arms, cursing inwardly at the twinge of pain running along his ribs at her snug fit. "Eye-candy is all you'll get tonight, sweetie. My body will revolt if I push it too hard."

Lynn caressed his tender back. "I'll take care of you," she murmured. "Don't worry."

He laced his fingers through her hair, tilting her head to meet his eyes. Hers were full of trust and sympathy. He pushed his lingering doubts aside.

"I have a gift for you before I get distracted–again." He slipped the necklace over her head and dropped a kiss on either side of the silver dollar settling between her breasts like a beacon, reminding him of everything she had done for him already. The lingering smell of soap and her unique scent assailed his senses.

Raising his head, he met her glowing eyes. "Come on. Let's go before we change our minds. The water's hot, but the air's a little cool."

"Sounds refreshing," Lynn whispered in his ear, nipping at the lobe and trailing her lips down his neck.

His crotch sprung to full attention. Good to know no damage done there.

Lynn slid out of his embrace and sauntered toward the patio doors, toeing off her socks along with her pants, and pulling her shirt over her head. In only a skimpy bra and thong, the silver necklace bouncing provocatively, she threw a mischievous smile over her shoulder. "Last one in has to make coffee in the morning."

He staggered after her, tearing off his T-shirt and sweats. Clambering together into the hot tub with all the finesse of bumper cars, her hands wandered over his bruises. He explored the spidery network of scars along her abdomen. His heart raced as she reached behind her and unsnapped her bra, flinging it aside.

Lynn shivered, the bracing night air rippling her skin and tightening her nipples. He pulled her deep into the soothing water and onto his lap. Twining her hair in his fist, he planted gentle kisses on the nape of her neck, following the links of the chain. She drove him crazy, all warmth and energy and generous giving of her very soul, along with her luscious body. Bracing her hands on his hard thighs, she rocked against him. His hips jerked up, but a shooting pain stopped him cold.

Eric groaned, setting her away from him reluctantly. "My spirit is willing, but my body just can't cooperate, honey."

"So that's what guys call it these days."

"Spirit or cooperation?"

"Does it make a difference?"

"Only if we're making a movie–PG versus X-rated."

"Hmm, I never saw myself as a porn star. But now that you mention it..."

Don's cameras! Had he disengaged them yet? "Yeah, well I think my director just yelled 'Cut!'"

She giggled. "Ah, another euphemism. Spirit, director–how many does an average guy use to name his...let's say prime...body part?"

"As many as it takes to get his woman to smile. How am I doing?"

She grinned, sinking to her chin in the frothy water. "You made the cut."

Spreading his arms along the patio deck, Eric relaxed against the hot pulses, willing his body back under his control. She gripped the side of the tub with her fingers and blue-tipped toes, letting her body bob to the surface. The moonlight spotlighted her scars, tearing at his heart for the pain she'd suffered. His eyes roamed where his palms itched to touch–over her shoulders, around her tantalizing breasts, along the length of her legs to the shadowy cleft in between.

"Eric?"

"Hmm?"

"If I were an egg, I'd be hard-boiled by now. You?"

"Definitely hard."

She quirked one eyebrow, a languorous smile spread across her face. "Change your mind?"

"Only if I can change my body. God, Lynn, you're tempting."

"I can wait." She tucked her feet under her and rose. Water sheeted off her in provocative waterfalls, drips gathering in peaks and valleys he ached to lick dry.

Grimacing, he stepped out of the tub onto the cold patio tiles. He grasped her hand and helped her up the slippery step, easing her into his embrace.

"How about joining me for a little under-the-blanket cuddling and then a lot of sleeping?" Draping his arm over her shoulder, he turned her toward the house. "After getting the stuffing beat out of me today, I could use your TLC to keep me company tonight."

Her arm snaked around his waist and held tight. "Sounds perfect. A few hours with no worries, and my own hero to watch my back. What else could a girl ask for?"

"A nightgown?"

She snickered. "Some hero. Won't you keep me warm enough without it?"

"I was aiming for making you hot."

"You already have." She twisted and placed a soft kiss across his lips.

He groaned, halting at the kitchen door. "Don't tempt me, woman. I might maim myself for life."

Tucking her arm in the crook of his, she led him down the darkened hall to his bedroom. "I can wait," she repeated in a soft voice. "Let's do it right this time."

"I can't do much. But what I can do, I promise I'll do right," he murmured, sliding his hand along her hip and easing her thong down her legs.

"Eric, are you sure?"

"Let me just show you how much you mean to me, sweetie." He prayed any little bit of intimacy would bond them. He couldn't wait any longer for just a taste of his personal quest, his private dream.

Chapter 57

Lynn blinked against the morning light seeping through the lacy branches of the pepper tree. Eric's arm weighed heavy against her waist. His chest rose and fell in easy rhythm, and his faint snore tickled her ear. She sighed, wishing they could stay like this for hours. Their physical connection last night had overwhelmed her. He'd accepted her scarred body with ease. He was so attuned to her sexuality, so willing to give. She wanted to rely on him, to create an emotional link that was too strong to break.

To love him, she realized with sudden clarity. Eric had earned her trust back. Had she earned all of his?

His leg jerked and he tilted onto his back. She peeked over her shoulder, confirmed he still slept, and slipped out of the bed. Tiptoeing to his closet, she grabbed one of his shirts, pulled it on and buttoned it against the morning chill. Fred's tail thumped against his blanket and he yawned, rising to his feet and stretching yoga-style. He followed her down the hall, into the kitchen, and wiggled through the doggie-door.

She stared at the empty coffeepot. Had she been the last one in the hot tub? Warmth flooded through her as she remembered their playfulness last night. Who cared who won the bet? She needed caffeine–now.

As she retrieved her phone, she settled into the breakfast nook and waited for the coffee to brew, scrolling through her emails.

Interesting...one each from Peter Baxter, Allan Fleming, and Simon Hays, bidding for control of her vote, couched in legalese. Hays offered an obscene amount of money–today–if she voted to stay the course for an IPO. Wasn't that bribery?

She rose, tapping her fingers on the counter until the pot finished its final hiss. Lynn poured the coffee into an oversized mug and added a liberal dash of cream. While settling back into the nook, she glanced at the incoming message from Bernadette.

Her stomach clenched reading the stark words. Mitch and Mom would travel to Phoenix next week for an indeterminate time to seek alternative treatment for his spreading cancer, something their insurance carrier refused to pay for. Bernadette wanted to go with them for moral support, but couldn't afford more than a weekend. Could Lynn help in any way?

Could she? Simon Hays' offer tempted her.

No more money coming in anytime soon. When had she let the client's wishes compromise her professional integrity?

When business came face to face with life or death. Hers...and Eric's.

On the bright side, now she was free from the baggage of Kip's manipulations. Legally, if she closed her company down, there were no assets to pursue from a disgruntled former client.

Unless they went after her personal assets. Which, if she were to believe Kip, could reach the millions after an SDS IPO.

He had to be wrong. The venture capitalists weren't offering anything close to that high a price for her shares. Kip was delusional again. Eric would tell her different if that were the case.

Wouldn't he?

Fred's head poked through the doggie-door, then his body struggled through and, finally, his wagging tail appeared. He dashed through the kitchen, skittering around the corner on his nails, his soft woofs echoing down the hall.

"Is that coffee I smell?" Eric called in a low, gravelly voice. He walked into the kitchen, scratching his bare chest, sniffing the air. Low-slung sweatpants hung off his lean waist.

Her mouth watered. "Didn't I lose the bet last night?"

"I hope not. I tried hard to make you win."

She laughed. "Another euphemism?"

He grinned. "The truth, honey." He lifted a mug from the drying rack and poured a steaming cup, settling his hips against the counter with a sigh. "Ah, exactly what the doctor ordered."

"How are you feeling?" She winced at his purpled stripes.

"Fantastic. Ready to conquer the world."

She arched her brow. "The whole world? Or just our corner of Silicon Valley?"

He dropped into the bench across from her. "How about just SDS' world today? Tomorrow we can take on more."

She studied his serious expression, fighting back the old familiar tension. "What aren't you telling me?"

"The SDS IPO is on hold," he said, avoiding her eyes. "I received a formal offer to buy us outright. I need to negotiate some terms to give fair consideration for all our shareholders, but I'm calling for a vote this afternoon."

"When did this offer come in?"

"Last night."

Of course. Why had she expected he'd tell her the full truth? "Why didn't you tell me then?"

He slurped his coffee. Sighing, he raised his gaze to hers. "Frankly, I wanted to forget about SDS and be with you. After all we'd been through yesterday, I thought we had earned a break."

Should she set a good example and tell him about all her emails? She chewed her bottom lip. Her conscience screamed "Yes!" Her fearful side reminded her she could get hurt.

Tough.

She took a deep breath. "Well, that makes the timing of these emails pretty darned interesting."

Eric narrowed his eyes. "What emails?"

"Oh, your buddies Peter, Allan and Simon all want to pay me big bucks so I vote for an IPO. And my family needs immediate help financially. What do you think I should do?"

He stared at her, frustration clear in his eyes. "I told you–the shares are yours to vote as you think right. I gave them to you, for you. Not for me to dictate your decisions or actions."

Wow! She didn't think he'd remembered his ideal speech of the other night.

But she remembered hers.

"All right then. Let's get moving, shall we? This promises to be a banner day." She dumped her coffee cup in the sink and waltzed out of the room, heart pounding in her chest.

Chapter 58

"I'm glad that's over!" Eric rumpled his hair, tired of dressing up for the cameras and bankers. Lynn had insisted they wear their best this morning for the impromptu press conference, but his tie felt like a tourniquet around his neck. Especially when his throat knotted up as he thanked Lynn publicly, and commended her professional integrity. Right after she admitted she had sent out a false press release and resigned. Her colleagues would never forgive that error.

Exiting the convention center's side door into the glaring sun, Rajiv led Eric and Lynn to his Mercedes. Rajiv opened the back for her, while Eric eased himself into the front passenger seat.

"Is everything set for the board meeting?" Rajiv asked, as he pulled onto the busy boulevard to avoid the stream of students exiting from Mission College. The thirty-two-foot-high, steel statue of the Virgin Mary seemed to bless their passing.

Eric would take all the help he could get at this point.

He glanced at his phone. "Yes, Baxter just texted. They all have a copy of the offer, and understand time is of the essence. We can conference in from my office rather than having to run up to Menlo Park, thank God. I think Baxter would throw the phone at me if I dared show my face. He never wanted any option but a hot IPO."

And what about Lynn? How desperate was she? Enough to take drastic action? Vote with Peter and the others? He couldn't quite squelch his niggling uncertainty.

"Life is full of hidden surprises," Lynn quipped. "We've had to handle our share. It seems only fair he takes a turn."

Rajiv chuckled. "My guess is he does not quite see it that way."

"Probably not," she admitted. "But it's true."

Arriving at SDS, they settled around the glass table in Eric's office, well supplied with coffee. Eric paused with his hand halfway to the phone.

"Rajiv, are you sure you're satisfied with the conditions I've laid out? I'll go to the mat to get them, but this is our only chance to negotiate."

Rajiv leaned forward and gripped Eric's shoulder briefly. "You have fulfilled both my current needs and my future desires," he answered. "I confess, sometimes I thought you were running this company as your own pet project, but in the end you are getting a phenomenal return on our investment. That is all I ever asked."

A self-deprecating smile flickered across Rajiv's face. "Well, this prestige to flatter my family does not hurt," he added. "But I trust you understand why. You have returned my loyalty tenfold, and I appreciate it. Not all my friends have." He grimaced.

"Lynn?" Eric clenched his teeth, keeping his face rigid and expressionless. "Are you ready?" He bit back the questions he really wanted to hurl at her. *Do you believe me? Will you support me? Will you let me help you, no matter what you or your family need?*

His chest tightened as he battled creeping fear from Don's warning.

Lynn studied him with a frown marring her brows. "Yes, Eric, I'm fine. Are you okay?"

Eric nodded curtly, not daring to meet her eyes. "Here we go."

The conference call was brief but to the point. Baxter confirmed everyone understood the terms of the offer. The engineering headquarters of SDS would remain in Silicon Valley, with Rajiv heading up the US technical division as general manager, at a generously increased salary, and a much broader scope of authority and responsibility. Then he started the roll call of votes, board members first, followed by Eric and Rajiv. Finally, it was Lynn's turn to cast her vote.

Eric held his breath.

"I vote to accept the offer." Lynn reached for Eric's hand and squeezed hard.

Eric exhaled his relief and couldn't resist lifting her hand for a brief kiss. His heart pounded at the implication of her final vote.

The venture capitalists lost graciously, offering whatever help was necessary to close the deal. Eric kept them on the line as he waited for Joshua to fax the signed acceptance of the new terms. Rajiv beamed when the approval came in and the board formally accepted the offer. With an ending flourish, Eric faxed the written acknowledgement directly to the Shanghai Stock Exchange.

Eric shook his head in wonderment. This must be how a woman feels after delivering a baby. A whole era has passed, and a new one is about to begin. Only the good moments are remembered, none of the pain and heartache.

It felt fantastic.

"Ms. Baker, would you help an old friend put together a press release announcing the sale of SDS to the Shanghai Stock Exchange?" he teased.

"No problem," she replied demurely, powering up her PC. "Only this time, you can't duck the reporters' questions."

"Let the new GM handle them. You did great this morning, Rajiv, when you announced the bug was found and fixed. You'll make your family proud," he added when he caught Rajiv tugging his ear, a glint of panic in his eyes. "And it's entirely appropriate. The kick-off to a new beginning–new company, new management, new focus. It's all yours now, buddy. I'll handle the details of the acquisition. That should keep me running around in circles for weeks, believe me."

Lynn wrapped up the draft of the release and presented it to Rajiv for review. She pulled Eric aside. "I already emailed my family. My folks need help, and I need to go home."

Eric nodded. "Grab the next flight you can. Like I said, I'll be tied up for a while settling things here."

Fifteen minutes later, he joined her in her office and closed the door behind him. She was busy separating documents into piles, returning the office to its lifeless, spartan functionality.

He slipped a check into her hand. "Here's payment for your full two-month contract, plus a bonus."

"Eric, that's not right. I only–"

He pressed his fingers against her lips. "Just take it, sweetie. You more than earned it. And it will keep you afloat until the deal concludes and the rest of the money comes in." Sliding his fingers over her cheek, he cupped her face. "We have a lot to talk about. Do you want me to come to Boulder when I'm done?"

She slid into his arms, winding hers around his neck and brushing his lips with hers. "Are you still throwing your Halloween bash?"

"Sure. Most of the people at SDS are staying on, and it'll be a good way to celebrate the buyout without becoming maudlin."

"If I can wangle an invitation, I'll come back for the party." She gave him a deep, soulful kiss. "We can talk then."

Eric held her tight. "You've been my silver dollar sweetheart for years. I guess I can wait another fourteen days–but that's pushing it." He kissed her with abandon, his passion turning into tenderness, then wistfulness.

Damn, he would miss her. He had so much to tell her.

Everything.

"I'll call you tonight," he murmured. Turning on his heel, he strode back to his office. The faster he got SDS turned over to its new owners, the better.

Chapter 59

SHANGHAI, CHINA

Zhu Zhien pointed his lit cigarette at the straight-backed chair across from his desk and frowned at the youngster hesitating in the doorway. He had called Sun Guibao to his office as soon as SDS faxed their acceptance. There was no time to waste.

Little Sun darted across the room and sank into the chair, keeping his eyes on his feet. Good, Zhu thought. Fear is a powerful motivator to force the truth into the open.

Exhaling a large plume of smoke directly into the young man's face, he watched for his response. No coughs, no uncomfortable squirming. This boy kept his head. He would be a fine addition to his inner circle. They needed someone with engineering know-how, if his plan were to succeed.

"Look at me!" Zhu snapped. The youngster's head popped up, his eyes wide but devoid of any emotion. "Tell me about all your dealings involving SDS."

"What do you mean, Director Zhu?" A long, telltale swallow betrayed his nervousness.

Zhu pointed his cigarette at his face. "I have a network of contacts, too, Little Sun. I traced the first press release to a military-backed software company. Somehow, you discovered the bug before anyone else did. Don't pretend you don't know what I'm referring to."

He cleared his throat and twisted his head without dropping his gaze. "Do we now own SDS?"

"Except for the final details, yes."

Little Sun let out a deep breath, his shoulders visibly relaxed. "I had many conversations with Joshua Stein about their technology. I also stayed in contact with companies using their software to understand how their product really worked in...unusual applications. You see, I wanted to be absolutely certain we had all the inside information, in case the deal faltered."

"Hmph. Likely story," Zhu scoffed. "I happen to know you also have ties to engineers and bankers who are not so interested in the Exchange's success. Is that not correct?"

He gulped, tensing again. "I was always taught that it is best to keep friends close, and enemies even closer. I am in a unique position to talk to many engineers from Silicon Valley. They love to boast about their new top-secret technologies. The bankers follow along in their wake, eager to discuss the real potential of each one with a Chinese expert."

"And how were you planning on using all this information, hmm?"

"Director Zhu, my plan was to share any appropriate disclosures with you, of course."

Zhu stubbed out his cigarette. "Good, because that's exactly what you will do in the future."

"Pardon me?"

Rising abruptly, Zhu strode around the wide desk. He hitched his hip over the corner and thrust his face to within inches of the young man's. "We now have a chance to make our Exchange the most successful one in the world. To do that, we will need accurate inside information on which companies are most likely to succeed before we encourage investment in their technologies."

Little Sun quailed. "What does that have to do with me?"

"You will continue as you have been, gathering contacts like a girl gathers spring blossoms. I expect weekly reports on which companies have garnered the most investment attention from the American bankers and VCs, so we can invest our money accordingly." Zhu slapped his hand on the desk. "Do you understand? We cannot afford to have any companies fail that we bring into the public marketplace!"

"I…I think so. But isn't it expected that some companies won't attract additional investors, and fail as a result of their product or management, not due to the Exchange's efforts?"

Zhu sighed at his new protégé's thick-headedness. "China can't afford a misstep introducing the concept of a public stock market to our people," he lectured. "The middle-class needs to see it as a way to improve their standard of living through investment, not just as another gambling venue. Otherwise, all of capitalism will fail, which will return us to the old days." He clenched his fist around the edge of the desk. "We must succeed. You will get us the information we need, no matter what the source. I will not tolerate failure."

Little Sun met his unblinking gaze, surprise etched onto his features. *Good.* The boy needed to appreciate there was more at stake than just their professional reputations. Zhu loved his homeland. He would continue his fight to keep it strong, even when it was not politically correct.

However, the youngster's astonishment was understandable. Zhu had deliberately cultivated a reputation of being heartless, dishonest, and ready to follow whatever orders came down from the Party. Only a select few were aware he was willing to risk his exalted, government-appointed position in order for this new economic system to succeed. Little Sun would have to come to grips with the consequences of discovering that closely guarded secret. There would be no turning back. Ever.

"Well?" He coughed loudly in displeasure.

"Of course," Little Sun hastened, still looking rattled. "My contacts are at your disposal. I will strive even harder to get the information you seek."

Zhu glared at him. "All of your contacts. In this country and out. In the government and out–including those in the military. You will pass on all inside information you uncover to me. Agreed?" Grabbing a rumpled pack of cigarettes, Zhu shook two out and tilted the pack forward.

With shaking fingers, his protégé accepted his offer and managed to get it lit. "Agreed…Boss."

Zhu smiled in victory, expelling smoke through his nostrils like a powerful dragon–watching every move, alert, and willing to pounce at the first sign of disloyalty.

Chapter 60

BARCELONA, SPAIN

"Where the hell are you?" Paul Freeman's voice reverberated through Kay's brand new cell phone, purchased just that morning. She had left behind all traces of her former life two weeks ago, praying it would make it harder for Du's group to track her down.

She'd even put off checking in with Paul Freeman, her boss at the Defense Intelligence Agency. Since he'd recruited her directly from college, Paul grudgingly granted her a lot of freedom in her undercover roles. But she'd really pushed the limit this time.

"Barcelona today. Tomorrow–who knows?" She kept her eye on Charlie's back as he bickered with a street vendor for tonight's dinner. He had surprised her. He reveled in the back and forth exchange with fish mongers in each tiny port they visited, proud as a schoolboy when he bested them for their prize catches. He even tried his hand at cooking the local dishes for their dinner. Like Kay, he preferred a low profile for now, and tooling around the Mediterranean on a leased yacht was no hardship.

"Uncle Sam has been very worried about you," Paul scolded. "Du lost a great deal of face with the Taiwanese Maoists when he didn't acquire the technology you promised him. Word on the street in Taipei is to enslave you for his embarrassment."

Kay sniffed. "All because he assumed a woman was easily controlled. Serves him right." She wiped the sheen of perspiration from her brow with her free hand. Even in her skimpiest sundress, the setting sun's rays set her aflame.

"Well, that's probably part of it," Paul chuckled. "But you did damage his reputation in Taiwan. Any Maoists still there sneaked back to join him on the mainland like whipped dogs, tails between their legs."

"Then we accomplished our mission–in a rather unorthodox fashion, I admit." She crossed her fingers that Paul's bosses would agree. "The Chinese military didn't get their hands on the SDS technology, and the Maoists are weaker. Instead of using the software to monitor the Maoists' new revolution, our friends at the CIA can follow the money through the Shanghai Exchange. Money always funds politics."

"Assuming it works as intended," Freeman cautioned. "Coleman promised a lot when he first came to us at DARPA, but it's been years. Who knows if his software is as good as he says?"

"Coleman delivered. You can bet on it. He never once swayed from his course." She scrunched her nose, regret sweeping through her. "It's too bad we had to use physical coercion though. When Simon Hays couldn't use the board to sway him, I had to pull out all the stops to keep the players interested."

"Yeah, well the upper ranks at Langley squawked at your tactics, but I convinced them it was necessary, given the stakes." Paul paused, as if giving her a chance to defend herself, but Kay kept quiet. The less said on that matter, the better.

Out of the corner of her eye, she watched Charlie wave as the fisherman wrapped up his catch in paper. Only a few moments of privacy left.

"Listen, Paul, I'm sticking close to Wilkins for a while. He has a whole network of contacts in China's black market, and he has to atone for losing this deal. Apparently, there's more than one company's software he's doctored. He's really low on funds, so I bet he'll try blackmail again soon. Getting screwed by SDS' private sale really hurt his ego—and his lavish lifestyle."

Kay waved back at Charlie and lifted one finger to give her another minute alone. "I did find out he convinced Tong Xiao's organization to release the false press release about the bug. With those kinds of military contacts, he could be tied into the biggest technology theft rings we're tracking."

"Doesn't he need U.S. security clearance for leverage with those contacts?"

"I'm not sure. Let's reactivate it so we can use him while I'm his shadow. Give him free rein just to see where he leads us."

"Agreed."

"You also need to pass onto DOD that I'll be tracking technologists now, not the financiers. I may run across more of their precious engineers with high clearances who aren't trustworthy. They'll have to deal with these leaks somehow."

Paul sighed. "They'd probably rather not know the truth."

"Tough! They're not the only ones concerned about national security," Kay retorted. "I bought a new laptop today with GPS. I'll activate my secure email account so you'll know where we are, and keep you updated via phone when I can."

"I'll pass that on to the senior division head. He's been desperate to get someone inside those technology circles ever since we signed that trade agreement with China. It kills him to see our intellectual property pirated."

"The Communist Party still doesn't get it. Intellectual freedom has to be part of the equation." Kay fought to lower her voice, passion rising from her very core. "If people are afraid to think for themselves in day-to-day activities, how will anyone feel free enough to innovate? Copying what comes out of America may be easier for growth in the short term.

But in the end, until free ideas flourish, the country will flounder. After all, isn't that what my great-great uncle fought for?"

Charlie was only fifty yards away, his bright yellow cotton pants and black flip-flops were hard to miss. She pivoted, staring out over the deep blue waters of the Mediterranean, buying herself a few extra seconds of privacy. "One more follow-up item. I expect to find an email waiting from Joshua Stein from his new digs in the Caymans and I'll send you his address. Turn the IRS loose on him."

Paul laughed. "Kay, you really are a piece of work, aren't you? Stein probably thinks you're ready to crawl on your knees for his help. And you're tattling to the IRS?" He chuckled again.

"Serves him right, just like Du!" Kay fumed. "A woman can be just as loyal and patriotic as a man, using different techniques. If subterfuge and espionage take in a crook, where's the harm? Besides, I don't need his contacts if I'm with Wilkins." Glancing over her shoulder, she saw Charlie approaching rapidly. "Gotta go!"

She swung toward Charlie and opened her arms wide, forcing a welcoming smile. He wrapped her up in a bear hug, and she relaxed into her other persona, the one that would keep her alive until she accomplished her current mission. Whenever that was.

Deep in her heart, she knew it would probably take her whole life to bring full freedom to her Chinese compatriots–to those who hadn't had a chance to flee the tyranny. She intended to help them in any–and every–way she could.

Chapter 61

Eric hovered near his front door, basking in the warm breeze glancing off the dry, grassy hills. He shoved his battered hat away from his eyes to fiddle with the collapsible fishing pole stuck into his belt. Shouts of hilarity reached the porch from the large crowd inside.

He glanced at his watch. What was keeping Lynn? She'd promised last night she'd be here before the Halloween party even started, and that was an hour ago.

Peering inside, he smiled at Scotty in a Star Trek uniform, and Stephanie as a nasty-looking witch, complete with pasty white face and truly unkempt tresses. Adults at play. Silicon Valley's best, letting down their hair and partying.

Twin headlights slashed the night. A white sedan pulled in behind his Mustang in the carport. He stiffened in anticipation. He'd made it clear in his invitation that everyone else had to park on the street, reserving that place for her.

The motor stopped and the lights went out. He peered into the sudden darkness.

One high-heeled leg jutted out from the car door. He'd recognize that sexy calf anywhere. Clattering down the steps, he kept his eyes fixed on the woman behind the wheel, staring at herself in the rearview mirror.

"Lynn?"

An uncertain smile surrounded by a mahogany mane greeted him. She shook her head, and a flowing cascade of vibrant highlights glimmered in the car's interior lamp. Biting her lips, she pivoted her hips and rose, stepping away from the car. His breath caught. She wore the same outfit she'd flaunted in San Francisco.

"I'm looking for Mr. Coleman," she teased, winking. She looked years younger, and the expression on her face was so full of hope, it squeezed his heart. This was how she had looked that day at Northwestern. Only more beautiful now. "I'm supposed to be his companion for the evening."

"Just the evening?" He reached for her and held her tight. "Not longer?"

"I guess that depends on how the evening goes." Her breathless voice matched her kinky outfit.

He smiled, pulling his hat down across his face to hide his lust. "Ma'am, can I interest you in a favorite rock of mine?" If she felt half the pulsing excitement he did, they'd better get to privacy fast.

"Is this rock somewhere near Lake Michigan?" She twisted her fingers in her hair, her eyes devouring him.

"Actually, I was thinking of the one hidden at the very rear of my yard," he whispered in her ear, leading her around the side of the house. She stumbled in the uneven grass, grabbing onto his wrist. He swung her up in his arms and carried her deep into the shadows, where the noise of the party became muffled and distant.

"God, I've missed you," he breathed. He lowered his head and possessed her mouth. She matched his hunger, her heart pounding against his. Gasping, he lifted his head and lowered her feet to the ground, keeping his arms locked around her.

"Lynn, I have a confession to make," Eric sighed into her neck. He felt guilty before he even started.

Lynn stilled. "What is it?"

"Umm, I haven't been completely honest with you about what happened at SDS. I wanted to tell you weeks ago, but I didn't dare talk to you about it over the phone. But see, the first chance I have, I'm telling you." He put enough space between them so he could read her eyes in the ambient light surrounding his pool and garden.

She met his gaze, pressing her lips together. Her expression was wary. Nodding in anticipation, she leaned back against the circle of his arms.

"You need to understand my upbringing. My father drilled into me that leaked military secrets result in lost lives. That's how he got killed on his last mission." He fought the lump forming in his throat.

Lynn cupped his cheek with cool fingers, her turquoise eyes awash with compassion. "I understand how hard life's lessons are, Eric. Especially those we learn as kids."

"DARPA required me to keep the strategic purpose of their funding a secret. It never occurred to me to tell anyone who wasn't involved in the project what was behind it all."

He paused, tightened his grip and dropped a brief kiss on her lips. "The DOD asked me to accomplish a very complicated and highly covert mission–to develop software that would allow them to monitor networks surreptitiously, and be attractive enough to entice foreign governments to buy it without official U.S. sanction. It took all of my focus. All of my dedication." His head sunk onto his chest. "I think it stole my soul."

She nudged his chin up and shook her head. "No, Eric. Your soul gave you the strength to keep going." Her eyes welled with tears. "God, you must have been lonely!"

With a trembling hand, he wiped away a sparkling drop from her lashes. "Don was the only one I could talk to about it. So I kept you alive in my mind, even when I couldn't find you."

He dropped a kiss on her right eye. "I remembered how generous you were at the lake." He kissed her left eye. "How you gave your good luck charm to a perfect stranger." He kissed the tip of her nose. "How right you felt in my arms."

Lynn kissed him on his mouth. "Then I have a confession, too. I did everything I could to forget you, to squelch my feelings, even though they were special. You were my hero. When you lied to me, I hardened over my heart...and my soul too."

"No more secrets. Forget my security clearance. I won't hide anything from you ever again, even if it means sacrificing my career. Agreed?"

She nodded, her eyes huge but still uncertain, as if she wasn't sure he had more to confess. He couldn't wait to put the usual spark back in her expression.

He waggled his brows. "Since I've told you my one deep dark secret, it's your turn. Is this a wig?" He played with the long tresses pouring down her back, enjoying her shivers as his fingers brushed against bare skin.

"No, I decided to try my original color. It's just a temporary rinse. Do you like it?"

"Actually, I've always admired the courage it took for you to show the world you overcame adversity." He caressed her stomach scars with a gentle touch.

Lynn's eyes filled with tears again. "Thank you. That means so very much to me."

He lifted her hand and kissed it with reverence, staring deep into her eyes. "I love your hair anyway you want to wear it. Because I love you, sweetheart." Her swift intake of breath was almost inaudible, but he felt her jerk in his arms. "Surprised?"

"Ecstatic," she corrected. "I love you too, but I . . ."

He cut her words off with his mouth, not caring what caveats she wanted to add. She loved him, and that was enough. He lifted his head to breathe.

"...wanted you to believe me when I said it," she gasped. "I'll keep your secrets safe, as long as you trust me enough to share them."

"I trust you," he assured her, holding her close. "You sacrificed everything for me, on just my word. How could I not return such confidence, so sweetly given?"

A warm smile blossomed on her lips and she relaxed in his embrace. Her eyes caught the reflection off the pool water, turning them a brilliant blue.

"So what do we do now?" Lynn lifted her hands and knocked the hat off his head. Twisting his hair with a carefree chuckle, she gave him an exaggerated smack on his lips.

"I have an idea." He slipped his hand under her skirt. He frowned in mock disappointment as silky fabric blocked his probing fingers. "Now here I thought you'd gone for the authentic costume tonight just for me."

"It is just for you, Eric. As far as authenticity, well, I didn't want to embarrass either of us. So I opted for a little prudence."

"No secrets, no barriers. Not anymore. Remember?" He delved under the tiny strap riding high on her hip, pushing the scrap of material out of the way.

"Are you sure no one can see us back here?" Her whisper held a mixture of excitement and shyness, but her bold fingers cupped him.

"It's just you and me. No one else to worry over. Nothing to think about. Just us and our sweet, sweet future together."

An ecstatic smile answered him, followed by a kiss so fierce it almost made him forget where they were. Almost.

"We need to stop, sweetie," he gulped, breathing hard. "I'm losing control here."

"Do you think anyone's even missed you?" She seemed to delight in tormenting him. "I mean, as the ex-president, they probably only care if you don't have enough munchies to go around."

Eric laughed, smoothing her clothes back into place and retrieving his hat. He tucked her under his arm, turning her toward the house. "Since

I'm hosting this shindig, I should spend some time with my guests. But later..." He squeezed her butt cheek.

"We have to get our minds off sex for the rest of the party!" She laughed. "Hmm, let's see, what can we talk about?"

"How about our future?"

"Have you made any plans yet?"

"Yeah. Bum around for a bit with my millions and get a life outside of work." He'd finalized the deal that morning, and he was just plain tuckered out. "Wanna join me?"

"Anywhere. I haven't come up with a plan either, but I need to. I have to pay off the rest of my debts and help my parents out. Mitch's treatment costs a boatload of money, but fortunately he's responding to it."

"Your bank account will be pretty hefty tomorrow."

"That's your money, not mine. I told you that already. You earned it all, not me."

"We'll share." He smiled down at her with all the love he was feeling.

"All right," she capitulated. "You've proven dreams can come true." She squeezed his waist tight before continuing in a hesitant voice. "Actually, I've been thinking about my next step for the last few days. What I'd really like to do is work with you again. I enjoyed it, and apparently I just can't seem to get enough of you."

They stepped onto the patio and wound their way into the house. "A perfect solution," he agreed. "No matter what kind of work, let's do it together. Only this time, work comes second. You come first. Now and forever. Okay?"

Did she understand the sanctity of his commitment? The casual words were inadequate, but this was neither the time nor place to tell her he intended them to be together.

"Okay!" Lynn breathed, meeting his serious gaze with a matching fervency—and joy.

A figure dressed in ball cap, T-shirt and hiking shorts stuck out his hand, halting them just inside the door. A giant-sized Snickers bar protruded out of one pocket and a granola bar poked out of the other. "Hello, Eric. Thanks for inviting me."

Eric studied him with a wrinkled forehead, and then grasped the offered hand. "Alex. Good to see you again. You remember Lynn Baker, don't you?" He smothered a laugh at the youngster's wide-eyed perusal of Lynn's outrageous costume. "How's it going for you?"

A self-conscious smile hovered on Alex's lips. He shook Lynn's hand and shifted his weight from one booted foot to the other. "My costume says it best, I guess. I'm a happy little camper."

Lynn's lips quirked upwards. She darted a knowing glance at Eric. "Good news?"

Enthusiasm lit his face. "I just got approval from a small venture capital firm who looked me up after the awards banquet. He'll fund my business, but he requires solid, senior people to advise me. I–I wondered if either of you would be interested. I mean, I'm just starting out, and I can only work in my spare time outside of school, but I really think I'm onto a market niche that's exploding soon."

Eric draped his other arm around Alex's shoulders and ushered him toward the relative quiet of his den, seeing Lynn's nod. "If you can handle both of us, Alex, you've got yourself the beginning of a board of directors. Why don't you tell us all about it? As sage old-timers, maybe we can make sure you don't make the same mistakes we did."

Alex's excited tones bounced off the den's walls. Eric drifted in and out listening to his business plan. He conversed with Lynn with his eyes only, giving and accepting offers for their own private future.

ACKNOWLEDGMENTS

Thanks to Killian, Pat, Mike, and Tim for their support and input. And a special thank you to Peiying, whose insight, expertise, and cheerleading proved invaluable.

A NOTE ABOUT THE AUTHOR

Chris Hardy Photography

Ann Bridges is the pen name of a Chicago native who fell in love with Northern California while attending Stanford University. Now a longtime resident of San Jose, Ms. Bridges creatively incorporates the dynamics of her Silicon Valley business experience into new works of fiction. Extensive insider knowledge of operations, finance and marketing in the entertainment, communications and technology industries form an authentic underpinning for her sexy, intelligent style of Silicon Valley novels.

Upcoming titles include the 2016 release of *Rare Mettle*, the sequel to *Private Offerings*, and the 2017 release of *Kit's Mine*, historical fiction set against the Bay area's rich, 19th century past.

Thank you for taking the time to read this book. Please leave a review and share your reading experience with others by posting on any or all of the following suggested sites:

- Amazon's *Private Offerings* page
- Barnes & Noble's *Private Offerings* page
- Disqus on the Author Profile page on www.balcony7.com

The authors and the production team appreciate all feedback you may share. Please follow Author Ann Bridges on these social media sites:

CPSIA information can be obtained at www.ICGtesting.com
Printed in the USA
BVOW08*1941140815

413151BV00001B/1/P

ML 9/2015